A Prelude To
The Most Dangerous Game...

"The prey! The prey!" The Hunters all burst forth into radiance, riders and mounts alike. A wheel of rainbow splendor, they turned in the air above the feebly swimming plesiosaur, almost fifty gloriously armored men and women from the court of the Tanu Battlemaster. To one side, aloof as rosy-gold comets, were Nodonn himself and his new bride.

The Hunt whacked shields, sounded crystal horns. "The prey! The prey!"

"To Vrenol," Nodonn decided, his voice storm-loud.

One of the riders plummeted, trailing sparks, and swooped over the brute writhing amid the deadly waves. The snakelike neck of the beast lashed out, and the rider thrust with his glowing sword. A ball of purplish fire flew from the tip to strike the marine monster between the eyes. The animal screamed.

A cheer was emitted by the circling Hunt.

"The entire concept is outrageously original...[and] it all comes to a climax that, to say the very least, is Wagnerian in scale. After that finale, how can May top it?"
Isaac Asimov's Science Fiction Magazine

By Julian May
Published by Ballantine Books:

THE SAGA OF PLIOCENE EXILE

The Golden Torc

Volume II of The Saga of Pliocene Exile

Julian May

A DEL REY BOOK

BALLANTINE BOOKS • NEW YORK

A Del Rey Book
Published by Ballantine Books

Library of Congress Catalog Card Number: 81-4126

ISBN 0-345-30838-7

This edition published by arrangement with Houghton Mifflin Company

Printed in Canada

First Ballantine Books Edition: September 1983

Cover art by Michael Whelan

For Barbara,
nurse and redactor and sternman

Open the door to us, and we will see the orchards,
We will drink their cold water where the moon
    has left its trace.
The long road burns, hostile to strangers.
We wander without knowing and find no place . . .

Before us is the door; what use for us to wish?
Better to turn away, abandoning hope.
We will never enter. We are weary of seeing it.
The door, opening, let so much silence escape

That neither the orchards appeared nor any flower;
Only the immense space where emptiness and light are
Was suddenly everywhere present, overflowed the heart,
And washed our eyes almost blind under the dust.

"The Threshold," Simone Weil
translated by William Burford

CONTENTS

SYNOPSIS OF VOLUME I

THE MANY-COLORED LAND

THE GREAT INTERVENTION OF 2013 OPENED HUMANITY'S WAY to the stars, giving the people of Earth unlimited lebensraum, energy sufficiency, and membership in a benevolent civilization, the Galactic Milieu. Humanity became the sixth of the Coadunate Races, a commonwealth of planet colonizers who shared high technology and the capability of performing mental operations known as metafunctions. The latter—which include telepathy, psychokinesis, and many other powers—had lurked in the human gene pool from time immemorial, but only rarely were manifest.

By 2110, when the action of the first volume in this saga began, a kind of Golden Age prevailed. More than 700 fresh planets had been colonized by exuberant Earthlings. Humans with overt metapsychic powers were slowly increasing in number; however, in the majority of the population, the mindpowers were either meager to the point of nullity, or else latent—that is, nearly unusable, because of psychological barriers or other factors.

Even Golden Ages have their misfits, and the psychosocial structure of the Galactic Milieu had its share. A French physicist named Théo Guderian unwittingly provided these square pegs with a unique escape hatch when he discovered an apparently useless phenomenon: a one-way, fixed-focus time-warp opening into France's Rhône River Valley as it existed during the

Pliocene Epoch, six million years ago. Certain that a prehistoric Eden must exist on Pliocene Earth, an increasing number of misfits prevailed upon Guderian's widow, Angélique, to let them pass through the time-portal into "Exile."

From her husband's death in 2041 until 2106, the rejuvenated Madame Guderian operated a peculiar establishment that the Galactic authorities reluctantly tolerated. Her French inn, l'Auberge du Portail, served as a front for transporting clients from Old Earth to a world six million years younger. After suffering qualms of conscience about the fate of the transportees, Madame herself ultimately passed through the one-way gate into Pliocene Exile. Operation of the time-warp was taken over by the Galactic Milieu, which had found it to be a convenient glory hole for dissidents.

On 25 August 2110, eight persons, making up that week's "Group Green," were transported to the Pliocene: Richard Voorhees, a grounded starship captain; Felice Landry, a disturbed young athlete whose violent temperament and latent mind-powers had made her an outcast; Claude Majewski, a 133-year-old paleontologist recently bereaved of his wife and colleague; Sister Amerie Roccaro, a physician and burnt-out priest who longed to become a hermit; Bryan Grenfell, an anthropologist in search of his lover, Mercy Lamballe, who had preceded him through the gate two months before; Elizabeth Orme, a Grand Master metapsychic operator deprived of her stupendous mental powers by a brain trauma; Stein Oleson, a misfit planet-crust driller, who dreamt of leading a Viking's life in a simpler world; and Aiken Drum, an engaging young crook who, like Felice, possessed latent metapsychic powers.

These eight people successfully made the jump six million years into Earth's past—only to discover, as other time-travelers had before them, that Pliocene Europe was under the control of a group of maverick humanoids from another galaxy. The exotics were also exiled, driven from their home because of their barbarous battle-religion.

The dominant exotic faction, the Tanu, were tall and handsome. In spite of a thousand-year sojourn, there were still less than 20,000 of them on Earth because their reproduction was inhibited by solar radiation. Since their plasm was compatible with that of humanity, they had for nearly seventy years utilized the time-travelers in breeding, holding Pliocene humanity in benevolent serfdom.

Antagonistic to the Tanu and outnumbering them by at least

four to one were their ancient foes, the Firvulag. These exotics were mostly of short stature and reproduced quite well on Earth. Tanu and Firvulag actually constitute a dimorphic race—the tall ones metapsychically latent, the short ones possessed of limited operant metafunctions. The Tanu wear mind-amplifiers, collars called golden torcs, to bring their powers up to operancy. Firvulag do not require torcs, and most of them are weaker in mental power than the Tanu.

For most of the thousand years that Tanu and Firvulag resided on Pliocene Earth (which they called the Many-Colored Land), they were fairly evenly matched in the ritual wars fought as part of their battle-religion. The greater finesse and more sophisticated technology of the Tanu tended to counterbalance the superior numbers of the cruder Firvulag. But the advent of time-traveling humanity tipped the scales in favor of the tall exotics. Not only did Tanu-human hybrids turn out to have unusual physical and mental strength, but humans also enhanced the rather decadent science establishment of the Tanu by injecting the expertise of the Galactic Milieu. The seventy years of time-traveling had seen nearly 100,000 humans transported to Pliocene Europe; their assimilation gave the Tanu almost complete ascendency over the Firvulag foe (who never mated with humanity and generally despised them).

The lot of humankind under the Tanu overlords is by no means grim; people who cooperate are treated very well. All rough work is done by ramapithecines, small apes who wear simple torcs that compel obedience. (Ironically, these "ramas" are part of the direct hominid line that climaxed in Homo sapiens six million years later.) Humans occupying positions of trust or engaged in vital occupations under the Tanu usually wear *gray torcs*. These do not amplify the mind, but do allow telepathic communication between humans and exotics; the devices also incorporate pleasure-pain circuits, through which the Tanu reward or punish their minions. The torcs are not easily made, requiring a rare barium component in their manufacture, and so they are not used on the majority of "normal" (that is, metaphysically nonlatent) humans, who are coerced into obedience by other means. If Tanu testing shows that an arriving time-traveler has significant latent metafunctions, the lucky person is given a *silver torc*. This is a genuine amplifier similar to the gold collars worn by the Tanu—but with control circuits. Silver-torc humans enjoy a privileged position; rarely, they may even be granted *golden torcs* and full freedom as citizens of the Many-Colored Land.

The eight members of Group Green, like all new arrivals, were taken for mind-testing to a Tanu fortress, Castle Gateway. Almost at once, the Group proved to be anything but typical. The starship captain, Richard, temporarily escaped and had a terrifying encounter with a Tanu slave-mistress, Epone, who administered the tests for latent metafunctions.

Elizabeth, the former farsensor and metapsychic teacher, discovered that passage through the time-warp had triggered restoration of the awesome mental powers she feared had been lost forever. Her discovery was noted with excitement by another Tanu, Creyn, who promised Elizabeth that a "wonderful life" lay ahead of her in the Many-Colored Land.

Stein Oleson, the huge driller, was driven temporarily insane by the trip back through time. Smashing the door of his detention cell, he was subdued only after killing a number of gray-torc bondsmen. To insure Stein's future docility, he was fitted with a gray torc of his own. His heroic physique made him a candidate for the Tanu-Firvulag ritual war, the Grand Combat. Still unconscious from his recapture, he was readied for a trip south to the Tanu capital city of Muriah.

Also torced—but with silver—was the trickster youth, Aiken Drum. The exotic testers had detected strong metapsychic latencies in him, which would be brought up to the operant level as he became accustomed to wearing the amplifier.

The anthropologist, Bryan Grenfell, possessed no significant mental latencies. But his professional talents seemed strangely valuable to the Tanu, with the result that Bryan was able to bargain his cooperation in return for Tanu help in finding Mercy—and a torcless status.

The old bone digger, Claude Majewski, showed no hidden mind-powers. With some disdain, minions of the Tanu informed him that he would be sent north to the city of Finiah, together with most of the week's bag of time-travelers, and put to work. He found himself incarcerated in Castle Gateway's "people pen," together with more than thirty other ordinary humans, awaiting the departure of the northern caravan. In the prison dormitory lay Richard, comatose from mental abuse by Epone.

The last members of Group Green to be tested by the exotic slave-mistress were Sister Amerie and Felice Landry. The nun had no important latencies. Faced with being tested next, Felice seemed seized by hysterical fear; her agitation made an accurate calibration impossible. Epone gave up on the girl, since she could be tested later in Finiah. Then, in an offhanded way, Epone informed the two of the Tanu custom of using human women for brood stock, dismissing their indignant protests with the promise that they would eventually accept the role and even be happy with their new life in Finiah. When the exotic woman left them, Felice's feigned hysteria vanished. She had succeeded in concealing her strong latent metafunctions from Epone, escaping the torc at least temporarily; and now she resolved in cold fury to "take" the entire Tanu race.

That evening, two caravans left Castle Gateway, traveling along the Pliocene River Rhône in opposite directions. In the northern group, bound for Finiah on the Proto-Rhine at the edge of the Black Forest, were the partially recovered Richard, Claude, Amerie, Felice, and the majority of the other human prisoners. They were escorted by Epone and a squad of gray-torc human troops. In the southern cavalcade, led by Creyn, were Elizabeth, Bryan, Aiken Drum, the wounded Stein, and two other silver-torc humans: a former juvenile officer from a colonial satellite, Sukey Davies, and a glum Finno-Canadian forester, Raimo Hakkinen.

At first the northern train made peaceful progress. Suffering from having to ride a huge Pliocene mount called a chaliko, Amerie searched her soul and began to understand the neurotic pressures that had led her to abandon her ministry. Richard, recuperating with the help of Claude, stewed in helpless rage when his position became clear. He was dubious, but subconsciously receptive, when Felice proposed a scheme for escape.

Two days out of Castle Gateway, Felice's plan was activated. She had three weapons: preternatural strength in a deceptively slight body, the ability to mind-control animals (an aspect of her metapsychic latency she had used during her athletic career), and a small knife that had escaped detection. Felice broke the chains holding her Group Green friends and those of four other prisoners. Then Richard, disguised in Amerie's religious robes, was able to stab the officer of the guard to death. Meanwhile, Felice mentally coerced the caravan's ferocious bear-dog escort, forcing the animals to attack the other soldiers and Epone. A wild fracas ensued, in which the freed prisoners, together with the mind-controlled bear-dogs, killed not only the rest of the soldiers, but the Tanu Epone as well.

In the moment of triumph, Felice sought to take Epone's golden torc, knowing it would release the latent metafunctions heretofore imprisoned within her brain. But a half-crazed time-traveler threw the device into a lake, where it sank in deep water. Felice was prevented from murdering the interfering man only when Amerie administered a powerful sedative from her medical kit, causing the little athlete to fall unconscious.

Bewildered and frightened, the ex-prisoners realized that telepathic news of the attack must have been flashed by the dying Epone. Most of the escapees elected to follow the mountain-climbing Oxford don, Basil Wimborne, who proposed to lead them in small boats across the prehistoric Lac de Bresse to safety in the high Jura. Claude, wilderness-wise from expeditions on wild planets of the Galactic Milieu, demurred. He advised taking to the forests of the adjacent Vosges Mountains, where it would be difficult for gray-torcs on chalikoback to pursue them. Only Richard and Amerie agreed to follow him, taking the still-unconscious Felice along.

From a high ridge, the four members of Group Green saw gray-torc boats in pursuit of their former companions. That evening, Amerie felt herself strangely attracted by Felice's violent behavior, which seemed to reflect some dark shadow within her own conventional spirituality.

While crossing a torrent on the following day, Amerie fell and broke her arm. The others made camp and tried to decide what to do. Felice seemed to take for granted that they would all lead a guerilla existence, harassing other caravans in the hope of getting another golden torc. Richard received this notion with scorn. The only sensible thing was to make for the sea, away from the regions that the Tanu were known to inhabit. Claude, knowing that Richard was right, but troubled at leaving the impetuous girl behind on her own, went off into the quiet woods to think. After burying his late wife's ashes, he fell asleep, waking at evening to find that a tiny Pliocene cat with illusions of domesticity insisted upon accompanying him back to camp. The cat, Claude felt, would be a valuable distraction for Amerie, who was becoming morbidly preoccupied with Felice.

Man and pet returned to camp to find that all trace of the others had vanished. Fearfully, Claude went up the riverside path. The time-travelers had been warned of the terrible Firvulag who inhabited the Vosges forest. Now it seemed that Richard, Felice, and Amerie must have been abducted by the shape-shifting little exotics—or else recaptured by minions of the Tanu. Hearing voices, then compelled against his will to reveal himself, Claude came upon the very desperados who had seized his friends. They were not exotics but human beings—*free* humans who had escaped from exotic bondage and now lived an outlaw life.

Their leader was a well-rejuvenated old woman wearing a golden torc; the widow of the time-gate's discoverer and the ultimate author of Pliocene humanity's degradation... Angélique Guderian.

On the last day of August, the four members of Group Green, Madame Guderian and her band, and some 200 other "Lowlives" (as the free humans proudly styled themselves) came to a hiding place in a giant hollow tree deep in the Vosges Mountains. The forest now swarmed with Tanu and their gray-torc henchmen, sent by Lord Velteyn of Finiah to search out the killers of his sister, Epone. Velteyn himself, proficient in the metafaculties of psychokinesis and creativity, was conducting personal sorties as the head of his Flying Hunt, a cadre of glorious Tanu knights in glass armor, made levitant by their lord's mental power.

Safe in their sanctuary, the Lowlives and Green Group engaged in mutual assessment. Madame told the newcomers of her grandiose plan to free all of Pliocene humanity from Tanu bondage, a task she had undertaken in expiation of her own guilt. She had engineered a fragile alliance between Lowlives and Firvulag against the common Tanu enemy; but the entente had been only minimally productive.

The Tanu were oddly invulnerable to the vitredur glass and bronze weapons commonly used by all three races. Tanu might suffer injury, but after a recuperative course administered by redactors—metapsychic healers—even the worst wounds would be cured. Madame and her chief fighter, a Native American named Peopeo Moxmox Burke who had once been a judge, were keenly interested in how Group Green had managed to dispatch Epone. Until this time, no Lowlife had ever been able to kill a Tanu. Felice displayed her little steel knife, and a fact that Amerie had already suspected became confirmed: Iron was poisonous to the Tanu, perhaps acting in some way to destroy the linkage between the exotic brain and the golden torc. (Felice looked upon Madame's own golden torc with some speculation at this point, but the intrepid old woman simply pricked herself with the blade to show that humans were made of tougher stuff).

At this point, a personage named Fitharn Pegleg arrived within the hollow tree. Resembling a short, sturdy human, he proved to be a Firvulag capable of assuming a monstrous shape, one of the Little People who had originally befriended Madame Guderian in the Pliocene. As she explained her plan to liberate enslaved humanity, Madame asked Fitharn to recite an ancient lay traditional among his people. It told of the original arrival of Tanu and Firvulag on Earth in a gigantic living spaceship that had as its spouse Brede, a woman from the exotic galaxy. In making the incredible journey across millions of light-years, the Ship was fatally strained. Tanu, Firvulag, and Brede escaped from the hulk in small flyers and watched the remains of the huge organism crash upon Pliocene Europe, forming a crater "too wide to see across." To consecrate the Ship's Grave, a ritual battle was fought by two heroes—Sharn of the Firvulag and Lugonn of the Tanu—the former armed with a photonic weapon called the Sword, the latter using a similar laser-type projector called the Spear. Sharn was defeated. The victor, Lugonn the Shining One, had the honor of receiving a blast from his own Spear between his eyes. Laid out in his golden glass armor, Spear at his side, Lugonn was left at the Ship's Grave to "captain it upon its final flight."

After a thousand years had passed, the remote location of the Ship's Grave had faded from the memory of Tanu and Firvulag alike. But the legend had sparked hope in Madame Guderian. The Sword of Sharn was now in Tanu hands, serving as a trophy awarded to the winner of the annual Grand Combat religious war. But the Spear of Lugonn must still be there beside the crater lake, together with the gravo-magnetically powerful flying machines that had carried the exotics from their dying Ship. If the Lowlives could secure the photon weapon or a flying machine—or both—they would gain an unprecedented advantage over the metapsychic barbarians who constituted the Tanu chivalry.

Lowlives and friendly Firvulag had searched in vain for the Ship's Grave. But now Claude, knowledgeable in future geology, told them where it must be. Only one astrobleme in Europe fit the description, a crater called the Ries that lay some 300 kilometers to the east, on the northern shore of the Danube River.

Jubilation greeted this intelligence, and it was decided to mount an expedition at once. With luck, the searchers might return before the end of the month. Then Firvulag would join Lowlife humanity in an attack against Finiah—provided that the fighting took place before the start of the Grand Combat Truce beginning at dawn on October first. The expedition would consist of Fitharn, Madame Guderian, Chief Burke, a dynamic-field engineer named Martha, a former gravomag repair technician named Stefanko, and three members of Group Green. Claude would guide them to the spot. Richard (over his protests) would pilot a flyer if one could be made operational. Felice insisted she would be useful fending off wild beasts with her special talent, as well as doing chores such as hunting for food. (She *had* to go; around the neck of Lugonn's skeleton was a golden torc.)

Fitharn proposed that the expedition receive official sanction from the Firvulag monarch, Yeochee IV. Before leaving the tree, Madame gave secret orders to a Lowlife metalsmith, Khalid Khan, to take a group of men to a site designated by Claude, where iron ore might easily be found. They were to smelt as much of the "blood-metal" as possible and bring it back to the principal Lowlife settlement of Hidden Springs as soon as the Tanu search parties withdrew. The iron was to be kept a secret from the Firvulag, since their loyalty was strongly tinged with expedience, and no Lowlife knew how long the shaky alliance might last.

Amerie would go to Hidden Springs and reside in Madame's own house. There her arm could heal and she could minister to the outlaw humans, who had lived for years with neither a physician nor a priest. Meanwhile, messengers would go to other Lowlife settlements thinly scattered about Europe, attempting to attract volunteers for the Finiah attack—now tentatively scheduled for the last week in September.

In the Firvulag stronghold of High Vrazel, the little expedition met with a skeptical King Yeochee, who warned that the regions east of the Black Forest were full of Howlers, deformed mutant Firvulag only nominally under his authority. He presented Madame with a royal order commanding the cooperation of Sugoll, reputed to rule the Howlers in the regions around the Danube headwaters.

On the fifth day after leaving High Vrazel, in the Vosges Mountains, the expedition arrived at the Rhine—and encountered disaster in the shape of a pig the size of an ox. This creature attacked from ambush, killing Stefanko and badly wounding Chief Burke. Fitharn urged that they turn back; but the humans feared that if they delayed, the Firvulag might seek out the Ship's Grave themselves. Frail Martha, who had been forced to give birth to four children in quick succession as a Tanu slave, began to hemorrhage. Nevertheless, she was firm in demanding that they press on—and so five of them did, with the dauntless Felice carrying Martha until she was well enough to resume hiking.

Slowly, the expedition made its way up the great escarpment on the eastern Rhine shore, into the eerie zone they named the Fungus Forest, which crowned the highland where the modern Schwarzwald lies. It was not until September eighteenth that they reached the Feldberg, home of the Howler lord, Sugoll. This individual, wearing a handsome illusory body to screen hideous deformities, toyed with the humans while his horde of goblinesque subjects projected hatred and fear of the interlopers, demanding their death.

Claude brought about a reprieve when he explained the cause of the Howler mutation to Sugoll: The population had split away from their western brethren hundreds of years earlier, and had inadvertently settled in a region rich in radioactive minerals. These, combined with the exotic sensitivity to radiation, had caused the terrible birth defects. There was hope for the Howlers, Claude said, if they would move out of this area and, using their powers of shape-shifting to assume a more attractive aspect, resume mating with normal Firvulag. The Howlers might further be helped by the skills of a genetic engineer from the Galactic Milieu; but unfortunately, such a skilled scientist would surely have been enslaved by the Tanu for their own purposes.

To express his gratitude, Sugoll assisted the expedition. The subterranean source of the Danube rose only a short distance away. A single day's travel on this would bring boaters to the open river, which flowed so swiftly and smoothly that they might hope to reach the Ries Crater in only a few days more.

Once again the five people set off. Richard's navigating skill told them when they had reached the approximate longitude of the Ship's Grave. On September twenty-second, they arrived at the crater, around the rim of which stood forty-three exotic flying machines, layered in dust and lichen. A cursory inspection convinced Richard and Martha that the exotic craft were indeed gravo-magnetically powered, quite similar to the machines of the Galactic Milieu. Cleaned up, refueled with distilled water, with the exotic controls deciphered, one of those thousand-year-old birds might still fly.

Felice found Lugonn—but the golden torc was not around the ancient hero's neck. Years ago, a ramapithecine had invaded the parked flyer where Lugonn rested and had stolen the glittering bauble. Frustrated again in her quest, Felice reacted with great violence.

Richard and Martha, who had become lovers during the long trek, set about to repair a single flyer and the photon-projecting Spear, which was found next to the skeleton in armor. Time was growing perilously short; but if even one day remained before the Truce on October first, the Firvulag would join with the Lowlives in an attack upon the Rhineside city of Finiah, source of the vital element barium, without which no type of torc could be made.

Richard tested the flyer successfully on the twenty-sixth. But Martha's old affliction had returned, and she weakened from heavy loss of blood. In spite of this, she and Richard made plans to flee together immediately after he had assisted in the bombardment of Finiah. Three days later, at dusk on the twenty-ninth of September, the flyer landed at Hidden Springs with the Spear ready for use. Martha was in shock from the hemorrhaging, and Amerie could only rush her away for transfusions, praying for a miracle.

Down on the western bank of the Rhine, a Lowlife army waited in a secret camp opposite Finiah. The city, gorgeously illuminated with twinkling lights, was still undisturbed at dawn on the thirtieth. Chief Burke was ready, together with several hundred free humans, many of them armed with iron. The Firvulag army under Sharn the Younger was also on alert—although still skeptical—poised to attack on two fronts should the promised aerial bombardment materialize.

Richard piloted the flyer to a position above the Tanu citadel. Screened by Madame Guderian's metapsychic power, the craft prepared to attack, with the photon weapon manned by the rock-cutting paleontologist. Claude fired twice and missed, but his third shot broke the Rhineside wall, allowing penetration by the Lowlives and a large unit of Firvulag. Changing targets, the old man demolished a wall on the other side of the city; Ayfa, general of the Warrior Ogresses, led in a second prong of attackers opposite the main strike. With power in the Spear running low, Claude knew that there only remained enough energy for a single great blast at the strategic barium mine in the heart of Finiah.

But now there came streaming up from the city a train of glowing knights mounted on chaliko chargers. Velteyn and his Flying Hunt had penetrated Madame's illusion and identified the enemy. The psychocreative lord sent balls of lightning soaring into the open hatch of the aircraft. Dodging, Claude fired, striking the mine squarely. Before Richard could get them away, the globes of psychic energy did their work: Claude was seriously burned, Richard lost an eye, and Madame lay on the floor of the smoldering flight deck, surrounded by toxic fumes.

Half mad with pain, Richard crash-landed the flyer at Hidden Springs. At the same time, a successful invasion of the Tanu city was being carried out by combined human and Firvulag forces. The battle of Finiah lasted twenty-four hours. At the end of that time the barium mine was destroyed, the city was in ruins, the Tanu population was slain or had fled, and the enslaved human inhabitants were faced with a choice that, for some, was oddly difficult: Live free or Die.

Richard awoke in Hidden Springs and discovered Martha's body laid out in the Lowlife chapel. Remembering the promises they had made, he took her up and stumbled to the still-operational flyer. Madame and Claude were going to recover, and no doubt the old woman would press ahead with her scheme to free humanity. But not Richard. He had a plan of his own. Waving farewell to Amerie, he launched the gravo-magnetic craft into an orbit thousands of kilometers above Pliocene Earth and began to wait.

Far below, Felice was trudging through the forest toward smoking Finiah. She was too late for the war, but somehow or other she would find a golden torc in the ruined city and fulfill her promise to *take* the Tanu.

The other four members of Group Green encountered an utterly different face of the Many-Colored Land.

Six weeks earlier, The Tanu overlord, Creyn, had mounted his chaliko and departed Castle Gateway. With a minimal escort of three soldiers, he had led Elizabeth, Bryan, Aiken Drum, Stein, Sukey Davies, and Raimo Hakkinen along the track toward the Rhône River. As they traveled, the Tanu man told these privileged prisoners something of the wonderful life that awaited them. They would take ship at the riverside city of Roniah, and after a journey of five or six days arrive in the

Tanu capital, Muriah. There Stein would be healed of the injuries suffered in his escape attempt. Aiken and Raimo and Sukey would learn how to use the metafunctions made newly operant by their silver torcs. Bryan would assist in a cultural analysis project that had been initiated by the Tanu King himself.

And Elizabeth . . . her destiny would be the most splendid of all. Never before had the time-gate admitted a genuinely operant human metapsychic to the Many-Colored Land. (It was prohibited by Galactic statute.) Elizabeth's mind might be convalescent, but when she recovered, her farsensing and redactive abilities would far exceed those of any Tanu Great Ones. Creyn, himself a skilled redactor, was humbly aware that her probing and healing powers dwarfed his own. Elizabeth would not receive the common initiation. No, she would go to the Shipspouse who was the guide and guardian of both exotic races; she would go to Brede.

The exotic healer's promises only filled Elizabeth with fear and dismay. There was a good reason why the Galactic Milieu forbade operant metapsychics to pass through the time-gate. In the Milieu, all persons with great mental power—human and nonhuman—were bound in a benevolent Unity, incapable of any selfish action that would harm civilization. But bereft of the Unity . . .

Elizabeth felt as though she were the only mature adult cast away in a world of children—and malicious children at that, who would seek to *use* her. This must not be permitted.

Elizabeth was roused from her reverie of despair by the necessity of rescuing Sukey. This young woman, who also had redactive power, had gone snooping into the mind of unconscious Stein. Discovering his longstanding psychic hurts, Sukey tried inexpertly to drain them. Only Elizabeth's intervention prevented the deeply traumatized Viking from crushing his would-be healer into imbecility. Temporarily postponing noninvolvement, Elizabeth began to teach Sukey proper techniques so that she would not harm herself or the man she was growing to love. Before the trip south concluded, Sukey was able to bring Stein genuine relief from mental dysfunctions that had plagued him from childhood. Stein in turn reached out and pledged himself to her. Their two minds, operating on the most intimate telepathic level of his gray, and her silver, torc, took each other for husband and wife. Such a union, Creyn had warned, was forbidden to silver-torc women on pain of death;

but the lovers hid their secret well. No one knew the truth but Elizabeth.

The madcap Aiken Drum's reaction to his new mind-power and the dazzling splendor of the Many-Colored Land was profoundly different. He gloried in both. In Roniah, he was the star of a rowdy debauch and the darling of insatiable Tanu women. Later, he and his new crony, Raimo, assumed the illusory forms of butterflies and took an impromptu tour of the riverside city. This ended with the partial destruction of the Roniah dock as part of a metapsychic practical joke.

Creyn programmed what he thought was a firm curb upon the trickster's metafunctions. However, as the journey lengthened, it became evident that Aiken—self-confessed Connecticut Yankee in King Arthur's court, mechanical genius, recidivist delinquent, charmer, wearer of a golden suit with a hundred pockets—was something far out of the ordinary run of latent metapsychic. The mental powers that had been chained in his skull for twenty-one years of misspent youth were of incredible potential. Elizabeth saw this clearly—and so, to a more limited extent, did Creyn.

The boat carrying the travelers plunged over a torrential slope, la Glissade Formidable, into the prehistoric Mediterranean Basin. Sailing over shallow lagoons, it approached the Tanu capital, Muriah, which lay at the tip of the Balearic Peninsula. Most of the human passengers were increasingly anxious as the voyage neared its end; but not Aiken Drum. His silver torc, instead of merely freeing his metafunctions, had acted as a trigger to a psychic avalanche. Control circuits that had easily held normal human minds in thrall burned out before Aiken's mental blaze; and his powers, unlike the gentle ones of Elizabeth, were fully oriented toward aggression. Behind the grinning face of the young man in the shining golden suit was a personality that might, in time, seek to dominate not only the exotic races of Pliocene Earth, but humanity as well.

Now begin Volume 2, which follows Aiken, Elizabeth, Stein, and Bryan on the sixth day after their passage through the time-gate into the world of Pliocene Earth.

PART I

THE
MÉSALLIANCE

1

THE DRAGONFLY HOVERED, A GOLDEN SPARK, JUST ABOVE THE bare mast of the motionless boat.

As the first breezes broke the water with cat's-paw dimpling, the dragonfly darted off. He zoomed powerfully into the sky and hovered once again. The boat below him was now transformed into a lonely speck amid a pastel expanse of shallow lagoons and saltflats, all blurred in pearly mist.

Higher! His shape-shifted wings lofted him into the dawn. Keen compound eyes that covered most of his head showed him the continental slope's dark rampart along the northern horizon: the brink of Europe punctuated by a single towering cloud that marked the cascade of the Rhône River, pouring down a vast slope of sediment into the nearly waterless Mediterranean Basin of Pliocene Earth that was called the Empty Sea.

Should he fly toward the mainland? His wings had the strength to carry him more than 100 kilometers per hour for brief sprints. He knew it would be easy for him to retrace the journey the boat had made on the previous day; or he could fly eastward to the upthrust mass of Corsica-Sardinia, where Creyn had said no Tanu lived.

He could go anywhere he liked. He was free now.

Gone were the mental restraints programmed upon him by the exotic slavemaster. This morning when he awoke, the silver torc at his throat was cold rather than warm, the neural circuitry of the psychocoercive device overloaded and rendered useless by his mind's new power. The metapsychic latencies that the torc had unlocked remained operant. And were still growing.

He reached out with his farsense, listening. He perceived the slow-cycling rhythms of the seven people asleep in the craft

3

beneath him, and farther afield, telepathic murmurs from other boats scattered about the Great Lagoon. In the distant south— he concentrated his farsense, clumsily attempting fine focus— was a conglomerate mental shimmer. Fascinating! Could it be coming from the Tanu capital city of Muriah, the goal toward which they had been traveling these past five days?

If he gave a hail, would anyone down there answer? Try!

There came a hard bright response, shocking in its eagerness:

O shining boymind who?

Well . . . Aiken Drum that's who.

Hold still littlemind so far yet so glowing. Ah!

No. Stop that—!

Do not pull away Shining One. What can you be?

Let go dammit!

Do not withdraw *I think I know you . . .*

Suddenly, he was overcome by an unprecedented fear. That distant unknown was locking onto him, coming at him in some manner down the pathway of his own mind's beam. He pulled away from the grasp and discovered too late that it was going to take almost all of his strength to sever the connection. He tore free. He found himself falling through thin air, his dragonfly shape shifted back to vulnerable humanity. Wind whistled in his ears. He plunged toward the boat, mind and voice screaming, and only managed to regain control and the insect form a scant moment before disaster. Trembling and funked out, he settled to the tip of the mast.

His projected panic had awakened the others. The boat began to rock, generating concentric ripples in the pale lagoon. Elizabeth and Creyn emerged from the covered passenger compartment to stare at him; and Raimo, with an expression of bleary incomprehension on his upturned face; and scowling Stein, with worried little Sukey; and Highjohn, the skipper, who yelled, "I know that's you up there, Aiken Drum! God help you if you've been playing any of your tricks with my boat!"

The boatman's shout brought out the last passenger, the torcless anthropologist, Bryan Grenfell, who was feeling testy and was aware of none of the telepathic querying now being hurled at the dragonfly by the others. "Is it necessary to rock the boat quite so much?"

"Aiken, come down," Creyn said aloud.

"Not bloody likely," the dragonfly replied. Wings abuzz, the insect prepared to flee.

The Tanu raised one slender hand in an ironic gesture. "Fly away, then, you fool. But be sure you understand what you're renouncing. It makes no difference that you've escaped the torc. We were expecting that. Allowances have been made. Special privileges have been arranged for you in Muriah."

A doubting laugh. "I've already had a little hint of *that*."

"So?" Creyn was unconcerned. "If you'd kept your wits about you, you'd know that you have nothing to fear from Mayvar. On the contrary! But make no mistake—even without the silver torc, she is able to detect you now, wherever you might go. Running away would be the worst mistake you could possibly make. There's nothing for you out there, all alone. Your fulfillment lies with us, in Muriah. Now come down. It's time we resumed our journey. We should arrive in the capital tonight, and you can judge for yourself whether or not I've told the truth."

Abruptly, the tall exotic man withdrew into the passenger compartment. The small group of humans remained on deck, gasping.

"Oh—what the hell," said the dragonfly.

It spiraled down, landed at the skipper's feet, and became a little man clad in a gold-fabric costume all covered with pockets. Self-confidence completely restored, Aiken Drum grinned his golliwog grin.

"Maybe I *will* stick around awhile. For as long as it suits me."

That evening, when the throng of Tanu riders came to welcome the boat to the shores of Aven, Bryan could think of only a single thing: that Mercy might be somewhere among the exotic cavalcade. And so he rushed from one side of the boat to the other while a team of twenty stout helladotheria, looking something like giant okapis, were hitched to the craft in preparation for its being hauled up the long rollered way to Muriah. There was a bright gibbous moon. A kilometer or so above the docks, which lay on a saltflat surrounded by weathered masses of striped evaporite, the Tanu capital city glittered on the dark peninsular height like an Earthbound galaxy.

"Mercy!" Bryan called. "Mercy, I'm here!"

There were numbers of human men and women riding together with the tall exotics, dressed, like them, either in faceted and spiked glass armor or richly jeweled gauze robes. The flameless torches that they carried cast beams of many colors. The riders laughed at Bryan and ignored the questions that he tried to shout amidst the tumult of the hitching.

So many of the human women perched on the great chalikos seemed to have auburn hair! Again and again Bryan strained to catch a closer glimpse of a likely one. But always when the beautiful rider approached it was not Mercy Lamballe—nor even one who really looked like her.

Aiken Drum stood on one of the boat seats posturing like a gilded puppet, throwing out teasing or challenging quips that provoked exotic hilarity and increased the bedlam. The Finno-Canadian woodsman, Ramio Hakkinen, hung over the pneumatic gunwale of the boat kissing the proffered hands of the ladies and toasting the men with swigs from his silver flask. In contrast, Stein Oleson sat back in the shadows with one huge arm curved protectively around Sukey, both of them apprehensive.

Skipper Highjohn came to stand beside Bryan in the bows. He fingered the gray torc around his neck and laughed out loud. "We'll be on our way any minute now, Bryan. What a welcome! I've never seen anything like it. Just look at your tricky little gold friend up there! They'll have a hell of a time taming that one—if they ever do!"

Bryan looked at the smiling brown face blankly. "What? I'm—I'm sorry, Johnny. I wasn't even listening. I thought I saw—someone. A woman I once knew."

With kind firmness the boatman pressed the anthropologist down onto one of the benches. Teamsters whipped up the hellads and the boat began to roll, accompanied by cheers and a bell-loud clangor from the escort, some of whom were beating their gem-studded shields with glowing swords. From nearly a hundred throats and minds came the Tanu Song, its melody oddly familiar to Bryan, for all that the words were alien:

> Li gan nol po'kône niési,
> 'Kône o lan li pred néar,
> U taynel compri la neyn,
> Ni blepan algar dedône.
> > Shompri pône, a gabrinel,
> > Shal u car metan presi,
> Nar metan u bor taynel o pogekône,
> Car metan sed gône mori.

Bryan's fingers dug into the boat's splashcover fabric. The fantastic panoply of riders swirled along the towpath as the boat mounted a long slope. There was no vegetation this close to the salty lagoon, but eroded lumps and pillars of mineral loomed in the wavering shadows like the ruins of some elfin palace. The train entered a depression between steep cliffs and bright Muriah disappeared from view. The hellad-drawn boat and its faerie escort seemed to move toward a black tunnel mouth flanked by huge broken cherubim. The Song echoed from overlooming walls.

An old imagery reasserted itself to Bryan. A cave—deep and dark—and a loved thing lost inside. He was a small boy and the time was six million years into the future: in England, in the Mendip Hills where the family had a cottage. And his kitten, Cinders, wandered off, and he searched for three days. And finally he had stumbled upon the entrance to the little cave, barely large enough for his eight-year-old body to wriggle through. He had stood staring at the fetid black hole for more than an hour, knowing that he should search it but terrified at the thought.

In the end, he had taken a small electric torch and wormed his way in. The passage twisted and angled downward. Scratched by sharp stones and nearly breathless with fear, he had slithered on. The stench from bat droppings was dreadful. All daylight vanished at a turn in the narrowing corridor; and then the crack opened into a deep cavern, too large to be illuminated by his little flashlight. He aimed the beam downward and saw no bottom. "Cinders!" he called, and his boy's voice reverberated in broken wails. There was a horrid rustle and a faint sound of squeaking. From the cave roof high above, a mist of acrid bat urine drifted upon him.

Choking and retching, he had tried to turn around, but the crevice was too narrow. There was nothing for it but to back out on his stomach, tears streaming down his cheeks, knowing that at any moment the bats might fly into his face and sink their teeth into nose and lips and cheeks and ears.

He dropped the torch as he hunched along. Maybe the light would frighten the bats. He kept going, centimeter by centimeter backward over rough stones, his knees and elbows getting rawer. The passage would never end! It was already much longer than it had been when he entered! And it was tighter, too, squeezing him beneath unimaginable tons of black rock until he knew it would press away his life . . .

He came out.

Too weak even to sob, he had lain there until the sun was low. When he was able to get up and stagger home, he found Cinders lapping a saucer of cream in the back garden. The ghastly trip into the cave had been for nothing.

"I hate you!" he had screamed, bringing his mother on the run. But by the time she reached him he was cradling the black kitten against his bruised and filthy cheek, stroking it while the sound of its purring helped slow his thudding heart.

Cinders had lived for another fifteen years, fat and complacent, while Bryan's boyish devotion to the animal dwindled away into vague fondness. But he would live forever with the horror of the loved thing lost, the fear and the gush of hate at the end because his bravery had been wasted. And now he was entering another chasm . . .

The friendly voice of the skipper drew him back. "The lady you're looking for. Did they tell you she was down here in Muriah?"

"An interviewer back at Castle Gateway recognized her picture. He said she had been sent here. Creyn seemed to hint that if I cooperated with the local authorities along professional lines, she and I might—meet."

He hesitated only for a moment before unbuttoning his breast pocket and taking out the durofilm sheet. Highjohn stared at Mercy's self-luminous portrait.

"What a beautiful, haunted face! I don't know who she is *here*, Bry, but then I'm on the river most of the time. God knows I'd never forget her if I ever did catch sight of her. Those eyes—! You poor bastard."

"You can say that again, Johnny."

"Why did she come here?" the skipper asked.

"I don't know. Ridiculous, isn't it, Johnny? I knew her only a single day. And then I had to leave her for some work that seemed to be important. When I returned, she was gone. All I could do was follow after. It was the only choice open to me. Do you understand?"

"Sure, Bry. I understand. My own reasons for coming weren't that different. Except that no one was waiting . . . But there's something you've got to expect, when you do find her. She'll be changed."

"She was a latent. They'll have given her a silver torc. I'm aware of that."

The big riverman shook his head slowly. Once again he

touched his own gray necklet. "There's more to it than a latent's becoming operant—although God knows, acquiring metafaculties all of a sudden has its hazards, so I'm told. But even us grays—without getting any metafunctions to speak of—gain something fantastic through this torc. Something that we never had before." He pursed his thin purplish lips, then suddenly exclaimed, "*Listen*, man! What do you hear?"

"They're singing in their Tanu language."

"And to you, the words mean nothing. But to us collared ones, the Song says well-met, and fear-not, and this-is-it, and we-you-us! When a human being becomes part of the torced society, he gains a whole new level of consciousness. Even us grays, with no operant metafunctions, can share in it. It's more than telepathy—although that's a part of it. It's a whole new form of social intercourse, this mind-to-mind intimacy. How the hell can I explain it? Like being a member of some kind of superfamily. You know you belong to this great thing that keeps rolling along and taking you with it. You'll never be alone in your pain again. Never be outside. Never be rejected. Any time you need strength or comfort, you can dip into the collective *resource*. It's not a smothering thing because you can take as much or as little of it as you choose—well, subject to limitations unless you're a gold-wearer. You obey orders, just like in the service . . . But what I'm trying to tell you is that wearing these things changes you deep inside. It doesn't happen right away, but it does happen. As you wear the torc, you're educated whether you want to be or not. Your lady is going to be a different person than the one you remember."

"She might not want me. Is that what you're trying to prepare me for?"

"I don't know her, Bry. People react in different ways to the torcs. Some of them bloom. Most of them."

The anthropologist did not meet the skipper's dark eyes. "And some don't. I see. What happens to the failures?"

"There aren't too many among us grays. The Tanu have worked out a fairish battery of tests to sort out the go and no go. Human psychotechnicians working under Lord Gomnol try to make sure that no normal human gets a gray torc unless his or her PS profile shows that the device will be generally beneficial to the individual's functioning. They don't want to *waste* the torcs because they're not easy to make. If your psychosocial tests show that you're a maverick, likely to whack out unless you're allowed to stew in your own independent juice, then you don't get a gray collar. They'll coerce you in more conventional ways to make you a productive member of their society—or else give up and toss you into the discard. But the real winners here in Exile are the torc wearers. The Tanu know they can trust us because they can share our thoughts and control our rewards. So we're allowed positions of responsibility. Look at me! Tanu are lousy swimmers. But I've had members of the High Table, the top Tanu administration, riding in my boat."

"With never a qualm, I trust."

"Okay—laugh. But I'd never do anything to endanger the lives of the exotics and they know it. It would be unthinkable!"

"But you're not free."

"Nobody is ever free," the skipper said. "Was I a goddam lily of the field back in the Milieu, piloting my ferryboat on Tallahatchie with Lee driving me crazy jealous? Here in this world, with this torc, I follow Tanu orders. And in return I get a share in the kind of mind-pleasures that only the metapsychics got in our twenty-second century. It's like seeing with a thousand eyes. Or going high with a thousand bodies all at once. I can't tell you how it is. I'm no poet. No psychologist, either."

"I'm beginning to understand, Johnny. The torcs are certainly more complex than I first thought."

"They make life a lot easier for the people who can stand up to 'em. Just take the matter of language. In our Milieu, the exotic sociologists knew how vital it was for each single race to have a single language. That's why we humans had to agree to become monolingual as a condition to Milieu acceptance— and Standard English won hands down. But with this mental speech, any kind of verbal misunderstanding is impossible! When another person mindspeaks to you, you know exactly what the message is."

Half to himself, Bryan murmured, "Barbaric. That's why the Milieu places such strict limitations on the metas. Especially the *human* metas."

"I don't get your point there, Bry. See what I mean? If you wore a torc, I'd know exactly what you were trying to say."

"Forget it, Johnny. Just my cynicism showing its fangs."

"To me, the mental unity seems ideal. But then, I'm just a dumb sailorman whose lover went over to another. Now if the two of *us* had been able to understand each other from the start . . . aw, the hell with it. Now there are thousands of people who love me. In a manner of speaking."

The skipper waved at the procession of riders. Almost all of them immediately waved back. Bryan felt something cold clutch at his bowels.

"Johnny?"

The skipper broke out of his reverie. "Mm?"

"Not all of the time-travelers are tested for psychocompatibility before being torced. Stein wasn't. They collared him when he became a menace."

Highjohn shrugged. "You can understand why. The torc can be used to subdue rebellious people on a short-range or long-range basis. Since your pal is still with us, I presume they have some plans for him. Certain types—medics and some other specialists who rarely come through the gate—they get collared willy-nilly, too. Essential occupations."

"And the metapsychic latents—people such as Aiken and Sukey and Raimo? They were apparently put into silver collars as soon as their latency was detected, without consideration of any adverse mental consequences."

"Well, the silvers are a special case," Highjohn admitted. "There's the matter of the genes."

Bryan looked at him.

"The Tanu use human women in their breeding scheme, Bry. Some human men as well. Normals, latents, both kinds get used. But the latents are the most valuable to them. I'm not too clear on the specifics of the thing, but somehow they figure that putting human latent genes into their pool will speed the day when the whole Tanu race goes operant. You know . . . just like the human race is going operant back in the Milieu."

"But the Tanu are operant now, with their golden torcs!"

"Limited, man, limited. Even the best of 'em can't measure up to masterclass metas in the Milieu. And none of the Tanu are a patch on our Grand Masters. Nope—they've got a long way to go in the mind-power game. But this genetic scheme is supposed to give them a boost. The Tanu are great schemers. Plotting and fighting are their favorite sports—followed closely by screwing, drinking, and feasting. The gene plan is just one of the ways they're trying to consolidate their advantage over the Firvulag. You know about the Little People, don't you? Racial brothers to the Tanu. No-torc operants—but only in illusion making, creativity, and some farsensing, for the most part. Firvulag genes are strong recessives among Tanu, so the Tanu mothers keep throwing Firvulag babies. And the little gnomies are physically tougher and reproduce a hell of a lot faster than the Tanu do. So if the Tanu want to keep control of Exile, they've got their work cut out for them."

"I'm starting to appreciate the situation," Bryan said. "But, come back to the silver-torcs. If they're indiscriminately collared, then some of them must whip out under the neural tension."

"True. Some go mad. Any kind of torc can do that if the personality of the wearer is fundamentally incompatible. Even the pure Tanu have their zonk-outs. Black-torcs, they call 'em. However, even if a silver goes bananas, the Tanu try to save the genes. A woman will be put on oblivion hold and used as brood stock until she breaks down. If she can't be restored by the healers, her ova can be transplanted to ramas. That often doesn't pan out because these exotic folks have a crude reprotechnology—but they try anyhow."

"And the male silver-torc dropouts?"

"Sperm is an easy keeper. As for the bonkered-out owner . . . well, there's always the Hunt. Or the life-offerings."

"I know about the Hunt." Bryan was grim. "But the life-offering thing is new. What is it—human sacrifice?"

"More like ritual execution of criminals and hopelessly unfit persons. As I understand sacrifices, the victim was supposed to be noble or pure or something. Well, the Tanu have *that* kind of ritual killing only once in a blue moon—like when there's a new King or Queen inaugurated. Like the regular life-offerings come twice a year. At the tail end of the Grand Combat in early November and at the Grand Loving, in May. It's more like a clean sweep of the jails and soft rooms than anything else. Uncivilized by Milieu standards, but not all that bad an idea when you get right down to it."

Don't read my mind, Johnny, Bryan thought. Aloud, he said, "How do the human silvers become golds?"

The skipper gave a basso profundo laugh. "There's ways and ways. Your weird little pal is a shoo-in candidate!"

Bryan was at a loss for words. Yes, Aiken might fit in very well in this mad world of wondrous powers and appalling barbarity. But what of Mercy, fey and fearful?

Tall Creyn, with his red-and-white robes billowing in the breeze, came into the bows area, followed by Elizabeth. "We're almost there, Bryan. You can see the High King's palace now—that complex with bars of golden light and the hundreds of bright lamps spaced along the façade. We'll be ending our journey there. After we've rested for a few hours, there'll be a supper feast in honor of you new arrivals. King Thagdal and Queen Nontusvel will be there themselves to bid you welcome."

"Do all newcomers get such a splendid reception?" Elizabeth inquired. Half hidden behind the towering Tanu, she was an unobtrusive figure in her red denim jumpsuit.

"Not all." Creyn smiled down at her. "Your arrival is a very special occasion. It's been an honor for me to escort you. I hope to be able to work with you at Redact House in later days."

The realization burst upon Bryan. Of course. The magnificent escort had really come to catch a glimpse of *Elizabeth*! And the banquet with the King and Queen in attendance would be primarily for her. What a priceless catch the exotic time-fishers had made in this quiet, repressive woman with the unfathomable mental powers. And what new plans the genetic schemers must be hatching! Poor Elizabeth. Bryan wondered whether she was yet aware of the kind of temptation that the Tanu were sure to offer; and whether she realized the deadly danger that she faced if she should decline to cooperate...

Creyn continued to point out features of the capital city to the two of them. "The largest of the structures, those with the surmounting towers and faceted beacons, are the headquarters of the five great Guilds Mental. You might think of them as metapsychic clans—for there is more of a family than a professional relationship among the membership. The violet and amber lights adorn the Hall of Farsensors, which is presided over by the venerable Lady Mayvar Kingmaker. The Guild of Creators has its headquarters lit with aquamarine and white. At the present time, this group is led by Lord Aluteyn Craftsmaster. However, his authority has been recently challenged and there may be changes made after the manifestations of power take place at the Grand Combat. The blue and amber lights symbolize the Coercer Guild, whose head is Sebi-Gomnol, a human wearer of the gold. Beyond that complex rises the home of the psychokinetics, the movers and shakers who are led by Lord Nodonn Battlemaster. He is at this time resident in his home city of Goriah. The PK Guild has rose and amber for its heraldic colors."

"And your association?" Elizabeth asked.

"The Guild of Redactors has its headquarters outside of the city, on the southern slope of the Mount of Heroes. The white-and-red illumination is not visible from this side of the peninsula. Our guild is headed by Lord Dionket, Chief Healer of the Tanu."

A small figure in a suit of metallic fiber came slithering forward. Aiken Drum doffed his hat and bowed. His grinning face was shadowed and masklike in the light of the escort's torches.

"I couldn't help but eavesdrop, Chief. How is it that a human being—this Gumball, or whatever his name is—can head up one of your big corporations?"

Creyn's reply was cold. "Lord Sebi-Gomnol is a person of extraordinary talents—both metapsychic and scientific. After you meet him, you'll know why we hold him in such high esteem."

"How did he get his gold?" Aiken persisted.

Even Bryan was aware of the palpable revulsion flowing from the exotic healer. "You'd better hear that from his own lips as well."

Aiken gave a wicked chuckle. "I can hardly wait. Old Gumball sounds like the kinda guy who could even give *me* a few tips!"

You will leave us Aiken Drum.

Anything you command Chief!

Elizabeth frowned at the retreating back of the golliwog youth. To analyze this interesting implication was going to take some patient work. She hoped Lord Gomnol would be present at the feast.

Bryan was asking, "Are the rest of the buildings in the city private, then?"

"By no means," Creyn said. "Muriah is a working capital. The persons resident here are primarily concerned with the administration of our Many-Colored Land. Our education facilities are here and certain other vital operations as well. But you will discover, Bryan, that we are not nearly so formal in these high matters as your Galactic Milieu will be six million years into the future. We have a small population in our High Kingdom and a fairly simple culture. Many workings of our government are handled family-fashion. You will be encouraged to study the social structure very closely. There are things you must tell us about ourselves."

The anthropologist inclined his head. "It'll be a fascinating project. I can't think of a Milieu culture even remotely resembling yours."

The boat was finally drawing up to a quasi-Babylonian edifice of white stone, lavishly adorned with flowering plants that dripped over stepped, lamplighted balconies. The portico of the palace fronted on a spur of the rollered way. There were no casual mobs of human onlookers to be seen, but a large group of liveried human attendants stood waiting, together with forty or fifty little ramas dressed in white tabards ornamented with the stylized golden male face, emblem of the sovereign. As the boat came to a halt, the mounted escort rode partway up a flight of shallow steps that led to the palace entrance. The riders sat straight in their saddles, raised their torches on high, and formed into ranks like an honor guard.

There was a gong sound and a flourish of trumpets. A stately Tanu woman dressed all in silver and attended by silver-armored human soldiers came to the head of the stairs. She held out both arms toward the travelers in the boat and sang a strophe in the Tanu language. The riders chorused a response at the top of their lungs.

Creyn interpreted. "The Exalted Lady Eadone, Dean of Guilds and eldest daughter of the Thagdal, greets you. Elizabeth will answer."

Skipper Highjohn had been busy amidships winding out a gangplank that settled onto the lowest step. He winked at Elizabeth and held out a big brown hand to assist her to disembark.

An abrupt silence fell. The brisk evening breeze whipped the pennons, capes, and robes of the chaliko riders. Elizabeth in her simple red suit looked lost in the midst of the pageant; but her physical and mental voice was firm and quite as impressive as that of the King's daughter.

She spoke a phrase in the Tanu language and then repeated it in English: "Thank you for welcoming us to this beautiful city. We are impressed by the splendor and richness of your Many-Colored Land, which is so different from the primitive world we expected to find six million years into our past. We greet you with all goodwill. We hope you will be patient with us as we learn your ways. And we pray that there will be peace between our two races through the length of the world's age."

Crash! went the drums and cymbals. The orderly scene dissolved into a carnival whirl. Chaliko riders galloped up and down the steps, cheering, laughing, and singing. After a courteous nod to Elizabeth, the Lady Eadone vanished into the palace. Attendants and ramas came swarming to assist the time-travelers and gather up their baggage.

Elizabeth came quickly back onto the boat before the wild

throng could engulf her. Distracted, all barriers up against the mental cacophony, she went forward to say goodbye to Skipper Highjohn.

Bryan was there, leaning against the doorframe of the wheel-house, a look of horror on his face.

Creyn passed Elizabeth, smiling. "It's quite all right. Highjohn did such a fine job in conveying us that I wanted to give him his reward immediately." The redactor stepped onto the gangplank and vanished into the crowd.

Elizabeth came and stood beside Bryan, looking into the wheelhouse. The boatman lay on the deck beside the steering housing. His old U.S. Navy cap had fallen from his head. His eyes were rolled back so that only the whites were visible. Ribbons of saliva were spun from his open mouth to his kinky black beard. The gray torc was slimy with sweat. Highjohn's hands scratched at the decking and his body arched up again and again in convulsive spasms.

He groaned in ecstasy.

Bryan whispered, "Are they all doing it to you, Johnny? All of them, curing the loneliness?"

With gentle firmness he drew Elizabeth back and closed the wheelhouse door. Then they followed the others into the palace of the Tanu King.

2

A GAUDY THRONG EDDIED AROUND THE FEAST-HALL ANTE-
room in anticipation of the arrival of what a courtier had called
Most Exalted Personages. Both humans and Tanu wore filmy
robes in different styles. Most of the women sported fantastic
wired and jeweled headdresses. Music filled the air, played by
an unseen orchestra that featured flutes, harps, and glocken-
spiels.

Bryan and Elizabeth and Stein and Sukey and Raimo had
met again after an interval of three hours, brought into a railed
enclosure separate from the rest of the crowd of dinner guests.
The time-travelers stared at one another and then burst into
laughter, so bemusing had been their transformation.

"But they took away my other clothes!" Raimo protested,
his face aflame. "And they told me this would be the kind of
thing the other guys would wear!"

Stein guffawed. "Talk about giving the ladies a treat—!
You look like a friggerty ballet dancer. Or Captain Marvel!"

"Steinie, shut up," said Sukey. "I think Raimo looks fine."

Glowering, the former woodsman tried to pull his skimpy
golden cape around his torso. He wore a scarlet leotardlike
garment with a faint diapré pattern of gold that looked as if it
had been shrink-wrapped about his muscular body. Golden
boots and a matching belt completed the ensemble.

He is packaged for display, Elizabeth realized. With his
meager psychokinetic ability and low level of intelligence, he
is destined to be a toy.

Raimo was scowling at Stein. "At least they got you out of
that mangy fur kilt."

The Viking only smiled. He looked magnificent and knew
it, having been decked out by palace servitors in a deep-green

17

short tunic of simplest cut, together with his own leather collar and belt studded with gold and amber. To this had been added an ornate baldric in similar style that supported a bronze two-handed sword in a jeweled scabbard. From Stein's great shoulders fell a cloak of sherry-colored brocade held by a greenstone brooch. He wore his bronze Viksø helmet with the curling horns.

Sukey clung to one arm of this incarnation of Norse divinity. Her gown was of white silken gauze with a trailing skirt and close-fitting sleeves. The simplicity of the dress was offset by an elaborate headdress resembling a silver halo, ornamented with glowing red gems. The ruby color of the stones was repeated in her narrow pendant belt and in the wide bracelets at her wrists.

"I think they dressed me in the heraldic colors of the clan I'm to be initiated into," Sukey said. "The redactors seem to wear red with white or silver. I wonder why you didn't get red-and-white regalia, Elizabeth?"

The farspeaker said, "I think I look very tasteful in black. Perhaps it has a special significance. They did spend a lot of time dressing my hair, at any rate. And when the wardrobe mistress saw my diamond ring, she came up with this nice little tiara."

"You and I make rather a set," Bryan observed. "Elegant restraint in the midst of these birds of paradise."

Elizabeth was amused. "And not bad at all, Doctor, now that you've shed those wrinkled bush-cottons and the imitation Aussie hat."

The once-drab anthropologist now wore garments cut from a glistening fabric of deepest blue-green. He had narrow trousers tucked into silver short boots, a well-tailored jacket piped in silver, and a long cape that matched the suit. Elizabeth's costume was also simple. Her loose gown of filmy black was adorned by a narrow neck-yoke of red metallic fabric; two free-hanging ribands of the same material, jeweled and embroidered, fell from the front and rear of the yoke. It was a style that many of the Tanu women wore—although none showed the black-and-red color scheme.

Sukey was looking around. "I wonder where Aiken is?"

Stein muttered, "I don't see how they could make *that* kid any fancier-looking than he already is."

"Speak of the devil," Bryan said.

A servant pulled aside the drapery covering the passage door that led to their enclosure. The missing member of the group was ushered in, and Stein's observation proved to be prophetic. Aiken Drum was still wearing his own golden suit with the hundred pockets. He had added only a black cape that sparkled like carbonado and a tall bunch of black feathers fastened behind the cockade of his broad-brimmed hat.

"The festivities may now commence!" the jester declared.

"Maybe we'd better wait for the King and Queen," Elizabeth suggested.

Raimo was indignant. "Would you believe it, Aik? They took my *flask*!"

"The fewkin' fiends! I'd bring it running to you on little bitty feet, Chopper, if I wasn't confused by the layout of this place."

"You could really bring it here?" the ex-woodsman exclaimed.

"Why not? You know what whisky means? And akvavit and all those other boozy words we know and love? They all translate as 'water of life!' All those old folks who put a name to strong drink thought that it put the life back into you. So why shouldn't I put a little life into the booze? Make it sprout legs . . . easy!"

"I thought they programmed a curb on your metafunctions," Elizabeth said. She probed gently and met a well-constructed defense.

Aiken winked. He hooked a finger around his silver torc and pulled. The metal necklet seemed to stretch—then snap back to solidity. "I've been working on that, sweets. Plus a few other things. Want to bet this is going to be one mother of a party?"

"Attaway, buddy!" Raimo cackled.

"I must say," the shining youth observed, "that the rest of you are really looking up, sartorially speaking. You're almost as gorgeous as me!" He studied Stein and Sukey in silence for a moment, then said, "And let me offer my largest felicitations on your union."

The Viking and his lady stared at Aiken with mingled fear and resolution.

Damn you Aiken, Elizabeth sent. I'll snap your synapses if you—

But the trickster swept on, black eyes alight. "The Tanu aren't going to like it, because they had plans of their own for you two. But I'm a sentimentalist. Romance must triumph!"

"Do you know what you're talking about?" Stein's voice was quiet. One ham-sized fist closed over the pommel of his bronze sword.

Aiken skipped close to him. Scandinavian blue eyes bridged a fifty-cent gap as they met those of the mischief-maker. Elizabeth was aware of an electric surge of mindspeech, well-directed along the intimate mode. She could not decipher it; but Sukey must have understood it, as well as her gigantic consort.

The background music ceased. A squad of trumpeters, their glass carnices hung with banners featuring the male-head motif, appeared in the arch of the feasting hall and sounded a fanfare. The butterfly swarm of guests paired off and a fuller orchestra began to play alla marcia.

Bryan caught the eye of a human courtier who was opening the gate of their enclosure. *"Wagner?"*

The gray-torc nodded. "Indubitably, Worthy Doctor. Our gracious Lady Eadone wished to make you feel more at home, insofar as that's possible. The Tanu are very fond of human music. The feasters will also use your own speech-vocal in consideration of your torcless status. If you please, your scholarly analysis of our society may begin this very night."

It began when I came through the damn time-gate, Bryan thought. But he only nodded to the man.

Aiken was asking the gray, "What do we do now, cockie? We don't want to commit any fox paws in front of the biggies."

The courtier said, "The Most Exalted Personages are enthroned at their own banqueting table. You'll be presented to them briefly, and then the supper will begin. Court etiquette is very informal in this society. Just carry on with reasonable courtesy."

They waited until the last of the privileged citizens of Muriah had entered the hall, marching two by two. Then it was time for their own entrance.

Aiken swept off his golden hat and made a mocking bow to Raimo. "Shall we, dear?"

"Why the hell not?" laughed the forester. "If this party is anything like the last one, the ladies'll be joining us inside!"

"This party," Aiken said, "is not going to be anything like the last one. But you'll have a great time, Ray. I guarantee it."

"How about the rest of us?" Stein asked. He had tucked his

helmet under one arm. He and Sukey fell in behind Raimo and Aiken.

"Make your own fun, my man," said Aiken Drum. He strutted through the ranks of trumpeters into the hall.

Wordlessly, Bryan offered his arm to Elizabeth; but all thought of the farspeaker and her fate had gone from his mind. As they stepped forward to the Tannhäuser cadences he felt only the stabbing thrust of his fixe: that Mercy would be there! There and safe within her silver. Not trapped, not struggling, but secure in the faerie family that enraptured the lucky ones among its captives.

Only let her be happy.

They walked into a great beamed and paneled room that was lit by brazen sconces full of honest fire. The sparkling little meta lamps were in use, too, but for decoration only, studding strange tapestries and metal sculptures along the walls. The feasting board made a great inverted U-shape, with the several hundred guests ranged along both sides of the lateral sections, standing at their places. At the far end of the chamber was the local version of the high table—actually somewhat lower than the two side boards so that the dignitaries enthroned there would be more visible to the guests. The wall behind the Exalted Personages had a huge reproduction of the male-head motif, crafted of gold and deeply set into a complex mosaic of the crystalline meta lights. Draperies of thin metallic fabric framed the whole emblem and merged into a canopy above the line of twenty thrones. Liveried waiters were poised behind all of the guests. The Personages were attended by a double line of servitors, much more sumptuously dressed than those who waited upon the lower orders.

Bryan and Elizabeth walked toward the table, past the ranks of smiling nobility. The anthropologist tried to be discreet as he scanned the throng; but there were such numbers on both sides of the room, and far too many of the human women had auburn hair . . .

"The Worthy Doctor of Anthropology Bryan Grenfell."

. . . And then the arbiter bibendi was presenting him, and he stepped forward and made his brief obeisance in the usual Milieu style, conscious that the people at the High Table were craning forward to study him and his female companion with an eagerness they had not vouchsafed to the four other honorees. Court etiquette evidently did not include the introduction of the Personages to *him*, but he had little curiosity about the glittering figures at the moment. Mercy was not among them.

Bryan stepped back and Elizabeth, pale and strained-looking, had her turn last of all.

"The Most Illustrious Lady Elizabeth Orme, Grand Master Far-speaker and Grand Master Redactor of the Galactic Milieu."

Bloody hell, marveled Bryan.

The standing guests raised their arms. Astonishingly enough, the Exalted Personages got up from their thrones and also joined in the salute. The entire asembly gave voice to a threefold hail:

"Slonshal! Slonshal! Slonshal!"

Hairs bristled at the back of Bryan's neck. Now *that* had to be a linguistic coincidence.

The most central of the male Personages gave a small twisting gesture. From somewhere came a jangling sound, as though a chain were being shaken. Silence fell.

"Let refreshment and fellowship prevail," intoned the male Personage. A magnificent physical specimen, he wore a white robe, completely unadorned. His long blond hair and flowing beard were dressed with exquisite care in braids and tiny thin curls. There was a distinct resemblance to the masklike heraldic emblem and Bryan knew that this must be Thagdal, High King of the Tanu.

The tableau broke into a confetti swirl as the guests flung themselves into their seats or went dashing about to exchange fresh greetings with one another. Human waiters and rama servers began loading the tables with food and drink. The six honorees were seated on low couches opposite the Exalted Personages and all formality went by the board as the Tanu aristocrats satisfied their curiosity by asking the time-travelers a torrent of questions.

Bryan found himself addressed by a formidable woman in white seated at the right hand of the King. Glorious red hair cascaded from beneath a close-fitting hood of golden fabric with upstanding jeweled wings. "I am Nontusvel, Mother of the Host and wife to the Thagdal. In courtesy I am your Lady, Bryan, and I bid you warm welcome to our Many-Colored Land and company. Now . . . what's this I see? Confusion in you? And perhaps a fear? I would ease that if I might."

The power of her smiling ur-mothermind was irresistible, strumming his memories like an expert lutanist. A dim control room high in a château tower and a face full of sweet rue.

Tears at a troubadour's song. And with that chord plucked, segue into another of apple blossoms nightingales moon rising flesh warmth auburn hair and eyes of the haunted sea so fey. And then the dissonant arpeggio. But where Gaston where's she gone where through the damn time-portal into Exile. Here I go Monsieur le Chat into the deep cellar...

Bryan's festive costume had inner pockets. Without volition, he reached a hand into the one over his breast and handed the durofilm to Queen Nontusvel. She gazed at Mercy's portrait. "You followed her here, Bryan."

"Yes." I did but see her passing by. Till I die I see her.

Nontusvel's metapsychic tendrils came weaving solace and diversion. "But your Mercy is safe, Bryan! Successfully integrated into our fellowship. And so happy! It was as though she had been born for the torc. As though she yearned unconsciously to belong to us and searched us out over the gap of six million years."

The Queen's eyes were as bright as sapphires, shining with an inner light, for all that they seemed to have no pupils.

"May I visit her?" he asked humbly.

"She is in Goriah, in that region you would call Brittany. But she will soon return to our City of the White Silver Plain and then you shall hear her tell of her life among us. And in return for this reunion, will you serve us willingly? Will you help us to gain the knowledge that we require, the insight that may be vital to our survival as a race?"

"I will do as I can, Exalted Lady. My training has been in the analysis of cultures and the evaluation of intercultural impact and the attendant stresses. I admit that I don't understand completely what you want of me, but I'm at your disposal."

Nontusvel nodded her winged golden head and smiled. The High King turned from Elizabeth and said to the anthropologist, "My dear son Ogmol will help you coordinate your researches. See him? That high-spirited fellow at the righthand table in the turquoise-and-silver robe, balancing the wine ewer on his head, the silly twit. There! Now he's done it... Well, even a scholar has a right to celebrate. You'll see his more serious side tomorrow. He'll be your guide. Your *assistant*, damme! And between the two of you, you'll make sense out of our conundrum before the Great Combat convenes or I'm a no-ball son of a Howler mule!"

He guffawed hugely and Bryan, overawed, could only think

of a particular virile Ghost of Christmas Present he had seen as a child on the Tri-D.

"If I may ask, King Thagdal—what is the basis for your sovereignty?"

Both Thagdal and Nontusvel laughed uproariously, the King to the point of coughing. Whereupon the Queen took up a great golden cup and soothed her husband with a draft of honey-wine. When the King was restored, he said, "I like that, Bryan! Begin at the top with the authority figures. And begin *now*! Well, it's simple enough, lad. I've got stupendous metafunctions, of course, and I'm a wiz in battle. But my most valued attribute is—fertility! More than half of the people in this hall are my children and grandchildren and great-grandchildren. And that's not to count the absent loved ones—eh, Nonnie?"

The Queen simpered discreetly. She told Bryan, "My Lord Husband is the father of eleven thouand and fifty-eight—and never a Firvulag and never a black-torc among them. His germ plasm is without peer, and for this reason he is our High King."

Bryan tried to phrase his next inquiry tactfully. "And you, Noble Lady, have a similarly distinguished reproductive history?"

"Two hundred and forty-two children!" trumpeted Thagdal. "A record among the royal spouses. And among them such many-talented luminaries as Nodonn and Velteyn and Imidol and Culluket! And the Exalted Ladies Riganone and Clana and Dectar—to say nothing of dear Anéar! None of my other wives, not even the lamented Lady Boanda, brought forth such riches."

And now Elizabeth entered the colloquy, saying softly, "Bryan—be sure to have His Majesty tell you about the *other* mothers of his children."

"Simple enough." Thagdal beamed. "Share the wealth! Propagate the optimal phenotype, as Crazy Greggy would say. Every gold and silver lady gets a whirl with the Old Man first time around."

Elizabeth said, "And after they're impregnated by the King, they may become the wives or mistresses of other Tanu nobles and have children by others. Isn't that interesting?"

"Very," Bryan said faintly. "But this—uh—genetic plan could not have been in force from the beginning of your race's residence on the planet Earth."

Thagdal stroked his beard. His bushy blond brows came together. "No-o-o. Things were a little different back in the beginning—in the Dark Ages, so to speak. There weren't too many of us then, and I had to fight for my Kingly rights if the lady wasn't willing. But of course I won most of the time, because in those days I was the best swordsman in more ways than one. You understand?"

Bryan said, "There was a similar custom during the ancient day of our Earth. It was called the droit du seigneur."

"Right! Right! I recall one of the dear little gorfie silvers mentioning it. Where was I?... Yes, the history thing! Well, with the opening of the time-gate and the coming of you people from the future, we tried to organize the propagation of the race more scientifically. Some of your folks were a great help along those lines. You must be sure to meet them, Bryan. I'd say they rank as near-godparents of the glorious Tanu fellowship you see here today! Dear old Crazy Greggy, of course— Lord Greg-Donnet, that is, our Eugenics and Genetics Master. And that marvelous woman, Anastasya-Bybar! Where the hell would we be if Tasha hadn't shown our decadent reprotechnicians how to reverse the sterilization of human women? Why— all of those precious latent ova would have been lost to us!" He dug an elbow into Nontusvel's junoesque torso. "And half *my* fun is persevering until I get that little bun safely into the oven—eh, Nonnie?"

The Queen simpered.

Bryan took an overlarge swallow of wine. He was conscious of Elizabeth's eyes on him. "And so—and so approximately seventy years ago, when the first time-travelers began to arrive, you started to hybridize with humans?"

"Get it straight, son. Only the human *males* contributed to the gene pool at first. Tasha didn't come through until— when?—say, ten years after the gate opened. Our ladies had their fun, of course, in those early years. And it didn't take long for us to discover that human-Tanu hybrids were less likely to go Firvulag—and more likely to be carried to term by our delicate little mothers . . . saving your presence, Nonnie love! Even our numbwit Tanu geneticists noticed that. Aluteyn and his people were on the lookout for someone like Academician Anastasya Astaurova. And sure enough—Compassionate Tana sent her to us with bells on! Literally."

Thagdal indulged in another fit of jollity, quenching it with heroic drafts of wine. All around the feasting hall, spirits were rising as cups were drained and refilled. The supper consisted mostly of meat dishes in bewildering variety, together with great platters of fruit, and breadrolls baked in odd shapes.

Entertainers, announced by the arbiter bibendi, did their turns in the middle of the U of tables, and the guests responded with showers of small coins or half-chewed bones, according to the quality of the talent displayed. The Exalted Personages supped in a more refined fashion; but down near one end of the High Table, where Aiken was seated opposite two nobles attired in rose and gold, there was a good deal of rowdy laughter and cupthumping going on.

The Queen said, "Tell dear Bryan about our gift of the *torcs*, Thaggy."

"Tell us both," Elizabeth said, with her most Mona Lisa smile.

The King wagged a finger at the farspeaker. "Barriers still up, little love? That'll never do, you know. Honey-wine is what you need. Is there anything else I can tempt you with?"

Nontusvel covered her mouth and spluttered with stately mirth.

"Your Majesty is a most gracious host." Elizabeth raised her goblet to him. "Please continue your fascinating history."

"Where was I? . . . Torcs for the humans! Well, you have to understand that true fellowship between us Tanu and you people wasn't something that could spring up full-grown in a year or two. There was the genetic compatibility, with advantages that were manifest but not well understood. We bestowed honorary golden torcs on Greggy and Tasha in gratitude for their efforts. They weren't latents, as it turned out, and not all that psychoadaptive, either. And then Iskender-Kernonn came through and domesticated the animals and we gave *him* an honorary torc."

"Poor dear Isky," the Queen lamented, emptying her goblet. A waiter filled it immediately. "Snatched from us by the Firvulag and their bestial coterie of Lowlives!"

"And then about forty years ago Eusebio came through and did such brilliant work improving the rama torcs—being a psychobiologist back in the Milieu and the first person who seemed to understand the *theory* behind the torcs. So we gave him a gold, too, and named him Gomnol. And damned if the man didn't turn out to be a superlative latent coercer, for all that he's an ugly little runt! What a shock for us!"

"You hadn't known about the human metapsychic latency factor before?" Elizabeth asked.

"We are an old, old race," the Queen admitted, "afflicted with a certain scientific languor." A tear stole from one sapphire eye and trickled down her flawless cheek, splashing into the cushioned depths of her corsage. She took consolation from the cup.

"As Nonnie says," the King resumed, "we're an ancient race. Rather decadent in certain disciplines, I fear. And our own small faction—which as you may know fled our home galaxy under duress—was even less scientifically inclined than the common ruck of Tanu . . . No, except for Brede (who doesn't really count), we didn't understand how the torcs worked to make our own metafunctions operant, and we didn't try very hard to understand the powers themselves. They were *there*, if you follow me. We didn't worry overmuch about the whys and wherefores, so human latency came as a complete surprise. As Gomnol pointed out, you humans didn't know your own minds and bodies for ninety-nine pip niner per centum of your racial history, either! So don't sneer at us. Where was I? . . . Oh, yes. Latent humans. Well, when Gomnol got his golden torc and went meta, *he* connected the whole thing in a flash. The Tanu are latents and so are normal humans—some more, but most very much less, even to the point of nullity. In your future world, the babies that are potential operants are detected and later trained up by farsensing and redactive practitioners such as this Illustrious Lady." He gave a courtly nod to Elizabeth. "Since no operants came through the time-portal in those days, and since our torc-enhanced powers are shaky in detecting human latents, Gomnol decided that we must make ourselves a mechanical device for mental assay of the human population. He worked out the gadget that tested you folks back at Castle Gateway. We have others at our principal cities to catch the latents that elude us because of mental turmoil during the initial testing. There are a fair number of slip-throughs." He scowled thunderously. "Including one that was an unmitigated *disaster*! Where was I? . . . Gomnol's brainstorm! Understand now—this chap is an inspired psychobiologist. He knew it would be dangerous to put gold torcs on human latents who weren't wholeheartedly assimilated into our fellowship."

"There are always," the Queen interposed darkly, "ingrates."

"So Gomnol conceived the silver torcs, with their built-in psychoregulators. And shortly after that, the gray torcs—to be used by so-called nonlatent humans who could stand very low-level metapsychic involvement. A whole new world of fellowship was born! Beginning in Gomnol's time, when it became possible to mass-produce the gray torcs—well, produce them with relative speed, at any rate—we of the Tanu were able to seize the ascendancy on this world. The vile Firvulag, those shadow-siblings of ours, were no longer able to contend with us on a virtually equal footing. We had armies of loyal human grays to crush their superior numbers! We had human mothers to counter the vulgar fecundity of their coarse little women! We had the noble silvers—our operant allies-mental! And as time went on, many of the silvers were advanced to full citizenship and given gold."

This can be done without psychic injury torcexchange?

Certainly cherishedElizabeth silvertorc removed without danger after gold in place.

"And think! The brilliant gray technicians have improved our economy by devising more efficent means of transport and goods production! Thanks to the mourned Lord of Animals, Kernonn, we have beasts to ride and beasts to haul and beasts to guard us from Firvulag depredation. And perhaps best of all . . . we have hybrid human champions in the Grand Combat." The King paused. He leaned across the table, upsetting his cup in the process, and took one of Elizabeth's hands.

"And now, Tana's bounty surpasses itself. She has sent us you."

Queen Nontusvel seemed to radiate a lunar benevolence. There was a different glow in the deep green eyes of Thagdal.

Impervious and calm, Elizabeth repeated, "And now Tana has sent me. But in our own world, the gifts of God are often ambiguously given. You don't yet see me as I am, King Thagdal."

"But that will come, dearest Elizabeth! You shall go to the most noble of us all for your initiation into our ways—to the Prescient Lady Brede Shipspouse, she of the Two Faces and the poetry. Brede will teach you and you will teach her. And in good time you will go to Tasha-Bybar and then you will come to me. Dearest Elizabeth."

"Dearest Elizabeth," came Nontusvel's echo. Surely it was as full of goodwill as it had ever been.

"A toast!" bellowed Thagdal, leaping to his feet. His cup had been speedily righted and replenished.

"A toast!" the several hundred guests shouted back. The arbiter shook the chain of silence.

"To the Tanu race and the human race! In fellowship, in communion, in love!"

The feasters raised their great golden goblets. "Fellowship! Communion! Love!"

"With an emphasis on the latter!" called out Aiken Drum.

There was laughter and shouting and a great swallowing and spilling of wine, with many a soggy embrace and a sipping from lip to lip. The royal couple, inflamed by the drink and festivity, now clung to each other murmuring and snorting. A corps de ballet of human women and men, dressed alike in bold magpie leotards, appeared as music struck up and began to lead the throng in elaborate contredanse patterns.

Elizabeth whispered to Bryan, "I'm going to have to leave you for a while. I must look into them while their inhibitions are down. If you like, I'll share the data with you later." She gave him a solemn moue, then closed her eyes and withdrew to some mental vantage point.

One of the female black-and-whiters tried to haul Bryan off his bench into the dance, where Aiken and Raimo were already whirling and leaping as though they had been doing the complex steps all their lives. Bryan shook his head to the invitation. He let the waiters fill his great cup again and again and tried to blot from his mind the realization of how it must be now with Mercy.

When he finally thought to examine the cup closely and discovered what the gold and jewels ensheathed, he was too drunk to care.

3

Steinie don't dance with them don't. Look what they do to Raimo myGod.

Allright allright littleone calm keep on hiding the two of us don't give way don't fear.

They are stronger especially this DionketLordHealer I could never keep him out of us without Elizabethhelp. They don't like that friendshipwall but afraid offend her too early. O Jesus. That beautybitchslut Anéar taking Raimo right there middlemob shame disgust furyhate . . . Steinie!

Calm calm shelterlove armsword bless Elizabeth. Atleast they no make Aiken dance their tune viceversa if anything.

Not toy like Raimobooby.

Nor I Sukeylove if you help.

"Are you sure you won't take a turn with the dancers?" The Lady Riganone smiled at Stein and Sukey. The magpies were back importuning them. "Your two friends are having a marvelous time."

"No thank you, Lady," Stein said. The magpies minced away with reluctance.

Sukey helped herself to another of the spiced tournedos. "These are delicious, Lord Dionket." She spoke shyly to the deep-eyed Chief Healer, who sat opposite her. "Are they made from venison?"

"Why, no, Little Sister. Hipparion."

"Those adorable little *horses*?" Sukey cried in dismay.

Lady Riganone tossed her head and laughed merrily. The pendants dangling from wires on her lavender and gold headdress clashed and pealed. "What else would we do with them? They're the most abundant meat source that we have—and the Goddess be thanked they're so delicious. Why—do you realize

30

that those poor people up in the Hercynian Forest, in Finiah and those other places at the end of the world, must make do with pigs and tough old stags and even mastodons? We southerners are so lucky. There's really nothing to compare with a roast loin of hipparion, seasoned with garlic and a hint of thyme and perhaps a little of that new *pepper*, all brown and crackling on the outside and oozing blood within."

"Don't be squeamish, Sukey," Stein told her, dipping out another helping from a bowl of rich stew. "When in Rome, you know! I don't know what *this* is, but it's sure got flavor."

Dionket poked a bony finger into the deep silver dish, then sucked meditatively. "Mmm...a promephitis ragout, dear warrior. I believe the Elder Earth equivalent for the little creature would be—"

Th mental picture flashed before Stein and Sukey.

"Skunk!" The Viking choked.

"Oh—there, there, Steinie," Lady Riganone exclaimed, radiating solicitude. "Did something go down the wrong pipe? Do take some wine for that coughing."

The Personage seated next to Dionket, a burly giant in a short jerkin of blue and gold, said, "Try some of these hedgehogs in burgundy to settle your tripes, Stein. Now there's a dish to make your belly take notice! And you know what they ay about hedgehog." He leered and the mental image of the prickly pun was distressingly overstated.

Coolly, Sukey shoved the platter of odd little dainties far out of Stein's reach. "The warrior is recovering from an injury, Lord Imidol. He mustn't overindulge. In anything."

Lady Riganone's fluting chuckles and her chapeau tinkled together. "Isn't she marvelous, Dionket? She'll be such an asset to your Guild of Redactors. But it was really very naughty of you to have reserved her from the bidding."

Mindsnap.

"What do you mean, Lady?" Stein asked.

"Have some more cherry brandy," the President of the Redactors urged. "Or would you prefer plum or raspberry?" He fingered his torc. Both Stein and Sukey were compelled to relax.

I couldn't help it Steinie he slipped through. O Elizabeth come back from there and help us before Stein finds out I won't be able to hold him!

...

Sukeywoman whatwhatWHAT dammit?

Steinie stop I can barely cover you if they perceive allthat inside they'll hurt you love O please calmrecedeflattentranquilize. Damn you ElizaMasterbeth come back from there!

Out in the middle of the floor, the arbiter bibendi was holding a length of glittering glass chain above his head and shaking it. The riotous dancing calmed and the music drained away. Revelers drifted back to their seats. Four Tanu ladies all but dragged the disheveled Raimo with them. Aiken Drum suffered no such indignity. He strutted back to his place at the High Table and sat carefully on the edge of his couch.

"Exalted Personages, most noble lords and ladies, and illustrious honorees!" cried the arbiter. "Pray silence! It is the hour for the contributions of the honored guests!"

Cheers, cup-thumping, and a clatter of knives upon golden plates.

The aribter shook the chain again. "Two of our guests"— the silver-torced exquisite bowed toward Bryan and Elizabeth—"are exempted from show by command of Their Awful Majesties. And one other"— he pointed at Raimo—"has already made his talents known!"

The ladies at the low tables screamed with laughter. A number of them began pelting Raimo with bananas, stopping reluctantly as the chain of silence rang once again.

"We will hear from Sue-Gwen Davies!"

Sukey felt herself impelled toward the center of the room. The soul within her was turned over and over helplessly by the examining psyches of the King and Queen and the other Personages. The Tanu were surprised at the deep barrier (for Elizabeth had returned to assist in the nick of time), but were disposed to be satisfied with the superficial revelations that were accessible to them. Dionket's mind spoke.

Dear little RedactorSister, apprentice comforthealer! Lend us a small solace this night sing of ElderEarth of ancient parentland.

Sukey's apprehension began to melt. Other minds all around her seemed to beg: Lull us.

Keeping her gaze on Stein, she sang a cradlesong in a small clear voice, first in Welsh and then in Standard English. After the first phrase, a single harpist accompanied her.

> *Holl amrantau'r sêr ddywedant,*
> *Ar hyd y nos.*
> *Dyma'r ffordd i fro gogoniant,*

Ar hyd y nos.
Golau arall yw tywyllwch,
I arddangos gwir brydferthwch,
Teulu'r nefoedd mewn tawelwch,
  Ar hyd y nos.

Love, fear not if sad your dreaming,
  All through the night.
In the mist bright stars are gleaming,
  All through the night.
Joy will come to us at morning,
Life with sunrise hope adorning,
Though sad dreams may give dread warning,
  All through the night.

Behind the words and music glowed the sheltering love of the caregiver. Her healing energy poured over the manchild to whom she had given rebirth, overflowed and spread in a great psychic pool throughout the hall. For a moment, the lullaby's softness quenched all the others' anxieties, soothed anger and lust, diminished grief and frenzy.

When the song was done the banqueters were silent. And then on an alien level of consciousness, which the torced humans could sense but not decipher, came a burst of declaration from many Tanu minds. It was cut off in full spate by the lofty voice of Dionket. The Lord Healer rose from his place at the High Table and held out his arms, forming a living tau of crimson and silver.

Mine. Reserved.

Sukey returned to her place, dazed, and sat down beside her husband. The arbiter bibendi shook his chain.

"We will know the talents of Stein Oleson."

It was the Viking's turn to be drawn irresistibly from his seat. He stood with his head uncovered and glared at the exotic nobility lounging at the High Table, feeling their minds come tapping, prying, snooping. And the Queen's motherthought, more compassionate:

He should *not* have been torced alas the briefliving!

And then the King: Suffice unto the Combat. Skillplay!

Two of the magpie dancemasters came bounding from the sidelines, carrying metal baskets full of fruit resembling large oranges. One pitched a bright globe overhand and it flew at Stein's head.

The bronze sword hissed from it scabbard, gripped in both the giant's hands. He smote the fruit neatly in two.

King Thagdal roared with jovian delight. The men in black and white began flinging oranges at Stein as fast as they could. His sword flashed like a golden wheel. He spun and leaped, chopping the flying spheres to bits. The King pounded the table while tears of mirth ran into his splendid beard. The company of Tanu screeched and cheered.

The chain of silence sounded.

The arbiter gushed, "Oh, a fair show indeed by our newest warrior! Well done, Stein!"

Bid.

Again the burst of exotic mindspeech. This time Elizabeth was attuned to it. Without surprise, she heard Stein being auctioned off to the highest bidder as a likely gladiator in a contest called the Low Mêlée. Since the ex-driller was one of the most impressive physical specimens to have appeared in Exile within the past decade, the sports-crazed exotics drove the bidding to what was evidently an unprecedented level. They were bidding their personal services to the Crown—nominal owner of all exceptional time-travelers—offering their metafunctions, their material wealth, their torced and untorced human subjects.

Three hundred grays for the Royal Guard!

My garnet mine in the Pyrénées!

The renowned dancing woman Kanda-Kanda and all of her suite!

A hundred racing chalikos caparisoned in gold!

The death of Delbaeth.

The King cried aloud, "Hold!" He rose from his couch and glowered over the startled assemblage. Out in the middle of the floor, Stein stood still, the point of his great sword resting on the tiles.

"What person has dared this bid?" asked Thagdal with silken softness. "Who esteems the strength of this warrior so highly that he will rashly pledge the destruction of the Shape of Fire?"

The crowd of banqueters held their tongues and minds.

"I do," said Aiken Drum.

There was a collective sigh, and a collective lancing out, and a mental gasp of stunned surprise as all of the mind-probes fell blunted. Thagdal began to laugh aloud and after a moment, so did Nontusvel and then all of the others. Reaction to the enormity rocked the hall.

Elizabeth came sliding into Aiken on the uniquely human mode.

What in the *world*?

Look Thaggymind yourself Elizababe fondest wish extirpation meanie FirvulagDelbaethShapeofFire. So bid.

For Steinie? Deranged clownAiken gaming with ourfriend's life?!

Elizadummybeth! I'd save Steinbuddyvulnerable. Tanu combatschool ferocitymindset recharge berserkerpsychoenergy irrevocably.

Damn . . . yes. I affirm.

Safe with me. Eventually get Sukey too. TurdflockTanu really bit it off when torced me. *You* know.

Suspected. But damn they get you if comdown mindunion crunch. Get us both if they decipher operant snuffsequence.

Distract distract distract.

The mental exchange between Aiken and Elizabeth had occupied a fraction of a second. The arbiter bibendi was frantically jangling the chain of silence as the prankster in the shining suit strolled from his place at the High Table to a position beside Stein. When the tumult died away, the King said, "Speak, Aiken Drum."

The little man swept off his hat and bowed. Then he began to talk; and as he spoke aloud his mind played a subtle descant that somehow gave his ludicrous words credence, painting them with a mesmeric plausibility that disarmed even the most skeptical of the exotic audience.

"Now I know that my bidding has surprised you, friends! For not only is the deed itself an impudent thing, but you scarcely can understand how I know enough of the horrid Delbaeth to suggest his removal. It seems incredible to you, doesn't it, that a newly arrived little silver-torc can propose to do what so many of your own champions have failed of.

"Well, let me tell you how things are! I'm a different kind of human! You've never seen my like. Now, this big fellow who stands beside me is my friend. And I fear that the Good Queen is right in saying that he's not the kind who can wear your gray torc long and live. The coaching style of your fighting-school would undo all the redaction done by the little Sue-Gwen and the Lady Elizabeth to restore his sanity. And to save Stein, I'd take him from you. But not without offering a fair price in return.

"Now you've been probing me and pinching me and trying

to peek inside me while I speak. And you've failed! Even King Thagdal has failed. Even *Elizabeth* can no longer probe me! And so you'd better know that the torc put on me at Castle Gateway set off a mental chain reaction that's still going on. I scared your Lord Creyn and I'm scaring you now. But don't fash yourselves! I don't fancy doing you any harm. In fact, I like almost all I see of this world, and the more I grow within, the better things seem to portend for all of us together. So wait until I have my say before you give in to the fear and try to swat me! First see how I can help you become even greater than before!

"Now, Delbaeth. I saw his Shape of Fire deep inside the Thagdal's mind. I was curious, and I studied it as we ate and drank and amused ourselves. And when the bidding started, I said to myself: Why not? And so I bid my services, following your own custom. I'm confident that I can exterminate this Firvulag menace. So I leave it up to all of you, friends-mental. And you, High King of the Tanu! I'll open myself for just a moment and let you look at what's growing in my skull. Then decide whether you want to treat me as a fellow mind-jouster, or as a slave . . ."

He expanded to them all and they went rushing in.

Elizabeth flowed over and around and through the exotics, rating an ironic acknowledgement from Aiken for her skill. The Tanu stumbled through incandescence, hardly aware of what the burgeoning mental sprouts showed promise of becoming. But Elizabeth knew.

Milieu well shot of you Aikenboy.

Pooh lass see how they run fewkin' psychelliptical blindmice.

No . . . one of them knows. See there?

Hah! Yes! . . . Who you anyhoo oldwomanmind?

I am Mayvar. I have been waiting for the likes of you since the coming of the Ship. I am ancient and I am ugly and I lead the Guild of Farsensors. Come freely to me for your initiation and it shall all be as you hope. Unless you are afraid . . .

The chain of silence clanged. The Great Ones and all of the piddling, timorous inspectors went fleeing out of Aiken. He politely waited while Elizabeth and Mayvar withdrew, before slamming down the barrier once more.

"Shall we allow him?" roared King Thagdal.

"Slonshal!" the assembly responded.

"Shall we send him to the test, and shall the boldest of us witness his victory or destruction?"

"Slonshal!"

The King's voice fell to the threshold of audibility. "And who among us will dare to take him to kin and teach him our way, this perilously shining youth?"

Far down at the left end of the High Table a wand-thin figure arose. She came into the center of the hall leaning on a tall golden staff. Her gown was of a purple so deep as to be almost black, powdered with gold stars, and having a hood that concealed her hair but let the amazing ugliness of her features be fully revealed to the two humans waiting for her.

"Mayvar Kingmaker will take him to kin," said the crone. "I'll see him to his gold and if he's kind, to more! Will you come with me, bright laddie? And will you bring your friend to learn the battlecompany's way, before the two of you together dare Delbaeth?"

"Stein!" cried Sukey.

The hag laughed. Her mind spoke to Aiken in the intimate mode.

Countercustom though it be I'll see that he alone has her if you fill your boast. Dionket and I are allied. Now are you coming?

The little man in the suit of gold extended both arms to the tall old Tanu woman. She bent to him and they kissed. Then they walked together from the hall, with Stein following as if in a dream a few paces behind. The arbiter bibendi gave a frantic signal and the musicians struck up a spirited dance tune. The magpies came cavorting to draw the stunned guests out onto the floor by sheer force.

At the High Table, Thagdal watched the strange trio leave through the door at the opposite end of the room. He had not moved so much as a muscle since the woman in purple had risen from the table. But then the opaque green eyes returned to life. Thagdal smiled and raised his cup and so did the remaining Exalted Personages occupying the thrones that flanked his.

"Shall we give Aiken Drum slonshal?" the King asked softly. "Or shall we wait a bit to see whether or not the Venerable Lady Mayvar has chosen rightly?"

His globlet tipped. Rasberry liquor poured onto the polished tabletop like fresh blood. Thagdal inverted his cup in the midst of the puddle, lurched to his feet, and vanished through a door concealed by draperies. The Queen hastened after him.

Sukey came to Elizabeth, mindweeping but with dry eyes. "What's happened? I don't understand. Why have Stein and Aiken gone with that old woman?"

Patience little Mindsister I'll explain—

"Kingmaker!" Bryan peered owlishly at the two human women, then raised his own jewel-eyed golden skull goblet with an unsteady hand. "Mayvar Kingmaker, Creyn called her! Bloody damn legend. Bloody damn world. Slonshal! Long live the King!"

He tilted the dregs down his throat and fell prone onto the table.

"I think," said Elizabeth, "that the party is over."

4

QUEEN NONTUSVEL AND THREE OF HER CHILDREN WALKED IN the garden before noon, while it was still cool, and if the royal lady was apprehensive, she kept her fear well veiled.

The Queen plucked a coral-colored blossom from a honeysuckle and held it out with an invitational thought. A hummingbird came, its feathers flashing iridescent blue and green when it darted through sunbeams. It drank nectar and suffered the Queen to tickle its avian brain. When it was done it hovered for a moment before her face, buzzing, and then whisked away into the lemon tree.

"Those things are vicious, Mother," Imidol said. "They'll go for your eyes if they catch even a hint of threat. We should never have allowed them out of the aviary."

"But I *love* them," the Queen said, laughing as she tossed away the drained flower. "And they know it. They would never try to hurt me." This morning she was wearing a soft blue robe. Her flame-colored hair was bound into a braided diadem.

"You're too trusting," Culluket said. And there it was, the opening wedge the other two had been waiting for.

Imidol, the youngest and most aggressive, rushed in with all the natural force of the metacoercive. "Even creatures that appear to be harmless can be dangerous. Consider human women! When they're cornered, when they're confronted with multiple psychic shocks, they may strike out rather than subside into the complaisant mode we've come to expect from them."

"This new operant one could be a serious menace," Riganone cautioned.

Culluket took his mother's arm as they came to a wide flight of rustic steps that led to a grassy area fully enclosed by flow-

39

ering shrubs. A small marble pavilion stood in the center of the lawn.

"Let's sit here for a moment, Mother. We must speak of this. It can't be postponed."

"I suppose not." Nontusvel sighed. Culluket was smiling his reassurance and she radiated affection in return. Of these three grown children, he resembled her the most physically, having the same wide-set sapphire eyes and high brow. But in spite of his beauty and his great redactive skill, members of the Host rarely sought him out for the healing, even though he was their brother. Was it true, what the others said, that Culluket was too zealous in his scrutiny of pain?

Nontusvel said, "Surely we have the resources among the Host to control this Elizabeth—for all her torcless power. When she sees more of our ways, she will surely unite with us. It's only reasonable."

O Mother misapprehend! Woe.

Screen up Cull? Listeners!

Upfast. Imi shunt those gardeners away. Riga show her.

"You mustn't whisper behind my mind," the Queen chided them. "This mental jumble—! I taught you better, dear ones. Now, an orderly disquisition, if you please."

Riganone the farsensor rose from the marble bench and paced back and forth, tall and mauve, without meeting her mother's mind in the intimate mode.

"Early this morning, as I had planned, I observed the awakening of the woman Elizabeth. I knew that her screens would be misty in half-sleep and hoped that I would be able to penetrate her deeply and without trace during the few moments that she was vulnerable. I undertook the task, rather than Culluket, because my combination of farsensing and redactive faculties is perhaps most congruous to Elizabeth's own, and thus least likely to be detected by her... I believe that I succeeded. I observed her reactions to the events that took place at the supper last night, as well as her later response to the removal of her hot-air balloon and other survival gear from her chambers. As to the first: She views our simple culture with condescension and disdain. She finds our manners barbarous, our mental patterns adolescent, and our sexual mores incompatible with the ritual monogamy and sublimation fostered among the metapsychic elite of her Milieu. She despises us. She will never willingly integrate. She rejects and abominates the role of royal consort. There was something deep within her motivation that I was unable to con, but the fact of her resolution was clear and immutable. She will never submit to the new genetic scheme hatched by Gomnol. As to our abstraction of her escape gear—she still hopes to flee from Muriah in some manner and become a Lowlife."

Reliefgratification! "But, my dears! We couldn't ask for a better outcome! My greatest anxiety was that she should aspire to be queen." And I . . . come at last to share the fate of Boanda and Anéar-Ia.

Never! cried the three sibling minds.

The Queen expanded to embrace them: Dearest children flowers of my Host.

Culluket said aloud, "Nevertheless, we mustn't delude ourselves. Even without ambition, Elizabeth menaces our dynasty. I have been farspeaking to Nodonn in Goriah and he agrees. As matters now stand, our noble brother is the obvious heir to the Thagdal even in spite of his flaw—and we shall amplify our power beneath Nodonn's aegis. But we could not hope to prevail against a line of operant metapsychics of the type that Elizabeth and the Thagdal would engender. You can be sure that Gomnol is quite aware of this."

The redactor projected two genetic diagrams. "The first shows the offspring if Elizabeth is homozygous. Greg-Donnet says that metapsychic operancy is an autosomal dominant with full penetrance."

"All of the children will be operant!" Nontusvel exclaimed in dismay.

Culluket continued. "The second diagram assumes Elizabeth has only a single allele for operancy. Half the offspring would then be operant. Inbreed the operants of the first generation, and the next yields three operants out of four. Continue the consanguineous matings, and you have a rival host of torcless metapsychics ready to oppose us in the third generation!"

Riganone's mind queried: Incest?

Culluket showed his sister a bleak smile. "The scheme is Gomnol's. He is hardly one to scruple at our Tanu taboos. And the Thagdal grows old and ever more subject to the filthy Coercer Lord's human wiles."

The four minds paused to reprise the old infamy. A human upstart as President of the Coercer Guild! Poor old Leyr hadn't had a chance against him.

"A good thing the wretch is sterile." Young Imidol's hatred

was vividly displayed. "Gomnol would go for Elizabeth himself! Defiler of our sacred blue and gold!"

We depart from the immediate matter Brother.

"Culluket is right," said the Queen. "But what are we to *do* with Elizabeth?"

Visions: A red balloon soaring eastward from Aven, over the Deep Lagoon to the long isle of Kersic . . . A sailing craft manned by Highjohn, or even by the woman herself, fleeing south to Africa . . . A furtive figure in a red jumpsuit making its way westward on foot along the high spine of the Aven Peninsula, guided by ramas into the wilderness of Iberia . . .

Consequents: The balloon swiftly spied out and pursued by flying psychokinetics loyal to the King rather than to the Host. The escaping boat retrieved with even greater ease by the same PK adepts, the sails of their cutters filled by mind-conjured gales. The woman fleeing on foot presenting a knottier problem—and how far could she go with the entire countryside aroused, and four hundred kilometers to travel before reaching the mainland of Spain? She would have to skirt the large city of Afaliah at the peninsula's base, escape its Hunt and plantation security forces. Still, if she did reach the Catalan Wilderness . . .

"She would be out of the Thagdal's reach and out of ours," Culluket said, "but subject to capture by the Firvulag or even the heretic Minanonn. And this last, I submit, would be an even greater calamity than the one facing us now."

The Queen's kindly heart shrank from the next question. "What is the solution, then?"

"She must be put to death," said Imidol. "It is the only way. And not only her mind but her body destroyed, so there is no hope of Gomnol utilizing her ova in his obscene contraptions."

Little olive-and-black finches warbled in the lemon trees. The breeze from the Mount of Heroes above Muriah was dying now and it was getting very hot. The Queen extended a ringed finger toward a tiny spider that was lowering itself from the rafters of the pavilion. Its web floated as in an unfelt wind, bringing the creature to a landing on Nontusvel's fingernail. She watched it stand there, combing the air with its front legs, its sparky predator's mind sniffing.

"It may not be easy," she said. "We know little of the offensive capability of such a one. If we sent her far away, she would not desire to return. She would be grateful to us rather than perhaps doing us great harm."

The spider began a wary descent from the Queen's finger. She sent it sailing safely to the branch of a remontant shrub rose. *Eat the aphis, little hunterkiller, so that the roses may thrive.*

Culluket said, "Elizabeth is strong only in farsensing and redaction. Her other metafaculties are negligible. She cannot spin concrete illusions nor conjure up psychoenergies. She has a small PK factor but it is useless for self-defense or aggression. There is no coercive power per se—but the redact is developed to a formidable degree."

Imidol sent an ironic thrust at his brother. "And you, if anyone, Interrogator, should know the potential for mischief in a corruption of the mindhealing power."

Imi we have no time for pettypushies! Aloud, Riganone said, "The Galactic Milieu placed limitations on masterclass metas after the time of their rebellion. There is not only an ethical restraint but also an imposed superego block, which I saw very clearly during my probing. Elizabeth cannot harm a sentient being except in the gravest defense of her *fellow humans.*"

Digestivemindpause.

"A nice point," Culluket mused. "If we had sufficient time . . . a compulsion to self-destruction would be effective. Do you agree, *Farspeaking Sister?*"

"Her emotional tone was deep gray," Riganone agreed. "She feels she is alone. Bereft."

And so she is, came the Queen's soft motherthought.

Imidol said, briskly, "Cull and I will design a suitable compulsion. We'll plan a coordinate thrust powered by the one hundred and nine members of the Host who are presently here in Muriah. If this isn't strong enough, we'll try again at Grand Combat time when the rest get here."

"We can't count on compulsions alone," Culluket said. "I'll try to work out some other options. And when Nodonn arrives, he may think of some better means of dealing with her."

"The Thagdal must never know!" the Queen warned them.

Nor Gomnol, Culluket's mind added.

"We have time for maneuvering," Riganone said. "Remember that Elizabeth must go to Brede first for the initiation, and that will take some time. Not even the King would dare to interfere with an initiate—or with Brede."

The enigmatic image of the Shipspouse hovered in all their minds. The guard and guide of their Exile, older than the oldest of them, some said she was the most powerful of them all and few would doubt that she was the wisest. But Brede rarely intervened directly in the affairs of the High Kingdom on Earth. It had been a shock to the entire company when the King announced that Elizabeth would become the Shipspouse's initiate.

"Brede!" Imidol exuded the contempt of the younger generation for venerable mysteries. "She has no allegiance to any faction. Still—Elizabeth is such a patent danger to us all, that perhaps if we appealed to the Shipspouse—"

Riganone laughed without mirth. "Do you really believe that Brede doesn't know? She sees everything, hiding away in her room without doors! She very likely ordered the Thagdal to send the human woman to her!"

"Damn Brede," said Culluket in vicious dismissal. "Let the Two-Faced One have Elizabeth for the time of initiation. What can she do? We'll get the human bitch somehow when the Shipspouse finishes with her. Elizabeth will never become queendam in your place, Mother."

Never, never, vowed the other two.

"Poor woman." The Queen arose and went out of the pavilion. It was time to seek the cool inner rooms of the palace. "I feel so sorry for her. If only there were another way."

"There isn't," said Imidol. Dauntless in his coercer's blue and gold, he offered Nontusvel his arm. The four of them went off down the garden path.

Back in the rose bush, the little spider was busy sucking the life juices from an aphis. When the finch swooped down on him, it was too late to duck.

5

"NOT SILVER . . . OF COURSE NOT SILVER, BRYAN. GOLD!"

Ogmol's high voice, incongruous in one of such heroic physique, was loud enough to carry over the normal clatter and buzz of the marketplace and cause shoppers and sellers to stare at him. There weren't that many Tanu wandering among the stalls anyway, and no males that Bryan could see. Here and there a willowy exotic lady, attended by a retinue of grays and ramas to carry the packages and hold the sunshade, bent over the offerings of an itinerant human jeweler, glassblower, or some other cottage artisan. There were a few silver-torcs among the browsers; but most of those who moved about the open plaza seemed to be torcless human householders or grays in the livery of the great houses, out to purchase fresh produce for the kitchen, flowers, live birds or animals, or other items not generally available in the many small shops that lined the perimeter of the Square of Commerce.

"I've been over this with Creyn," Bryan said patiently. "No torc for me." He stopped to examine a table crowded with a jumble of oddly assorted twenty-second-century artifacts; canteens, half-empty jars of cosmetics, tattered page-books, worn articles of clothing, broken musical instruments, defunct chronometers and voicewriters, a few common decamole appliances and vitredur tools.

"It would help you in your work," Ogmol insisted. He took belated notice of the flea market wares Bryan was looking at. "These things—the usual castoffs. The more unusual and valuable items from your era may be disposed of only through licensed dealers. But there is a black market, of course."

"Mm," said Bryan, moving on.

Ogmol returned to the previous tack. "There are no coercive

or dispositive circuits of any kind in a golden torc. In your case, since you have no significant latencies, the torc would merely enhance your telepathic ability—the metapsychic power every human has—and allow you to mindspeak with us. Think of the time we'd save! Consider the semantic advantage! You wouldn't miss a single nuance of your cultural immersion. The scope of your analysis would be broader, less prone to subjective error—"

A vendor in a straw sombrero grinned and waved a skewer of small, freshly roasted birds. "Barbecued larks, Exalted Lords? My own Texas-style chili sauce!"

"Popcorn," croaked a withered old woman in the stall next door. "New crop tetraploid. One kernel a snack in itself."

"Only a few Périgord truffles left today, Lord."

"Attar of roses! Orange-water to cool your temples! Just for you, Lord—a rare flagon of 4711!"

Ogmol grimaced. "It's a fake. They ought to do something about these fellows . . . But as I was saying, with a torc—"

"The only working conditions I'll accept are those affording complete freedom." Bryan kept his good humor. Ogmol made a gesture of resignation and led the way to a building on the shady side of the square. A sign designated it BAKERY-KLEIN-FUSS-CAFÉ.

The crowd of shoppers parted respectfully before them. Tables were set on a flower-decked terrace fronting the bakery. A rama in a red-and-white checked tabard came trotting up, bowed, and took them to a table, where Ogmol collapsed in a wicker chair.

"This walking in the heat of the day! I hope we can engage in less strenuous researches for a while, Bryan. I'm still a bit hung-over from the party last night. I don't know how you manage to look so bright."

The rama swiftly produced two cups of coffee and a large tray of pastries. Bryan chose one.

"Why, there's a pill. Our race had to wait a long time, but we finally developed an instant cure for overindulgence just in the last year or so. Tiny little pills. I packed a good number in my rucksack. A pity I didn't think to bring them this morning."

"There!" moaned Ogmol. "The very thing I mean. If you wore a torc, you'd *know* how I was suffering without my having to tell you in so many words." He downed his coffee in a long gulp and the rama refilled the cup. "And you'd be able to make your wishes known to the ramas as well. See? That little chap almost warmed up your cup before you were ready for it—but he'd never do that with me. You can't do much verbal communication with ramas, you know. Just 'come' and 'go,' that kind of thing. Persons without torcs have to use sign language with the little apes—and that can be very awkward for all but the simplest commands."

Bryan only nodded, eating his pastry. It was delicious, evoking Vienna's best. Small wonder that the interior of the Bakery Kleinfuss was crowded with take-out customers. "As I understand it, the golden torc can't be removed once it's in place. And I also have learned that some personalities become seriously disturbed through wearing the thing. You can understand why I don't want to risk my sanity, Ogmol. There's no reason why my torcless status should limit my researches. I was a competent worker in the Milieu without metafaculties, and so were most of my colleagues. All that's necessary for a valid analysis is dependable source material."

The Tanu's eyes shifted. "Well, yes. We'll try our very best to obtain that for you. My Awesome Father has given explicit orders."

Bryan tried to be tactful. "Some of my investigations are bound to touch raw nerves. I can't help it in a study such as this. Even my superficial observations have begun to reveal a pattern of profound stress resulting from the impact of human and Tanu cultures."

"The very thing my Father wishes to evaluate, Bryan. But the researches could be done so much more—gracefully on the mental level. Words are so *dense*." He downed another cup of coffee, squeezed his eyes closed, and pressed the fingertips of both hands to his golden torc. Many of the exotic men had faces of transcendent beauty; but Ogmol's was refreshingly handsome. His nose had a knot at the bridge, and his lips, between the short-cropped beard resembling tawny plush, were too thick and red. He resembled the King only in his deepset, jade-colored eyes—now lamentably blood-webbed. For the sake of coolness he was attired in a short sleeveless robe of cyan-blue and silver, symbolic of the Guild of Creators. His arms and legs were furred with wiry tan hair.

"No use trying to psych the miseries away." Ogmol tapped his knuckles against his brow. "Plum brandy will have its revenge. You *will* let me have a pill or two for future use, won't you, old man?"

"Of course. And I'll try to be as judicious as possible in

my investigations. It might take a little longer that way, but we'll get on."

"Feel free to be as direct as you please with *me*." Ogmol gave a rueful chuckle. "My sensibilities are quite expendable."

"Why do you say that?"

"It's my duty to assist you. My honor. And as a half-blood, my skin isn't quite as thin as that of the—uh—isolate fraction."

"Your mother was a human?"

Ogmol waved away the rama and leaned back in his chair. "She was a silver. A sculptor from the Wessex world. She passed her latent creativity along to me, but she was too emotionally unstable to last long in the Many-Colored Land. I was her only offspring."

"Would you say that there was significant prejudice against those of mixed heritage?"

"It exists." Ogmol frowned, then shook his head. "But— damn *words!*—the disdain in which we're held by the Old Ones is strongly tinged by other emotions. Our bodies aren't as finely formed as theirs, but we're stronger physically. Most purebloods can't swim, but *we* have no difficulty in the water. Hybrids are more fertile, in spite of the fact that the full Tanu have a more urgent libido. And we're less likely to engender Firvulag offspring or black-torcs." He repeated the uneasy little laugh. "You see, Bryan, we hybrids are actually an improvement on the original model. That's what's so insupportable."

"Mm," the anthropologist temporized.

"As you can see, my body is superficially very similiar to that of a pureblood: light hair, fair skin, typical light-sensitive eyes, elongated torso, attenuated limbs. But the ample body hair is a human heritage, and so is my more robust skeletal structure and musculature. Only a minority of the pureblooded men have this type of physique . . . the King and the battle-champions. Back in the home galaxy of the Tanu, a heroic body was rather an anachronism. A reminder of the crude origins of the race."

"But the very heritage," Bryan observed, "that the exiled group was determined to revive. Interesting."

The rama came running up with a large napkin, which Ogmol used to wipe his brow. It really was a pity, Bryan thought, that he had left the aldetox back at the palace.

"But don't you see, Bryan, how difficult it is for the Old Ones to accept the fact that human genes optimize their racial survival on Earth? Hybrid vigor is a putdown to them. The Old

Ones are very proud. It's illogical—but they seem to be afraid of us mixed-bloods."

"The mind-set wasn't uncommon even in my own era," Bryan admitted. He swallowed the last crumb of pastry and finished his coffee. "You said we might visit Lord Gomnol's establishment. Shall we go there next?"

Ogmol grinned and fingered his torc. "You see? Another advantage! Give me a minute."

The rama waiter stood passively beside the table, a monkey-child with intelligent, sad eyes. As Ogmol made his telepathic call, Bryan fished in one pocket for some of the local coinage he had been given and held out a random assortment. Solemnly, the hominid fingers extracted two pieces of silver. "No tip?" Bryan wondered. He looked around at the other tables. Not a single person without a torc was seated on the terrace. The barenecks had to make do with a self-service bar inside where human clerks took their verbal orders.

"Good news," said Ogmol. "Gomnol is free and would be delighted to conduct you around his laboratories person-ally! . . . I see you've paid. Just let me—"

The rama gave a little yip of pleasure and everted its lips at Ogmol. "*Mental* largesse, Bryan."

"I should have guessed."

They took a cab, drawn by a helladotherium, to the large complex on the northern edge of the city that housed the Coercer Guild. On the way down the wide boulevards they passed many small shops and neat attached dwellings. There was none of the quaint "Munchkin Tudor" architecture of the outlying set-tlements to be found in Muriah. Here the buildings had a clas-sical elegance of line that was almost Doric. The white and pastel masses were softened by lavish plantings, tended by the ever-present ramapithecines. The human inhabitants of Mu-riah—artisans, shopkeepers, service workers, troops, and functionaries—were universally well-fed and prosperous-look-ing. The only persons who could be classed as shabaroons were the peddlers in the open market, the caravan drovers, and trav-elers newly arrived from the hinterlands; even these seemed only temporarily grubby. Bryan saw no evidence of disease, privation, or maltreatment among the torcless element. On the surface, Muriah looked to be an idyllic small city. Ogmol told him that the total permanent population included some four thousand Tanu, a few hundred gold-torc humans, under a thousand silvers, about five thousand gray-torcs, and six or seven thousand torcless. The ramas outnumbered the people by at least three to one.

"We classify as Tanu any person who *looks* exotic," the brawny scholar explained. "Officially, there is no discrimination among purebloods and mixed. And, of course, a gold-torc human is the social equal of a Tanu. In theory, anyhow."

Bryan suppressed a smile. "Another reason for your urging a collar on me? Your association with a bareneck must be a trifle déclassé. I noticed that the vendors were giving me a fishy look back in the market."

Rather stiffly, Ogmol said, "Any person of consequence knows who you are. The others don't matter." They rode in silence for a while. Bryan considered another possible motive for the King's having commissioned the anthropological study. He was glad that Ogmol was unable to read his thoughts.

They came to a handsome group of buildings at the very edge of the dropoff to the Catalan Gulf. The white marble of the Coercer Headquarters was inlaid and ornamented with blue and yellow. The forecourt had mosaic pavement with abstract designs. The roofs were sheathed in striking azure tiles with gutters and other fittings that glistened like gold. Squads of well-armed gray-torc guards in half-armor of blue glass and bronze poised stoically in the entry archway and at all of the doors. As the carriage passed and Ogmol emitted some unheard telepathic hail, the men thumped the butts of their vitredur halberds in salute. A detail stood by as Bryan and Ogmol alighted, making sure that the human cabdriver did not linger in Guild precincts.

"The Coercers seem quite security-conscious," Bryan remarked.

"The torc works is here. In a certain sense, this place is the very keystone of our High Kingdom."

They passed into cool corridors, where more guards stood like living statues—any boredom presumably assuaged by their gray torcs. Somewhere a deep-toned bell sounded three times. Bryan and Ogmol ascended a staircase and came to a pair of tall bronze doors. Four guards on station lifted a heavy ornamental bar so that the two researchers could enter the antechamber of the President's office. There behind a console equipped with constructs of glowing crystal sat an exotic woman of singular beauty. Bryan felt something like an icy needle whisk behind his eyes.

"Tana's mercy, Meva!" said Ogmol irritably. "Would I bring a hostile here? Doctor Grenfell was vetted by Lord Dionket himself!"

I was? Bryan wondered.

The woman said, "I only do my duty, Creative Brother." She gestured to the door of the inner sanctum, apparently opened it by psychokinesis, and returned to whatever esoteric work their arrival had interrupted.

"Come in! Come in!" called a deeply pitched voice.

They came before Gomnol, Lord Coercer, who inhabited a world all his own. The room was chilly in spite of the tropical climate of Muriah. A few coals smoldered in the grate of a manteled baronial fireplace, above which was a stark canvas that had to be a Georgia O'Keeffe. A Chihuahua dog eyed the newcomers dyspeptically from its cushion in front of the fire. The walls of the rooms were paneled in dark wood, interrupted by shelves crowded with leatherbound pagebooks, Tanu crystalline audiovisuals, and plaques of the twenty-second century. A stand held a copy (surely it was a copy?) of Rodin's sinister little Tentation de Saint Antoine. Chairs and settees of tufted, wine-colored leather stood before a huge reproduction of a rococo-revival desk, upon which rested a green-shaped oil lamp, a tarnished silver inkstand with quill pen, a fruitwood humidor, and an onyx ashtray overflowing with cigar butts. A walnut credenza in the same ornate style as the desk, flanked by fern stands, held a dozen cut-glass decanters, a tray of Waterford tumblers, a soda siphon, and a small tin of Cadbury biscuits. (And what time-traveler had surrendered the last treasure to the Lord Coercer's irresistible demand?)

In the midst of a cloud of fragrant smoke sat Eusebio Gomez-Nolan himself, wearing a quilted jacket of gold brocade with lapels and cuffs of midnight-blue satin. While perhaps not the "ugly little runt" deprecated by King Thagdal, he was only of medium stature by the standards of the Old World, with a nose that was not merely aquiline but verging on the bulbous. His eyes, however, were a beautiful luminous blue with dark lashes, and he smiled at his visitors, showing small, perfect teeth.

"Be seated, colleagues," he said in a casual tone, gesturing with his cigar.

Bryan asked himself how the devil this ordinary-looking little fellow had managed to install himself as President of the Coercer Guild.

And Gomnol heard.

Once in years long past, Bryan had sailed his small yacht into a hurricane that had broken loose from the weathermakers and wandered close to the British Isles. After enduring hours of battering, he had relaxed in a respite—only to see rising before his craft a mountainous green sea with a breaking crest that appeared to be at least thirty meters above him. Deliberately, this huge wave had curled over his yacht, pressing it under with a monster insouciance that he knew must end in annihilation. And so it was now with Gomnol's psychic force impinging upon his own stunned consciousness, pressing him easily toward a final darkness.

The great storm-surge had unaccountably released his broken but still seaworthy yacht. With a similar mannered fillip, Gomnol let loose of Bryan's mind.

"That's how," said the President of the Coercer Guild. "Now. How may I assist your researches?"

Bryan heard Ogmol explain the task that the High King had set and the techniques that they hoped to use to gather data for the culture-impace analysis. Lord Gomnol could help, if he would, not only by explaining the pivotal role of the torcs, but also by sharing his personal reminiscences, uniquely valuable because of his privileged human status. And if the Exalted Lord would prefer to confer with Dr. Grenfell alone . . .

Smoke rings drawn around a friendly smile. "I believe that would be best. My congratulations on your delicacy of feeling, Creative Brother. Why not return and join us for dinner—say, in three hours? Splendid. Assure our Awesome Father that I'll take the very best care of the worthy Doctor of Anthropology."

And then Gomnol and Bryan were alone in the pseudo-Victorian snuggery, and the psychobiologist was clipping the end off a fresh cigar and saying, "Now, then, my friend. What the devil is the likes of you doing in Exile?"

"May I—have a drink?"

Gomnol went to the decanters and lifted one containing a nearly colorless liquid. "We have the Glendessarry, but no Évian water, I'm afraid. Or would you care to try some of our homebrews? Five whiskies, a vodka, any number of brandies— the preferred tipple of our Tanu brethren."

"Straight Scotch is fine," Bryan managed to say. When the whisky had restored his nerve a bit, he said, "I hope you won't regard me as a threat. Really—I'm not at all certain of the motivation behind the King's request myself. I came through the time-portal for the most ordinary of reasons. I was following the woman I loved. I had expected to become a fisherman or a trader in a primitive Pliocene world. The interest in my profession by my Tanu captors was a complete surprise to me. I'm cooperating because I've been told this is the only way I'll get to see Mercy."

Gomez-Nolan lowered one black brow in a half-scowl, seeming to scrutinize something floating in the air in front of Bryan. "*That's* your Mercy?" he inquired cryptically. "Good God." Not bothering to explain himself, he lit his cigar. "Come along. I'll show you the factory and tell you the Changeling's Tale."

A slab of the paneling swung aside, revealing a long, well-lit passage. Bryan followed Gomnol in a wake of smoke. They came to a great gateway of bronze bars that folded aside of its own volition as Gomnol strode heedlessly into it.

"Oh, yes. I have PK, too," the psychobiologist said. "And farspeak and redact. Not as strong as the coercive faculty, of course, but enough to be useful."

They came into a large room filled with what appeared to be jeweler's benches. Human and Tanu men and women in blue smocks, wearing magnifying eyelenses, were making golden torcs.

"This is the heart of the place, right here. All handwork for these. Subassemblies—the crystalline chips with the circuitry—have to be grown, then spattered and etched and sent here for installation within the metal shell. The Tanu brought only a single crystal-growing unit and chip etcher with them from their home galaxy, but I was able to build more to permit an increase in production of about tenfold."

A rama went by, trundling a cart with containers of glittering components. Gomnol waved his cigar, causing a pink wafer to fly out of a box and into his fingers. "This little widget is my own psychoregulator that I developed for the silvers and grays. It puts the wearer at the mental disposal of any gold."

Bryan could not help but envision Aiken Drum.

Gomnol brightened. "A fascinating case. I wasn't at the feast, but they told me all about him. Too bad old Mayvar has him locked up over in Farsense House. Both Culluket and I are itching to interrogate him."

"He worries the establishment?"

Gomnol laughed. "The more naive elements. He doesn't worry me. The boy sounds like he must be a mental nova. Flash-in-the-pan pseudo-operant. The phenomenon wasn't unknown in the Milieu. Certain latents can be shocked into operancy by some profound trauma. We've had it happen here once or twice before, although none of the cases was quite as memorable as this Aiken Drum seems to be. The temporary operant status of the brain overrides the controls of the silver torc. But the thing can't sustain itself and eventually burns out—googol to gaga, just like that."

"I've heard about the sad cases who couldn't adopt to the torc. But I understand you've been wearing one for forty years without suffering a mental burnout."

The man in the smoking jacket only smiled around his cigar.

They wandered among the benches, watching the painstaking work. It took almost a week for a technician to complete one of the golden neck-rings—even longer for the delicate little torcs worn by Tanu children. These came in four sizes; and when a larger one was put on, the smaller could be safely removed and used on another child.

"No silver torcs for children?" Bryan asked.

"Tanu women don't have human offspring—not even when they mate with human males. And human women—whether gold or silver or gray or bareneck—are only permitted to conceive by Tanu males. All of their offspring are exotic as well, but with a much smaller percentage of Firvulag phenotypes in the litter than Tanu women produce. The Tanu hybrids vary greatly in metapsychic faculties, of course. So far, all of them are latent. But in time, the race will produce natural operants, just as humanity has done. The human advent was quite a genetic leg up for the Tanu, as you can imagine. On their own—without any human admixture—they wouldn't have gone operant for millions of years. The human-Tanu matings speed up the evolutionary process drastically. Given the quality of the latent stock coming through the time-gate, Prentice Brown had calculated that the Tanu would go reliably operant in only fifty generations. Of course, now . . ."

"Elizabeth?"

"Exactly. When we got word of her arrival, Prentice Brown and I recalculated the heritability of the different meta genes based upon Elizabeth's presumed genetic assay and the results were astounding. You can get the details from Prentice Brown himself over at Creation House. He's called Lord Greg-Donnet, you know."

Bryan couldn't help thinking: Crazy Greggy.

Again Gomnol laughed, teeth tightly clenching the cigar.

"Some sooner, some later. Come along through here. The silver torcs are basically similar to the gold. But we've been able to automate a bit in the manufacture of the gray and rama types."

"How," Bryan asked, "do the Firvulag fit into your genetic enterprise?"

"They don't, as yet. A great pity from the eugenic viewpoint, as you've already deduced. The Little People are genuine operants, even if their powers tend to be limited. Unfortunately, both races have a horrendous taboo against interbreeding—and no Firvulag would touch a human with a barge pole. But some of us are working on the problem. If we could only convince the Tanu to keep their Firvulag children instead of passing them over to the Little People, we might have a chance of changing the mating pattern. It's fraught with possibilities."

They did a quick run through the area where the gray torcs were made. There was more of a factory atmosphere in this workshop, where several simple stamping machines were turning out torc shells and ramas were performing some of the assembly. Gomnol explained that the gray torcs were a variant of the device originally used on ramas by the pioneering Tanu, which he himself had modified into a psychoregulator suitable for humanity.

"We still have some problems with the torcs, as you heard. But by and large they're much more effective than the docilization implants that were used on sociopaths in the Milieu. And the pleasure-pain circuitry and the farspeak augmentation are completely innovative." Gomnol's eyes darted sidelong. In a neutral tone, he added, "I designed the original docilization device at Berkeley, you know."

Bryan's forehead furrowed. "I thought Eisenmann—"

Gomnol turned away. In a tight voice, he said, "I was a graduate student working under him. A young fool. We had a touching father-son relationship and he was so proud of me. My work was promising, he said, but its potential might remain unrealized because I lacked the cachet necessary to attract Polity funding. However, if I worked under him . . . there would be no problem. I was grateful and he was clever and the work was a resounding success. And now the entire Milieu knows Eisenmann the laureate. A few even remember Eusebio Gomez-Nolan, his faithful little assistant."

"I see."

The other man whirled around. "Oh, do you?" he flared. "Do you, indeed? Just forty years, and I've shaped an entire culture—turned these exotics from a path of feckless barbarism toward civilization! If the genetic manipulation with Elizabeth comes about, they could become transtechnological, superior to the Unity of our unborn Galactic Milieu! What would Eisenmann and those Stockholm idiots think if they could see all *this*?"

Oh, God, Bryan thought. He tried to keep his own mind as blank as possible. What had Elizabeth told them back at the auberge? Count! Onetwothreefour onetwothreefour onetwothreefour . . .

But Gomnol was not attempting to read the panicked anthropologist's thoughts. He was fully occupied with his own inner vision. "Many years ago, during the time of the Rebellion, a small number of other operants came through the time-gate. I wasn't ready. My position was still unconsolidated and the Tanu culture was in such a state of flux that matters were taken out of my hands before I could act. But I'm ready now! There are people working with me who share my views. With a new generation of operants standing with us, we'll prevail."

Onetwothreefour onetwothreefour. "It's a remarkable ambition, Lord Gomnol. Given the cooperation of Elizabeth, I don't see how it can fail." Onetwothreefour.

The psychobiologist seemed to relax. He blew a smoke ring, then gave Bryan a hearty clap on the shoulder. "Keep an objective eye, Grenfell. That's all I ask."

They moved into another area, where the crystal modules for the mental-assay machines were being assembled. "Care to have your soul microanalyzed?" Now Gomnol was jovial. "We can do a much better job here than at Castle Gateway. Prototype of an improved model coming up. I could furnish you with your complete psychosocial profile as well as a latency analysis. It would take only a few hours."

Onetwothreefour. "It wouldn't be too useful to you, I'm afraid. Lady Epone wasn't impressed when she tested me back at the castle."

An expression of wariness clouded the Lord Coercer's smile. "Yes. It *was* Epone who checked your Group out, wasn't it." He fell silent, and after a perfunctory stroll through research and testing facilities, where Gomnol was evasive about the exact nature of the work being done, they went down a long ramp that led from the factory to an atrium open to the sky and cooled by the jets of a spectacular fountain. They sat at a shaded table and rama servants in blue-and-gold livery brought a drink resembling iced sangría.

"One of your Group was a young woman named Felice," Gomnol said. "She's been involved in a serious accident. Can you tell me anything about her background?"

Onetwothreefour.

Bryan recapitulated all that he could remember of the girl's career as a ring-hockey player, her attack on the auberge counselor, her great physical strength and obvious deviation from the psychosocial norm. "I never saw her profile. But her ability to control animals is certainly suggestive of latency. I'm rather surprised that she didn't rate a silver torc. Was she badly injured in the accident?"

"She wasn't hurt at all." Gomnol's tone was studiously neutral. "The travelers in her caravan staged a revolt on the way to Finiah. The Lady Epone, a powerful coercer, was killed, together with the entire escort of gray-torc troops. The prisoners escaped, but most of them were later recaptured. They agreed under interrogation that your friend Felice had been the ringleader of the affair."

Onetwothreefour! "That's incredible. And did she—did you recapture Felice?"

"No. She and three other members of your Group are still at large. Most of the Tanu Great Ones are inclined to think that the affair was a fluke. There have been other minor uprisings from time to time, sometimes abetted by the Firvulag. But never before this have bare-neck humans been able to kill a Tanu. If Felice engineered it, I must find out how."

Onetwothreefour onetwothreefour. "I don't think there's much more I can tell you about her that would be useful. She struck me as a peculiar and dangerous child. She's only about eighteen, you know."

Gomnol sighed. "The children are *always* the most dangerous . . . Finish your drink, Bryan. I think we just have time to visit the classrooms of the apprentice coercers before the end of the afternoon. You'll enjoy meeting my youngsters. I have the highest hopes for them. The very highest."

Puffing his cigar, Eusebio Gomez-Nolan took Bryan off to view fresh marvels.

6

SUKEY'S FEAR HAD LESSENED NOW BUT THERE WAS STILL THE underlying sense of terror at being separated from Stein. But she no longer worried that he might be in danger; Aiken Drum, that inexplicable jester, would take care of him.

But what would become of *her*?

Creyn had come for her—friendly, familiar Creyn, the only person besides Elizabeth that she would have willingly followed. (And how had they known?) She rode now with the exotic healer in a hellad-drawn calèche to the College of Redactors, which was situated high above the city on a road that led up the forested Mount of Heroes. Olive trees heavy with plum-sized fruit grew along the verge and in the walled compounds of handsome white villas. She saw groves of citrus and almond; and, higher up the slope, rows of grapevines were being dressed by ramas. To the west the land of Aven stretched in a crazy quilt of greens and golds to the Dragon Range dimly visible on the horizon. Most of the region seemed under intensive cultivation, a striking contrast to the salt flats and pale bluish lagoons of the surrounding Mediterranean Basin.

As the carriage climbed higher, Sukey was able to see the peculiar topography of the ancient seabed south of Balearis. A scarp nearly 100 meters high fell off sharply on that side of the peninsula. Below lay an undulant slope of snow-white dunes, broken here and there by buttes and eroded pillars of what seemed to be pastel-colored salt. A small river coming off the peninsula slightly west of Muriah had carved a canyon through sparkling sediments. The watercourse wandered over the barren bed of this gorge, whose walls showed pale strips of color, and eventually reached the southern arm of the lagoon. East of the river channel and extending below the tip of Aven were flats that reflected the sunlight with a mirror dazzle.

"The White Silver Plain," Creyn told her. "We hold the Grand Combat down there, setting up cities of tents on either side of the Well of the Sea. Nearly ten thousand Tanu and human fighters come to the Combat from all parts of the Many-Colored Land, together with five times that number of noncombatants. And the Firvulag come as well, all tricked out in their bright and fearsome illusions with the black armor hidden beneath, carrying monstrous effigy standards hung with dyed scalps and festoons of gilded skulls."

Her mind's eye gaped at the picture he conjured up—first of the preliminaries, where the Firvulag played their uncouth games while the Tanu contended in splendid tournaments and races with chalikos and chariots. And then the manifestation of powers when the battle-leaders were chosen, and finally the High Mêlée itself, with Tanu and human and Firvulag thundering toward one another, shining hero versus hideous demon in battles pitting arm against arm, mind against mind, for three days—with the seizing of banners or standards and the taking of heads, the whirl of glass and bronze and leather and sweating flesh, the victors howling and glowing in the dark like torches, while the losers lay silent, spilling their blood back on the salt . . .

"No!" Sukey cried. "No—not Stein!" But he would love it—

Peace flooded through her.

Be at ease littleSistermind. It is a ways away and things may happen and not allTanu revel in its bloodshed O no not all.

"I don't understand," she said, searching Creyn's shuttered face. "What are you trying to tell me?"

"You're going to have to be strong. Bide your time until the proper moment and take a long view of matters. Keep hope high even when . . . distressing things happen to you. Stein and Aiken Drum have a hard way ahead of them, but yours may be harder."

She tried to probe him, to discover what lay behind that walled and kindly gaze, but it defeated her. She fell back into the simpler comfort that he offered, hardly caring any more what happened to her so long as there was a chance it might come right in the end.

"There *is* a chance, Sukey. Remember. And be brave."

Walls and turrets of silver and scarlet loomed over their carriage. They passed beneath an arch of marble filigree and halted before a white structure with pillars of red marble. A Tanu woman gowned in filmy white came out and took Sukey's hand.

Creyn introduced her. "The Lady Zealatrix Olar, who will be your teacher here in the House of Healing."

Welcome Daughterdear. What is your name?

Sue-Gwen.

"A goodly name," said the woman aloud. "We will give you the honorific Minivel, and you will rejoice to know that the lady who bore it last lived for two thousand years. Come with me, Gwen-Minivel!"

Sukey turned to Creyn, lips trembling.

"I leave you in the best of hands," he said. "Courage."

And then Creyn was gone, and Sukey followed Olar into the headquarters of the Guild of Redactors. It was quiet and cool, the décor mostly a chaste white and silver with only occasional accents of the heraldic red. Only a few people were to be seen; there were no guards.

"May—may I question you, Lady?" Sukey asked.

"Certainly. Later there will be the testing and the discipline. But now, at the beginning, I will show you the work that we do and answer your queries as fully as possible." *And correct and guide and light.*

"Persons like me—with silver torcs, or gold. How long may we live in this world? Is it as you imply—"

Smile. Come see. Anticipate!

They descended into arched catacombs within the rock of the mountain, lit with ruby and white lamps. Olar opened a thick door and they entered a circular room, quite dark, where a lone Tanu redactor sat on a central stool with his eyes closed in meditation. Slowly, Sukey's vision accommodated itself to the dimness. What she had mistaken for white statues ranged around the wall proved to be people, their naked bodies completely shrouded in transparent, clinging cauls that resembled some plastic membrane.

May I examine?

Freely.

She moved around the room, looking at the standing figures. Here was a gold-torc human male, reduced to a virtual skeleton by cachexia. Beside him was a Tanu woman, apparently lost in serene sleep, one pendulous breast distorted by a tumor. A

Tanu child, motionless, her eyes wide open, had one arm severed below the elbow. A robust goldenbeard, smiling as he
dreamed inside the artificial amnion, displayed the slashes and
punctures of a hundred wounds. Another warrior type had both
hands burned away. Next to him stood a human woman in late
middle age, her body sagging but unmarked.

"The more severe cases are dealt with on an individual
basis," said Olar. "But these our Healing Brother may minister
to en masse. The membrane is a psychoactive substance we
call Skin. Through a combination of psychokinesis and redaction, the practitioner is able to muster healing energies from
the patient's own mind and body. Injuries, disease, cancers,
the debilities of age—all respond to treatment if the patient's
mind is strong enough to cooperate with the healer."

Limitations?

"We cannot restore brain injuries. And it is against our ethic
to restore those who are decapitated in combat or ritual obser-
vances. If a person is not brought to treatment before full brain-
death, we cannot help. Nor can we restore the aged whose
minds have been allowed to deteriorate beyond a critical point.
Given these limitations, we are not as advanced as the science
of your Galactic Milieu, which could regenerate an entire cer-
ebral cortex if only a gram of tissue remained, or rejuvenate
even the most decrepit if their will was strong."

"Still—this is marvelous," Sukey breathed. "May I hope
to do this kind of work some day?"

Olar took her hand and led her from the room. "Perhaps,
child. But there are other tasks. Come and see."

They looked through one-way windows into rooms where
the mentally deranged were undergoing deep-redact. A large
percentage of the patients were young people, and Olar explained that these were mostly Tanu-human hybrids experiencing difficulties adapting to the torc.

"We treat human golds and silvers as well. However, some
human brains are fundamentally incompatible to the long-term
effects of the torc's amplification. Bringing such patients to
full sanity may be impossible. Lord Gomnol has provided us
with devices that indicate feasibility. We may not waste the
time of our talented redactors on hopeless cases."

"I don't suppose you waste time on gray-torcs, either,"
Sukey said in a low voice. Elizabethstyle barrier firmly in place.

"No, dear. Ordinarily not. Valuable as our grays are to us,
they are ephemerides—here and gone in a brief flash of vitality.

The healing is a difficult and time-consuming process. It is not for them . . . Now, come and see our babies growing!"

They ascended to the upper reaches of the huge building and came to sunny rooms full of bright-colored play equipment. Beautifully groomed female ramapithecines romped and lolled under the benevolent eyes of human and Tanu keepers. In adjoining rooms, ramas were eating or sleeping or submitting to various kinds of care. Every one of the little apes was pregnant.

"You may know," Olar said in an offhand manner, "that we Tanu women have experienced difficulty reproducing on this world. Early in our Exile, we utilized ramas as nurturers of the zygote. Ova fertilized in vitro are implanted within these animals and nourished. The ramas are too small to carry the fetuses to term, of course. But when development has progressed as far as possible, the infant is delivered by caesarian section. The mortality is nearly eighty percent, but we feel that the precious survivors are well worth the struggle. In the earliest days, these surrogate mothers seemed to be our only hope of racial survival. Fortunately, that situation no longer applies."

They left the ramas and tiptoed through a darkened ward where premature infants slept in sheltering glass crèches. Sukey was amazed to see Firvulag as well as Tanu babies receiving devoted care.

"They are our shadow-brethren," Olar told her. "We are obliged by the most ancient precepts of our way to rear them to term and subsequently turn them over to their own folk."

And then hunt and kill them?

You will understand one day littleSistermind. It is our way. If you would survive it must become your way.

"And now," Olar spoke out loud, "we will visit the Lady Tasha-Bybar."

Behind her mental screen, Sukey cried out.

"The procedure is very brief, but it is usually some weeks before the menstrual cycle reasserts itself normally. We will take care of this small matter before beginning your apprenticeship so that there will be a minimum of delay in your initiation."

Keeping a firm grip on herself, Sukey said, "I—I protest. To be *used* in this fashion."

Peacecalmsolace. "It is your lot. Accept it. There is so much joy to be gleaned in compensation! And the Lady Bybar is very skilled. You will feel no pain."

Olar stood still for a moment, fingers resting on her golden torc. She nodded, smiled, and took Sukey up a winding stairway into one of the high turrets. The room at the top was fully thirty meters in diameter, commanding a fantastic view of the surrounding countryside and the misted, glaring salt.

In the middle of the polished black floor was a long golden table surrounded by small trolleys with jewel-bright objects gleaming on their open shelves. The reflector dish of a huge lamp, unlit, hung above the equipment.

"The Lady Bybar will first dance for you, Gwen-Minivel. She does you great honor. Wait here now until she comes, and comport yourself with a dignity befitting your silver torc."

With that, Olar left her alone.

Hesitating and fearful, Sukey approached the central table. It was! There were clamps and stirrups. And the jewel-bladed things were just what she had suspected.

Tears blinded her and she stumbled away from the apparatus. She cried out secretly: Stein I would for *you*.

Or she could still run . . .

Olar's mind-grip caught her. She was forced to stop, to turn around, to watch in stunned incredulity as Tasha-Bybar entered and began her dance.

The human body was as pale and as lush as that of an houri— and so exaggerated in its sexuality that Sukey's instinct told her it must have been artificially enhanced. There was hair only upon the woman's head, and this flared like a blue-black cloak when she spun and leaped, and rippled almost to her knees when she was momentarily still.

All that she wore was bells, and the golden torc. The bells were small and round, fastened to her living flesh in graceful twisting patterns. They had differing notes; and as the dancer's muscles flexed and extended, an elfin melody born of the movement itself sounded in the huge, nearly empty room. The rhythm was that of Sukey's pulse. She stood frozen and helpless as the dancer approached in great fluid leaps, arms beckoning as they wove their eerie song, feet stamping with an accelerating insistence that compelled Sukey's heart to beat faster and faster.

The dancer's sunken eyes were as black as her hair. Nearly colorless lips drew back in a rictus above her teeth. Around and around Sukey the dancer spun, increasing the tempo of the music until Sukey was dizzy, nauseated, trying in vain to close her eyes and ears and mind to the flashing chiming gyrating thing that seized her and whirled her into oblivion.

7

"YOU'VE FIXED IT! YOU'RE A BONNY BOY, MY SHINING ONE."

Mayvar the Hag watched in delight as the tiny figures on the timepiece came sliding out on their tracks and circled one another. The turquoise-and-jet dragon flapped golden wings and lunged, clashing its jeweled fangs. The knight in opal armor fended off the little monster, then raised his glittering sword and struck; once... twice... three times. The clock told the hour. The dragon expired, chopped into three sections revealing ruby entrails. The entire turntable at the front of the timepiece revolved, carrying the tableau back inside golden doors.

Aiken Drum stowed tools back into pockets. "It wasn't that hard to fix. Crud in the drivetrain, a worn tooth on one of the little gears. You ought to have a glassblower make a dome to cover it, sweets. Preventive maintenance."

"I will," the old woman promised. She lifted the elaborate toy from the table where Aiken had been working on it to a safe place on a high shelf. Then she turned to him and held out both hands, grinning.

"Again?" he protested. "Insatiable old bag, aren't you?"

"All we Tanu women are," she cackled, pulling him toward the bedroom, "but there's few that can rise up to Mayvar and live, my Shining One, as you should know by now. So when I find such as you I must test and prove him. And if he lasts— ah, then!"

The room was very dark and cool and the awful old woman only a shadow waiting. Free of the golden suit, floating in the air, he came to her and was devoured. But there was no fear in him or cringing—not after the first time had shown him what lay beyond the repellent husk.

O amazing Hag with your hidden cauldron of near-deadly

rapture! You'd take the entire measure of life-force if I'd let you—snuff me after I'd fed your ancient nerve-fires and stoked them to youth again! But I won't die, Hag. I won't burn out. I'm up to you, old Mayvar, and beyond and above you, drawing you along with me while you scream. Come along and don't falter, Mayvar! Cry to die, Mayvar! Then burst and tumble down when you've had your surfeit of the Shining One who meets your test again and laughs . . .

The golliwog put on his golden boots and gave her ugliness a touch of pure affection. "You know, you're pretty good yourself, Witch."

"Once the Thagdal said the same." She uttered a long sigh. "And my darling Lugonn, that I had such hopes for before he died." She showed him the way it had been, back at the Ship's Grave, when all of them had first arrived in the Many-Colored Land.

"What a funny race you are," Aiken said. "Not civilized at all. You'd be in a fine mess by now if humans hadn't come through the time-gate and organized things for you. You should be grateful instead of resenting us!"

"*I* don't resent you," Mayvar said complacently. "Come close, my bonny boy." She took it from under the pillow and held it out to him.

"Do I need it?" he asked her, mouth quirking with the old mischief. "Would you have even more of me, glutton Mayvar?"

But this time she was serious. "You've still a way to go and a way to grow before you're a match for the greatest of the Host, Aiken Drum. There are those who can kill you— make no mistake. If you're wise, you'll go about this prudently and follow my counsel. Take it."

He settled the twisted golden ring around his neck and snapped the ends shut. Mayvar's gnarled fingers unfastened the old silver torc and dropped it beside the bed.

"I'll do as you say, Witch dear. And savor the fun to the fullest every step along the way."

She got up from the bed and he helped her to don the purple robe. Then they went out into her sitting room, where he combed her white hair and called for refreshment, which they both stood in need of.

"You've proved yourself to me," Mayvar said at length, "but you must also prove yourself to *them*. They must freely accept you. This is our way."

A tinkling fanfare came from the golden clock on the shelf.

Once again the dragon slithered forth and the knight came stalking him; and this time, the bejeweled prey was hewn into four sections to mark the striking of the hour.

"You want me to go and do likewise," Aiken observed. "Show all the folks what a grand barbarian warrior I am by making good on my monster-killing boast."

"It'll be a significant proof, the slaying of Delbaeth." She began to rock back and forth, chortling, hands clasping bony knees through the fabric of her gown. "Oh—you caught their attention with that offer, lad! Tana herself must have put the notion into your mind."

His response was laconic. "Your High King was so loud broadcasting his anxiety about the spook that it was impossible to resist."

"Ah! But, you see, there'd be talk of how the Thagdal himself should deal with Delbaeth! And since he's really too old, he'd have to ask Nodonn to do it. And that would obligate him to the Host, and—ah, you'll know about the politics soon enough. But as for Delbaeth—this Firvulag is one of the most powerful sort. He's a giant, not one of the little kind. He's been rampaging around burning up plantations outside of Afaliah, on what you'd call the Spanish mainland, for nearly a year now. Much of our provisioning here at the capital comes from the Afaliah region, and we also count on those farms for the extra supplies needed during Grand Combat time. Now, Afaliah's Lord is Celadeyr. He's a First Comer and a feisty old shit-kicker of a Creator-Coercer—but no match for Delbaeth. None of us are—if you match power for power. Old Celo's tried to Hunt down the Shape of Fire, but he gets outwitted every time when the Firvulag runs off and hides in the caves of the Gibraltar Isthmus. Things are getting serious, with the Grand Combat nearly on us, and Celo has demanded the assistance of the High King. The Thagdal is obliged to respond."

Aiken nodded. "I get it. But the King is getting a bit long in the tooth for that kind of adventure. Rogering maidens is more his style these days."

"He may properly designate any champion as his agent to deal with Delbaeth. But you forced him to send you! Do you see how galling it must be? An outsider—a human!—taking on a job that's defeated Tanu stalwarts. And all by accident, you've put one up Nodonn, too, since he was too wily to volunteer before the King asked him! If you succeed in killing

Delbaeth, wearing the gold and all, you tell the world that you think you're as good as any of them."

"Just as Gomnol did?"

She half-closed her pouched eyes, simultaneously projecting a vision of the long-ago triumph of the human Lord Coercer for Aiken's study. She looked out over the White Silver Plain where it had happened. "Gomnol would have aspired higher," she said softly, "but I spurned him, even though he could have sated me. Sterile! Or more correctly, so riddled with lethal genes that even the science of your Galactic Milieu had been powerless to correct his faulty plasm. The Kingmaker rejects such offal . . . Needless to say, I've already determined that you have no such deficiency."

Hands on hips, he threw back his head and laughed. "What a cold-blooded witch you are! And I thought it was all for sweet passion's sake."

Destiny rules passion in us both ShiningOne.

"You weird old crone!" he cried. "Meddling old bag of bones! Power-hungry ballbreaker! Get your stringy old ass to Redact House and crawl into the Skin and have them make you young again. We'll go and screw 'em all together, Lovie!"

Grasping one of her hands, he spun her tall figure around— then stopped short at the expression on her face and the vision that accompanied it.

"I've been lucky, Aiken. Most of my kind are only able to choose once. But I picked the Thagdal, and I chose his successor as well—although Tana's will took dear Lugonn before my choice could be made manifest. After he was gone, I waited these thousand years, weighing the hopefuls as it's my duty to do. But all of them fell short in one way or another. And so I had settled on the best of the rejected, Nodonn Battlemaster of the Host. His mind is stupendous and his heritage is acceptable—but ah what a meager flame he kindles, for all his jealous pride! What a poor stick to the engendering of a race of heroes! But he was the best we had until . . ."

"Silly Hag."

The knotted fingers stroked his golden torc, sending sweet fever rushing through him.

She crooned, "Lucky Mayvar! To see the third one come after all. Ah, but I've reached my limit with you, bright laddie! Three thousand three hundred and fifty-two of your years I've lived and done the love testing for the Tanu. You'll be the death of me, Aiken Drum. But not, please Tanu, until I've seen you safely installed."

"First things first," he said, divesting himself of her mental caress with some reluctance. "This Delbaeth. You realize that I don't have the faintest idea how to go about killing him? I talk a good game, but when push comes to shove, the spook might just burn the fewkin' gold britches off me! Wouldn't that be a nice end to our schemes?"

Mayvar gave a gay titter. "Would I send my own Initiate away unprepared? You'll be taught to use your powers properly before you go on the Delbaeth Quest. Two weeks under my tutelage—and that of mighty Bleyn, and Alberonn Mindeater, and the mistress of illusion, Katlinel the Darkeyed—and you'll be more than a match for this Firvulag . . . And to be on the safe side, I'll give you something else as well. What you would call an ace in the hole."

"Witch!" He sniggered. "What is it?"

"You'll never guess! No true Tanu would dare to use it because of the mortal danger to himself. But it'll be harmless to you, my bonny boy, and it'll dispose of Delbaeth if you but track him down. You must keep it secret from the others if you love your life—but with you as clever as I know you are, it should be no problem."

"What is it, for God's sake?" He grasped her by her bony shoulders and shook her as she continued to tantalize him, dangling a small mental image just out of reach.

At last she sobered. "Come along to the cellar, then, and I'll show it to you."

Stein was in an uneasy and dangerous mood, his great hands white-knuckled as he gripped the railing and pretended to watch the apprentice fighters larruping each other out in the arena. The upper level of his mind listened obediently to the running commentary of the Lord of Swords, who pointed out the technique—or lack of it—displayed by the young gray-torcs. Beneath the veneer, however, Stein was raging. Bluff Tagan, preoccupied with his exposition of martial arts, never noticed; but the gold-torc human woman who had been delegated by Mayvar to shepherd Stein on a tour of Muriah was all too aware of the giant's growing impatience. With a farspeaker's tact, she insinuated herself.

FriendStein are you weary of viewing fighterschool? Had hoped it would amusedistract.

Something wrong Sukeywife. WhatWHAT Lady Dedra I will know!

". . . and observe that young ox in the rust-colored kilt, Stein. Kurdish stock. Splendid musculature and as game as they make 'em, but he won't last five minutes in a Low Mêlée if he doesn't learn to stop telegraphing his ripostes. You don't need a torc to read that one's mind! Now, if you want a real study in finesse, keep a close eye on those two Maasai types sparring with vitredur lances. That's the kind of work that makes an old fighter's blood sing . . ."

Calmcalm relax Stein. Remember VenerableMayvar's directivepromise + that AikenDrum: no harm to Sukey.

Disbelief! FURY. I *hear* her she is crying afraid bellspun falling reach out Lady Dedra to her find her tell me why she cries!

Verywell I will look but do not betray yourself TaganCoercer freshaware your inattention.

Aloud, Stein said, "Those fellows have the moves, Lord Tagan. I'm no expert, but they look damn impressive. But I don't see how they'd have much of a chance in a contest against one of your Tanu brain benders."

"Most of this lot will only fight in the Contest of Humans— against one another. It's only the best who get to fight side by side with the metapsychic warriors in the High Mêlée against the Firvulag. Brave and strong-minded grays have managed to give a good account of themselves in the High. It's a matter of resisting the fear-provoking illusions of the Little Folks and keeping your mind on business. Of course, ultimately most of the grays . . ." The vision winked out almost as soon as it formed in Tagan's telepathic projection; but it had been clear enough to Stein.

The Lord of Swords peered obliquely at the Viking. Tagan looked more weather-beaten than most of the other Tanu, with a drooping gold mustache, and shaggy brows hedging sunken green eyes. "There have been exceptions to the usual fate of the gray fighter. A really superlative gladiator can expect a reprieve. And not just until the next year's Combat, either. Permanently. To serve on my staff here at the school."

Dedra said, "You know, Coercive Brother, that Stein's assignment must come ultimately from the Lady Mayvar, who has taken to kin the Candidate Aiken Drum." Putative master of this perhapsbriefliving gray.

The blue-armored Tanu gave a mental sneer, dismissing both Mayvar and her upstart protégé. "We'll see you in the

Combat one way or another, Stein. You're a natural, boy! I saw you at the supper. Just a few weeks of work here..." The coercer reached out: comradeship, adrenalin, challenge, release, gore, sweet shattering fatigue! "How about it, lad?"

Stein opened his mouth to curse the Lord of Swords. But what he said was, "I thank you, Lord Tagan, for thinking that I might be worthy to study under a great champion such as you. After my master and I dispose of the loathsome Delbaeth, we'll be free to think of the upcoming Combat. My master will confer with you in good time."

I didn't speak *you* spoke damnedDedra let me go let me go let me—

"We will leave you now, Coercive Brother," Dedra said, bowing and drawing her lavender chiffon cloak about her slender body. The sun had gone down behind the rim of the arena, which might have explained why she had begun to shiver. "You may be sure that Stein and his master, Aiken Drum, will consider your generous offer most seriously." Stop it! Stop fighting me you great blockhead!

Tagan smote his armored breast with a sapphire gauntlet. "I salute you, Farspeaking Sister, Exalted Lady Mary-Dedra. Remember me to your President... And you, valiant Stein. We hold the City Games thrice weekly here and at the Plain of Sports. Join us! Tomorrow our top wrestlers will test the first of the giant apes that were recently captured in the North African hills. It promises a bit of excitement!"

Stein was forced to remove his horned helmet and abase himself before the Lord of Swords. And then he had to hurry along after the gold-torc woman through cold, echoing passages that led beneath the arena to the carriage-yard where their calèche waited. The corridors were dark and deserted. Stein called for Dedra to wait for him, but she threw a glance over her shoulder and began to run instead. Her mind, operating on the coercive mode, reiterated:

You will submit to me you will be calm you will submit—

"Something's happened to Sukey, hasn't it?" he cried out.

You will submit to me you will be calm—

"You're afraid to tell me!" His stride lengthened. "I can't hear her calling me any more!"

Youwillsubmit youwillsubmit YOUWILLSUBMIT!

The pressure of his rage built into a great igneous flood, undermining her restraints, melting them. "They've killed her— haven't they?" the berserker roared. Dedra dodged away from him, almost falling on the damp stone floor. "Answer me, you stupid bitch! Answer me!"

YOU WILL...

Stein gave a shout, mingling pain and triumph, as the last of the mental shackles dissolved. A single leap brought him up to Dedra and he snatched the human woman into the air, spinning her around so that the panic-stricken, lovely face stared up helplessly. He bent her spine backwards and drew her into a dark niche, clammy and odorous, at one side of the corridor.

"I'm going to break your back if you make one sound! And don't call out in the farspeak mode, either, because I'll hear you. Understand? *Answer* me, dammit!"

Stein O Stein you misapprehend we wish no harm we would help—

"You listen to me," he hissed, relaxing the tension slightly. "There's no one down here but you and me. No one to come and save you. Mayvar should have given me a stronger keeper than you, Dedra. She should have known you'd never be able to hold me."

"But Mayvar would—"

He gave her a brutal shake. "Stop trying to get back into my mind, bitch!" She moaned and her head lolled sideways. "I want to know what's happened to my wife! You know and you'll tell me—"

"She's alive, Stein." Jesus God man you're crushingbreaking me ease up the spinalnerve bruising ahhhh...

He relaxed, propping her sagging body against the rough stone wall. She hung there like a cut-string marionette, belly swelling against her rucked-up lilac gown, lavender-and-gold headdress awry. Her mental explanation came rushing out.

As with all silvertorchumanwomen yourSukey gone to Bybar for fertility restoration.

"They promised me she wouldn't be harmed! Mayvar promised—and that bloody little gold grannybanger. They *promised*!"

Tears white arms reaching compassionbalm... "She hasn't been hurt, Stein. Can't you understand? We had to treat Sukey like an ordinary candidate. If an exception had been made before Aiken's position among the battle-company was affirmed—*don't*! Don't hurt me again! Can't you see I'm telling you the truth? Mayvar and Dionket must move cautiously at this stage or all the planning goes for nothing. There's more at stake here than you and your wife!"

Stein let her go. She sank to the dirty floor. Her mind was numb, shallowly adrift. The violet human eyes looked at him from amidst runnels of tears. "We never meant Sukey to go to the Thagdal. There's time. At least a month before her female cycle is reestablished."

"When will *your* Tanu bastard be born, bitch? To hell with Mayvar and Dionket and their schemes! To hell with all of you! I could hear Sukey calling me, dammit, and now she's stopped. You prove to me that she's alive and unharmed or—"

Take him to her.

Stein gave a start. His hand dropped to his sword hilt and he looked wildly about. The corridor was empty.

"I warned you, Dedra!" His face clouded again with fury.

She raised one shaking finger to her golden torc. "It's Mayvar. She's seen and heard. I'm to take you to Sukey. *Now* will you believe that we're on your side?"

He pulled her to her feet. Her gown was snagged and stained. Swiftly, he unpinned the brooch of his own short green cape and flung the covering garment about her shoulders. "Can you walk?"

"As far as the carriage. But give me your hand."

Outside, the bareneck gaffer who waited with their calèche was dozing as the cicadas turned up for their evening performance. Ramas were going about with short ladders and slow-matches, lighting the streetlamps. The broad promenade that skirted this side of the stadium had only a few cabs rolling along and no pedestrians except for the busy little apes.

Respectfully, Stein handed the Lady Dedra into the carriage before going around to the other side and climbing in.

"Where to, marm?" the driver croaked, coming to life with reluctance.

"Redact House. And quickly."

The driver whipped up the hellad and they trotted off. The carriage drove through the central city and its western suburbs before reaching the road that led to the heights. Muriah had no city wall. The natural isolation of the Aven Peninsula was deemed protection enough here in the southland where the Tanu were most powerful. Dedra did not speak and Stein sat stiffly at her side, not looking at her. Finally, when they were well above the city, the woman said, "There's a fountain ahead. Will you let me stop to clean up? If I enter the precincts of the redactors looking like this, there are bound to be questions."

Stein nodded and she gave instructions to the driver. After a few minutes they pulled into a deeply shadowed wayside. Some kind of bird was going *doink doink* among the crags. A spring emerged from the yellow limestone into a triple-tiered basin and the hellad was permitted to drink from the lowest pool, after which Dedra had the driver lead the beast to where it could crop from the thick shrubbery. She bathed her face in the central basin and produced a small mirror and a golden comb, which she used to repair her straggling coiffure. The ornate headdress was badly crushed. After a futile attempt to restore it, she threw it into a waste receptacle.

"Let some trash collector have a treat. I think my hair will do for now, but we'll have to hope Tasha is too stoned to notice my gown."

"Can you stop her reading our minds?"

Dedra gave a sour little laugh. "Ah! You don't know about our dear Tasha-Bybar, the Anastasya Astaurova that was, prime benefactress of the Tanu breeding scheme. Well, relax, lover. She has no metafaculties at all! Her gold torc is honorary—a token of Tanu esteem. Tasha is the human gynecologist who first showed the exotics how to reverse our sterilization some sixty-odd years ago. There are about a dozen other gut choppers doing the work now as well as Tash, of course, but none as competent as she is. She does all of the silvers herself. Literally keeps the old hand in."

A picture of the bell-dancer was projected before Stein's mental eye. "I've seen a few," he muttered. "But that's a different shade of kink!"

Dedra dipped one hand into the topmost pool of the fountain and drank from her cupped palm. "She's quite insane now. She must have been borderline when she passed through the auberge . . . Don't give me that old-fashioned masculine look, lover! I think she's a traitor to the human race, just as you do. But what's done is done. Most of us women make the best of it."

Stein shook his head. "How *could* she?"

"There's a crazy kind of logic to it . . . How do you like frustrated motherhood for starters? Here's this too dreadfully sexy bod that can't grow babies—so why not be a mother by proxy? All these perfectly healthy female time-travelers could have lovely Tanu children if only some good doctor repaired the mischief done by those gyn-folk with the little laser scalpels back at the auberge. The fix is quite tricky, because Madame's people seem to've anticipated some kind of jiggery-pokery among the philoprogenitive. But dear Tasha perseveres! Finally she gets it right, and she passes on her skills to a select squad of Tanu students. And here we all are, ready to be plowed and planted."

"If she's such a wiz of a doctor, why doesn't she have one of her prize pupils fix *her* up?"

"Ah! That's the too-barfmaking tragedy of it all, lover. Within that voluptuous female form with the enhanced secondaries and the estrogen implants there beats the heart of a true XY."

Stein glared at her in impatience. "What the hell are you talking about?"

Dedra climbed down from the fountain and sent an imperious mental command for the carriage. "An XY, lover. Tasha is a transsexual. Oh, you could stow away some real woman's fertilized egg in her fake uterus, and maybe shoot her full of preggy hormones, if you could get them in this primitive world— and perhaps the embryo would live a few weeks before dying. But that's all, lover. Maternity is a marvelous and tricky symbiosis. And of course, no one in our Galactic Milieu or anywhere else has ever made a *true* mother out of a male."

She stepped lightly into the calèche without assistance. "Well? Don't just stand there. Do you want to see your wife, or don't you?" Stein climbed in and they rode away.

When the red and white lights of the Redactor Guild buildings were quite close, Dedra said, "You're going to have to be careful when we get inside. Tasha can't read you, but there will be plenty of others who can. Heavy screens aren't my specialty, although I'll do the best I can for you. But if you start thrashing around and break through me it's going to be *both* our asses in a sling."

"I'll relax," he promised. "Sukey taught me things when we—on the trip down the river when we wanted privacy."

"Trust me," she pleaded. Looking up at him in the dusk, she tried to find one small scrap of empathy; but all that mattered to him was the safety of his precious, funny-faced love.

"I'm sorry I hurt you," he conceded. But that was all.

She stared straight ahead at the slouched beanbag shape of the old driver. "Think nothing of it. My fault for standing in the tornado's path. Lucky little Sukey . . ."

The carriage drew up to the entrance. Once again, Stein played the solicitous gray-torc esquire and Dedra, the Exalted

Lady. There were two guards in garnet-colored half-armor on station beneath the portico. A peevish silver male came to escort them up to Tasha-Bybar's eyrie.

"Most unusual," he fretted. "The routine is completely upset, Farspeaking Lady. You know, it was necessary for the Lord Healer himself to use his good offices—"

"We're very grateful to Lord Dionket, Worthy Gordon. It's a matter very important to the Venerable Mayvar Kingmaker."

"Oh, well, of course then. Along through here and up we go. Gwen-Minivel will still be groggy, you know. Lady Tasha likes them to rest well afterward."

"I'll bet," growled Stein. He lurched slightly as Dedra administered a psychic correction.

"We'll not be long, Worthy Gordon. How peaceful it is in your precincts at night! It seems we at Farsense House never really seem to settle down. In and out, in and out. Someone always has an important message or a data-search or a surveillance or a lost dog or something even more vital. I must say, I prefer your tranquil atmosphere."

"Indispensable in a house of healing," Gordon said. They had reached a landing just below the topmost floor of the tower. "The recovery rooms are arranged around the perimeter. The Candidate Gwen-Minivel is resting in Three."

"Please don't trouble yourself to wait." Dedra was firm. "We'll find our way out, and we'll only stay a very few minutes."

Gordon received this suggestion dubiously, but after arguing with the farspeaker for a few minutes, he bowed and retreated, leaving them standing before the door marked 3. Slowly, Dedra slid it open.

Stein pushed past her into the darkness. "Sue? Are you here?"

Someone moved on a chaise near the open window and sat up, dark against the lights of Muriah outside. "Steinie—?"

He knelt down beside her and took her face between his hands. "Have they hurt you? *Have* they?"

"Hush, love. No." *Gently gently my darling ah how did you know? How could you hear me?*

Muffled, he said, "I did and I came."

You broke Dedra/Mayvar control O Steinlove how did you break free how is it possible O mydear so wilduntamedrashmadloving!

They will not tie me separate us never until I die.

"Stein," she whispered, and began to weep.

From one corner of the darkened room, the one farthest from the door, came a small sound. The tinkle of a tiny bell.

"So you like to spy, too, do you?" Stein's voice was very soft. He rose to his feet and stood motionless.

"So *tall*! So *strong*!" The bells shivered up the scale and down. One with a lower note began a languorous rhythm. The dancer came, fluid as a shadow, and undulated before him. "So you want her? How sweet." It was a song the dancer sang, accompanied by the suddenly discordant chiming. "You want to take her, to take her, to take her!"

In Stein the white-hot anger was born again, an eruption of primitive psychoenergy howling wrath against the mocker and her music. Stein uttered a low cry and reached out to stem the peril; and Dedra, with her back against the closed door, threw her mind against him, too, even though her restraints were even weaker than Sukey's against that uniquely masculine tidal bore.

"Don't, Stein!" Sukey cried aloud. "Oh, don't!"

"You want to take her," laughed the bell-dancer, bending and thrusting. "But why why why? Take her her her?"

The bell sound and the laughing blended with twisting lights—the glittering bits of metal that rippled over white skin, the pulse quickening with the danger that made it more sweet—and then the music and dance ended in a shuddering finale and she opened to him as Dedra moaned and Sukey made one last futile try to prevent what was going to happen.

"Take *me*," invited Tasha-Bybar.

And the bronze sword did.

There was a great silence. Quite calm now, Stein wiped his blade on the draperies, sheathed it, and lifted Sukey into his arms. He stepped over the thing on the floor. "Get out of the way," he told Dedra.

"You can't!" the farspeaker wailed. *Mayvar! Mayvar!*

The door to the corridor opened, admitting a wide swath of light. An immensely tall man stood there, flanked by two servitors in the scarlet-and-white livery. "I warned Dionket that this was a mistake," Creyn said, his tone weary. He came into the room, gestured, and turned on festoons of the small cold-light lamps. A grim smile played over his lips as he looked beyond Stein and Sukey to the fallen dancer. The coarseness of his mental comment brought a gasp from Sukey and a surprised bark of laughter from Stein.

"You're on our side," marveled the Viking.

"Put Sukey down, you great ass," Creyn told him. "Thanks to you, your wife must be hidden away until the Grand Combat . . . and we'll have to move even faster than we'd originally planned."

8

NODONN SENT THE THUNDERBOLT DOWN INTO THE DARK WATERS of the Gulf of Aquitaine, where the wavelets reflected the moon and an unsuspecting monster chased a school of tunny not far beneath the surface.

As lightning struck, the sea boiled and belched clouds. Fifteen of the big fish went belly-up, electrocuted instantly. The plesiosaur, however, was only stunned. It broke through the maelstrom, raised its wattled head, and bellowed.

"Oh, you got him!" Rosmar cried. "And a big one!"

"The prey! The prey!" The other Hunters all burst forth into radiance, riders and mounts alike, now that there was no longer a need for concealment. A wheel of rainbow splendor turned in the air above the feebly swimming beast, almost fifty gloriously armored men and women from the court of the Tanu Battlemaster. And to one side, aloof as rosy-gold comets, were Nodonn himself and his new bride.

The Hunt whacked shields, sounded crystal horns. "The prey! The prey!"

"To Vrenol," Nodonn decided, his voice storm-loud.

One of the riders plummeted, trailing sparks, and swooped over the brute writhing amid the deadly waves. The snakelike neck of the plesiosaur lashed out and the knight hauled his chaliko up just in time to escape the dagger teeth. The rider thrust with his glowing sword and a ball of purplish fire flew from the tip to strike the marine monster between the eyes. The animal screamed.

A cheer was emitted by the circling Hunt. "At him, Vrenol!" some woman urged.

The Huntsman waved his sword in jaunty acknowledgment—which was a mistake. With its attacker distracted, the plesiosaur sounded with a simultaneous push from all four paddlelike limbs, leaving the discomfited Tanu knight poised in the air above a surge of evil-smelling bubbles.

"Oh, hard luck," an anonymous voice drawled. One of the armored women blew a derisive triple toot on her animal-headed glass trumpet.

Now Vrenol was faced with the dreadful expedient of pursuing the beast into the water—that element so abhorred by his race—if this first attempt at a kill were not to end in humiliation as the prey escaped.

"Ah, the silly young juggins," said Rosmar. "Bring the leviathan back up, my Lord!"

The blazing face of the Battlemaster smiled upon his bride. "If you ask it, vein of my heart. But Vrenol deserves to dunk for his foolishness." Nodonn reached out to discern the monster's position. "Oh, you'd sneak away, would you?" A blue bolt of energy split the gulf's water, causing the chalikos of the circling Hunt to rear and squeal. The plesiosaur surfaced once more and this time Vrenol went for it with his lance.

"He's got it!" Rosmar exclaimed. "Right at the base of the neck! Let's go down for the kill!"

The Lord and Lady of Goriah spiraled toward the water, the wheel of light fracturing respectfully before their passage. Now the individual Hunters poised waiting for the end. The plesiosaur, paralyzed by the wound, was still able to open and close its great jaws slowly. The seven-meter bulk of it wallowed amidst spreading bloodstains, lapped by small waves and glistening from the moonlight and the radiance of the killer hovering above.

Vrenol gripped his sword in both hands. The blade flashed down. The Hunt cried, "A trophy! A trophy!" One of the ladies descended, her lance couched, and with easy expertise pierced the floating severed head and hoisted it high. She presented the trophy to Vrenol. His glowing form changed from rainbow to neon-red and he was off like a scorching bolide to draw triumph figures among the stars.

"Well, he's young," Nodonn observed tolerantly. "We must make allowances." But on the command mode of the mental speech he warned the others:

Don't think the rest of you will be permitted such sloppiness! These beasts are getting scarce with overhunting and I'll not have them wasted.

The shining troupe responded: We hear Lord and Battle-master!

Aloud, Nodonn said, "Then back to Armorica and the Tainted Swamp. I require heads from the Firvulag Foe on your lances this night, for they are growing bold. And we must find, if we can, one of the great armored reptiles. It is urgently needed for the arena in the capital."

"On with the Hunt!" cried the sparkling riders. They formed a fiery procession again, with the scarlet figure of Vrenol now leading, and vaulted into the sky on the way to the mainland of Brittany.

Nodonn and Rosmar followed more slowly. He said to her, "There came to me just now a farspoken message from my Lady Mother. You and I must go to Muriah—and the reptile with us. We will take only a small escort to see to the beast."

"You are troubled," she said.

"It's nothing that can't be dealt with." But his deep thoughts on this matter were heavily screened.

Rosmar lifted the flashing glass helmet from her head and hung it from the horn of her saddle. "That's better. The wind in my hair! How I love to ride beside you, my daemon lover! Shall I ever learn to fly without your help?"

"In time you may learn. It's a shallow enough trick. We reverence you more for your gentler powers." And he smiled on her.

"My powers are for your service," she said. "But tell me what is happening in Muriah."

"There are matters touching upon our dynastic hopes. I must go down to assist other members of the Host of Nontusvel— for our Tanu people only respect the display of power."

"Is it the Firvulag?"

"There is a certain Delbaeth," he said, "whom I shall have to deal with before another does, shaming our House. But the real danger comes from newly arrived humans. Damn the time-gate! When will the others understand its perils?"

Rosmar laughed. "Do you think we humans should be locked out of Exile? Do you think the Tanu could survive without us?"

He reined up his steed and halted hers, so that the two of them drifted a moment in apparently motionless air. The sound of surf against the coastal rocks reached them, a faint booming.

"Some humans belong in the Many-Colored Land. People like you, Rosmar, my green-eyed, gray-eyed love, who never truly fit into the world of Elder Earth. But not all members of your race who come through are willing to accept the Tanu as masters. There are those who'd take the land away from us . . . or failing that, destroy it."

"Let's fight them together!" she said, wild with excitement. "Yours is the only world I want to know." Her soul opened to the bright Apollo, showing that what she said was true. Their two minds embraced in an ardent lifting.

"My daemon lover," she laughed.

And he said, "My own Mercy-Rosmar."

9

Jump Elizabeth.

Jump Elizabeth.

She stood on the headland above the White Silver Plain, looking down on the phantom cavalry of cloud shadows racing there on the empty moonlit salt. At the rim of the grassy terrace was a low railing. Beyond that a few stunted, picturesquely deformed pines at the precipice edge overhung a sheer drop of perhaps 100 meters to the Mediterranean abyss.

Jump Elizabeth jump to peace.

"Do you hear it?" she asked Brede.

A dark shape sitting on a stone bench stirred. Its topheavy headdress with the padded brim inclined in agreement.

"They're farwatching me from the palace," Elizabeth continued. "See what happens when I approach the brink—"

Jumpjumpjump! Be free abandoned onlyoneofkind! Poorforlorn thing Elizalonelybeth. Jump to release. Escape undesecrated while yet possible. Jump . . .

Palms resting on the balustrade, she leaned far out. Night winds brought the scent of the distant lagoon to mingle with the orange blossoms of Brede's garden. Out here on the land's end of Aven, far from any freshwater influx that would encourage simple algae and hardy crustaceans to flourish, there was no fishy-iodine smell of marine life—only the bitter alkali of the Empty Sea.

Elizabeth said, "They worked on me all afternoon while I was locked in my suite, trying to set up what they thought would be an appropriate emotional basis for the suicide impulse. Trading mostly on motifs of despair and dignity-threat, mixed with a good dollop of old-fashioned funk. But their whole foundation is spurious. The motivations are unacceptable to my metapsychic ethic. If they'd gone for the self-sacrificing altruism angle they'd have been nearer the mark—not that *that* would have worked, given this exile situation."

Brede's mental voice, so formal and lacking in the elisions and concatenations of ordinary mindspeech, said:

The masterclass metapsychics of your Milieu embraced a common ethical formula?

Elizabeth let amiable affirmation shine through the barrier she had maintained between herself and the Shipspouse since her first meeting with the exotic woman two hours earlier. "Most of us followed a system consonant with the philosophy of an evolving theosphere. Are you familiar with this concept? With the major religions of the later human era?"

I have studied your people since their first timefaring. Some of their professed philosophies have dismayed and repelled me. You must understand that the Tanu embrace a simple, unstructured monotheism without any priesthood or established hierarchy. We have been quite willing to grant religious freedom to those humans whose faith was nonmilitant. But there have been zealots who persisted in disrupting the King's peace—bareneck ones, of course—and these were speedily granted the martyrdom they subconsciously craved . . . But none of the humans I have studied was able to shed light on the Unity of your Galactic Milieu. And this is understandable, for only a true metapsychic can know it. In humility I request that you enlighten me.

"What you ask is virtually impossible, Brede. A young meta usually begins training before birth. The mental enlargement is intensified in early childhood—this is the kind of work I devoted my life to before my accident. A person with masterclass potential must expect to spend thirty years or more adapting to the full Unity. Enlighten you? . . . You invited me to inspect your intellectual potential and I'll agree that psychounion between us two is not utterly impossible. But that torc of yours presents a wall and a snare all at once. You think of yourself as operant. But, believe me—you aren't. Not truly. And without genuine metafunction you can't know the Unity or any of the rest of Milieu essence."

The calm thought came: It is foreseen that one day my people will partake of this essence.

"Foreseen by whom?"

By me.

Elizabeth came away from the railing and stood in front of the Shipspouse. Upon their first encounter Brede had revealed

that she belonged to a race different from that of the other
exotics. She was of less than medium height, with eyes that
were carnelian-brown instead of blue or green. Her face, the
lower part exposed now that she had once again removed her
baroque respirator, lacked the preternatural beauty of the ruling
Tanu race but was comely enough, appearing middle-aged.
Brede wore a gown of metallic red fabric that was styled in a
different manner from the thin flowing robes of the Tanu. It
was trimmed with red-and-black beading and over it she wore
a black coat with trailing bell sleeves and borders of red flameshapes. Her huge chapeau, also black and red, was aglitter with
jewels and had a black veil floating from it. The costume,
except for the ornate breathing equipment, reminded Elizabeth
of one of the tapestries from the Middle Ages that had adorned
the grand salon back at l'Auberge du Portail. There was an
archaic arura about the Shipspouse, a flavor of something con-
spicuously absent from the other exotics. Brede was no barbarian, no oracle, no priest-mother. All of Elizabeth's attempts
at analyzing her had thus far proved futile.

"Tell me what you want from me," the human woman said.
"Tell me who you really are."

The Shipspouse lifted her bowed head, revealing a sweet,
patient smile. For the first time, Brede voiced her thoughts
aloud.

"Why will you not mindspeak with me, Elizabeth?"

"It would be imprudent of me. You're more formidable than
the others. As both of us know."

Brede rose from the bench. Her breath began to come painfully again and she raised the respirator for relief. "This atmosphere—so suitable for my Tanu and Firvulag people—is
rarified for one of my stock. Will you come inside my home?
The oxygen is enriched within, and we can also seclude ourselves in my room without doors, and these hostile minds will
no longer be able to weary you with their importunities."

Jump Elizabeth! Don't let Twoface Brede fool you take you
from onlyescape. She worst of usall! Go back cliffside and
jump jump . . .

"The compulsion is getting rather annoying," Elizabeth
agreed. "But I'm capable of dealing with it."

"The attack of the Host represents no threat to you?"

"In order for their compulsion to work, it would have to be
strong enough to completely override my superego and will.
They'd almost have to dismember my personality and reinte-

grate it on a lower, complaisant level. There's a crowd of them
pecking at me now and the directing intelligences are respect-
ably strong. But none of them—not severally and not working
together—can summon the power to compel my suicide. Who
are they? Can you recognize any of them?"

"The four directors are leaders among Nontusvel's Host.
The PK adept is Kuhal, Second Lord Psychokinetic to Nodonn.
Imidol is the coercer, a battle-champion with small mental
subtlety. The farsensor is Riganone, a female warrior who sees
herself as the successor to Mayvar—an amusing conceit! The
fourth, the redactor, represents a more serious challenge, although perhaps not in the compulsive mode. He is Culluket,
the King's Interrogator, whose loyalty lies with his mother
Nontusvel and her Host rather than with his father, the Thagdal.
Culluket's faculties for deep-probe and mind alteration are second only to those of Dionket the Lord Healer. But healing is
not the work for which Culluket is known. It would not be
wise for you to encounter him at close range until you are
conversant with certain aggressive techniques in use among our
less principled element."

"Thanks for the warning. A perverted redactor might be
able to get into my autonomic nervous system while I was
asleep or emotionally distraught. I'll have to spin a special
stem-shield—maybe a trap, too. We had problems along this
line many years ago in the Milieu, before the Unity had reached
full maturation, with all human metapsychics assenting to the
common moral imperative. The self-defensive maneuvers are
still taught to young metas . . . just in case."

The compulsion now built to a near-hysterical crescendo as
Elizabeth walked at Brede's side on the path through the orange
grove. There were lurid threats of Tanu gang-rape and muti-
lation; visions of suffering, exploited daughters yet unborn;
wheedlings that promised death-peace and a reuniting with
Lawrence; even—belatedly—logical arguments for self-destruction based on the genetic ramifications of the situation.

Elizabeth turn back! Better for you for allhumans in Exile
allTanu as well if you die! Don't listen Twoface Shipspider-
spouse lies! Turn back and jump! Jump!

There were oranges on the ground, for Brede was not served
by ramas. The distinctive smell of citrus-mold blended with
the flower perfume; the trees carried blossoms simultaneously
with the fruit. Elizabeth reached up and picked a pendant globe.

The mental voices keened at ultimate strength: *Don't!* Don't turn away from release! Don't lose opportunity Elizabeth! Escape impossible within roomwithoutdoors! Turn back! Jump! Turn back . . .

BE GONE.

(Bubblesnapripplequench.) (Withdrawal.)

Brede's amplified voice said, "Now they know you were fully aware of their attack."

"They had to find out sooner or later. I prefer sooner."

"They'll try again. More of them. Queen Nontusvel has more than two hundred surviving children."

"Let them try! The compulsion-aggression would be ineffective if they amplified their efforts a thousandfold. Your people and their torcs! They don't achieve true mental synergy at all! They can't marshal the proper force behind a multimind thrust. They're primitive and sloppy—out of phase and out of focus. And out of their league, if you follow my idiom."

O cruel in aloof superiority O proud Elizabeth.

She paid no attention to the unspoken reproach. It had been an irritating day. As they walked toward the small white villa, Elizabeth peeled the orange and ate the small segments. The flesh of the fruit was dark in the moonlight, adding another brick to the edifice of her indignation: It was a blood orange.

Elizabeth's voice was snappish as she said, "You won't get anywhere being subtle with me, Brede. I never was much good at diplomatic byplay, even back in the Milieu. I want to know whose side you're on and what expectations you have of me. And just what is this room without doors?"

"You need have no fear of it. It cannot hold one such as you. But it will keep the Host away from you, body and soul, for as long as you remain within its sanctuary. I had hoped that you would stay with me. We could . . . teach one another. There is ample time, nearly two months before the Combat, where I foresee a climactic resolution."

The last pieces of orange rind fell from Elizabeth's hand. She slowed as they came out onto a small patch of lawn in front of the villa. Brede's house bore none of the usual Tanu faerie lights, but stood in Grecian simplicity framed by cypresses. It was a dwelling fit for the mystery woman, lacking any exterior openings.

The half-masked face of the Shipspouse looked up at her, entreating. It seemed to say: More than all the rest, we two are exiled.

"What happens if our attempted meeting of minds is unsuccessful?" Elizabeth inquired.

"Then you will do what you must." Brede was apparently unperturbed. "Shall we go in together?"

Side by side, the two of them crossed the grass, came onto the pillared porch of the little house, and passed through the smooth marble wall.

Into peace.

Elizabeth could not help letting a great sigh escape her lips. Mental as well as physical silence enveloped her—the kind that had once provoked such anguish back at the Metapsychic Institute on Denali, where the therapists had tried in vain to reestablish contact with her regenerated brain. But now—how welcome the stillness! It brought surcease from the background noise of all those lesser psyches that had mumbled and squealed and droned and piped their thin discordancies even when they were not actually reaching out in childish insolence or daring a frontal attack against her very ramparts. They couldn't reach her, of course; but there was still the battering . . . In the Milieu, such mental static was shut out by the overwhelming harmony of the Unity. Here, until now, there had been relief from it only in that cocoon of fire that was the last terrible refuge of a suffering, self-centered soul.

But this—

"Do you like my room?" asked Brede.

"I do," said Elizabeth. Both her mind and countenance smiled.

The exotic woman lowered her respirator. "There is an elevated partial pressure of oxygen here, which promotes euphoria. But the mental stillness is the most precious attribute of this room without doors. We two may reach out, but none may enter."

The exterior of the villa had been modest, with classic perpendicular lines; but the walls inside curved and arched away into immense distances. They were midnight-blue with ever-changing fragile patterns of faint carmine and silver, reminiscent of oil-sheen on deep water. There were pictures—projections, rather—of two deep-space vistas: a barred-spiral galaxy trailing two great arms, and a planet whose landmasses wrinkled into high mountains, having blue seas in rounded basins resembling lunar maria.

The furnishings of the room were simple, nearly invisible because they were made of the same dark stuff as the walls.

There were a few chests, shelves holding colored glass cylinders with magnetic imprints that were Tanu audiovisuals, a pair of long couches, several featureless cubes the size of footstools. Hovering at eye level against one wall was a small piece of sculpture, an abstraction of a female figure. Three blue lights were ranged around it. In the center of the room (or what might have been the center, if the walls had not approached or receded as one concentrated on them or ignored them) stood the most striking piece of décor: a low oval table that glowed milky white, flanked by two dark padded benches. On the table was a glass model that Elizabeth assumed represented some intricate protist organism such as a marine radiolarian.

"An image of my Ship," Brede explained. "Let us be seated and I will begin the sharing by telling you of our journey."

"Very well." Barriers firm, Elizabeth sat with clasped hands, looking not at the Shipspouse and her room of wonders but at the small diamond ring on her own right hand.

Aeons ago in our distant galaxy [Brede said] there lived a sentient race on a single small planet orbiting a yellow sun. When this race first achieved a written history it had but a single body form and a single mental pattern. With the passing of millennia it developed a high technology and the gravomagnetic transport, which enables vessels to travel at velocities approaching that of light without being restricted by the limitations of inertia. Suitable planets within practical range were colonized and a federation established. But then there was an interstellar war, and for long years the shattered colonies were separated from their mother-planet not only by the gulfs of space but also by a profound deterioration of culture. One daughter-world alone—my own planet of Lene—retained limited space-travel capability, using primitive reaction engines for brief forays into its own solar system.

Back on the mother-planet, which was called Duat, the great war had provoked melancholy changes. Damage to the land and atmosphere led to climatic alterations. The high mountains became a wilderness of snow; the precipitous valleys, though semitropical, were largely overcast and foggy. Over a thousand generations, the native people evolved two body forms, both different from the parent stock that had colonized the daughter-worlds so many years before.

The upland race, the Firvulag, dwelt in wintry austerity for most of the year. They were mostly small in stature and physically tough. Their culture was simple, with the technological conservatism and cooperative social patterns that often prevail in harsh environments. Isolated for long periods in their snow-bound caves, they consoled themselves not merely with handicrafts but more especially with mental diversions designed to preserve sanity. They developed the ability to conjure entertaining visions and pseudomaterial manifestations, as well as many other refinements of the psychoenergetic metafunction that you of the Milieu term "creativity." They also achieved a form of farspeech and farsight that enabled them to contact distant brethren without venturing into the deadly storms. The Firvulag became true, if limited, metapsychics, and they prospered.

Meanwhile, in the lowlands of this same Duat, a second racial type flourished—tall and slender and pale-skinned, with light-sensitive eyes, as was suitable in a warm climate with heavily overcast skies. This ancestral Tanu population struggled slowly back to a level of high technology. They never evolved into operant metafunction, as the Firvulag did; instead they developed the mental amplifier you know as the golden torc, which made their latent metafunctions imperfectly operant and gave them a crude but satisfying simulacrum of psychounity— the "mind-family" relationship that you have observed among our people and among the golds and silvers and grays of this Many-Colored Land . . .

There was always a strong strain of aggression in the people of biracial Duat. The Tanu and Firvulag were perennial antagonists, although neither group wreaked more than superficial damage upon the other because of a reluctance to penetrate far into enemy territory. The ritual battles became the basis for a simple religion that prevailed for another sixty generations— until Duat was contacted once again by explorers from the reborn Interstellar Federation.

Yes . . . we regained the stars, we daughter-worlds. While our ancient home-planet went its separate and peculiar way, we rediscovered the gravo-magnetic drive. But there was more! We entered into a wonderful symbiosis with the titanic sentient organisms that came to be called Ships. They were capable of superluminal travel through the exercise of their own minds, generating what you would call upsilonfields by means of a unique ultrasense. If the Ships were suitably motivated, they would carry a thousand or more of our people along with them in an implanted capsule, soaring to the uttermost parts of our galaxy in minutes—hours, at most. As you may have already guessed, the Ships could be motivated only by love. And each Ship that served us had as Spouse a woman of my race.

The dimorphic population of Duat was welcomed into our federation. Their golden torcs proved to be compatible with the minds of many, but by no means all, of the people living on the former colonial worlds. A torc-wearing elite came to power; and after only four generations, our confederation was experiencing a Golden Age of cultural and technoeconomic expansion.

Like all Golden Ages, ours came to an end. Descendants of the original Tanu and Firvulag, who were zealous endogamists, carried their ancient enmities to the stars, precipitating a new series of ruinous wars. After much suffering, peace was restored; but our federation decreed that the remnant of Firvulag and Tanu purebloods must abjure the battle-religion and mingle their genes so that the basis for the old hatred would be obliterated. Most of the dimorphic population eventually agreed to this. But one diehard segment refused and demanded the right to emigrate to another galaxy. This request was denied and their unconditional surrender required. They fled, only a thousand Tanu and Firvulag, to a remote world near the tip of one spiral arm, where they prepared to battle to the death among themselves in a last gesture of apocalyptic defiance.

One person only was sympathetic to their original plea for exile. This woman was blessed—or afflicted—with more than the ordinary Shipspouse's share of the metafaculty of prolepsis. You would call this prescience or foresight. She foresaw that the small mob of malcontents, so useless in their own galaxy, would have a catalytic effect in another star-whirl younger and less mentally evolved, where the great longevity and mental power of the exiles would have a beneficial influence on the slowly coalescing local Mind. The vision was a cloudy one. But it was sufficient to inspire this person to offer the services of herself and her Ship to carry the exiles away...

Thus we came.

And the human time-travelers came.

And *you* came.

"At this point," Brede admitted, "my prescience fails me. The arrival of people from Earth's distant future gave me great concern, upsetting as it did the Tanu-Firvulag balance of power that had prevailed up until about seventy years ago. I still have not fully assessed the impact. The survey now being conducted by your friend Bryan will possibly provide data necessary for my ultimate judgment—although neither King Thagdal nor any of the rest have thought deeply on what would have to be done should the verdict be unfavorable to further human participation."

"Humanity," said Elizabeth, "occupies a similarly equivocal position among the coadunate races of the Galactic Milieu."

"The human advent has brought about many advantageous changes—and not merely technoeconomic and eugenic. Factions among both the Firvulag and Tanu—especially *hybrid* Tanu—have begun to weary of the traditional contention and reach out toward a more civilized philosophy. It may well be that the assimilation of latent humanity into the Tanu population is a desirable thing. But you—!"

"No anthropological survey will assess my impact."

"Perhaps it is appropriate that you contribute your priceless heritage to our racial evolution at this point. The Thagdal believes this, as do Eadone Sciencemaster, Aluteyn the Lord Creator, Sebi-Gomnol, and a number of others among our Great Ones. But you and your genes for operant metafunction might just as easily be a potential lethal factor—as the Host of Nontusvel perceives you. What is to be done? I am at a loss to know how to proceed."

Slowly, Elizabeth rotated the diamond ring on her finger. "Some other would-be manipulators of humans have known the feeling."

10

ISOLATED FROM THE MAINLAND ON ITS LONG PENINSULA AS the Tanu capital was, its citizens were restricted in their ability to engage in Hunts. Long before humans came to the Many-Colored Land, all Firvulag had been exterminated or driven from Aven; citizens hankering for blood sport had either to travel to the Iberian mainland or content themselves with the organized events that took place in Muriah's huge open-air arena or at the Plain of Sports, a great green field northwest of the city that was laid out with grand- and petit-prix race-courses. In addition to the thrice-weekly contests, there was held midway in each month, excepting those of the Grand Combat and the flanking Truce, a much larger Sport Meeting that attracted contestants and spectators from all parts of southern Europe.

It was at the September Sport Meeting that Aiken Drum and his man-at-arms Stein Oleson were ordered to demonstrate their newly acquired martial skills. If the two of them passed muster in the arena, they would be allowed to participate in the Del-baeth Quest—which was now scheduled to be conducted by the King himself. After frantic maneuvering on the part of the Queen and her Host, it was decided that not only Aiken but also Nodonn Battlemaster, Lord of Goriah, would pursue the elusive monster under Thagdal's designated agency. All of the noble sports fans who could manage to get away would accompany the expedition to Spain to watch the fun.

Opening odds on Aiken to take the Shape of Fire were 300 to 1.

A nasty driving rain swept over Aven on Meeting Night. A team of PK stalwarts led by Nodonn's twin brothers Fian Sky-breaker and Kuhal Earthshaker mobilized efforts to deflect the downpour from the stadium by means of psychic energies. It was expected that the Battlemaster himself would arrive at the capital in time to witness the testing of the Candidate Aiken and his Viking henchman.

In the royal box awaiting the parade of contestants, Queen Nontusvel glanced up at a crooked discharge of natural lightning that flashed above the transparent roof generated by the psychokinetics.

"Such unusual weather for this time of year. I hope Nodonn and dear Rosmar won't be delayed." She turned to Eadone Sciencemaster who sat beside her, austere in unadorned silver. "Gomnol theorizes that our Flying Hunts may be disrupting the ozone layer and changing the climate."

"Twaddle," said Eadone, secure in her position as Dean of Guilds and eldest child of the King. "It's nothing but a freak storm. Perhaps the remnant of some tropical cyclone from the South Atlantic that managed to cross the Gibraltar Isthmus."

"Let's hope so, August Daughter," boomed Thagdal. "If this rain settles in to stay, it'll mean poor sport for our Delbaeth Quest. The old Shape of Fire might just stay home in his cave with his pipe and slippers if the crops at the plantations get all soggy and nonflammable. We'll have a devil of a time tracking him if he stays underground."

"Here's Bryan!" exclaimed the Queen. She now spoke in Standard English, a courtesy followed by all of the Tanu Great Ones in the presence of the torcless anthropologist. "And Greggy, and the Craftsmaster, too! Quite drenched, poor things. Aluteyn, darling! Couldn't your PK cope?"

"I'm a creator, Awful Lady, not an umbrella merchant," grumped the stout old Craftsmaster. "What's wrong with a little rain, anyhow? We Tanu ought to stiffen up and shake our silly water phobia. Whoever drowned in the rain?"

Bryan bowed to the royal couple. "It wasn't at all bad until we were forced to make a run from our carriage to the arena entrance. There are so many people here tonight that the ramas holding canopies over the new arrivals kept tangling up with one another."

Someone giggled, a sound approximating that of a strangling bantam chicken. A human male in a golden torc, wearing a clawhammer cutaway in the colors of the Creator Guild, stumbled moistly toward the King and Queen, spattering the other occupants of the royal box as he waved his arms in greeting.

His marmoset face was full of blithe innocence; he seemed to be about sixty years old.

"Aluteyn spun us an *illusion* of dryness!" this personage declaimed, executing a kind of curtsy that ended just short of his pitching over the rail into the arena. "But can illusion ever mimic truth? Especially when a canopy full of water tilts and—"

"Oh, shut up, Greggy," said the Craftsmaster, looking tired. "It's been a long day, Great Ones," he told the King and Queen.

"And did you take good care of Bryan? Show him all the wondrous secrets of your Guild?" The good Queen's solicitude warmed all three of the arrivals and dried their wet feet.

"A most impressive tour," Bryan said. "The facilities for training artists and scientists reminded me of certain universities of my own era. And of course Lord Greg-Donnet conducted me around the research laboratories of his own Genetics Department—"

"And wasn't it marvelous? Wasn't it?" The former Gregory Prentice Brown gave a small skip and clapped his hands. "I can't tell you what a joy it is chatting with a colleague who could fill me in on some of the latest developments of Milieu science! Do you realize, Majesties, that the percentage of operant metapsychics among last year's newborn humans in the Galactic Milieu has risen from two to *four*? I simply must replot my study of the latency coefficients! I had based my original prognosis on the assumption that the population was in equilibrium . . . but Grenfell says it's not! The implications are *enormous*."

"I'm sure they are, Greggy dear," said the Queen. "Do sit down and relax. Look—here come the clowns!"

"Oh, goody!" Lord Greg-Donnet cried. "I hope the exploding one is here tonight." He plumped down onto a seat and appropriated a plateful of finger-bananas from the royal snack table, eating them skin and all.

Eadone asked Bryan, "Is what Greggy says true?"

"I should think so, Lady Sciencemaster."

She frowned. "But for a replot, we'll need the computer."

"But we *have* the computer," Bryan said. "Ogmol and I have been using it to store our data."

With some stiffness, Aluteyn said, "The kid fixed it."

"Tana's toenails!" exclaimed the delighted King. "Maybe I misjudged Aiken!"

The Queen sat watching the cavorting entertainers with a fixed smile.

"Aiken Drum has been busy about many things," the Crafts-master continued in a voice heavy with irony. "He was able to show some of my people at the glass works how to restore the large annealing machine. He and Gomnol have been conferring on ways to improve the mental-assay device—which as you know has always been dismayingly fragile. And he has also introduced the vulgar nobility to kite fighting and three-dimensional chess. The new diversions have swept Muriah in the past two weeks."

"H'm," mused the King. He did not look delighted any more.

"Oh, the *animals*!" Greggy squealed. "Just look at that gigantopithecine! Will he fight? Will he?"

"Not to the death, darling," the Queen said. "We must save him for the Grand Combat. But there'll be elephants, and giant bear-dogs from the Catalonian Wilderness. And—look there, in that wagon. Another new monster! Isn't it dreadful? Like a cross between a sabertooth and a huge hyena!"

"Hyainailouros," Eadone said. "Another specimen brought back by the African expedition. The last delayed shipment arrived today."

Now there was a flourish of brass and tympani, punctuated by thunderclaps. The night's contestants paraded forth: first the lesser grays on foot, wearing different kinds of gladiatorial gear; then the higher-ranked grays, the silvers, and the human and Tanu gold-torcs in resplendent glass armor of many colors and styles. The chaliko steeds they rode were also armored and trapped richly, and many of the animals had their coats dyed yellow or crimson or blue.

The applause of the throng swelled almost to the pain threshold. Through the entrance and into the arena came two riders, side by side. One was a gigantic human male riding a coppery-red chaliko. His full armor was crystalline green studded with roundels and spikes of glittering topaz. The visor of the horned emerald helmet was up and Stein grinned at the shrieking fans and smote his shield with the flat of a huge vitredur axe. Beside the Viking rode a diminutive figure who seemed all plated in gold, astride a great black mount. As the ladies began to throw flowers he gave a bound and stood upright in his saddle, bearing aloft a lance from which floated a long purple pennon with a golden symbol on it.

"A banner with a strange device," Bryan murmured. "Is that charge really a digitus impudicus?"

"The Venerable Mayvar," said the Queen in a neutral tone, "allowed her Candidate to choose his own armorial bearings. Am I right in presuming that the hand-gesture motif represents a certain raffish defiance?"

"Your Majesty is quite correct," said Bryan, keeping a straight face.

The parade now ranged in a great circle all around the arena. The Marshal of Sport and the Lord of Swords entered last of all, together with their attendants and the corps of referees. When these functionaries came to the great fenced stairway in front of the royal box, they made their duty to Thagdal and Nontusvel and led both contestants and spectators in a loud salute.

Thagdal's mind and voice bellowed: "Let the games begin!"

The audience settled down while the principal fighters and animals retired to sideline areas. Preliminary events and circus acts began to warm things up. The King asked Bryan, "How does your survey go, Worthy Doctor?"

"I've gathered a considerable body of data, as Lord Ogmol has doubtless reported."

The King nodded. "Oggy's fighting tonight, but he tells me you've been running him all over town—and into the countryside."

"It's important to include agriculture, especially since it has become your policy to delegate operation of the plantations entirely to humans. I was surprised to find so many torcless workers employed in nonmenial positions. It's interesting that most of them seem productive and happy."

"Were you surprised to discover that, Bryan?" inquired the Queen. She took a napkin and dipped it into a goblet of white wine, then wiped mashed fruit pulp from Lord Greg-Donnet's face. The Genetics Master smiled adoringly at her.

"The apparent assimilation is significant. I understand that malcontents are relatively few—at least in the Aven area. Will I be allowed to compare these data with similar surveys of other metropolitan regions—say, Goriah, and Finiah?"

"Unfortunately," the King said, "there will not be time. We will require your completed analysis before the Grand Combat. You must make do with the material you're able to gather here— even if it does tend to be loaded with positive factors."

"We gather the crème de la crème of humanity for Muriah,"

said Greggy, looking smug. "Hardly anybody runs away down here. Not even the women. I mean—where could they go?"

"Kersic, mostly," said Eadone. She applauded an exhibition of roping and hog-tying of elk-sized antelope, performed by cowboys in orange lamé. To Bryan, she explained, "That's an island east of here. In your future world it has split into Corsica and Sardinia."

"And the—outlaws live there?"

"A few," the King said, waving a dismissive hand. "Gangs of sickly bandits preying on each other. Every few years we mount a Hunt and clean them out. Not much sport, though."

"Look! Look! The hoe-tuskers!" The Genetics Master, and most of the rest of the crowd, jumped up and down and screamed. Handlers with long goads brought on six colossal proboscideans with downcurving tusks. The largest stood nearly four meters high at the shoulder. Tanu knights afoot, armed only with vitredur lances bearing large banners, performed an exotic corrida with the animals. One luckless fighter botched a pase and was trampled. The rainbow blaze of his unbroken armor dulled abruptly, as though a switch had been thrown.

Greg-Donnet tittered. "Snapped his neck. Well—there's one for Dionket's baggie-bin!"

The Queen told the appalled Bryan, "He will be restored, dear boy, never fear. We're a very tough race, you know. But that poor fellow will be sidelined for the Grand Combat while he heals within the Skin. He's lost great prestige by being so clumsy."

The deinotheria and the surviving knights retired to applause.

"None of the animals are to be killed?" Bryan asked.

"There will be only two battles to the death tonight," said the Queen. "Ah. That's the end of that. And now . . ."

An elablorate blast of brasses sounded. The Marshal of Sport came to the steps in front of the royal box and Aluteyn translated his announcement for Bryan.

"Be pleased, Awful Majesties, to accept the homage of the Novice-at-Arms Stein Oleson, loyal servant of the Candidate Aiken Drum!"

Stein cantered out on his chaliko, rode up to the steps, lowered his long-hafted glass axe, and saluted by touching his gray torc. The cheers were loud but tentative. When the King arose and made a gesture, the crowd fell silent.

Stein turned his mount to face the chosen antagonist. Animal handlers on the other side of the arena opened a stout gate on the wheeled cage that held the hyainailouros.

The beast seemed to flow across the pocked and stained expanse of sand. It had the snakey neck and relatively small head of a polar bear. Its body, however, bulked at least twice as large as that of the unborn ursid. The hyainailouros might have weighed a ton or more; it moved with speed and agility, flattening its large rounded ears against its head and heading directly for Stein in a kind of galloping slither. The animal's mouth hung wide open, displaying a pair of oversized upper canines that were longer than Stein's mailed hand.

"Oooh!" shrilled Lord Greg-Donnet.

Following the obligatory etiquette of the arena, Stein came at a gallop to meet the creature, swerving aside at the last second to whack it on the rump, en passant, with the flat of his glass axe. It whirled, giving a kind of hissing hoot, and slashed with one clawed forefoot, then the other. Stein returned to count more coups, attacking and retreating, smacking the animal on flanks, back, neck—even gently tapping its flat skull. The hyainailouros spun about in a frenzy, trying to disembowel the chaliko or catch the tormenting rider in its gnashing jaws. The spectators greeted each coup with a roar of approbation. Finally, when the sabertoothed beast was beginning to reel with vertigo and frustration, scattered voices among the fans started to shout: "A kill! A kill!"

Stein spurred his mount and galloped in a tight circle around the swaying creature, which had risen to its hind legs. It uttered a series of short, high-pitched bleats, like demon laughter.

Thagdal stood up once more and gestured.

"A kill!" howled the crowd in unison.

And then there was silence, except for the thud of the chaliko's clawed feet as Stein guided it away from the hyainailouros, and the rasping exhalations of the winded prey waiting for its enemy to return. Stein dismounted. At the end of his axe was a stout lanyard; the advancing Viking began to swing the weapon by this cord, whirling it around and around his horned head. He approached the now rampant brute with every facet of his armor aglitter and the rotating vitredur blade all but invisible. Then he sprang, his body's trajectory timed to coincide with the swaying of the sabertoothed prey, and scythed its head off.

The spectators erupted in a mental and vocal tumult, shouting, clapping, and stamping. Thagdal opened a wicket in the

front of the box and descended the stairway that led into the
arena. Down below, the Marshal's attendants threw wide
the gate in the protective fence so that Stein could approach
the sovereign. The Viking took off his emerald helmet and
clumped forward.

And then the crowd gasped. From the other side of the
stadium came thundering a black steed bearing a small rider
armored in gold-lustred glass. Just as Stein paused in front of
the King, Aiken Drum reined up in a sliding halt scarcely a
meter behind his "servant," grinning like the personification of
Jack O'Lantern.

"And he did it all himself!" the jester said. "No assists from
mighty Me!"

The Marshal of Sport had been obliged to act fast with his
PK to keep the great dust cloud Aiken had generated from
enveloping the disconcerted King. Now the official stepped
forward and declaimed: "Pray silence for the accolade of His
Awful Majesty!"

"Yeah," said Stein, giving Aiken a look. "You'll get your
chance."

Thagdal produced a large chained medallion embossed with
the heraldic male face. He raised it. As the crowd cried, "Slonshal!" he hung it around Stein's neck.

"Accept this our accolade, and be forever our faithful man-
at-arms."

The people cheered, and Queen Nontusvel sent down a
napkin threaded through a magnificent ruby thumb ring (Stein
didn't mind at all that it was a little messy with banana), and
the Tanu ladies exuded concupiscence, and *very* guarded hostility emanated from the Tanu gentlemen, and a hostler brought
Stein's chaliko to him, and he rode away. Aiken followed after,
broadcasting, "That's my boy!" on a highly amplified farspeech
mode.

When Thagdal returned to the box there was a distinct atmosphere of jovian pique.

"Now, Thaggy," soothed the Queen.

"Didn't you *love* it?" Greggy squealed.

A great crack of thunder rang out. "My sentiments exactly,"
growled the High King of the Many-Colored Land. "You will
all excuse me. I am going for a royal leak."

"He doesn't really care for humans, you know." Lord Greg-
Donnet's cheery infant face was illuminated by momentary
sanity. "No more than you do, my Queen, and all your Host.

The King endures humanity as a necessary evil. But *you* would rather the timegate had never opened."

"Shame on you, Greggy," said Nontusvel. "Some of my best friends are human. You mustn't talk like that, naughty boy. What will Bryan think? Here—have a nice hard-boiled egg."

The Genetics Master took the proffered silver dish and stared into it, apparently puzzled. "Eggs? Eggs? But they, dearest Lady, are the matter of contention! A quarter of a million of them tucked within her human ovaries! So generous, so wasteful, so providential of Mother Nature to stuff every human female with such a superabundance of ova!" He peered sideways at Bryan, took up an egg and dipped it into a jar of Grey Poupon mustard before taking a meditative bite. "Do you know, Dr. Grenfell, that in the Pliocene, dear Mother Nature's name is Tana? . . . Or Té, if you're of the Firvulag persuasion."

"Don't talk with your mouth full, Greggy dear," said the Queen.

Tears began to trickle down the madman's smooth cheeks. "If only we could clone her!" And Bryan was quite aware that the Genetics Master no longer referred to Mother Nature. "You wouldn't believe, Grenfell, how primitive this outfit really is compared to my old lab back at Johns Hopkins."

"Watch the tournament, Greggy," Nontusvel urged. "See? There's Ogmol coming into the lists."

The Lady Eadone Sciencemaster gave Bryan an appraising glance. "And what preliminary conclusions have you been able to draw in these first weeks of your culture-impact survey, Doctor? Genetic considerations aside, we're worried that the Tanu may be becoming too dependent upon human workers and human technology. As you've noted, none of our young people choose a career in agriculture any more. The same is becoming true in other practical disciplines: mining, architecture, civil engineering, manufacturing."

"All activities that fall into *my* province," Aluteyn put in, looking harried. "Creation House is overflowing with musicians and dancers and sculptors and apprentice couturiers. But do you know how many signed up for bioluminescence technology this year? Five! Another couple of hundred years and we'll have to light our cities entirely with olive oil and reed pith soaked in tallow!"

"You may have grounds for your concern," Bryan said carefully.

The indignant Craftsmaster said, "There's even talk of separating the arts and sciences entirely—spinning off a new Guild, if you please!—with mostly gold humans in charge of technology!"

"Gomnol's idea, of course," Eadone remarked, entirely sedate.

"I've been in harness since the old days," Aluteyn said. "I was one of the First Comers who defied the federation and made contact with Brede. There aren't many of us left now among the Tanu—the Thagdal, Dionket, Mayvar, Lady Eadone, the Lord of Swords, poor old Leyr sulking in the Pyrénées . . . There! Even *I* give the damn mountains their human name! Just sixty-odd years of the time-gate and a millennium of Duat culture nearly gone down the drain. Even the best *fighters* these days are mostly hybrids! The world's gone to hell in a nightsoil cart."

"Compose yourself, Creative Brother," the Queen said.

Greg-Donnet showed his teeth in a wide grin. "You can't stand in the way of progress."

"Oh, really?" said Nontusvel.

A gray-torc usher opened the curtains at the rear of the royal box. He announced: "The Exalted Lord Nodonn Battlemaster and his consort, Lady Rosmar."

A towering form in rosy-golden armor stood in the doorway, almost blinding Bryan with sunrise radiance.

"My son!" cried the delighted Queen.

"Mother!"

"I'm so glad you're in time for his testing."

The visage of Apollo displayed an ironic smile. "I wouldn't have missed it for the world. I've brought a little present for Mayvar's fancyboy."

The Queen had risen from her seat to kiss her eldest child. Now she took the hand of a human woman dressed in a splendid costume and headdress of auroral hues and led her to the still-dazzled anthropologist.

"And here's a surprise for you, Bryan. Just as we promised! Dear Nodonn will want to go down to the arena to witness the trial of Aiken Drum, so you two must sit together and get reacquainted. You *do* remember Bryan Grenfell, don't you, darling Rosmar?"

"How could I ever forget?" Mercy said. Tenderly, she bent and kissed the anthropologist on the lips, then raised a playful eye to her resplendent Lord. "You mustn't be jealous, my daemon lover. Bryan and I are old, old friends."

"Enjoy one another," said the Battlemaster.

He opened the wicket and descended the stairs to the arena. The stadium crowd and the stormy sky thundered together in a concert of adulation.

Watching from the opposite side of the stadium, Aiken asked the Lord of Swords, "Who's the badass archangel?"

"You'll be finding out shortly! I understand he's brought something special for your testing from the marshes of Laar." Tagan went out of the sideline dugout to meet the Tanu champion. The jousting had come to a standstill in the uproar attending Nodonn's appearance.

Stein, free now of his glass armor and gnawing the roasted leg of some large fowl, called from the passageway leading to the dressing rooms. "Hey, kid! Somebody here to see you. Your old pal, the B.C. stud."

Raimo Hakkinen slid furtively into the dugout, pale eyes darting. None of the human or Tanu warriors was paying any attention to him, but he spoke in an anxious whisper just the same. "Only a minute of your time, Lord Aiken. That's all—"

The trickster was aghast. "What's this fewkin' *lord* bullshit? It's me, Chopper—your li'l bitty buddy!"

Aiken sent a quick probe behind bloodshot Mongol eyes . . . and found chaos. There was hardly a sensible thought to be found in that bog of weariness and dread that was Raimo's mind. Somehow, the silver torc had exacerbated the personal devils of the former woodsman. His experiences during the previous two weeks combined with this functional derangement to drive him to the brink of brain-wreck.

"The women, Aik! The goddam man-eating Tanu bitches! They been squeezing me like a lemon!"

Stein slapped one great thigh and gave a roar of cruel laughter.

Raimo only hung his head. He looked as if he had lost ten kilos. The formerly arrogant Finnish face had gone pinched and blotchy, the blond hair hung lank beneath a jaunty cap, and the once powerful body was shrunken within a costume that mimicked Italian Renaissance styling with its puffed sleeves, trunk hose, and codpiece. Raimo paid no attention to the Viking's derision but raised clasped hands and fell on his knees before the mischief-maker.

"For the love of God, Aik—help me! You can! I heard how you got this fuckin' town eatin' outa your hand."

Redaction was not Aiken's long metapsychic suit, but he plunged in to do the best he could for the tottering psyche. Some of the Tanu contestants for the games had begun to stare curiously, so Aiken pulled Raimo out into the corridor. Stein trailed after, chewing his bone.

"They been passing me from one to the other," Raimo said. "All the ones who don't have kids—and there are a coopful! They try out all the silver guys—grays, too, if they like the looks of 'em. But if it turns out that you don't knock any of 'em up, they quit being nice and get their buzz by—by—Jeez, Aik! D'you know what they can *do* to a guy wearin' this friggin' torc?"

Aiken saw. He moved quickly through the limbic system of the humiliated, hagridden brain, turning off pain circuits and putting up a temporary mitigating structure that would help... a little. When things were at their worst, Raimo would be able to retreat into it and stay sane. As the woodsman's twitching features calmed, he pleaded, "Don't let 'em get me, Aik. We were buddies. Don't let the Tanu bitches ball me to death."

A sudden burst of conversation and laughter sounded from the other end of the long passageway. Six tall apparitions of unearthly beauty, all rainbow chiffon and sparkling gems and floating blonde hair and on-the-gad pheromones, came gliding toward the three men with eager exclamations.

"We farwatched you and knew you'd be hiding here!"

"Wicked, delicious Raimo, to run away!"

"Now we'll have to punish you again, won't we?"

"Sisters! Do you know who the big one is? It's Stein! Let's take him, too!"

There was a perfumed scurrying and a clash of coordinated coercive power against a mind-shield of gold, followed by mental giggles and impudent tweaks that set Aiken and the Viking on fire even though the psychic barriers were up. A single moan: "Don't let 'em." And then Raimo and the Tanu women were gone.

"Holy shit," whispered Stein.

Aiken shook his golliwog head. "Back in the good old Milieu, I'd of said, 'What a way to go.' But you wouldn't believe what was rattling around in that poor bastard's skull.

A genuine fate worse than death! He just can't keep cutting it with those crazy broads!"

Stein said, "Too bad you don't give lessons."

"*Aiken Drum!*" came the mental and vocal command of the Lord of Swords. "You are required to demonstrate your power before the King and the nobility and populace of Muriah."

"Oh-oh. I'm on." The trickster looked up at Stein, serious for once. "If they nail me out there, Mayvar will bring you to the place where Sukey's hidden."

"Go stick it to 'em, kid," the Viking told him.

"Be pleased, Awful Majesties, to accept the homage of the gold-torc human Aiken Drum, sponsored Candidate of the Venerable Mayvar Kingmaker, President of the Guild of Farsensors."

Aiken rode up on the black charger to pay his devoirs. The plaudits were nearly as wild as those that had greeted the Battlemaster.

Nodonn himself stood at the foot of the stairs with Tagan and the Marshal of Sport, his head bared and an expression of benignity on his glowing face. When the cheers had completely died away, he said:

"Aiken Drum—your Venerable Patron has acquainted us with your considerable metapsychic talents. But these are not the qualities we seek to assess tonight as we weigh your candidacy. Instead, we would test the fundamental attributes that must characterize those of our battleworthy company—courage, resolution, intelligence. Demonstrate these as you meet the antagonist I have chosen for you . . . His name, according to the sages of Goriah, is Phobosuchus. Most of his kind have been extinct for nearly fifty million years. But a few survive as living fossils in the regions south of my city, in the vast estuaries of the River Laar where the long-necked sea monsters come to bask and breed. By my mind's power I have subdued and transported him here to try your skill. But I charge you, Aiken Drum, to remember our conventions of sport! You may use no overt mental force in your combat with Phobosuchus— only bodily strength, bravery, and natural cunning. Violate our precepts and the massed scorn of this noble company will annihilate you."

A low-pitched sound swept over the crowd. Conflicting farspoken sentiments eddied around the little figure in the golden armor: some hostile, some mocking or fearful, but others . . .

I'll be damned, Aiken thought. I think most of them want me to win!

Nodonn's admonitions having ended, the King signaled that the contest should begin. With one hand Aiken raised his pennoned lance, saluting first the royal box and then the mob of spectators. With the other hand, as he spurred his chaliko around to face the center of the arena, he repeated to the Battlemaster the finger gesture depicted on his banner.

There was a great cheer. A heavily barred doorway beside the animal pens swung wide, revealing a dark cavelike opening. Nodonn cried out in simultaneous vocal and mental command:

"Phobosuchus, come forth!"

A dragon raced into the arena, then stopped in the middle of the field to gape its jaws and give a hiss like an erupting fumarole.

The spectators responded with screams of awe and frenzied applause for the novelty, the like of which had never before been seen in the arena of Muriah. Phobosuchus was a monstrous crocodilian. Its skull measured two meters in length and the teeth in the bluish-gray mouth were the size of large bananas. At rest, and watching the approach of Aiken's black charger with a sardonic catlike eye, Phobosuchus squatted on the sand with bowed legs; the body was at least fifteen meters long, the dorsal surface armored with ridged bony scutes. The whimsy of the Battlemaster had augmented the natural pale-green-and-black banded pattern of the beast with painted designs of his own heraldic colors, rose-red and gold.

Infuriated by the mob's screeching, the bright lights, and the painful mental goad that Nodonn's coercive faculty had just administered, Phobosuchus sought whom it might devour. It lashed its serrated tail, releasing a noxious blast of musk from its cloacal glands. Then it hoisted its huge body high off the ground and started running toward the most likely target at a brisk gallop.

The pioneer "Scottish" planet of Dalriada where Aiken Drum had been nurtured had no native crocodilians, nor had the ecology engineers deemed that particular reptile order a suitable addition to the local biota. And so Aiken really hadn't the foggist notion of the type of creature that was charging toward him. He decided that it *had* to be a dragon. A dragon that could run like a racehorse and was thoroughly pissed. Game etiquette decreed that he meet the oncoming monster with bold resolution. He took a firm grip on his lance and thumped spurred heels upon his mount's wide shoulders...

...and quite forgot to hold onto its mind.

The black chaliko gave a ringing scream of fear and threw him. It fled for its life to the opposite end of the arena while the young man in the golden glass armor scrambled to his feet, snatched up his lance, and took to his heels with Phobosuchus in pleased pursuit.

After a silent beat of stunned horror, the spectators began a hilarious riot of cheering. The heavens added to the noise with a fanfaronade of thunder, which inspired the crocodile to bellow in response. It did this with its mouth closed, chasing Aiken up one side of the arena and down the other while clowns, referees, animal handlers, manure shovelers, Tanu knights in spiky jeweled armor, and dignified officials tumbled over one another and leaped or levitated into the front-row seats, trying to escape the racing monster.

As he approached the stairway to the royal box, where Nodonn, Tagan, and the other high-ranking observers stood like a collection of huge carved-gemstone chessmen, Aiken suddenly changed course. He streaked in a flat curve for the center of the arena with Phobosuchus two or three meters behind and beginning to get a trifle winded. Aiken thrust the butt of his lance ahead of him, sank it deeply into the sand, and went hand over hand up it in a fluid pole vault that sent him arcing through the air like a golden missile. He landed a monster's length to one side of Phobosuchus. The creature hesitated, then shied at the lance and its banner, which still quivered, embedded in the earth.

Phobosuchus halted, belly to the ground. It swung its awesome gape toward the golden manikin dancing around its flank. Aiken dashed toward the rear end of the great crocodile before it could shift its bulk and finally attained its blind spot. Skipping lightly as an autumn leaf, he ran along the knobbed and enameled expanse of the animal's back, keeping his balance like a logrolling champ while the reptile writhed and spun in an effort to discover what this peculiar prey was up to now.

Abruptly, the crocodilian froze. The crowd drew a collective breath. Aiken flung himself prone onto the gaudy cobbled hide and clung to a pair of scutes with a death-grip. Phobosuchus exploded into a fit of bucking and twisting, furious to dislodge the human pest that adhered to its back. Its jaws clashed with a noise of rending timbers; it bounced and squirmed and flung its three-ton body about with the agility of a basilisk, trying in vain to claw Aiken off with the black scimitars that tipped its feet. The reptile's tail churned up clouds of dust that momentarily hid both dragon and golden sticktight; but when the beast finally paused to rest, Aiken was still in position, lying on his armored stomach between two lines of scutes just aft of the front legs.

Phobosuchus lowered itself to its belly again and hissed exasperation. As the mouth, approximately as long as Aiken's body, closed, the trickster suddenly sprang to his feet and dashed up the neck, between the eyes, and down the length of the prostrate skull to leap off the tip of the snout. The monster watched in a kind of stunned fascination as Aiken sprinted for his lance and wrenched it out of the ground. He came running back to retrace his madcap route up the reptile's head and onto its shoulders, purple banner streaming raggedly above his dusty golden helm.

"A kill! A kill!" trumpeted the crowd.

Phobosuchus bellowed in despair. The jaws opened and the huge skull tilted above Aiken like the span of a nightmare drawbridge. Lance at the ready, the little man looked into the dragon's upside-down eyes. Aiken's farsense showed him the structure of the skull beneath the thick, ornamented hide— the two parietal openings behind the eyesockets.

Aiken chose the right fenestra, plunged his lance in, and immediately leapt from the creature's back and retreated to a safe distance. Once again Phobosuchus erupted into a paroxysm of thrashing, and this lasted for some time because dragons do not die easily. But at last the great body lay jerking in the dust and Aiken plucked the shattered lance with its ruined pennon from the bleeding brain. He walked very slowly to the royal stairway.

There was King Thagdal waiting for him. And the Queen, smiling, and off at one side the Battlemaster, aloof and glorious. And there was also a tall stooped figure in a plum-colored robe who cleaned his dusty armor with a gesture of her hand and gave him a fresh ensign, violet plumes, and a cloak like the spangled purple-black of the twilight sky to wear as he stood before the King.

Three times the Marshal had to cry: "Pray silence for the accolade of His Awful Majesty!" At last, the spectators were still.

The Lord of Swords stepped to the side of the sovereign

and held out a scabbard, from which Thagdal drew an amethystine sword. Holding the blade in one hand and the golden hilt in the other, the King poised the weapon in front of the face of the shining youth.

"We tender to you this our accolade, and bid you be forever our faithful knight. What name do you choose for your initiation into the noble battle-company of the Tanu?"

Mayvar's mental voice pervaded the arena with its muted tone.

He may not choose his name. I will choose his name at the acceptable time. But that time is not now.

The royal mouth tightened and static stirred the blond tendrils of the King's beard. "I defer to my Venerable Sister, your Patron and Lady. You will retain your human name until that time which she . . . foresees comes to pass. Receive this sword then, Lord Aiken Drum, and bear it in my service on the Delbaeth Quest."

Grinning, the golliwog accepted the vitredur blade. The Lord of Swords fastened the scabbard and its baldric and the crowd cried, "Slonshal!"

Up in the royal box, Lord Greg-Donnet hung over the rail cheering and scattering crumbs of egg yolk. "Good boy! Good lad! Well done!" He turned to the Craftsmaster, who watched the ceremony below with stony restraint. "Now we know that the lad is brave as well as talented in the métafunctions. Perhaps Mayvar wasn't quite so out of line as we feared, eh, Aluteyn?"

"Stop talking like an ass, Greggy. There's the Shape of Fire. The kid hasn't a chance of taking him."

Greg-Donnet chortled. "You think not? The bookies are giving three hundred to one on him. Or they were, before he polished off the dragon. Can I interest you in a side bet at those odds?"

Down in the arena, Mayvar was embracing her protégé. The King and the Battlemaster mounted the stairs to the box, looking unaccountably grim.

"A bet?" Aluteyn Craftsmaster was startled, then thoughtful. "Oh, no, Greggy. I don't think so. In no way."

"I was afraid of that," sighed the madman. He reached for another egg.

11

THE TRIMARAN FLEW WESTWARD BENEATH THE OUTTHRUSTING arm of Aven, skimming the shallow salt lagoon by virtue of the metapsychic gale Mercy had whistled up when Bryan protested that the day was too calm for sailing.

For what seemed like hours they took turns at the helm. She sang the oddly familiar Tanu Song, and the red-and-white sail bellied before them, hiding the distant mainland and the snow-crowned eastern end of the Betic Cordillera.

So strange, he thought, exulting in the nearness of her and the speed and the sunshine. So strange to realize that this was Earth. The Dragon Range of Aven, which would one day become the heights of Mallorca, had its lower slopes dark with tame forests and meadows where hipparions and antelopes and mastodons ranged in royal preserves. Those tawny hills, half-shrouded now in haze to starboard, would in six million years be islands named Ibiza and Formentera. (But never again would he race a yacht through azure waves off Punta Roya, for the Pliocene waters were pale as milk, and so her wild sea-reflecting eyes.) So strange.

The peninsular mass of Balearis rose from thick deposition beds of salt and gypsum and other sediments that had been laid down during the numerous regressions and inundations of the Mediterranean Basin. Streams flowing southward from Aven carved the minerals into canyons and buttes, spires and hoodoos, striped with pastel colors and sparkling in faerie splendor... and all of it would be gone without a trace by the time of the Galactic Milieu, drowned under unimaginable tons of water that would press the very bed of the sea two kilometers deeper and more, making abysses where now the Pliocene shallows glinted in the trimaran's wake. So strange.

109

After a long time the flats closed in around them and then folded into blinding gypsum dunes shimmering with mirages, among which weathered turrets of igneous rock poked up. There were hills and cliffs. The boat sailed up an eerie long fjord where whiteness gave way to purple and gray-blue, eroded slopes of ancient ash and volcanic scoria, broken cindercones lightly clothed in coniferous forest. The fjord was deep, the water now flowing from some western source. But Mercy's tame wind let them press on, breasting the current, until they emerged at last into an open expanse of saltmarsh, a green and living everglade that seemed to stretch on forever into the misted west.

"This is the Great Brackish Marsh," she told him. "A Spanish river pours in fresh water off the Betics, the high peaks we'll call the Sierra Nevada."

The diminished salinity of the marsh produced an environment much less inimical to life than the shores of the Mediterranean lagoons. Here grasses and sedges and mangroves throve in the shallows and there were many scattered islets with shrubs and hardwoods and swags of flowering vines. Gulls and gaudy pigeons wheeled overhead. Pink-and-black flamingos left off straining crustaceans from the pools and fled with honking cries when the invading trimaran glided by.

"We'll stop here," Mercy said. Her psychokinetic wind died away to the lightest of breezes. They hauled in the spinnaker and steered to a beautiful anchorage where a tall limestone outcropping crowned with laurel and tamarisk gave them shade from the sun.

"The Southern Lagoon proper ended when we came into the Long Fjord," she said. "This marsh stretches westward for another hundred and fifty kilometers or so, and beyond it are dry lakes and sand and alkali deserts all the way to the Gibraltar Isthmus. It's all far below sea level except for Alborán Volcano and a few smaller cones. Nothing lives in there but lizards and insects."

She coiled lines neatly. Leaving him to cope with the other sails, she went into the little cabin to get the basket with the lunch he had packed: a bottle of genuine Krug '03 from Muriah's black market, a wedge of the local cheddar equivalent, goose-liver sausage, sweet butter, a long loaf, and oranges. It had been too late in the season for black cherries.

"If only you'd waited for me back in the future," Bryan

said, "we'd have eaten this off Ajaccio. I had it all planned. The cruise, the supper under the Corsican moon . . ."

"The obligatory lovemaking. Dear Bryan!" Her wild eyes had become opalescent.

"I wanted to marry you, Mercy. I loved you from the first time I saw you. I still love you. That's why I had to follow, even though it meant coming this far."

One of her hands reached toward him, touching his cheek. The breeze moved the heavy fall of auburn hair that was tied back with a narrow bandeau. She was not wearing exotic clothing but rather a simple sunsuit of green and white, cut in the style of their own era. Only the torc, gleaming in the V-neck of the halter, recalled to him the gulf that now separated Mercy from Rosmar.

What did that matter? What matter any of the changes— the intrigues of the exotics, the cynical entrusting of her to him by the Tanu lover as he departed on his preposterous Quest. Mercy was here with him and real. All the rest was a fantasy to be forgotten . . . or at least postponed.

But change the earth or change the sky, yet will I love her—

"Have they made you happy?" he asked.

She cut bread with a glass knife and sliced the cheese. "Can't you tell, Bryan?"

"You're different. More alive. You never sang in our world."

"How did you know?"

He only smiled. "I'm glad you can sing here, Mercy."

"I never fit into the world we were born into. Don't laugh! There are more of us changelings than you might think! Misbegotten ones. Atavisms. No amount of counseling or brain chemical fiddling or deep-redact ever helped me to feel contented or satisfied. No man—forgive me if this hurts you!— no man ever gave me more than momentary comfort. I never knew a human being I could truly love."

He was pouring champagne. The words she spoke had no meaning and so they brought no pain. She was here with him. Nothing else mattered.

"It was the latencies, Bryan. I know that now. The people here have helped me to understand. All those strong metapsychic tensions locked away unused and unrealized. But pulling me—do you see? The operant metapsychics of the Milieu have their Unity, but there was none of that for me back on the Elder Earth. I belonged nowhere. Rested nowhere. Found peace nowhere . . . I found a little solace in drugs, a little more in music, in my work with the medieval pageants in Ireland and in France. But it was really no good. I felt I was an outsider, a misfit. Just a bit of nonviable scum on our famous human gene pool."

"Mercy—" I would love you any way. Every way.

"None of that, now!" She laughed lightly and took the glass of bubbling wine from him. "You know quite well that I was a hopeless mess, banging about like a moth around a streetlight. I played my games at the château and found other lost ones to share my bed, and suffocated quite a bit of the pain in a fog of sinsemilla. An old-fashioned vice. You smoke it as a euphoric. I brought some cuttings with me to grow—never dreaming that here I'd have no need of it ever again. This place, these people, *all* of this is what I yearned for without knowing."

"All I wanted," he said, "was you. If you can't love me, all I want is your happiness." She put her fingers against his lips, then lifted her own champagne glass for him to drink from.

"My dear. You are a rare man, darling Bryan. In your own way, perhaps as uncanny as I."

"I won't intrude on you if you're happy with him—"

"Hush! You don't understand how it is here. It's all new. A new world with new ways. A new life for you as well as for me. Who can say what might happen?"

He raised his eyes from the wineglass and met her wild glance, still not knowing what she was saying.

"Do you know what they've freed in me?" she cried. "What this golden torc has done? I've become a creator!... Not the kind who spins illusions or invents things or fashions works of art. A better kind! The highest of the Tanu creative ones are able to gather energy and channelize it. I can do that. Throw lightning, project beams of light, make things go hot or cold. But I can do other things as well—things no Tanu is capable of! I can take air and moisture and drifting dust and any old kind of rubbishy matter you can imagine and knead it and stir it and transform it into something all new! Look—just look!"

She sprang up, setting the boat to rocking, and reached toward the sky, a goddess summoning wind and mud and marshwater and cellulose and sugars and acids and esters from the grass. A flash of flame, an explosive report—

She held cherries.

Laughing, almost giddy, she let the black-red fruit dangle

from her fingers. "I saw them in you mind! Your favorite fruit that you wanted to lavish on your true love! Well—here they are, to complete the picnic that we've had to postpone for so long. We'll have them together with the golden apples of the Hesperides!"

It was not real, he told himself. Only she was real in all this world. And so he was calm and smiling as she dropped the cherries onto a large napkin they had spread on the chart table. The fruit was cold; drops of condensation beaded the juicy heart shapes.

"I'm still learning to use the power, of course. And there's no guarantee I'll pass it along full-blown to the children, because these high faculties are unpredictable. But who knows? Perhaps some day I'll be able to manipulate the genes themselves! Nodonn thinks it's possible, although Gomnol and Greggy don't. But even without that, I'll do marvelous things. Miraculous things!"

"You always were a miracle," he said. (Alas the child whose child?)

"Ah, silly!" she exclaimed, pretending anger. "The Thagdal's, of course, as the first must always be. You know about our jus primae noctis. And does it matter to you?"

"All that matters is that I love you. I'll always love you, no matter what you are."

"And what do you think I am?" She looked into his mind and the anger that blazed out now was real. "I'm *not* Nodonn's concubine. I'm his wife. He's taken me and no other."

And sixteen Tanu women and four hundred human latents of high talent before you . . . "I don't care, Mercy. Stop reading me! I can't help the way the thoughts come. They have nothing to do with my love for you."

She turned away from him and looked out over the marsh. "He'll be king one day when the Thagdal's finished. When he feels he has the full support of the battle-company, he'll challenge the old man in spite of Mayvar and win in the Heroic Encounter. And I'll be his queen. None of his other women had metafunctions to match mine. The exotics were barren except for five who had daughters and died. The humans . . . were beautiful and fertile but none of their talents are as fine as mine. They've all been discarded. I won't be. After I've borne this child for the Thagdal I'll have Nodonn's. Even if I can't manipulate the genes, I *can* learn to split the zygote with my psychokinesis and have twins, triplets even, just as easily as a single child. With the help of the Skin I'll have them safely and painlessly again aand again and again. I could have hundreds! And live for thousands of years. What do you say to that?"

"If you want it, I wish it for you."

Her indignation melted as she saw how forlorn and hopeless he had become before the prospect of her apotheosis. He stood there, moving slightly to keep his balance as the boat rocked, and she came to him and put bare arms around his neck and let her softness rest against him.

"Bryan, Bryan, don't be sad. Didn't I tell you it was a new world? I can't promise to be yours alone, my dear, but you needn't fear I'll drive you away. Not if you'll be gentle and discreet. Not if you'll . . . help me."

"Mercy!"

She closed his lips with her own. The warmth and brightness of her flooded suddenly over him, carrying far away the doubts and fearful promptings of logic. He kissed and shut her wild eyes and his own vision of the real world faded before her opening blaze. As their minds merged, so did their bodies, easily and perfectly as though angels were coupling instead of man and woman. He lifted and exalted her and she in accepting drew him even higher until each had consumed the other in a sunburst of joy.

"That's the way it is with us," she told him. "When mind and body are in sweet harmony it happens like this between lovers. And you're spoiled for the other kind forever."

"Yes," he agreed. "Yes."

"And you will help me?"

"Always. In any way."

"Remember your promise when you wake up, my dear. If you really love me. If you really want me to be happy. I have enemies, my dear. There are people who can hurt me, who can see to it that I never reach the thing I've been promised. You must help me. I'll show you how. I need you."

He heard himself say, "Only let me stay."

"Of course." Now the sun-flood gentled, became soft and dark as he was carried into the depths. "You'll stay with me and love me. As long as you can."

12

THE BODY IN ITS TRANSLUCENT SHROUD LAY IN STATE UPON a plinth of black glass in the great hall of Redact House.

These were the Great Ones of the High Table who came to pay homage: Queen Nontusvel, Eadone Sciencemaster, Dionket the Healer, Mayvar Kingmaker, Aluteyn Craftsmaster, Sebi-Gomnol the Lord Coercer, and Kuhal Earthshaker, a son of the Queen who was deputy to Nodonn and second among the psychokinetics. And others of the High Table included Imidol the Deputy Coercer; Riganone, second among farsensors; Culluket the King's Interrogator; and Anéar the Loving—all children of Nontusvel; and Katlinel the Darkeyed, half-human daughter of the deposed Lord Coercer Leyr. And those Great Ones absent on the Delbaeth Quest were Thagdal the High King, Nodonn Battlemaster, Tagan Lord of Swords, Bunone War-teacher, Fian Skybreaker, Alberonn Mindeater, and Bleyn the Champion.

The rulers of the Many-Colored Land looked upon the dead Anastasya Astaurova, linked minds, and sang the Song.

The caul clung tightly to her wide-open eyes, the arched nostrils, the clenched teeth visible through parted lips, the graceful neck with its golden torc. White as the salt and as cold were her splendid breasts and torso all beaded with tiny round bells, the belled legs and belled arms and ingenious surgeon's hands.

Mental speech, flickering and nuance-filled, passed among the assembled mourners with electric swiftness.

NONTUSVEL: Tasha-Bybar, farewell. So lovely to die, alas, thou
strangest of Earth's gifts to us, never understood and never

115

sated, in torment even after thy refashioning, dancing to find release in grotesque death.

DIONKET: A variation of her sabre dance with an unforeseen climax. Or was it?

GOMNOL: She was a genius! She should have been saved!

DIONKET: Teams of my redactors strove for three weeks to restore her within the Skin, but her mind was never able to cooperate. There were too many adverse factors: the massive trauma of the impalement, her longstanding unsanity— burned out as she was from our loving—the subconscious desire for obliteration. Even at best she was an insecure vessel of life-force, maladapted, unhelped by her transsexual conversion.

ALUTEYN: None other had her skill with the operation.

GOMNOL: No Tanu surgeon could equal her. No other human surgeon could/would do the great work she did.

EADONE: She was the opener of human wombs, the guarantor of our Tanu survival. Before her coming, our race dwelt precariously beneath this ferocious sun, multiplying slowly, so slowly. But she showed us a way to conquer our biological limitations, to burst forth in an explosion of life that has given us mastery of the planet. Praise to the departed Tasha-Bybar for having saved us!

ALUTEYN + GOMNOL: Praise.

MAYVAR: Given time, we could have saved *ourselves*.

EADONE: With the rama surrogates? Hardly!

ALUTEYN: Even now, Venerable Sister, the Firvulag outnumber us four to one.

MAYVAR: Nevertheless, what I say is true.

NONTUSVEL: Listen to Mayvar. She tells the truth, although her vision of it may differ from that of my Host. Oh, yes . . . we can and will survive of ourselves. As to how, I point in humility to the fruit of my own womb, the children of the Thagdal and Nontusvel: strong men and women, of the pure Tanu strain without human admixture, sitting at our High Table, leaders within our Guilds. *They* are the true salvation of our race! These children—my Host—and their own offspring are living proof of Tanu viability here on Earth, our guarantee of racial continuity. I will not deprecate the good work of Bybar nor the contributions of our other human benefactors. But let it be noted that the Tanu are survival-fit even without the mingling of human genes! The Host of

Nontusvel, two hundred and forty-two strong, has proved fully adapted to life on this planet.

KUHAL + IMIDOL + RIGANONE + CULLUKET + ANÉAR: Let the Queen-Dam's words be noted. It is in our Host that true survival resides!

EADONE: Your offspring's reproductive rate is still far below the optimum, Queen and Sister. But we may concede that your strain is the strongest among fullbreeds.

GOMNOL: You still can't deny that human genes saved the Tanu genetic bacon! In the sixty or so years of interspecific mating the Tanu population growth rate has increased tenfold. And the hybrids include most of your best fighters, your top creative people, and a majority of the coercers.

CULLUKET: Nevertheless, we now question the wisdom of continued dilution of our heritage.

IMIDOL: And above all, Coercive Brother, we question your scheme concerning the human operant, Elizabeth.

GOMNOL: So that's it.

ANÉAR: Dear Adopted Brother: we of the Host harbor only goodwill toward those of mixed Tanu and human blood. And we embrace the loyal human golds, such as yourself, who have so enriched our lives upon this planet. But we must take care lest we squander our inheritance by engendering more and more hybrids.

RIGANONE: Tana's will would be better served by an increase of purebloods. The vigor of the Host has proved that the original Tanu strain may reproduce itself adequately, albeit at a slower rate.

KUHAL: Disaster awaits us if we continue to mate with humans! Our noble Brother Battlemaster warned us of this decades ago. But we were so bedazzled by the benefits offered by humanity that we would not listen to his admonitions.

CULLUKET: The prospect of children by the Thagdal and Elizabeth has forced us to listen.

GOMNOL: The King endorses my plan fully. Eagerly!

EADONE: As Aluteyn and I have done. And yet . . . I must admit to some misgivings concerning the role of humanity in our High Kingdom. The Thagdal, too, has pondered this matter. For this reason we have commissioned the human anthropologist Bryan Grenfell to conduct a culture-impact study so that we may better understand the patterns of the psychosocial currents, both beneficial and inimical.

KUHAL: We of the Host have no need for human anthropology!

Our racial instincts alone are sufficient to show impending calamity!

IMIDOL: We and our Mother have seen what must be done if the Tanu heritage is to survive. Once Elizabeth's genes merge with ours, the true Tanu will be doomed. We say: Put an end to all bastardization! Return to the ancient way before it is too late!

ALUTEYN: Throw out the babies with the bath water? Piffle! You and Nodonn are only afraid your precious dynasty might get nudged out of power.

EADONE: Nevertheless, Craftsmaster, our Coercive Brother Imidol has raised a serious point.

NONTUSVEL: Dearest Sister—we are convinced of its seriousness!

GOMNOL: O Adopted Kinfolk, look at this matter rationally. This yearning for the good old days is futile. I've studied the records of the Lord Historian Seniet. Have you forgotten how it *really* was before the coming of humanity? Would you go back to living in crude strongholds in the wilderness? Would you revert to the hunter-gatherer culture of the Firvulag? You lived like savages before we shared our technology and our genes with you!

NONTUSVEL: Not really, Gomnol dear. It was a simpler life, that's true. Not nearly so grand. But we had the ramas to serve us. And our young people were interested in crafts then—

ALUTEYN: Not like the damn dilettantes nowadays. Wasn't for the humans and the hybrids, the whole economy'd go to pot.

NONTUSVEL: Now, Aluteyn. You exaggerate. I am a First Comer like you, even though I have only been Queen for eight hundred years. We had a good life in those early days. We hunted for food as well as for sport. There was some trading with the Firvulag for gems and furs and useful herbs and trinkets. And we bartered our splendid textiles and glass armor to them. Do you remember how valiantly our warriors fought when the Grand Combat was celebrated fiercely afoot, hand to hand, with no human levies standing between our fighters and the Old Foe? Do you remember those battles on the Firvulag's Field of Gold, and how we would rejoice when we captured their Sword of Sharn and bore the trophy home in triumph? And perhaps they would wrest it back from us in the year following, but we would train and scheme and strengthen our brains and muscles for the next Combat—and win! Those were the days, dear Craftsmaster! But now . . . for forty years running we have bested the Firvulag in the Combat with the aid of human and hybrid warriors. How stale the victory becomes. What if the Foe become so discouraged that they refuse to fight?

MAYVAR: It would show that they, at least, had evolved.

DIONKET: Morally, if not mentally.

CULLUKET: Lord Healer, you cannot expect me to sit unprotesting as you and the Venerable Kingmaker flirt with heresy against our glorious ideal of battle!

ALUTEYN: Dip your heresy in chaliko flop, boy! I say, what we need are fewer head-wallopers and more technicians! These simple joys of barbarism are all very well. But I'm the one who'll have to keep the glass-ovens stoked and the food and drink coming to the table. I remember how it was, chivvying Tanu crafters who were more interested in battling and screwing and Hunting than in getting a day's work done. Oh, the old-time ways had their charm! I'll concede that I wallowed in gore and flung thunderbolts with the best of 'em. But you can't give up progress any more than you can pretend the time-gate never opened. It did! The humans came. We used them. And now the good old days are gone.

NONTUSVEL: We could restore the best parts of them.

KUHAL: We are not against material progress, Craftsmaster. Only against the erosion of our Tanu ideals and their replacement with alien human values. The pacifistic sentiments of Lord Dionket and Lady Mayvar and their factions are well known—call them heresy or moral evolution. But the majority of us don't share their philosophy. It is a philosophy of weaklings, of hybrids, and of *humans*!

GOMNOL: Our Psychokinetic Brother distorts reality. All torced humans, excepting a few abnormals who have not reacted favorably to the mental amplification, are loyal to the Tanu race. As to the erosion of your ideals . . . when have you been stronger? You rule the world! And my plan can only make that rule more glorious. I will admit that times have changed—but this is not the planet of your origin. You have adapted, and you'll continue to adapt, to Earth. This is fully in accord with Tana's will.

KUHAL: We are grateful to the Lord Coercer for explaining our religion to us.

GOMNOL: Your suspicions of my plan are groundless. It poses

no threat whatsoever to your dynasty. Would the Thagdal approve it if it did? Do you question the vision of your own King?

EADONE: The plan involving Elizabeth is exciting. I am fascinated by the prospect of speeding our race's mental development—from latency to operancy—by incorporating her heritage within our own. To be free of the artificial action of the torcs! To see our offspring grow up to be true metapsychics! To see them possessed of godlike powers, perhaps even greater than those of the Milieu metapractitioners! There would be no more black-torc tragedies, no more burnt-out young Tanu brains unable to withstand the torc's amplification. With Elizabeth's genes, we could take an evolutionary shortcut, a leap across the aeons. Instead of waiting thousands or even millions of years to achieve operancy, we could see it within our own lifetimes...

ALUTEYN: I admit: a magnificent dream.

GOMNOL: No dream! A reality—if you don't turn your backs on my plan because of superstitious fear or racial chauvinism or petty politics. The anthropologist will prove to you that the coming of humanity to the Many-Colored Land has done you far more good than harm. I'll stake my life on it.

IMIDOL: You may, at that.

NONTUSVEL: Now...we must keep our tempers.

GOMNOL: You Host talk of racial purity. A thoroughly unscientific notion! Any biologist of the Milieu would tell you that. Just take an objective look at your allegedly pure Tanu heritage—! Firvulag recessives popping up like mad in every third birth.

KUHAL: Take care, Lord Coercer! Our Mother's strain is untainted. Never once has she given birth to one of the Foe.

GOMNOL: If that's true, you're very likely throwing out the very alleles you want to fix! And you want to use the Host as prime brood stock! Damn it, the Firvulag strain is the *operant* one! Ask the Lady Sciencemaster. Greggy and I have given up trying to sell you on mating with the Foe. But Elizabeth represents a unique genetic opportunity! A human operant has genes that not only enhance general survival, as the latents have done, but also give you the grand evolutionary leap that Lady Eadone spoke of. My plan leads to the fulfillment of Tanu destiny!

KUHAL: Again you presume to interpret Tana's will.

NONTUSVEL: It would be more *fitting* for the Goddess to work through our own Tanu line. We're afraid that Elizabeth's genes will turn us into humans, you see. Or at least into a race that is quite non-Tanu.

KUHAL + IMIDOL + RIGANONE + CULLUKET + ANÉAR: We do not need humanity! Better that we fulfill our destiny without humans!

GOMNOL: Then why has Nodonn himself taken to wife a woman of my race?

(Confusion.)

GOMNOL: Perhaps you'd better read your Crown Prince a refresher course in Tana's holy will.

NONTUSVEL: Do not descend to blasphemy, Lord Coercer. We have made it clear that we acknowledge the benefits that human genes have vouchsafed: the more powerful bodies, the increased fertility, the enhancement of coercive and creative metafunctions. And in the case of the precious Rosmar, we have embraced a rare and wondrous refinement of the creative power never seen among our Tanu adepts. *She* is the unique one! The value of her genes is self-evident. We welcome her as a fit consort for our future King. Dear Nodonn has had many wives—and as he is scarecely eight hundred years old, he may have many more if it pleases him. But let us not wander from the original matter at hand. Your plan, Adopted Son, proposes to go far beyond the mating customs that already obtain between the two races. The woman Elizabeth is not a talented latent such as yourself or Rosmar. She is a masterclass operant whose genes must be formidable indeed. Lord Greg-Donnet postulates that it is likely that all of her offspring would be operant—although perhaps not so powerful as their mother. He has also urged that, for the speediest achievement of race operancy, we should implant her ova in surrogates. But not ramapithecines! Human and Tanu women are to bear these wonder children! Who can assure us that this large new generation of torcless hybrids would be loyal to Tanu ideals? They will be a *new race*. It is logical that they would owe first loyalty to their own kind.

EADONE: There is a danger.

ALUTEYN: That possibility hadn't occurred to me. And I know Greggy never talked up artificial implanting to the King. That's not the Thagdal's idea of fun.

GOMNOL: This is ridiculous! Elizabeth's children would be as much Tanu as any hybrids. Education would see to it.

KUHAL + IMIDOL + RIGANONE + CULLUKET + ANÉAR: The Host does not concur. There is only one way to secure the safety of the Tanu heritage. The operant woman must die.

GOMNOL: You must not destroy her genes! Do you want to wait millions of years to achieve operancy? Future generations might call you worse than shortsighted! And if you come to your senses later on, it will be too late. There may never be another like Elizabeth to come through the gate!

NONTUSVEL: Alas. If only *she* hadn't come.

GOMNOL: She's here. I say it's Tana's will that she not be wasted... And don't you start twitting me about religion again, Kuhal! Not until the Goddess gives you her blueprint stamped APPROVED! My plan is as likely to coincide with divine will as your own.

ALUTEYN: Damn all this talk of becoming operant in millions of years! We *know* what's going to happen here on Earth in millions of years. The ramas will have evolved into humans. And we'll be extinct! There's Tana's will for you! Maybe the Thagdal *is* right about Gomnol's plan. At least it would give our people a good long run at playing metapsychic before the last snuff. Jack up our brainpower to operant status and we'll likely figure a way to get off this flatulent orifice of a planet!

NONTUSVEL: Aluteyn, dear. Control yourself.

ALUTEYN: If only we could be sure. These damn precious genes of Elizabeth's. If only they weren't so... human.

GOMNOL: How many times must I prove my motives to you? I have only the Tanu best interests at heart. I have had, from the beginning!

NONTUSVEL: There's still the vexing question of possible overdependence upon humanity by our race. I confess that I await the results of Bryan's survey with some trepidation.

KATLINEL: And what happens if the survey *does* show that the culture impact was largely unfavorable? Will you of the Host demand the death of all humans? Will you kill hybrids like me as well? Is this the secret solution that you've had in mind all along?

NONTUSVEL: Oh, Katy. How can you think it?

KATLINEL: The rest of them do, Queen-Mother.

IMIDOL: Nonsense.

CULLUKET: You are overwrought, Creative Sister. Let me administer a calmative.

KATLINEL: No, thank you, Redactive Brother. No, thank you!

EADONE: When the Thagdal returns at the time of Truce, we must have this out. Surely there can be a compromise.

KUHAL + IMIDOL + RIGANONE + CULLUKET + ANÉAR: Never on Elizabeth!

. . .

ALUTEYN: There's another factor nobody's even mentioned. As long as we're discussing genetic menaces, what about the other one? How would *he* fit into Gomnol's scheme? Or has Aiken Drum slipped the Lord Coercer's mind?

GOMNOL: I've assured King Thagdal and I assure you, too, that the boy is nothing but a mental nova. His mind will burn out as quickly as it flared up. He'll be a puling idiot inside of another month.

IMIDOL: You've tested him with your psychometric gadgets and proved this, Coercive Brother?

GOMNOL: You know very well that the Lady Mayvar wouldn't consent to my meddling with her great and good protégé, Coercive Brother.

IMIDOL: So much for guarantees. Tell us, Venerable Sister: On your honor as Kingmaker—is the youth Aiken Drum a mental nova?

MAYVAR: No. But he is no menace to our race, either.

GOMNOL: Even if he doesn't burn out, he's only a harmless nuisance—a practical joker with a certain crowd-pleasing charm. You people just haven't seen this type of human being before.

ANÉAR: I should hope not.

RIGANONE: Nodonn doesn't take Aiken Drum lightly. Why else would he have insisted on sharing the Delbaeth Quest with him?

EADONE: That is not the important question. What we really must know is why this charming, harmless prankster has been taken to kin by Mayvar Kingmaker. Let us be blunt. Will Aiken Drum challenge in the Grand Combat?

MAYVAR: If Tana wills that my golden laddie survive the Delbaeth Quest, then he will.

EADONE: Is Aiken Drum fertile?

MAYVAR: He is.

EADONE: Would he challenge Nodonn?

MAYVAR: You must ask him that.

NONTUSVEL: A *human*? A human challenging my Nodonn?

KUHAL + IMIDOL + RIGANONE + CULLUKET + ANÉAR: Tana forfend!

EADONE: Are Aiken Drum's metapsychic powers of sufficient potential to defeat the Battlemaster?

MAYVAR: Only Tana knows.

ALUTEYN: You know what would happen if the boy *did* win, don't you, kinfolk? He'd challenge the Thagdal! Is that the game you're playing, Venerable Sister?

MAYVAR: Beware, Aluteyn Craftsmaster. I play no games! I only do my Making as the Goddess commands me, and neither you nor the Host nor the entire battle-company of the Many-Colored Land may tell me how to fulfill my ancient office . . . Or would you?
(Dread.)

ALUTEYN: Well, you blew it once before with Lugonn, so it's no certainty.

MAYVAR: It is no certainty, as you say, Craftsmaster. But the Combat alone may prove the Goddess's will in this matter. Let no one here presume to interfere with my Making.

CULLUKET: No one will interfere—if your motives are true to the Tanu ideal.

MAYVAR: So once again, Young Redactor, you accuse me of heresy.

CULLUKET: Do you deny you have long opposed the battle-philosophy? Do you deny your sympathy for the traitorous heretic Minanonn, who betrayed his office as Battlemaster by preaching that Tanu and Firvulag should be brothers in sun as well as shadow?

MAYVAR: Poor Minanonn was ahead of his time, and imprudent. And he has paid for his rashness these five hundred years.

CULLUKET: But you and Dionket are cool hands! You're willing to play a waiting game until your human puppet is on the throne.

DIONKET: The Venerable Kingmaker and I are loyal to the Tanu race and resolved to see its destiny fulfilled in glory. And I admonish you to keep a respectful turn of mind, Redactive Brother, when addressing your elders.

NONTUSVEL: Oh, dear. This is all so confusing! Culluket, my son, you can't accuse people of heresy simply because they prefer the quiet life to Hunting and fighting. There have always been gentle ones among us.

IMIDOL: And they grow more numerous. Especially among the hybrids.

KATLINEL: We hybrids are loyal to the Tanu race! It is our race!

But if it's heresy to persuade the Thagdal to look afresh upon the old violent customs that originated on a forgotten planet in an inaccessible galaxy—then perhaps we *are* guilty!

NONTUSVEL: Of course you aren't, Katy. I'm sure Cull didn't mean it that way. Why—many of the Host are of a peaceful temperament, unless the Firvulag do something hopelessly provocative...

MAYVAR: And even then, there are those who eschew the pleasures of punishing villains such as Delbaeth in favor of remaining securely at home here in the capital while others do the Questing.

ALUTEYN: That's one on you, Cull. You never were one to do your own dirty work.

NONTUSVEL: We will not quarrel! There will be no more talk of heresy. I forbid it.

EADONE: Our Awful Queen is wise. Listen to her.

NONTUSVEL: There is still another potential consequent of the Aiken Drum matter to be considered. Let us look again upon the plan of Lord Gomnol. Suppose it happened that, in the uncertain future, the operant genes of the woman Elizabeth merged not with the seed of our beloved Thagdal, but with that of this *fully human male*?

EADONE: Tana have mercy! There is the true threat to our racial destiny!

ALUTEYN: The penalty for bearing a human child is death for parents and offspring.

NONTUSVEL: How could this be enforced if Aiken Drum were High King?

IMIDOL: A race of operant humans contending against us!

RIGANONE: We would be crushed.

CULLUKET: Let our loyal Lady Kingmaker explain this away!

MAYVAR: I can only do my Making as the Goddess prompts me.

IMIDOL: And Gomnol! Is our *human* brother manipulating the lot of us in some new experiment, as he has been manipulating us ever since he came through the time-gate?

GOMNOL: Perhaps you would like to challenge me for the Guild Presidency in the manifestation of powers, Coercive Brother?

NONTUSVEL: Oh, *no*! Now stop this, all of you! There is only one way we will ever untangle this muddle.

EADONE: Tell us, Sister and Mother.

NONTUSVEL: We must demand a ruling of Brede.

EADONE + ALUTEYN: Excellent. The Thagdal will surely agree.

RIGANONE: But there's no telling what that weird old Two-Face will say! She *never* involves herself in the affairs of the High Kingdom. She's no true Tanu at all . . . she's something else altogether.

ANÉAR: Something dreadful.

EADONE: Listen to me, you fearful young ones. Brede is the oldest and wisest, our guide and our first benefactor when an entire galaxy was arrayed against us. She had the original vision that inspired transport of the first Comers to our Exile here.

KUHAL: True, Lady Sciencemaster. But let us also remember that Brede brought *both* Tanu and Firvulag to this Earth. In some deep way she is linked in destiny to both races. We cannot be sure—

NONTUSVEL: We can only hope that she will choose what is best for both. We may even pray that she will choose what is best for all three races! . . . And now, my dearest ones, I would have you link minds with me once again. But this time you will not sing the Song for our poor dead sister, Bybar, but for all of us living on this planet, exiled and afraid.

13

AFTER NEARLY TWO WEEKS OF QUESTING IT HAD COME TO this: a vast black hole in the mountain and a nasty choice.

"What's wrong with chasing him underground?" Aiken Drum asked.

Nodonn bestowed a pitying glance on his diminutive rival. "On foot? With no bear-dogs to help catch his scent and distract him?"

The two of them were sitting on thoroughly winded chalikos, waiting for the other leaders of the great Hunt to reach the ledge in front of the cave. Several dozen amphicyons milled about yowling their frustration. None ventured more than two or three meters into the cavern entrance, from which a chill, dampish exhalation flowed.

"Let's take a peek at what's inside," Aiken suggested. He conjured up a fulgurant ball of energy like a floating star shell and sent it wafting into the dark cleft. The two Hunters followed its progress with their farsight. It came into a huge chamber all fanged with stalactites and stalagmites where there was a broad lake. On the far side a low arched passageway led deeper into the mountain and Aiken guided the psychoenergetic flare into this opening, through which an underground river flowed. The tunnel pinched and the roof lowered after about half a kilometer, and finally the stream flowed over a precipice into a void so black that the light of the flare could not illuminate it. For a moment the two metapsychics saw with their mind's eye a waterfall dropping like a length of gauze into nothingness. Then the flare was suddenly extinguished.

A faint sound of laughter floated from the depths.

"And up yours, too," Aiken said to the faraway Shape of Fire.

The King's mount came scrambling up the rocky slope, followed closely by Stein—whom the monarch had taken a liking to, Lord Celadeyr of Afaliah, Lady Bunone Warteacher, and fifteen or so others of the party possessing the PK power to assist their faltering steeds in the climb. Because of Delbaeth's habit of bombarding pursuers with fireballs, it had not been possible for the Quest to take to the air.

"Well?" growled Thagdal.

"Gone to ground," said the Battlemaster.

The King removed his diamond helm, slouched in the saddle, and chewed his golden mustache. "Damn it all to hell. After chasing him all this way."

"He does it every time," Celadeyr of Afaliah remarked, shrugging aquamarine-armored shoulders. "Leads you from one plantation to the next. Lets you think you've got him trapped, then pops up outside your line, fries a few grays and anybody else he catches with his pants down, and then off to the races again. Daring you to nail him! That's our Delbaeth. But it always ends the same way—into some bloody cave, and the laugh's on you."

"Damn smart for a Firvulag, Celo."

The Lord of Afaliah spurred his chaliko through the rabble of bear-dogs to the cavern mouth. "Would I have asked for your help against an ordinary spook? Good thing for us Delbaeth is a maverick and doesn't fight in the Combat! . . . This is a new bolt-hole. At least we've managed to chase him farther west than ever before. This part of the Cordillera is way to hell and gone out on the Isthmus."

The King spat. "Don't know *where* the devil we are, not being able to reconnoiter from the air. Steinie—you got any beer left?"

The Viking passed a large canteen.

Celadeyr said, "Now that the Shape of Fire's underground, it's safe to fly if you wish, Majesty. He'll stay holed up for several days now to rest. There'd be no danger at all flying back to Afaliah."

"Give it up?" cried Stein. "We still got three days clear until the friggin' Truce! There's still a chance we could get him."

The mounted assembly laughed. Bunone Warteacher, awesome in a silvery bascinet that made her look like a bird of prey, said, "Delbaeth isn't coming out. Would you and your saucy master follow him *in*?"

"Why not?" Stein asked, and once more the Hunters laughed.

Aiken said to the King, "I told you I'd get him for you. I promised it, in fact. If I don't get Delbaeth, I'm screwed for the Grand Combat—right?"

"Oddly phrased," said the King. His smile was affable. "But the conclusion is accurate. You've had ample opportunity to carry out your boastful proposal on this Quest. If we return to Muriah having failed, I'll consider your service-bid for Stein null and void. It would be proper to punish you for the insolence of having made the bid in the first place, but in consideration for your repair of the computer and several other worthwhile accomplishments, I feel disposed to generosity. You'll be eligible to fight in the High Mêlée with the other gold-torc human warriors. But you may not aspire to the Heroic Encounters."

"It is fitting," said Nodonn, glowing in the advancing dusk. A few bats began to zip out of the cave on their evening forays.

"If we're packing it in," Celadeyr said, "Let's get down the mountain before any others ruin their mounts trying to climb up here."

"Now just a damn minute," Aiken protested. "I didn't say I was giving up. There's still three days before the Truce . . . I'm going after Delbaeth. Into the cave."

"And I'm going with him," Stein said. "Nobody's gonna auction me off like a prize steer again!" The mental and vocal babble greeting their declarations made it possible for Aiken to screen off Stein's unspoken thought: *So what if I get killed? If any Tanu takes me for a slave, I'll never see Sukey again.*

"Make your foolhardy gesture if you must," said Nodonn. "Show us, if you can, that you know how to beat the Shape of Fire on his own home ground." Most of the Tanu crowded onto the ledge roared appreciation of the Battlemaster's remark. "The rest of us will return to Lord Celadeyr's castle for refreshment, then fly on to the capital. Delbaeth will keep until after the Grand Combat. Should we discover your bones when we finally penetrate to his lair, we'll conduct suitable obsequies and sing for you the Song."

More laughter. But in the midst, a protest.

"So you object, Bleyn and Alberonn?" inquired the Battlemaster.

Two riders urged their beasts to the fore. Bleyn the Champion was a hybrid, powerful in both PK and coercion, who sat at the High Table. Alberonn Mindeater, another hybrid, was one of the best warrior-illusionists. Both were of the faction of Mayvar and both had helped to train Aiken and Stein in martial arts for their initiation.

"It is not fitting that this company desert Lord Aiken here in the wilderness while he descends to challenge Delbaeth," Bleyn stated. "Shame on those who would hold a brave man's endeavor up to mockery."

Nodonn only smiled.

Alberonn said, "We two will await the return of Aiken and Stein. We will camp before this very cave mouth, praying for their success. We will wait for the three days, so that the time originally allotted for this Quest may be honorably fulfilled."

"I also will wait," decided Bunone, "and my three warrior-maids. Aiken Drum is a man of singular talents! We, too, will pray that he survives."

The High King threw up one flashing hand in a gesture of resignation. "Oh, very well! What's three more days? We've earned a little rest after chasing that damn spook the length of the Betics and never once daring to take to the air for fear of his fireballs. But if we stay here, Celo, you've got to fly us in some decent food and booze."

The Lord of Afaliah said, "We can set up camp in the meadow below, near the torrent, where the attendants and the baggage train now wait. My son Uriet himself will lead a squadron of levitants to bring refreshment."

"That's that, then," said the King. He glowered at Aiken. "Three days only! You hear me?"

The golden manikin leapt from his saddle, knelt on one knee before the royal chaliko, and grinned under his golden visor. "Thank you for your patience, Awful Father. We'll bring you Delbaeth's balls for biddy-swabbers!"

And then, while the Questers watched in incredulous silence, Aiken Drum and Stein took off their armor and stacked it in a pile just beside the cave entrance. They left all their weaponry except Stein's bronze sword and took from their saddlebags only the Viking's parcel of snack foods, the canteen of beer, and a thin golden box about the size of a pen case, which Aiken stuffed quickly into the front of his undertunic.

Waggling an admonitory finger at Nodonn, the golliwog said, "No fair peeking after us, Sun-Face. Don't you chase us with flares."

"I will not," the Battlemaster promised, his smile undimmed.

"Then—goodbye, all!" said Aiken Drum.

There was a soundless snap.

Two extra bats joined the flock wheeling over the heads of the Hunt. After taking a few minutes to get used to their wings, the pair swooped down and disappeared into the darkness of Delbaeth's cave.

"Hey, kid!"

"Shh. Gotta be sure nobody's farsensing us. Wouldn't trust that fewkin' Archangel one AU's worth."

"... Kid, what about the friggerty monster?"

"*Will* you shut your snoose-chompin' yap? It's tough work, doing these different kinds of mind-bendery all at the same time."

"Sorry."

They hung from the roof of the cataract shaft by their tiny claws. The world was utterly, appallingly black. The waterfall made a hissing sound as it sprayed into the mountain's gut. A faraway rumble down below announced its drainage into an abyssal sump.

The two bats could "see" by means of the sounds.

At last Aiken said, "It's okay. They're all going down to the campsite. Nobody's making a real effort to farsense us. The least little screen'll take care of them now ... Trouble is, Steinie, I don't really know how good at farsensing any of these Tanu biggies are. I'm certain that most of the exotics can't farsee underground. That's why the Firvulag live in caves and burrows. But the King, Nodonn, that damn Fian who does the PK stunts—they just might be able to figure some way to spot us through a klom of solid rock ... just like I can."

"Jee*zuss* God. Will you lay off the bragging and scan out where that torch-ass spook is holed up? Or don't you care if we get incinerated?"

"We're not gonna get incinerated. Delbaeth isn't waiting in some cranny to ambush us. He's gone home. He knows nobody in this Exile world is stupid enough to follow him into the caves."

"Ha ha. All right, Ace. Now that we're here—where the hell are we?"

"We're in a better position to nab the spook than we were before, hemmed in by that mob of exotics. This is just the kind of chance I hoped for ever since we took off on this dumb monster hunt! A chance to go after Delbaeth without the rest of 'em watching how I kill him!"

"You're not gonna zap him with your superbrain?"

"Betcher sweet ass I'm not. I wouldn't have a chance in a mind-to-mind with Delbaeth. Neither would any of those Tanu turds—unless the Firvulag was taken completely by surprise. And fat chance of that happening, with that friggerty circus parade of three hundred knights of the Round Table whooping after him. Nope! There's only one way to take the Shape of Fire. My little old sweetheart, Mayvar, knew it."

"Well how, for chrissake?"

"I'm gonna cheat. Come on. Let's get outa here to some place where it's flat and dry and I'll show you."

The two bats spiraled down the shaft. At the bottom they turned into pallid eyeless fish and went whisking through the flooded tunnel of the sump, "seeing" the twists and turns of the rock pipe by means of pressure changes and the reflection of water currents, rather than the echolocation they had used while they were bats. They traveled for more than a kilometer before the stream broke into a large airfilled space. One fish leaped from the water—flopped back. Then both jumped up and metamorphosed into bats. A few moments later they were in human form again, sitting on a rock shelf beside the underground river while a small ball of incandescence hung in midair to furnish light. The cave ceiling two or three meters above was covered with a fantastic growth of crystal soda-straw formations, thin and delicate, each with a pendant drop of water at the tip.

Aiken wasted no time admiring the scenery. He took the golden box from his shirt, manipulated the lid in some tricky PK fashion, and showed Stein what was inside: a single thin gray object about twenty cents in length, vaguely resembling a silvery length of punk with a wire stem.

Stein frowned. "You know what that looks like? When I was a kid back in Illinois we had—"

"That's what it is. Just one of these little things is gonna kill that shitfire Firvulag stone dead. A long time ago, some poor sucker brought this through the time-gate, thinking he'd liven up the Pliocene a little bit. Since they're perfectly harmless, the people at the auberge had no objection. But when the guy stepped into Exile, his stuff was confiscated—and all but this one destroyed before Mayvar got hold of it. You know why? Because here, things like this are deadly! Not to humans—not even torc-wearing humans—but to the exotics."

"Iron." Stein was awestruck. "No iron tools here, no iron

implements, nothing iron at all. All glass, vitredur, bronze or other alloy, silver, gold, whatnot. But never any iron! Hell—why didn't anybody notice?"

"How much iron did we use back in the Milieu in places where it showed? We were almost out of the iron age. You know what the Tanu and Firvulag call the stuff? Blood-metal! One prick and they're goners. Or, in the case of this thing—"

"Jeez, yes!" Stein exclaimed. His expression became intent. "You're gonna do it, kid. I'm a believer at last. And after we finish off this Delbaeth, you're gonna help me escape with Sukey. And if any dumb Tanu tries to stop us—"

"You stupid squarehead! You forgot your gray torc? And Sukey's silver one? The Tanu could track you anywhere. Relax! I got other plans. We'll all make it if you don't pull any more great moves like you did with Tasha."

Aiken closed the golden box and put it back into his shirt. "Now sit still and shut up. I gotta track Delbaeth, and this X-ray vision thing is a hell of a lot tougher than you might think. Good thing these mountains aren't granite."

"Naw. Limestone, sandstone, medium-grade schists, and other metamorphics down below at this end of the Med. Don't forget I used to work these rocks when I was a crust driller."

"Shut up, dammit."

The two of them sat there in their underwear. The psycho-energy flare went out as Aiken concentrated all of his power in his seeker sense. The only sounds were the drips from the slender calcite pipelets.

Could I reach out, too? Stein wondered. Sukey had told him it was love that did it before, that broke through Dedra's coercive control. Was love strong enough to cross the thousand kilometers that separated him from Sukey, hidden back there in Muriah in the catacombs beneath Redact House? First, visualize her in the mind's eye. (Easy when your optic nerves are getting input zilch.) There she is. Now tell her that you love her, that it's going to be all right, that you're safe, that you're going to come back, that you're going to win...

"I found him, Steinie! I found the fuckard!"

The astral light snapped on. Stein passed a great hand over his eyes and wiped it on his hip. The attempt at farspeech hadn't worked. His head hurt.

Reddish hair standing up like a charged mop, eyes seeming to snap with excitement, the trickster sprang to his feet and pointed toward a solid rock wall. "That direction. Maybe eight, nine kloms and a couple hundred meters lower down. There's this fuzzy blob—a mental aura, I guess. Only living thing anywhere around. It's gotta be him."

Stein sighed. "And all we have to do is walk through the wall."

The golliwog was apologetic. "That's not my act, Steinie. I can't do interpenetration. Can't zap mountains, either, not so's you'd notice. We'll have to walk, fly, or swim. If Delbaeth got there from here, so can we. This whole lousy range is honeycombed with caves. It'll take a while finding our way through the maze." He looked grim. "But it better not take too long or we'll be into the Truce. That's when Firvulags go outa season until Grand Combat time."

Stein looked at his wrist chronometer. "Half past eighteen hours, September twenty-seven, six million B.C."

"Checko."

"Just tell me one thing before you do your Dracula act, kid. Do we *really* turn into bats and fish and things when you say shazoom, or is it some kinda shape-shifting illusion thing and do we keep our regular bods all the time?"

"Damned if I know," said Aiken Drum. "Hang onto that food and beer, pally—we're off!"

They searched.

Tunnels dry and flooded; great galleries where flowstone and stalactites and rippling curtains of thin rock fell like frozen creations of peach and vanilla ice cream; constricted slots and tortuous low corridors studded with sparkling calcite teeth; tumbled rockfalls where a cave ceiling had collapsed into piles of house-sized chunks; partially drained streamways gleaming with mud; dead-end holes that had to be retraced; tempting passages that took them in the wrong direction.

They ate, and after a while, they slept. They woke and continued flying, swimming, walking, climbing. The food and beer were finished midway through the second day. There was plenty of water, but no bugs for bats, no edible bits floating in the subterranean waters that the men-fish could swallow to assuage the all-too-real spasms of their possibly illusory stomachs.

Aiken's mental screen was now projected only between them and the concentration of psychic energy that presumably marked Delbaeth. This hardly seemed to shift position at all now; perhaps the Shape of Fire took very long naps between sorties, or perhaps the fuzzy aura marked something else altogether . . .

The bats flew down a long, sloping tunnel. For the first time since their descent, they were aware of a current of air against their flapping wing membranes. The mental voice of Aiken spoke to Stein on the intimate human mode:

Don't think one solitary thing. Keep your mind quiet if you value your sweet ass. I don't think he can hear me on this mode but any squeak outa you would hit him S9 and wall to wall.

The two bats, now totally enveloped in the heaviest mindbarrier that Aiken could conjure, came to a ninety-degree bend in the corridor. They fluttered around the corner and saw light ahead—orangey yellow and flickering gently. The passage was dry. There were huge footprints in the dust.

Drifting among the rock formations, the bats approached the lighted area. It was a large open camber full of looming monoliths almost like shrouded human figures, together with complex tiers of flowstone that resembled gigantic gilled fungi. The bats flew up toward the ceiling to a ledge that jutted far out over the central area of the floor. There, hidden from the sight of anyone below, the bats turned into Aiken and Stein.

Silence. Don't move. Don't rattle that damn sword scabbard. Don't do one friggerty thing.

Aiken crept toward the edge of the formation on his stomach and peered down. A large fire burned within a well-made circular hearth. Piles of barkless tree trunks were neatly stacked in an alcove. Other parts of the cavern were furnished with a table, chairs, a bedstead of gargantuan proportions having a canopy and side curtains of the finest Tanu brocade, and any number of carved wooden chests and shelves. Leathern bags bulging with mysterious contents stood at the base of one pillar. Near another was a framework hung with fish netting edged with wooden floats. The floor was carpeted in glossy pelts—some dark, some spotted. Most of the dirty dishes on the table seemed to be large mollusk shells.

Drawn up close to the fire was a species of overstuffed chair upholstered in gray hide. In the chair, quite asleep, was a humanoid exceeding the tall Tanu in height and vastly more robust of build. His head had a tangled brick-colored mane of hair and a bushy beard. He wore a leather shirt with the front lacing open, showing the reddish pelt of his chest. His breeches were scarlet. He had taken off his boots and extended his huge feet toward the fire. Now and then the toes wiggled. A cyclic noise reminiscent of a malfunctioning ore crusher told Aiken Drum that Delbaeth, the Shape of Fire, most formidable wild Firvulag in the southern reaches of the Many-Colored Land, was snoring.

Aiken opened the golden box and removed the pencil-slim gray object. Hefting the little thing, he seemed to calculate a trajectory. He ignited the tip of his secret weapon with his creative metafunction.

The sparkler burst into vivid white light, throwing out glowing iron filings like tiny meteorites. Aiken held the firework at arm's length.

Down below, Delbaeth surged from his chair, bellowing. His body, nearly three meters tall, was transformed into a blazing mass that reached fiery arms toward the ceiling ledge and began to mold a ball of fire between incandescent paws.

Aiken threw the sparkler, guiding it with whatever PK he could muster through the thick psychic screen he had erected around Stein and himself. Delbaeth's fireball arced up, dead on target, and bounced.

There was another echoing cry from the monster. The fragile firework struck his flaming form and fell to the cave floor, still spitting sparks. Delbaeth's fire was extinguished. He crumpled slowly, almost seeming to melt into the ground, and did not move again.

"Come on!" Aiken cried.

The two bats flew down and became men once more. They stood beside the awesome carcass, and Stein said, "See where it hit him? Right on the forehead, because he was looking up. One tiny little burn with a hot iron wire!"

There was a leather bucket full of water beside the table. Aiken hoisted it and poured a stream over the still-coruscating sparkler. It hissed and went out. A hole had been burned in one fur rug, ruining it.

"You did it!" Stein swept up the little man and crushed him in a bear hug. "You did it!" Dropping Aiken, Stein howled to the stalactites: "Sukey, babe, we *did* it!"

Aiken frowned, then laughed out loud. "I'll be damned, Viking. She did hear you! Maybe you can't pick her up, but I get this little weak farspeak whisper. Aw . . . you'll never guess. She loves you."

Stein grabbed up the bucket and emptied it over Aiken.

"Thanks," said the golliwog. "I needed that. Now cut off

his head and let's get out of here. We've gotta find the shortest route to the open air and fly back to bedoozle the royalty. Not to sweat, though! We're one whole day early!"

Stein began to draw his great bronze sword from its amber-studded sheath. But when the blade was halfway out he froze and tilted his head. "Listen! Hear that?... It's a lot clearer now than it was up next to the ceiling with that spook snoring."

Aiken cocked an ear. A slow, deep *boom* vibrated the rocks. Several seconds passed. *Boom*. Like the tolling of some huge bell the sound repeated. *Boom*. Slow. Inexorable.

"Do you know what that is, kid?" Stein asked. "It's surf. Somewhere just the other side of that rock wall is the Atlantic Ocean."

THE END OF PART ONE

PART II

THE
CLOSURE

1

FELICE WALKED THE RUINS OF FINIAH.

By the time that the Truce was in its third day, the minor eruption of lava from the old Kaiserstuhl volcano had come to an end. Streams of once molten rock solidified into clinkery masses—fat, rounded, and branched like monstrous roots where they had flowed out from the central mineworkings into the streets and arcades of the devastated city. It had rained heavily. Buildings that had been white or golden and rose, or blue-green and silver with the colors of the Creative Lord Velteyn, were now streaked and smeared with ashy mud. Ash had smothered the gardens and blasted the foliage from most of the ornamental trees. The central plaza, where Felice prowled, was a tangle of burnt-out shops, shredded awnings, broken carts and tradesmen's booths, and bodies half-buried in cinders and muck.

Giant ravens as long as Felice's arms pecked at the swollen remains of chalikos, hellads, ramapithecines, and people. The scavengers were not disturbed by the passing of the small woman dressed in shining black. Perhaps they took her for one of themselves.

There were noises. The ravens uttered their *pruk pruk* calls. A broken water conduit gushed and flooded down a flight of stairs, washing clean the corpses of gray-torc soldiers and Lowlife invaders. In a cul-de-sac near the palace of Lord Velteyn, nearly a dozen uninjured ramas in ruined aquamarine tabards huddle together, whimpering. A sound of human groans came from a porter's house adjacent to the main palace approach. Felice ignored it and walked toward the entrance of Velteyn's mansion, an iron-tipped arrow nocked and ready in her compound bow. She had many other arrows in a shoulder quiver, all with stained shafts. There had been a few stubborn grays

141

down at the river landing determined to fight on, even though their Tanu overlords had fled; and down in the artisans' quarter, a bareneck woman had come rushing out of a devastated glass-crafter's workshop, brandishing a vitredur machete and crying vengeance on the despoilers of Finiah even as Felice shot her in the throat.

Humans were too irreligious to hold to the Truce. Long after the Firvulag and Tanu had quit the burning wreck of the city, Lowlife warriors continued to fight against those of their fellow humans who remained loyal to the exotics. Captured grays, as well as the few silvers who fell into the invaders' hands, were hustled before a guerilla tribunal where a Lowlife officer showed them an iron chisel and an iron knife and bade them choose: "Live free or die." A surprising proportion had opted for death rather than the removal of their mind-amplifying collars.

Felice entered the palace. The carrion birds were absent here, but there were flies, swift-scuttling rodents, and an appalling stench. The bodies of guards and servitors were heaped behind improvised barricades of furniture and demounted doors. Many of the defenders had died without a mark upon them, faces contorted by the mind-blasting attack of the Firvulag.

Except for the buzzing of insects, the rustle and squeak of rats, and the sighing sound of wind through smashed panes of colored glass, the palace of Lord Velteyn was quiet in its ruin. The little woman in black penetrated deeper into the apartments of the Great Ones, leaping over the piled corpses of human retainers who had fought an increasingly desperate rearguard action as the invading army hunted their trapped exotic masters.

Felice came to a great open door of bronze, studded with green stones. Bodies in Lowlife buckskin and homespun mingled with those in palace livery to clog its threshold. And here, for the first time, there were also Firvulag bodies, some squat, some taller than humans or Tanu and as burly as fairytale giants; all were attired in the gold-chased obsidian armor of Pallol One-Eyes's elite corps and all had been dispatched by iron-tipped weapons that Velteyn's human guard had presumably wrested from the Lowlives.

Calmly, Felice pulled a spear from a dead shape-shifter and used it for an alpenstock as she climbed over the noisome mound blocking the doorway. Inside the room, which was an elaborate bedchamber reduced to a shambles by the fighting, were six bodies attired in colored-glass armor. Four men and one Tanu woman were bloodied, transfixed by iron-pointed arrows. The second woman, a gold-torc human armored in sapphire blue, bore no wounds and had presumably succumbed to mental assault.

Felice removed her hoplite helmet and set it upon a large bedside stand. On a lower shelf, incongruous in undisturbed tidiness, were a golden ewer and basin. The girl filled the basin with water and set it on top of the table. For a moment, she stood looking down at the corpse of the human woman. In death, her azure eyes showed wide pupils, oddly emphatic in a face as pale as chalk. Long chestnut hair spread on the carpet in a nimbus around the bare head; her helmet lay nearby. The slender fingers in jeweled blue-plate gauntlets were hooked over a golden torc.

Like an acolyte enacting a ritual, Felice knelt. The rigor had left the dead hands and the torc was easily freed from their grip. The knobbed front catch clicked. The girl pivoted the collar on its back hinge and slipped it from around the livid throat. Rising, she went to the basin, dipped the gold several times, and dried it upon a soft towel.

Then Felice fastened the torc about her own neck.

The reality opened to her. She uttered a piercing cry.

This . . . so it was like this. All of it had been hidden within her, battened down and denied, so feared by the weaker ones all around her. But now open, released, and ready to be used.

She went out onto the balcony of the death room. Trembling, vision partly blurred by the tears of her joy, she looked over the ruins of Finiah. There was the wide Rhine, the heights of the Vosges, High Vrazel itself on the western skyline, where King Yeochee and Sharn-Mes and the other Firvulag were doubtless still celebrating the triumph over their ancient Foe. There were the high passes she had come through alone, too late for the war, passing Chief Burke and Khalid Khan and the remnant of the Lowlife force conducting newly liberated human survivors of Finiah to the bottomland camp where they would await the judgment of Madame Guderian.

Gold warm at her throat, Felice began to laugh. The sound swelled on the wind until it reverberated over the wasted city. The ravens, shocked out of their aplomb, took wing.

2

SHARN-MES THE YOUNG CHAMPION REGARDED THE RIOTOUS
scene in the Hall of the Mountain King and shook his head in
humorous wonderment.

"Just look at that gang of stewed fewmets. It'll be at least
three days' sleep to work off this three days' drunk. You know,
Ayf, this is going to play havoc with our travel schedule. The
armor and weaponry will have to be refurbished before we head
south unless we want to go into the Grand Combat looking like
a tatty rabble."

"There's still plenty of time." Ayfa, leader of the Warrior
Ogresses, tossed off her bumper of mead and helped herself
to a refill. "The lads and lasses are entitled to a celebration.
It's been forty years since we've had anything worth getting
drunk about. Who cares if we miss some of the prelims down
at the White Silver Plain? The high-ass crowd aren't about to
start any main events without us."

"I suppose," Sharn agreed, "that we do deserve a party."

The two great captains were sequestered in a snug gallery
that ordinarily accommodated musicians at formal feasts. But
there was nothing formal about the action now taking place
below them. All of the Firvulag veterans of the brief Finiah
campaign, together with most of the rest of the citizenry of
High Vrazel, seemed to have crowded into the royal audience
cavern to cheer the unexpected victory.

Brown ale and mead and cyser and blackberry brandy foun-
tained up from hollow stalagmites right into the waiting mugs
of those merrymakers who were still on their feet. Enough
pastries, meats, and other party food remained to make the
oaken tables creak under the weight. One mob in front of King
Yeochee's empty throne was playing a type of blindman's bluff

in which the hooded female protagonist had taken the game's title quite literally. Another hilarious crowd surrounded the two heroes of the battle, Nukalavee and Skinless and Bles Four-Fang, who vied with one another to see who could create the most ridiculously obscene illusory body. Points were awarded by the cheers, jeers, and occasional retchings of the onlookers.

More serious-minded revelers (and the maudlin drunks) gathered about a crookbacked goblin bard who had reached the one-hundred-sixty-fifth verse of a lugubrious ballad of doomed Firvulag lovers. Cheerier souls were concocting ingenious new stanzas to the soldiers' beloved drinking song, " A Princess Must Never Have Fleas," detailing those eccentricities that the royal demoiselle might legitimately expect to get away with. Warriors of the walking wounded, cosseted by plump little wenches, bragged of their late derring-do. Superannuated stay-at-homes muttered into their beer that the reduction of Finiah couldn't possibly compare to certain ancient affrays in which *they* had participated during the good old days.

Queen Klahnino supervised the safe retirement of fallen celebrants, who were dragged away into alcoves and packed cheek by jowl to sleep it off. King Yeochee wandered around in bare feet and a stained golden robe, his crown tilted over one ear, kissing all of the ladies and quite a number of the gentlemen as well. Pallol the Battlemaster, still disdainful of the enterprise but always ready for a party, had succumbed to a surfeit of sidecars—another legacy of the insidious Lowlives. He lay snoring in the King's crystal grotto, his huge head resting in the lap of the resigned concubine, Lulo.

"Yes," Sharn repeated himself at length. "We definitely deserve a celebration . . . What do you suppose the Lowlives are up to?"

"I'll look," said Ayfa, who possessed more farsight than the majority of her race. She was a handsome creature if one overlooked the excessively developed arm muscles, a concomitant of her prowess with the two-handed sword. Her hair was apricot-colored and her broad face freckled. Like most Firvulag, she had dark, twinkling eyes. She had shed her armor and wore a rumpled kirtle and blouse of madder rose, which clashed with her hair.

"Yes, there they are. The human prisoners, or refugees, or whatever you call 'em, are installed in the old staging-area camp. But Burke and his cronies are slogging along through

Ravine Pass toward Hidden Springs. They're getting rained on."

"Good," said Sharn. "Maybe it'll rust their perishing iron." He took a pull from his beaker and wiped his lips with a furry paw. "Dammit, Ayf, that's a bad business—using the blood-metal. Unprecedented! You know, when we trapped that bunch of Tanu engineers near the smeltery, one of 'em let off a really heavy curse before he died. I can still hear it: 'The Goddess will avenge us. Accursed through the world's age be those who resort to the blood-metal. A bloody tide will overwhelm them . . .'"

"Well, it seems to me that the curse is for the humans, not us. We'd always planned to put the Lowlives to the sword once they'd served our purposes."

"But we're only too willing to use them—*and* their iron—in the meantime! I hate it, Ayfa. It's a Lowlife way of doing battle, not our way. Old Pallol was bitching about how we'd surrendered our ancient honor just by fighting alongside humans . . . and how the iron was so obscene that it made a travesty of our whole combat-philosophy. I can't help agreeing. How can war be glorious with such an ignoble weapon? It puts the mightiest Firvulag or Tanu hero on the same level as some half-starved human pipsqueak with a compound bow. It's unfair!"

Ayfa grunted. "I suppose the Tanu have been fighting fair . . . with their chalikos and bear-dogs that have turned the Hunts into massacres! Or the human cavalry and charioteers in the Grand Combat who've been whipping the shit out of us for the past forty years!"

"Aaah. You women never did appreciate the fine points of chivalry!"

"No—we're willing to fight dirty to win." The female warrior served herself another great tankard of mead. "And speaking of that—did you see how the Lowlife infantry dealt with the mounted Foe in Finiah?"

Sharn acknowledged the fact with a surly nod. "Unsporting! That's not our *way*."

"Screw our way. The chalikos weren't the Tanu way, either, until that human animal tamer came along . . . Now you listen to me, big boy. There won't be any iron weapons to help us in the Grand Combat this year, but you can bet your sweet filberts that we *will* adopt those new antichaliko tactics of the Lowlives. This go-around, those gray-torc troopers are in for a helluva surprise! I've already got the armorers working on the modification. Easiest thing in the world."

"It could make a difference," he conceded. "If we can get the warriors to accept it."

"I'll leave the persuasion to you," she told him, smiling. Then her expression changed. "Keep still for a minute while I go back to my farsight of the Lowlives coming from Finiah . . . I get a few under three hundred surviving irregulars going over the pass and maybe twice that many captives and casualties down in the Rhineside camp. Most of the refugees are barenecks . . . No—wait. Some are too well dressed. By damn, they've got to be ex-grays or silvers with their torcs chiseled off! Noncombatants. Maybe scientific types, special-talent artificers. Old Madame Guderian will make good use of *them*, you can bank on it!"

"I wonder just how loyal to her those liberated townees will be, though?" Sharn was skeptical. "The humans who craved freedom the most tended to be the newcomers and the psychos. The people who'd been here for a while settled down under Tanu domination even without being torced. A life of freedom in the wild greenwood is going to be as appealing to those easy-goers as a case of hives."

"Hush. I'm looking for Felice."

"Oh, *that* one. The one you'll have to take into your crew if—"

"—if she finds a golden torc and goes metapowerful. I could strangle that Yeochee for pushing the dirty work off on me! As if the Combat wasn't tough enough for us women these days . . . Oh-oh."

"Spotted her?"

"She's in a room of Velteyn's mansion. Wearing a torc. And she's looting a body of its glass armor. So much for Yeochee's idea. This kid is way ahead of him, making her own Combat plans!"

"Cheer up." Sharn climbed to his feet, yawned hugely, and scratched his hairy chest through the open front of his tunic. "You're rid of her, anyhow. It'll take her a while to get used to the torc. And there's no guarantee that her latent metafaculties will measure up to her nerve, in any case. Even if she did mastermind Epone's killing and help bring back the Spear, she's still only a young girl. Maybe coercing animals is the only power she's got."

Ayfa's eyes came back into focus. "Té only knows. I guess I'm just too tired now to give much of a damn."

Sharn gave her a hand and hauled her up. "It's been a short war and a long party. What say we make our duty to the King and Queen and amble on home?" He gathered their black-glass armor by the straps and slung it onto his back.

"Good thinking," Ayfa agreed. She clapped her companion on one shoulder and, rising on tiptoe, kissed the end of his grubby nose. "I hate to think of the overtime we're going to owe the babysitter."

3

THE GUARDIANS IN THEIR WHITE TUNICS STOOD READY AROUND
the square of bare granite that had been marked off with rounded
stones. There were soldiers as well this morning, in consideration of the visit of the Most Exalted Personages. Thagdal,
Eadone, Gomnol, and the two brothers Nodonn and Velteyn
kept well back from the vicinity of the time-portal and waited
for the manifestation with the stoicism that dignitaries invari-
ably assume when they are obliged to inspect some important
but depressing activity taking place at an inconvenient hour.

Pitkin the Castellan said, "It's just dawn, Exalted Ones.
Here they come."

A block of air above the granite began to shimmer as if
suddenly heated. Four figures materialized within the singu-
larity and hovered some thirty centimeters above the surface
of the rock.

"Sindbad the Sailor, a Joe Meek mountain-man type, one
moribund hash aficionado complete with hubble-bubble, and
a classic British birdwatcher," Pitkin rattled off in snap appraisal. "The drugger's for the discard, I'm afraid; wasted to
a shadow. But the others will serve."

The guardians had darted forward to seize the arms of the
time-travelers and assist them as they stepped down the gap
that separated the invisible floor of Professor Guderian's device
from the solid ground of Pliocene Earth.

"Fortuitous that they don't materialize inside a mass of bed-
rock, isn't it?" Pitkin remarked. "This region has undergone
many vicissitudes, geologically speaking."

Sindbad had been separated from his scimitar, and the other
dazed timefarers were being frisked for iron by a guardian with
a metal detector. Pitkin said, "That new iron-sniffer of the

149

Craftsmaster's is a great improvement. No more worries about missed contraband... Ah. There goes the tau-field back for the second lot."

On the next cycle the time-portal admitted a young man in a suit of white denim carrying a crossbow; a goateed chap costumed as Queen Elizabeth I, whose farthingale skirts were a dreadful nuisance to his fellow embarkees, a deeply tanned woman wearing an Atalanta peplum and buskins; and a well-rejuvenated black man in a dacot lounge suit, draped with a dozen extremely expensive AV recorders.

"All serviceable stock," Pitken said. "Don't be fooled by Good Queen Bess. There's probably a useful technician under that pearl-studded red wig... Now let's see what kind of impedimenta we rate today."

The temporal field sprang into existence once more and guardians hastened to remove three large containers labeled MEDICATIONS, a case of Canadian Club, a papillon dog yapping hysterically inside its mesh carrier, a twenty-liter carboy of "Joy," a set of Larousse's *Grand Dictionnaire Universel du XIXème Siècle Français*, and a contrabassoon.

"After these new arrivals are processed, they go to the holding area, as you know, Exalted Ones. Because of the emergency, we have set up a temporary stockade by walling off sections of the outer ward, transferring the bear-dogs to exterior pens. In this way we can accommodate most of Lord Velteyn's refugees from Finiah in relative comfort within the castle proper until they are able to move on to Muriah. It's fortunate that this disaster took place at Truce time when there are extra supplies and transport available for those traveling down to the games. And of course the security matter is much more easily dealt with at this time as well."

"Sounds like you've got things in hand," the King muttered grudgingly to the Castellan.

"We have Lord Gomnol to thank for the initial disaster-relief planning. Castle Gateway was the logical receiving area, of course, and we were able to rush help northward in time to meet the refugees on the eastern shore of the Lac de Bresse just five days after the—uh—exodus from Finiah. Now, if you'd care to step into my office, Exalted Ones, I can go over the revised distribution system for the time-travelers that compensates for the temporary suspension of the Finiah run. There are also preliminary overviews of Castle Gateway's role in laborforce procurement for the reconstruction and pacification operations."

"Thank you, Pitkin," Gomnol said. "We won't trouble you for that now. I'll meet with you later myself to finalize the concentration of time-travelers during the Truce interim."

The Castellan bowed, excused himself, and hurried back up the path leading to the fortress. Only the five Exalted Personages and a small squad of soldiers waiting at a discreet distance now remained in the time-portal area. The sun was well over the brow of the eastern highlands.

"Sometimes," the King said, looking after Pitkin with a peeved expression, "the efficiency of you humans really depresses me. No righteous indignation. No avowals of vengeance or fealty. Just revised distribution systems and preliminary overviews!"

The Lord Coercer laughed in a genial fashion. "Vengeance is the Battlemaster's department. Mine is making certain that this disaster is confined to the Finiah region and neutralized as quickly as possible to minimize its impact on the socioeconomy. If it weren't for the importance of the barium mines, I'd be inclined to write Finiah off."

"Why, you arrogant little squeakpoop!" Velteyn's face was suffused with a red glare. "You're talking about my home! The cradle of Tanu culture on this planet! The City of Lights!"

"The lights," Gomnol said, unperturbed, "have gone out. Finiah is in ruins. The Foe used brilliant strategy to attack it. It's awkwardly situated, on the wrong side of the Rhine and too far away from our other population centers. There are Firvulag on one side of it and Howlers on the other—and Madame Guderian and her rustic irregulars making merry in between. Of all our cities, it was the ripest for surprise attack."

"I've kept it safe for five hundred years!" Velteyn shouted. "Once we get the walls back up and some reinforcements for the Flying Hunt, we'll have it as secure as ever. We'll wipe out Guderian's outlaws by organizing a Quest through the Vosges to destroy their settlements. Once the Lowlife nests are burned out, the Firvulag will crawl back into their own holes just as they've always done. They never would have mobilized for the attack at all if it hadn't been for that obscene old woman and her damned iron."

"It may not be as easy as you think to put down the hostile humans, Creative Brother," Eadone told Velteyn. "And I'm afraid that Lord Gomnol raises a serious point about the isolated position of Finiah. In the early years, when there were fewer of us and fewer Firvulag, your little walled city on the promontory was at a strategic advantage. But today it is trapped within a web of inimical forces. Now that the humans are aware of the power of iron, they'll make dreadful use of it. Even a handful of Lowlives will be able to waylay caravans and troop columns, attack your plantations, perhaps set up a blockade in the river that could reduce your citizenry to starvation. There is no way you can be supplied by land. The Black Forest massif behind you is too formidable a barrier. Neither could your armed forces be reinforced by land. Soldiers would have to cross the Rhine to reach you from our other northern strongholds—from Goriah, Burask, or Roniah. Even rebuilding your city will be a very difficult task because of the length of the lines of supply."

Velteyn's flaming face went almost purple. "But we *must* rebuild! The destruction wasn't total. By no means! Almost all of our noncombatant Tanu citizens survived. Six hundred and eighty-nine airlifted to safety by me, by Lady Dectar, and by our gold-torc human brother Sullivan-Tonn."

The King said, "But you lost most of the knights. And more than four thousand humans—silvers, grays, and barenecks—and every single rama! The whole damn working populace either dead, taken prisoner by that Tana-bedamned old harridan, or run off into the bushes where the Howlers or the wild animals will finish them off."

"The plantations are still secure! And the military outposts. We can rebuild, Awful Father! We can make Finiah impregnable. We'll bring in more PK and coercer adepts to strengthen our mental capability."

For the first time, Nodonn Battlemaster spoke. "We will have to reopen the mine. That is self-evident, unless we discover a new source of the vital barium ore. But there can be no thought of restoring Finiah to its former glory. Its day as a gracious and venerable seat of culture has passed. In future, it must present an austere but secure face to our Foe. We will rebuild it as a fortified mining settlement . . . but that's all."

Velteyn's entire body reacted as if from a physical assault. His mind screamed.

O my Brother what do you say how can you woundsoulflay me disgracedegrade me before mypeople a battlechampion fallen unavengedunrestoredabandoned to human/Firvulag derision + Tanu pityscorn . . .

Nodonn turned away. He walked to the empty granite platform of the time-portal and stood in the middle of it, aurora-hued robes bright in the sunrise. His immense voice rang in their minds and ears.

"Blame *this*! From this came your pain, Brother! From this source of rottenness and deadly peril that has seduced us from our ancient way! Cursed be the woman who first opened the time-gate to invading humankind. We will all of us be mourning for a world forever lost unless we have the courage to shut the humans out before it is too late. If we continue our fatal dependence upon them, the death of Finiah will be nothing in comparison to the death of the Many-Colored Land!"

Eadone said, "I could almost believe it now. And yet—"

"You're wrong, Nodonn!" Thagdal said. "You've been trying to sell that prophecy of doom ever since they first started coming. But look at us! We're stronger now than we ever were before. It's a damn shame about Finiah. The city was a shrine to our pioneer heritage. But, let's face it—a bloody inconvenient place to get to or from, for all its picturesqueness and charm and pretty lights and all!... Tell you what, Velteyn, son! We'll build you a new city in some better place. How's that sound?"

Gomnol joined the King in persuasion. "Perhaps on the shore of the Lac de Bresse. We can cut a new road from it to Goriah and open a whole new region for exploitation. Just as soon as the Combat is behind us, we can begin the planning. All of the other cities will contribute to its building, and you can have every one of the time-travelers for the next two years as a population base. We'll build you a new Finiah even better than the old. Proper streets and drains, proper water system and access, proper urban planning and defensive works. What do you say to that?"

Nodonn said: Proper/*human*?

Gomnol said: Rather wattledaubhuts handcrafted You?

Eadone said: Take comfort our Mourning Brother. We will see you restored never fear. Go now to your LadyWife + sorrowing folk and bid them hope.

"Yes." Velteyn lifted his head and the psychic luminosity faded. He spoke aloud. "It is a good plan, Awful Father, and I stand humbly grateful before your generosity." And to Nodonn: "If you think me lacking in courage, Brother Battlemaster, I'll prove differently at the Grand Combat. I confess that the battle-joy went out of me with this disaster... but by game-time I'll be a warrior restored. The Firvulag will pay a thousand times over for their unholy alliance with the Lowlives. As for the human despoilers—iron or no iron, we will see them screaming in the Great Retort as they offer their lives to the Goddess at the Combat's glorious end!"

"Well said," observed the High King. "And now that the future is assured, I believe it is safe to go into the Castle for breakfast."

4

THE REFUGEE CAMP AND FIELD HOSPITAL HAD BEEN SET UP IN the former invasion staging area in the Rhine bottomland. With the Tanu withdrawal to Castle Gateway and the retreat of Finiah's loyalist humans to the lake forts, the riverside was secure enough while the Truce prevailed. The wisdom of Old Man Kawai had dictated that the unfortunates not be sheltered in Hidden Springs village.

"It is a matter of simple psychology," he told Peopeo Moxmox Burke. "If we bring them to our canyon they will want to stay there, where there is ready-made housing and a vestige of civilization. But we cannot feed five or six hundred people indefinitely, nor will our buildings and sanitary facilities accommodate such a number. And the Firvulag bring in fresh stragglers every day! No—these refugees must be motivated to establish new settlements of their own. For this reason we must assemble them in a spartan campsite, care for their disabilities, furnish them with equipment and guides, and disperse them as rapidly as possible before the post-Combat Truce ends and the Tanu begin their countermeasures."

It was Khalid Khan who came up with the suggestion for the Iron Road. The metalsmith pointed out that the wilderness smeltery should become the site of a new human stronghold. Other smaller settlements could be strung along the bank of the Moselle to secure the trail between the iron workings and Hidden Springs.

"Provided the Tanu don't return in force too soon after the Truce's end," Khalid had said, "we can secure this whole region for Lowlife humanity by producing quantities of iron. The refugees can support themselves by making it after we help them to get established. I think we can bank on the Howlers

155

clearing out once word of the iron is passed around. But a massive Tanu Quest would be another matter, of course."

"If the next two phases of my plan succeed," Madame Guderian had said, "there will be no Quest."

Seven days following the attack on Finiah, Madame Guderian and Chief Burke came on chalikos to meet with Kawai for a last inspection tour of the refugee camp before proceeding south. The old woman and the tall Native American dismounted and tied their beasts to bushes near a stream, then walked with the aged Japanese into the grove with its rows of palmetto-thatched lean-tos and other rather squalid shelters. The area was becoming garbage-strewn and fetid.

"We have tried to have the refugees police the area," Kawai said in a low voice, "but many are still in a shocked and depressed state and indifferent to personal hygiene and orderly behavior. There was a bit of trouble yesterday, as Chief Burke has doubtless told you. A group of perhaps forty, led by five de-collared gray soldiers, insisted upon being allowed to proceed to Fort Onion River on the lake. We procured an escort of Firvulag and sent them away. It would have been useless to detain them."

"We did not lose any of the doctors?" Madame was anxious. "Or the glass technicians?"

"The medical personnel remained with us," Kawai said. "They were not willingly enslaved. One glassblower is gone. We have also lost the printer, several skilled stonemasons, some weavers and jewelers."

The old woman attempted a chuckle. "We will not miss the latter, at any rate." Her voice was hoarse and she coughed often. During the aerial bombardment of Finiah, when she lay unconscious on the floor of the flyer, she had inhaled fumes from cabin materials set on fire by Velteyn's lightning balls. Unlike Claude and Richard, she had not been seriously burned; but Amerie was deeply concerned about damage to Madame's lungs, which could not readily be treated with the medications and equipment on hand. Also, the old woman refused to rest and was obstinately determined to participate personally in the next phase of her plan. The youthful appearance brought about by her rejuvenation had begun to fade away, and there were now deep furrows in her forehead and beside her thin mouth. Loss of facial substance had thrown her cheekbones and her beaklike nose into gaunt prominence. The golden torc rolled loosely about her thin, corded neck.

Kawai said, "There remain with us in the camp some five hundred and fifty souls, most of them in good physical health in spite of their confused mental state. It is my opinion, as well as that of the three liberated physicians, that these people will recover once they embark on a course of positive action. We will begin dispersing the strongest within the next three days. They will travel with Homi and Axel and Philemon to the site of the Nancy iron workings. Others of our own people and some of the volunteers who remain will accompany this group with supplies. If all goes as planned, we will have at least the shell of a stockaded village erected within two weeks. Several smaller settlements will be built between here and Nancy as soon as Philemon and Axel can train the workers."

Madame nodded. "Bien, entendu. But remember—production of the iron must be given priority! Let nothing be spared in the encouragement of those refugees who are willing to undertake this work. We must equip all of the Lowlives with iron weapons as soon as possible."

They walked among the improvised huts toward a tributary of the Rhine, where the hospital tent had been set up. Many of the refugees came out of their shelters and stood in silence, watching Madame go by. She nodded to them and sometimes spoke a name, for almost all of these people had passed through the auberge during her tenure—and even those who were not known to her personally knew very well who *she* was.

Some of them smiled. A number of faces displayed open hostility and one man spat and turned his back on her. But most watched with a spiritless torpor that made the old woman's heart shrink.

"It was right, what we did!" She hurried along between Burke and Kawai, arms held stiff at her sides. "They had to be freed. They will become accustomed to it soon and then they will be content again."

"Of course," said Chief Burke gently.

Kawai said, "They are still profoundly shocked. We must make allowances for them. Later they will appreciate their release from bondage."

"Many will continue to hate me, though." Her voice was toneless. "First for having sent them into slavery, and now for having freed them, casting them into fresh uncertainty. Their misery lies heavy upon my conscience. If I had not permitted them to pass through the time-portal, this tragedy would never have taken place."

"They would have found another way to make themselves miserable," Burke said. "Look at me! The last of the shmohawks, for God's sake. No more Wallawallas after the Big Chief passes into the Happy Hunting Grounds—so I dramatize the damn shame of it by calling a press conference and telling the rotten paleskins, 'I will fight no more forever.' Not a dry eye on the Tri-D in a dozen Yankee planets as the noble Native American jurist makes his gesture. But later I got a note from the tribal council of the Yakimas telling me to get the hell back on the bench and quit being such a damn kvetch."

Old Man Kawai said, "We have all of us been foolish, Angélique. But you are not to blame. Without your time-gate as an honorable exit, I would likely have taken my own life. That is perhaps true of many of us exiles. But I came here instead—and it is true that I endured much suffering at first, while I was a captive of the Tanu. But later, after my escape, I knew also a great joy. I have learned that there is happiness to be found in service to others. Without you, without your time-gate, I would have ended my days as selfishly as I lived most of them. I am still a fool, perhaps. But I am a fool who has known good friends and true peace."

Madame's head lowered. "Nevertheless, I will not find my own peace until I atone in the way that I must. The slavery of the gray and silver torcs must be abolished. And the time-portal must be closed. We have made a beginning here at Finiah—but I will see it to completion or die!"

She began to cough violently and her face went bluish white.

"Goddam it!" muttered Burke. He scooped her up and went striding toward the shelter of the field hospital, a great tent made from dozens of durofilm tarps zipped together into a pavilion with screened sides.

"Put me down, Peo! I am quite all right." She struggled in his arms.

Kawai, trotting ahead, brought a swarthy man with tired eyes and a stethoscope held at the ready. "Put her on the plank table," the physician said. After examining the state of the old woman's lungs, the doctor said, "You don't take care of yourself, you're gonna drown in your own glop! Hear me? You been doing the drainage exercises Amerie prescribed?"

"They are undignified."

"Mashallah! Will you listen to the woman?" He scratched at an irritated ring of skin beneath his Adam's apple where the gray torc had been. "You guys—talk some sense into her!"

He produced a minidoser and applied it to her jugular.

"That will help some. But only rest will let your body get that fluid out of your lungs. Now are you going to behave?"

Madame said, "Hélas, Jafar chéri! There are matters that require my attention." Ignoring his protests, she got down from the table and toured the hospital, where most of the faces looked warmly upon her. One obviously pregnant woman, lying on a cot in the remnants of a splendid court costume, seized Madame's hand and kissed it.

"Thank God you freed us." The woman began to weep. "Twelve years. Twelve years of a living nightmare—and now it's over."

Madame smiled and gently extricated her hand from the woman's grasp. "Yes, for you it is over, dear child. You are free."

The woman hesitated. "Madame . . . what am I to do with it when it comes? There are other women, too, carrying *their* children. I am too close to delivery. But the others—"

"You must make your own choices. The tenets of my own faith would counsel me to bear the child. It is, after all, innocent. After that . . . perhaps the wisest action is that followed by the Tanu themselves."

The pregnant woman whispered, "I should give it back to them?"

"The Firvulag will help you." Madame raised her eyes to the doctor. "You will see to it, if this is what she decides?"

"I will."

The old woman bent and kissed the forehead of the expectant mother. "I must now undertake a long journey. Perhaps you will pray for my . . . safe arrival at my destination."

"Oh, yes, Madame. And I'll tell the others."

With a small gesture of farewell, the old woman turned away. The doctor followed her to the door of the tent where Kawai and Chief Burke waited.

"They are now in your hands, Jafar chéri. You and Lucy and Lubutu must take care of them, since Amerie will go south with us."

The physician wagged his head in dismay. "You're still determined to go?" He looked helplessly at Burke. "It's insanity."

"I must carry out my plan," she insisted. "We leave early tomorrow morning. Only three weeks remain of the Truce and there is no time to waste."

Burke said, "If you won't consider your own welfare, think of the rest of us! Having to worry about you and take care of you. Amerie would probably act sensibly and stay in Hidden Springs if she didn't feel you needed her."

Angélique Guderian looked up at the huge red man with affection. "You do not trap me with your forked tongue, mon petit sauvage. Now that Felice has returned from Finiah with her obedient herd of chalikos, we will ride south in comfort. As for Soeur Amerie, she has her own reasons for wishing to participate in the operation, as have the other volunteers. And so we march! Au 'voir, Jafar. We go now to the village to complete the last arrangements." She began walking toward the hospital door.

The doctor called out, "Reconsider, Madame!" But she only laughed.

Old Man Kawai shrugged as he started after her. "You have seen that it is useless to argue with her, Jafar. And perhaps, when you are as old as Peo Burke and I, you will understand why she thinks she must finish this affair herself."

"Oh, I understand," said the doctor. "Only too well."

He went back into the ward, where the expectant mother had begun to moan.

5

MARIALENA COOKED THE FAREWELL SUPPER HERSELF, LAYING places at Madame's table for the eleven who were going south, plus one for Kawai, who would take over as Freeleader in the morning.

When all were seated, the Frenchwoman said, "The Reverend Sister will ask a blessing."

Amerie said in a low voice, "Lord, bless this food. Bless this company. Bless this crazy undertaking."

"Ameen," said Khalid Khan.

The others, excepting Felice, said, "Amen." Then they heaped their plates and passed stoneware jugs of chilled wine.

"I thought Pegleg was coming," Khalid said.

Madame confessed, "I told him to meet us tomorrow before we set out. Perhaps you will think me a foolish old woman, mes enfants, but I judged it would be better to confer one last time tonight among ourselves. I know that Fitharn has seemed a faithful comrade during this perilous time. Nevertheless, we should not forget that his first loyalty is to his own Firvulag race. And I have never trusted the arrière-pensée of King Yeochee and Pallol One-Eye. There is always the chance that they plan to use us treacherously once we have succeeded in destroying the torc factory and closing the time-portal."

Vanda-Jo, the plainspoken Public Works Chief, gave a cynical hoot. "We'd be fools to let 'em know every card in our hand. If we bring this double-barreled blast off, the Firvulag will benefit. They don't need to know our planning details. All they have to do is help us with the traveling and hiding out."

"Too bad outlaw humans aren't covered by the Truce," said the nun. She dropped a piece of meat to her little wildcat, which lurked under the table.

"Fat chance," said Peo Burke. "Pass the burgundy—or whatever that is. My old wound needs anesthetizing."

"Speaking of wounds," Amerie went on, "I realize it's useless to urge Madame to stay behind. But Claude and Khalid are another matter. Claude's burns are just beginning to dry and a week isn't nearly enough recovery time for Khalid's concussion and arm and leg wounds."

"You need me," the Pakistani said. "I'm the only one who's ever been to Muriah."

"Ten years ago," the nun corrected him. "And via the Great South Road, not on the Rhône."

"The capital can't have changed much in that time. Besides, I'm looking forward to the boat trip. Gert and Hansi used to kayak on the river back in the future."

Hansi laughed grimly. "It should be a real pleasure cruise for invalids. But there's no escaping the fact that we need Khalid's knowledge of the city. Things will be tricky enough without getting lost."

"This is true," said Madame. "I am distressed that you must go, Khalid, after you have already done so much, but your help might be crucial to our success . . . Claude, on the other hand, is merely being stubborn when he maintains his indispensability!"

"I suppose you're the only one capable of pushing that amber message carrier through the time-warp!" the paleontologist snapped. "I'm fitter than you are, Angélique, and I've earned my place on this mission if anybody has."

"Mulet polonais! Stay home and recover your health."

Felice whacked her spoon handle on the table. "Now don't you two start that again! You're both a pair of sick old coots with no business out of your rocking chairs, and if we had any sense we'd lock you in a shed together and go off without you."

"Fortunately," said Uwe Guldenzopf, taking a placid pull on his pipe, "we have no sense."

Madame glared at Claude. "It is my duty to go! I, who sinned in opening the time-portal, must atone by closing it."

"Hogwash," said Claude. "You've got a death wish, that's what."

Madame flung down her knife. "Will you, of all people, impugn my motives? Look to your own death wish, Monsieur le Professeur!"

Claude took a prim sip from his mug of wine. "Honi soit qui merde y pense, sweetheart."

"Order, dammit!" Chief Burke pounded his huge fist on the table. "As Warlord in Chief of this flea-bitten crew, I declare that there will be no more discussion of motives! All of us have volunteered. All of us have proved that we can be useful in one way or another—either at Castle Gateway or down in Muriah at the torc-works caper . . . Now. I want to know whether there are any more *serious* questions before we wrap it up for the night."

"I have thought of one thing," Basil said with some diffidence. "As a newcomer to the group, I've hesitated to suggest any major modification of Madame Guderian's original scheme. And until Felice returned yesterday morning with her golden torc and the chalikos and said she would go with us, the point was moot anyway. What I'm trying to say is—how about the Spear?"

The others looked at the alpinist don with blank incomprehension. Basil had been liberated in the fall of Finiah, having spent a month in the city dungeons following his recapture on the lake. His place in the new expedition had been assured when he declared himself willing to use his mountaineering skills in scaling the walls of Castle Gateway, the Coercer Headquarters in Muriah, or any other fortress the group might care to invade. He was also, he admitted, "frightfully keen to teach the Tanu a lesson for having spoiled my Pliocene holiday."

Old Man Kawai now shook his head in regret. "The Spear's powerpack is completely discharged, Basil. You couldn't get a glim out of a micro-LED with the juice that's left. I had a stab at trying to open the pack myself, but I simply could not improvise a suitable tool. It needs a craftier hand."

"Still," Basil persisted, "if we *could* get the pack open, there's a good chance we could recharge it. Am I right?"

The former electronics manufacturer lifted his skinny shoulders. "The flyer was water-fusion powered. Why not the zapper?"

Felice said, "Jeez, guys, I'm not sure I can fine-tune my PK enough yet to break into the thing without ruining it."

"That wasn't what I had in mind," said the alpinist. "What you could do is carry the Spear south much more easily than the rest of us could do. It would be priceless for the assault against the torc-making establishment."

"He's right about that," Khalid agreed. "The factory is in the Coercer Guild Complex, locked up tighter than a Lylmik's virtue."

"Lest we forget," Amerie interposed, "the Spear is dead."

Basil said, "I have an idea who might resurrect it. Claude told me all about him one long hot afternoon weeks ago when we spent some time together in quod at Castle Gateway. Your talented little friend in the gold suit."

"Aiken Drum!" said Felice. "Little tricky-pockets!"

Claude's greenish eyes flashed. "He could! If anyone could decipher that antique photon weapon, Aiken could . . . But *would* he? They made him a silver, remember. He might have thrown in with them by now. He was always out for the main chance."

"He was our friend," Amerie said. "He's a human being. He's got to help us against those monsters!"

"Felice could twist his arm," Claude suggested, his smile bland. "Or isn't that your style any more, little girl?"

The athlete ignored him. "Basil—I think your idea is a winner. We'll take the Spear, even if I have to shlep it on my back the whole thirteen hundred kloms down to Muriah. One way or another, we'll get Aiken Drum to make us a can opener."

Chief Burke said, "We can hope for the best . . . Anything else?"

Nobody said anything. Uwe tapped the dottle from his pipe into the empty bowl before him. "Marialena is always furious when I do this. But perhaps one last time?"

"She'll forgive you," laughed Gert.

Chairs scraped back. Everybody got up and stretched. Those with cottages in the village prepared to leave. The others would spread sleeping bags upon Madame's floor.

Amerie laid a hand on Kawai's shoulder as the old man turned toward the door. "One favor, old friend."

"Only name it, Amerie-san."

The nun picked up the tiny pet wildcat. "If you could give a home to Deej—"

He bowed gravely and took the little animal into his arms. "I will keep her safe for you until you return to Hidden Springs. And you will. I have made a most formidable vow to the Martyrs of Nagasaki."

"Crazy old Buddhist," said the nun, pushing him out the door.

6

"THIS JUDGMENT THEY DEMAND OF ME CONCERNING YOU," Brede began.

"Yes?" Elizabeth replied aloud, as always.

"It must be made consonant with their own racial destiny here. I have foreseen my dear Tanu and Firvulag people united and operant. This is my vision as of the most ancient days, before we ever came to this galaxy, to this planet of the Many-Colored Land. This destiny will happen, even though my prolepsis fails in showing me the how and when . . . I would like to think that we have become friends, Elizabeth. I am deeply aware of your desire for noninvolvement in our affairs. But I cannot believe that you are an extraneous factor here! You are part of the pattern! And so are all of these others, your companions of Group Green, who have so gravely influenced Tanu and Firvulag and even the poor lost ones of the northern wilderness. I can see the lines of destiny reaching toward a sure convergence at the Grand Combat in three weeks' time. I see it, I tell you! And your role . . . is strongly interwoven. But if not as racial genetrix—then what?"

"Brede, I will not be used." Even with her mental screens firm, the determination behind Elizabeth's statement had an adamantine luster.

"Then *choose* to help us," the exotic woman pleaded. "Your own human race, your own close friends, are bound up in this climax."

"No judgment you make concerning me will satisfy all of the Tanu factions. You know that. Your High King wants his new dynasty. But the Host of Nontusvel won't be satisfied until I'm safely dead. As for my friends . . . they seem to be in better control of their own destinies than I am! Why won't you consider strict justice for me for a change, rather than viewing me as a chess-piece in your proleptic game? Let me go free and harmless away from this place if that's what I choose."

And I do. Soaring the world alone splendid at peace.

"But—the pattern! I tell you, I see it! If it is not your genes that are to influence us, then there must be some other factor. O Sister of the Mind, help me to focus my faltering vision!"

"Prescience was not a metafunction that was understood in my time. It was a wild talent. Unpredictable. The foreseeing was dangerous enough . . . but any attempted manipulation of future events foreseen was known to us to be futile. Whether I go free or not, your vision must come to pass. So let me go."

Brede seemed not to have heard. They were sitting together in the limitless room without doors where the ambient atmosphere was enriched to the exotic's special need. But she had gone rigid and gasped in shallow exhalations while her features worked and her partly open mind showed a whirlpool of faces— human and Tanu and Firvulag and Howler—all gyrating and pulsing around Elizabeth's own image, and that generating filamentous probability lines forming and reforming in what was almost a Lissajous fabric of incoherence—unordered, *un-unified*.

"The psychounion!" Brede cried. "Not the genes—the mental Unity!" The mind of the Shipspouse brightened in such sweet hopefulness that even Elizabeth faltered in continuing to refuse empathy.

"What—are you saying, Brede?"

"That is your role! It doesn't matter when my people achieve their coalescence with the local Mind. It *will* happen. And when it does, I must be able to guide them into the orderly levels of metapsychic union that were the basis of the governing forces of your own Galactic Milieu, the reconciliation of divergent intellectual energies into an operant organic whole. *You* are to teach me how this is to be done! That is your role among us. You guided young children of your own time into the Unity. This was the focus of your life's work, as you have told me. In your Milieu, immature metafunctional minds were not left to flounder and make their own way. They were taught, led, enlightened. Show me how this was done. So that I will be ready. And then, if you still desire it, I will help you to . . . leave us."

"You don't know what you're asking of me, Brede."

"But this *must* be the solution! So elegant, so logical an

extension of the work I have already done for my dear ones. Consider them as they are now, in their disunity! My poor Firvulag, operant but weak and impotent, their psychic energies diffused into silly byways. Their kinsmen, the Howling Ones, festering in bitter despair. And will the Tanu be any different when they in turn achieve true operancy, delivered from their golden torcs? Your operant human race on the Elder Earth might well have perished if it had not been helped in its extremity by other entities who were wiser. Help me to help *my* people. And then, when they are ready, I also will be ready."

"You foresee this outcome?" Elizabeth inquired, dubious.

Brede hesitated. Again the pained, gasping breaths. "I have—always been the guide and teacher of my people. Even in times when they were unaware. Whence shall the Unity come, if not from me? And where can I learn, if not from you?"

"The difficulties would be enormous. Not only is your mind exotic and therefore unfamiliar to me, but you are also a mature psychic entity conditioned to the torc device over thousands of years. I have never worked with any but humans. Almost all of them were very young children, still flexible and able to absorb the training with a minimum of painful catalyst. I can only compare the process with a child's first acquisition of language. This is a process that seems nearly effortless to a baby; and yet when an adult attempts to learn new languages without using sophisticated ancillaries, he labors and suffers. The bringing of latent metafunctions to fully adept operancy is infinitely more difficult. First, you would have to become operant—and then make the much greater leap to adept status before absorbing the masterclass teaching techniques. There would be atrocious suffering."

"I will endure whatever is necessary."

"Even if you survive my education with your sanity intact, there is no guarantee that you will attain full operancy—much less the adept level. If your strength failed at any point, you would surely die. And then what would become of your people?"

"I will not die," said Brede.

"There are other . . . technical difficulties. The catalyst I spoke of. I can't think of an algetic source of sufficient intensity that would be available to us here in your room without doors."

"Pain? Is this the only way that the psychic enlargement can be accomplished?"

"The only sure way. There are others. In my own world,

latent humans have attained operancy when certain psycho-
barriers were overcome through sublimation of the will to the
cosmic Unity. But these other roads are uncertain—and in any
case, I'm only qualified in the one technique. It has its roots
in the preliterate cultures of my own era. The primitive people
of Elder Earth were fully aware that pain, endured steadfastly
and with dignified acceptance, acted as a psychic refining agent
that opened the newly sensitized mind to wisdom otherwise
inaccessible—as well as the individual spectrum of metafunctions."

A panorama of pre-Milieu adepts flashed before Brede's
mental eye. Elizabeth showed her monks and nuns and prophets
and yogis, shamans and warriors and consecrated leaders, ab-
original healers and seers from all of the wild places of pre-
Intervention Earth—humans enduring self-imposed ordeals in
the belief that they would emerge transfigured.

Elizabeth said, "As we humans attained high technology,
the creative use of suffering was nearly lost. Most high-tech
civilizations are zealous in the eradication of pain, both physical
and mental. Up until the time of the Intervention, very few of
our intellectuals would have placed any value on it—this despite the teaching of earlier philosophers and the clear evidence
to be gleaned from anthropology and even from developmental
psychology itself."

"My race was as yours in this respect," said Brede. "Understand that I speak of my original home planet—not of these
Tanu and Firvulag, who are different. The best of the dimorph-
ics still celebrate life-passages with ordeals. The very Combat
itself has roots therein."

"But still perverted! Immature! Among the advanced human
cultures of pre-Milieu times, we had comparable kinks. One
form of physical suffering that was esteemed was that endured
by athletes. Ritual game playing. Do you see the parallel? But
our human race never valued any form of *psychic* pain. That
attendant upon the normal education process was tolerated as
a necessary evil—but there were constant attempts to amel-
iorate it or eliminate it altogether. It never occurred to our
primitive educators that suffering per se had a positive influence
upon mental growth. A few religious groups did discover how
pain worked as a tool for mental enlargement. My own church
had a rather muddled concept of algetic offering that at least
produced the proper endurance-discipline. But the faithful saw
algetics only from the spiritual angle. When certain practition-

ers happened to levitate or read thoughts or perform other metapsychic functions, everybody was highly embarrassed."

"Yes . . . yes." The great jeweled headdress nodded. Exotic reminiscences floated through Brede's mental vestibulum. "We of Lene also held to the belief that suffering was evil. And those who denied it were sadomasochists and hopelessly anomalous. For example—these exiles! My dear foolish people. I have never, until now, completely understood my deep motives for adopting them and helping them to escape from our galaxy. But now it becomes obvious that my prolepsis recognized that tiny kernel of psychic validity in their aberrant mind-set. The Firvulag, especially, who endured the greatest rigors in their natural environment, were keenly appreciative of ordeals. And yet—they stalled in their mental evolution. As did the Tanu, seduced by their torcs, and most of the other people of our federation as well . . . As I have told you, all but the incompatibles embraced the mind-amplifying device after the last of the wars."

She paused, touching the gold at her own throat that was half-hidden behind the lowered respirator. "And this torc, which seemed such a boon, resulted in a dead end for the Mind of an entire galaxy. Unless . . . the evolution continues here. And it must! But, Almighty Tana, why is my vision so *dim*?"

Elizabeth said, "The time-dimension may be much greater than you ever suspected. Our Milieu perceived the past manifest in the present, the present manifest in the future."

"Elizabeth!" Brede's voice caught. "Six million years? Ah, no!"

"We had legends. And there is the compatibility."

"And the Ship," Brede whispered. "I told my dearest one to choose the best."

She raised her glittering mask. Tears fell onto its red metallic smoothness, losing themselves in the crystal ornamentation. The women sat silent for a long time. Between them on the table rested the exquisite glass model of the interstellar organism that had been Brede's mate. Together the disparate spouses had shared a kind of psychounion that, inadequate as it was, had partaken in a small measure of the true mental conjugation Elizabeth had known among her own kind. But Brede's Ship was dead. And she—like Elizabeth—was alone.

"Whatever the risks," came the amplified voice from the hidden mouth, "you must teach me. I know that the Mind of my people will mature, just as I know that the destinies of

Tanu and Firvulag and humanity are interleaved. Perhaps the Unity of my people will perfect itself soon and perhaps late. But there must be a teacher. And if not me, then you."

Elizabeth flared in anger. "Oh, no you don't! Damn you! Can't you understand the way it is with me? I don't want to sacrifice myself for your people. Not even for my *own* people! Can't you accept that operancy doesn't equate with sainthood?"

"There have been saints among you."

The person behind the mask seemed to melt, to change. Elizabeth stiffened, shocked by the metaphoric thrust that she instantly repudiated.

"No! You can't trick me that way. You're no saint and neither am I! I'm an ordinary woman with ordinary flaws. I once was able to do unusual work because my natural talents were trained up for it. But there was never any . . . consecration. When I seemed to lose my abilities, I didn't offer up the loss and make the best of it. I chose this Exile route. I'm a flyaway and glad of it! My being trapped here in the Pliocene, separated forever from the Unity, with my metafunctions restored and monsters nipping at my heels, is a cosmic joke. And you are, too, whoever you are! And I *still* want my balloon back!"

And that is enough for you loving none loved by none O highflyingfleeing Elizabeth?

"I loved once and suffered the loss. Once was enough. Love costs too much. I won't be a mother to your people. Not physically and not mentally."

Brede's mind and mask mirrored only Elizabeth.

Bitter mind-laughter underlay the vocal speech of the human woman. "Oh, that's clever of you, Two-Face! But the ploy won't work. I know all about my sin of Olympian selfishness. But you can't prove that my duty lies with your people, or with exiled humanity, or with any hypothetical merging of the races."

Brede raised her hands. The mask came down and there was only the sad, patient smile. "Then help me to fulfill *my* duty, which does lie with them all. Teach me."

"We—we don't have a pain source of sufficient intensity."

"We do." Brede's determination was unshakable. "There is hyperspatial translation. My body can be sustained in the superficies of the continuum for as long as necessary. I have the legacy of competence from my Spouse. I require no mechanism whatever to span the width of this galaxy. I have never considered using the translational power before this, simply because there was no question of deserting my people. And of course I would not actually leave them now. I would return."

"If the attempt at mental enlargement doesn't kill you."

"I am willing to risk all, to suffer all."

Elizabeth exclaimed, "How can you love these wretched barbarians so much when they can never appreciate what you do for them?"

Only the smile, and the invitation to enter the mind.

With great reluctance, Elizabeth said, "There's another thing I haven't touched on. The teacher...shares the ordeal."

O Elizabeth. No I did not realize. I have been presumptuous and you must forgive. I see now that I have no right—

Elizabeth broke into the protesting thought with brusque words. "Brede, I'm going to die. Even if I fly out of here, your dearly beloved people are going to track me down sooner or later and finish me off. And so...why not? Perhaps, if I succeed with you, it would be a kind of epitaph. If you're willing to chance the ordeal, I'll take you. You'll be my last student. And if your vision of joint racial destiny is fulfilled, perhaps you can even be my justification."

"I never intended to cause you more pain. And I commiserate."

"Well—don't waste it." Elizabeth's tone was wry. "Every bit of suffering is valuable!... Are you sure you can work the translation?"

Brede's mind showed her. Elizabeth would not physically accompany the exotic traveler, of course. But her mind would remain meshed with Brede's to channelize the neural fires.

"Whenever you are ready," the Shipspouse said, "we can go forth."

The ceiling of the room without doors opened. There toward the south was the milky river of the Galactic Plane. And behind its dust clouds, the Hub; hidden beyond that lay the other arm of the spiral, almost a hundred thousand light-years distant.

"All the way across," said Elizabeth. "Now."

... And there they were, in an instant and forever, stretched on a rack the width of the starry whirlpool, poised between gray limbo and black, distorted, spangled space. The atoms of Brede's physical body had become more tenuous than the rare atomic fog that floats in the void between the stars and vibrates still with the birth cry of the universe. The mind of the Shipspouse shrieked on the same frequencies as the agonized particles. And in this manner, the enlargement began.

It would be all the more difficult because Brede's latent powers were so great. All of the well-worn psychoenergetic circuits leading from the torc would have to be rerouted through the syncytial mazes of the right cortex, reeducated to operancy within the refining flame of the ultimate pain that the universe could inflict upon a thinking, feeling creature. By enduring, Brede might pass in a short time through a process that ordinarily took many years. But the pain in itself was worthless unless discipline could be maintained and the divarication of the mental network kept firmly under control. This was where the guidance of a skilled teacher was all-important. While Elizabeth's great redactive power clamped around the pulsating psyche and kept it from disintegrating, she also directed Brede's flaring limbics as though they were countless metapsychic torches burning away the accumulated cortical debris of a lifetime 14,000 years in length.

The mind of the operant, steadfast in the mutual anguish, led and braced that of the aspirant. The two of them hung locked together in the inferno between true space and hyperspace, where there is but a single dimension, an afferent input that sentient beings of all races apprehend only as pain . . .

The process went on and on, simultaneous and eternal according to their shared subjective consciousness. Brede knew in her agony that changes were taking place within her soul—but she could not rise above the fire long enough to study herself. She could only accept and affirm and continue to be strong, hoping that when the suffering was done her mind would still live in the physical universe.

The pain lessened.

Now Brede felt Elizabeth's binding energies soften to gentleness. She became aware of other life-forces besides their own two, appearing to sing amidst the diminishing flame. How odd! And what was *that*? There, so far away, beyond the gray and the black and the humming megatonal song and the rack of invisible waning fire was a glimpse of brightness that might have been approaching; and the clearer her perception of it, the more irresistible it became. Brede abandoned discipline, forgot all self in her sudden eagerness to reach it, to see and join with it, now that she was capable of the Unity . . .

Return.

O no Elizabeth not now let me go on—

We have reached the limit. Return with me.

No no we exiles together continue on with me to the end of it and join beyond pain where it waits for us loving . . .

We must return. I'm going to draw you back. Don't resist.

No no no no—

Let go. Stop looking. You may not have that and live. Come back now from there submit to my redaction fly back across the expanse don't struggle Sancta Illusio Persona Adamantis ora pro nobis wherever you are submit Brede submit to my guidance rest in me we are almost there . . . there . . .

The Shipspouse sat unmasked across the table from Elizabeth. "Gone. It's gone. You took me away from it."

"It was necessary for both of us. And the culmination of the pain in your ordeal. Which was successful."

Tears steamed down Brede's face. There was a slow rekindling after near-extinguishment, and regret that would be a part of her until, at last, she died. In the silence of the room without doors Brede recovered.

There was an opening and an invitation. Brede ventured in, then cried aloud as she knew the first true Union with a mind of Earth.

So that is—how it is.

Yes. I embrace thee Sister.

The exotic woman put fingertips to the lifeless gold at her throat and unfastened the catch. She held the open torc at arm's length for a moment before laying it on the table beside the Ship's likeness.

I live. I function freely feeble an infant tottering on first legs but the metafunctions are released and such richness and the Unity is twoinone now but later when I know the loved Mind—

There will be spontaneous growth with joy instead of pain until you are filled to capacity. This last is subject to the limitations of your physical body as well as the state of the local Mind. Since you already love the Mind, you will be able to pour forth without diminishing. This is something I cannot do.

And *that* which I saw—

What most of us operant or no shall see and possess ultimately. Not many aspirants catch a glimpse of it. Fortunately.

Once more the two women sat in mental silence.

"There is no memory of anguish," Brede finally said out loud. "But I can see that there would not be. The guiding and the acceptance are all-important in differentiating unproductive misery from creative purgation. And after that comes joy. Yes— that, too, is what one would expect. Not mere absence of pain, but ecstasy."

"Almost all mature humans are aware of the thin line dividing the two—even if they can't understand what to make of it. If you wish, as part of your further education, I'll share some concepts of the Milieu essence that our philosophers and theologians debated."

"Yes. You must show me all that you can. Before you— go."

Elizabeth refused the gambit. "The psychology of each sentient race savors the theosphere in a unique way. We might study the possible niche that your people might occupy. And now that there are two of us, we can do what no single operant mind can do—partake together of the essence in a limited fashion. It will be dilute because the Mind of the Pliocene is still so infantile, but you'll find it wonderful."

"It is already wonderful," said Brede. "But the first thing I must do with my enriched newness is look once again along the lines of probability in search of the all-important pattern that was unclear. Will you join me?"

The teacher and sister vanished. Mental doors slammed. "I might have known! Brede, you're an incredible fool."

The exotic woman's mind was fully open but Elizabeth would not go in, would not look.

"I'm leaving your rooms without doors," Elizabeth said. "I'm going to find your King and tell him your judgment concerning my fate. Your new judgment. And I'm going to find the balloon, and in my own sweet time I'm going to leave this place."

Brede bowed her head. "I will give you your balloon. And if you wish, I will deal with the Host of Nontusvel. Please— let me go with you to the King."

"Very well."

The two of them went out and stood again briefly on the promontory above the White Silver Plain. The salt was crowded with miniature lights. As the time for the Grand Combat approached, the tent-city of the Firvulag grew. Even though it was the middle of the night, supply caravans flanked by rama linkmen could be farsensed as they crept down the slope south of the city toward the temporary encampment. Landing stages at the shore of the lagoon were illuminated and there were lights on the water as well.

Brede studied the scene, masked and inscrutable. "Only three weeks until the Grand Combat, and then it will be resolved."

"Three weeks," Elizabeth repeated, "and six million years."

7

AT THE TIME OF THE GRAND COMBAT TRUCE, ALL ROADS IN the northern regions of the Many-Colored Land led to Roniah. Through this city passed Tanu and Firvulag alike on their way to the games—the Great Ones of both exotic races traveling via riverboat while the humbler majority followed the Great South Road that paralleled the west bank of the Rhône all the way down to Lac Provençal and la Glissade Formidable.

Most of the travelers from northern regions broke their journey at the Roniah Fair. There the ancient enemies mingled freely in a once-a-year orgy of commerce that extended through the middle two weeks of the pre-Combat Truce, day and night without a letup. Booths were set up along the great pillared midway and among the surrounding exterior gardens of the river city. The peripheral area became a huge campground where human and Firvulag entrepreneurs presided over tented caravanserais and dining establishments catering to the tourists.

This year it was the Finiah refugees, well supplied with money but almost completely bereft of possessions, who were the most eager customers at the Fair. To bolster their spirits they spent lavishly for the luxury goods that were the stock-in-trade of Firvulag crafters: polished gems and amber, jewelry, novelties carved of ivory or semiprecious stone, gold and silver gewgaws, begemmed headdresses and garment trims, fancy tack for chalikos, ornate belts and scabbards and battleharness, perfumes and unguents and scented soaps derived from wildflowers and herbs, peculiar liqueurs, psychoactive flycap and panaeolus fungi, and delicatessen such as wild honey, candies with alcoholic syrup centers, truffles, garlic, spices, gourmet sausages, and that paramount exotic delectable—wild strawberry preserves. More-staple goods were purveyed by human

vendors from Roniah and the other Tanu settlements: fine textiles and readymade garments, dyestuffs and other domestic
chemicals, glass tools of every description, glass tableware and
containers, glass armor, and glass weapons. From the Tanu
plantations flowed quantities of beer, wine, and spirits packaged in wooden casks or leather bottles, smoked and preserved
meats, dried and pickled fruits and vegetables, and a wide
variety of nonperishable cereal products such as flour, groats,
and plain and flavored hardbreads. The food was not only sold
to the travelers, but was also sent down the river to aid in the
provisioning of the Grand Combat itself.

Late on October fourteenth a certain refugee party came
riding down the crowded highroad and arrived at the Roniah
Fair. It made its way into the private campground area where
petty Tanu and Firvulag nobility could erect their own pavilions
separate from the commonalty. The group of travelers was
unique only in that it consisted entirely of humans. There were
two gold-torc ladies who might have been mother and daughter—
the elder wearing flowing emerald gauze robes and an outra-
geous jeweled chapeau, the younger in full blue coercer's armor
and a golden cloak, bearing a lance from which floated a banner
of gold with a raven displayed sable. The ladies' entourage
consisted of five bronze-armored soldiers led by a captal of
gigantic stature, an elderly steward, two handmaids, and a
gnarled little one-legged wrangler, in whose presence the pack-
chalikos and remounts seemed unaccountably skittish.

"Yes—we lost everything in the Finiah disaster," the gran-
dam told the sympathetic human campmaster as they signed
in. "All save a few treasures and these faithful gray-torc servants are gone, leaving my daughter and me sadly destitute.
Still . . . there is the possibility that we may recoup our fortunes
at the Combat, for the Lady Phyllis-Morigel has trained dili-
gently and shows great promise as a warriormaid, and so we
may gain both riches and revenge at the White Silver Plain, if
Tana wills."

The campmaster saluted respectfully. The lovely young face
of the Lady Phyllis-Morigel smiled at him beneath the raised
visor of her helmet. "Good fortune will surely attend you in
the lists, Lady. I can feel your mighty coercive power even
though you've got it leashed back."

"Phyllis, dear," the old woman chided. "For shame."

The girl blinked and the wave of coercion receded. "Your

pardon, Worthy Campmaster. I didn't mean to press you. This will be my first Combat and I'm overexcited."

"Small wonder," said the man. "But don't you worry, little Lady. Just keep cool and you'll come out a sure winner in the prelims. I've got a feeling about you."

"You're kind to say so, Campmaster. I feel that I've been waiting all my life to participate in the games..."

"Ladies, it's late," interrupted the old steward, who had been fidgeting in the saddle during the chitchat. "You must rest."

"Master Claudius is right," said the huge captal of the guard. "Tell us our allotted space, Campmaster, so that we can rest our bones. We've been on the trail six days and we're worn out."

"Six days," tsk'd the campmaster. "Then you weren't with the refugee group that was sheltered at Castle Gateway?"

Hastily, the captal said, "We were too late to join the train led by Lord Velteyn. There is great confusion still in the northland."

The campmaster studied a board-map. "Most of your fellow citizens from Finiah who are still here are camped in the riverfront spaces, which are the most attractive sites that we have. I can place you down there for only a slight surcharge—"

The old woman was firm. "Much as we would like to join our compatriots, it is necessary that we economize so that we will not run short of funds at the Combat itself. Furthermore, we should be embarrassed among our friends because we are unable to reciprocate any entertainment they might offer us. Therefore, good Campmaster, indicate to us a modest place sufficient for our two tents and the picketing of our animals. One would prefer high ground, if this is available."

Slightly disappointed, the man restudied his board. "Well, there's Number 478 on the northern edge of Section E. High and breezy—but you'll have to carry water."

"It will do splendidly. My noble daughter will bring us water by virtue of her psychokinetic power. The fee? Ah. Ça y est. And now we bid you good night."

The man took the coins and threw a shrewd glance at the warriormaid. "So you have PK, too—eh, Lady Phyllis? Now I'm positive you'll do well in the lists! I'll watch for you and risk a few bob. As a rookie, you should get nice long-shot odds. Yes, indeed!" He waved a cordial farewell as the party rode down the lamp-bordered lane into the hurly-burly of the crowded campground.

"You dummy, Felice," said Chief Burke. "What's the idea letting loose your coercion? Now that man's going to remember you."

She gave a light laugh. "He'd remember us anyway, Peo. At least now he knows I'm a genuine gold. You should have seen your face when that guy suggested we camp next to the Finiah crowd!"

"This is our worst danger," Madame said. "Felice and I may easily delude any torced persons by pretending to be half-deranged with grief because of our misfortunes. But the rest of you, with your sundered gray torcs, are sure to be detected as interlopers if Tanu or torc-wearing humans attempt to communicate with you mentally. You must stay close to Felice and me at all times so that we may intercept and turn aside any telepathic importunities. The purchase of supplies and forage must be undertaken tonight by Fitharn. Unless he is deliberately probed by a powerful metapractitioner, he will be above suspicion."

"I still think it's risky camping in here," said Vanda-Jo.

"We've been over that," Burke said, "This far south, it would be suspicious if we tried to camp anywhere else."

"No more Firvulag tumuli to shelter in down here, missy," Fitharn said. "The Little Folk in these parts don't dare have large settlements, the way we do up north. Only single-family burrows for the most part, well-hidden in the wildest regions far from the trails. Folks around here are leery of strangers—even ones that come recommended by King Yeochee."

"We have already had hints," remarked Madame with some tartness, "that the royal authority becomes exiguous in the hinterlands."

Fitharn grinned. "Our King's sovereignty is a little less formal than old Thagdal's. We've an elected monarchy, you know. But we Firvulag are loyal in our fashion. And unlike some other people I could mention, we'd never stoop to using a deposed ruler as a life-offering."

The party came into a region where the tents and campfires were more widely spaced. There were large rock outcroppings and fewer trees and the lamp-bordered trail led increasingly uphill. That they traversed the low-rent district was obvious from the small number of chalikos and hellads that were pegged out among the campsites. The shelters were mostly black Firvulag tents or the motley lodgings of elderly Tanu bachelors. Unlike the noisy conviviality of the central area, this part of the campground was somnolent except for the calling of insects and snorts and grumbles from domestic animals.

Fitharn said, "Here's 478. Nice and secluded." He, of course, could see in the dark better than the humans could see by daylight. Hopping easily on his pegleg, he went up the rocks that hemmed the space on three sides and ascertained that the adjoining sites were empty. "Our closest neighbors are Firvulag, Madame. Looks like a perfect spot. I'll hobble the beasts for unloading and take a pair of remounts to the Fair for supplies right away."

Felice swung down from the saddle of her tall steed. "And I'll set up the tents." She came over to Amerie's mount and smiled up at the nun, who, like Vanda-Jo, was disguised in the blue-and-yellow-striped robes of a gray-torc serving woman. "Still feeling creaky? Let me help you."

Amerie was levitated out of the saddle and floated gently to earth.

"You're learning how, all right," the nun observed.

"Oh, yes. By the time we reach Muriah, I should have it pretty well figured out."

"How about Madame and me?" Vanda-Jo was letting her irritation show. "And poor old Claude and Khalid could use a leg down, too."

The athlete bent her psychokinetic power to the unseating of the others. Then, as Peo and Basil and Gert and Hansi unloaded the pack-animals, the girl erected the two Tanu-style tents, with their telescoping poles and guy-lines, simply by putting her mind to it. Another mental exercise brought waters streaming through the air from the Rhône, which lay nearly half a kilometer away, into three large decamole tubs that the men had set inflated and ready. An entire deadwood tree, plucked from the cliffs behind the camp, came sailing down and landed without a sound at the edge of the site.

"Now comes the dicey part," Felice said, concentrating. "My creativity isn't under control yet, so everybody stand back while I blast the tree into firewood. I hope! If I bobble it, we'll end up with charcoal or ashes, so cross your fingers."

Zap.

"Oh, well done," said Basil. "Split her right down the middle. Now off with the branches, my dear."

Zap zap zap. Pammedy-pow-pow-pow.

"Slice 'er like bratwurst!" Uwe urged. The girl's small-scale mental lightning flared again and again, cutting the tree into convenient billets. When the pile of wood lay there, steaming gently, most of the party applauded.

Madame said, "One can perceive that your three primary metafunctions are developing to a formidable degree, ma petite. You will exercise prudence, will you not?"

"Haven't I behaved myself on the trip from Hidden Springs?" Felice inquired reproachfully. "Don't worry. I won't go wandering away to show off. I want to see these Tanu bastards screwed just as much as you do, Madame. I won't jeopardize the plan."

The old woman looked exhausted, but she said with determination, "C'est bien. Then let us have a small council of war before our good friend Fitharn returns. The time has come for important decision making."

"We can gather round the campfire," said Felice.

A dozen stool-sized rocks came flying through the darkness and formed a circle. Pieces of wood arranged themselves into a cone and ignited when a glowing ball of psychoenergy materialized beneath them. Within perhaps ten seconds, the fire was ablaze. The conspirators sat down on the rock seats and began divesting themselves of armor and other superfluous gear.

"We have arrived," Madame said, "at a critical point in our enterprise. The usefulness of Fitharn and his Firvulag confrères is virtually at an end, since they will not violate the Truce by participating directly in any attack upon the Tanu. We, of course, have no such scruples. We Lowlives are ever outlaws, protected by no Truce. We know what we may expect if we should be captured. Nevertheless, the exotic enemy will not expect us to strike again so soon after Finiah. Tanu intelligence is doubtless aware that most of our irregulars have dispersed. They will expect us to consolidate our position in the north— which we are doing, of course—but they can scarcely dream that we would be so bold as to move against them in the south, on their own home ground."

Chief Burke said, "The presence of Tanu refugees has worked in our favor. There are so many ill-equipped exotics on the road that our group, dressed in the stuff Felice liberated at Finiah, attracts no particular attention."

"Things have progressed smoothly thus far," Madame agreed. "But now begins the most dangerous part of the operation. The new moon is on the twentieth, six days from now. This is also the last day of the Roniah Fair, after which there will be an emptying of this campground as the exotic people hurry on to the White Silver Plain. It is my belief that the torc factory strike-force should embark at once for Muriah via riverboat. It is possible to make the trip in less than four days—perhaps only three—if a skilled skipper is obtained and one can conjure up psychokinetic winds."

"We'll find us a good boatman," said Felice, peeling off her sapphire shell. "And he'll do exactly as we say, once Khalid puts the chisel to his gray torc."

"You're sure you'd rather not try to mind-bend him?" the metalsmith asked Felice.

"I'm still too clumsy to work through the torcs. If he fought me, I could accidentally kill him. Don't worry—I'll be able to tame him barenecked."

Madame continued. "We may hope that you will arrive in Muriah around the dark of the moon, obtain the assistance of Aiken Drum if possible, and mount your attack at a suitable time. Let us say, early on the twenty-second. In the small hours of the morning. And at dawn, I myself will put the message through the time-portal."

There was an uncomfortable silence.

"So you're still determined to make the grand gesture," Claude said.

The firelight showed Madame's face tightened into its most obstinate expression. "We have been over this. There are only two of us capable of approaching the time-gate under the cloak of invisibility—and Felice would be wasted in the Castle Gateway operation. Her great talents can best be used in the southern thrust, while my more meager ones are quite adequate for the castle action."

"You'll have to wait around here for a week," Claude said. "What if you come down with another pneumonia attack?"

"Amerie has given me medicines."

"So you'll just stroll up to the time-gate and toss the amber inside!"

"Au juste."

"Velteyn is still at Castle Gateway coping with his refugees," Chief Burke warned. "He may not go south until the last minute. We know that he has no difficulty seeing through your illusions. You may be able to approach the gate without being detected—but I doubt that your creative metafunction would be able to operate within the taufield itself. Once you throw the message carrier inside, it will become visible to the guardians and soldiers standing nearby. They'll sound the alarm."

Claude added, "And Velteyn or some other high-powered Tanu will come running and melt your personal invisibility screen like the snows of yesteryear."

"I will have accomplished my task," the old woman said.

"And died!" Claude exploded. "But it's not necessary, Angélique! I've thought of another way." And he told them.

Uwe nodded his bearded head. "That just might march, Claude. You should be able to do the necessary work without difficulty, and it would solve the problem of finding a place for Madame to hide out as well. And you'd be a backup for her in case—"

Claude broke in. "You guys don't need me down south. I'd be a nuisance—I admit it. But up here, I can be an asset."

"We know your motives, all right," Felice said. "Chivalrous old poop."

Madame glanced around the circle, then made a small gesture of resignation. "We will revise the castle action as Claude has recommended, then. At dawn on the twenty-second, when we two make our attempt against the time-gate, the rest of you will already have accomplished the assault on the torc factory."

"Sit deus nobis," muttered the nun.

Chief Burke said, "Our iron will be a secret weapon in any hand-to-hand fighting with the Tanu, but it will have no special advantage over human enemies—especially gold-torcs. We have only two weapons with really large destructive potential for the blasting of the Coercer Guild stronghold. There's Felice's psychozap—which may or may not be powerful enough to do the job—and the Spear."

"Which is nothing but a pretty glass clothespole," Khalid reminded them, "unless we get Aiken Drum to help us recharge it . . . How about it, Felice? Do you think your energy projection will build up strong enough to break down thick masonry and bronze doors?"

"As of now, I doubt it," the girl said. "I get better every day, but we'd damn well better not plan on that kind of attack. But, listen—as I understand it, our primary target isn't the whole headquarters building but just the factory part. Wouldn't those torc components be delicate little gadgets? Could be, all we'll have to do is bring the roof down on 'em and it's bye-

bye, baby! Vanda-Jo could tell by looking at the building just what spots I'd have to hit. Right?"

"I might be able to," said the Public Works Chief, but her tone betrayed doubt.

"I've seen that place," Khalid said. "It doesn't look anything like the fairytale towers of Finiah did. It's a bloody great cube of marble and bronze about as vulnerable as the Polity Bank in Zürich! Unless Felice checks out as a mountain mover by next week, she's going to find it a helluva tough zap."

The little athlete had removed almost all of her glass armor and its padding and sat on her rock attired only in a white chemise and a pair of sollerets with golden spurs. She swung her blue-shod feet. Reflections from the gemmed plates of the footgear danced over her delicate face. "I don't know what I'll be capable of next week. But whatever I've got, I'll lay all over those Tanu friggers."

"You will follow Peo's orders, child," Madame said sharply.

"Oh, yes." Felice's eyes were wide.

Basil said, "Whatever Felice's eventual firepower, our best chance of success still lies in the photon weapon. If we can recharge the Spear, we might even demolish the Coercer Guild complex from a distance with a minimum of hazard to our party. We could do it from out in the lagoon, couldn't we, Khalid?"

"The building is on the northern edge of the city, west of the place where the main rollerway comes up from the docks. One wall of the keep structure is flush with the escarpment. There's a sheer drop of maybe a hundred meters on that side of the peninsula, then a klom or so of dunes and carved-up sediments before the shore of the Catalan Gulf . . . What do you think, Claude? You fired the damn thing."

The paleontologist said, "With a steady platform for the shot, you could zap the building to kingdom come. Or even shoot the cliff out from under it."

Amerie's voice was low. "If we do it in the wee hours of the morning, perhaps the casualties will be minimal."

"Getting cold feet, Sister?" the big Native American inquired. "This is war. If you're squeamish, you'd better stay with Madame and Claude."

The old woman's face was troubled. "It might be best, ma Soeur."

"No!" said Felice. "You agreed to help where you were needed most, Amerie. And that's with us. We can't risk another stupid disaster like Peo's pig screwing up the assault. This time, the doctor goes along."

"I'll do my best," the nun insisted. "I told you that I would. Just settle on a plan and I'll follow it."

"Let me suggest," Basil said, "that we rethink the role of Aiken Drum. Is it really necessary for us to wait until we reach Muriah before contacting him to enlist his help?"

The rest of them looked at the climber, not understanding.

"We might try to farspeak him from *here*," Basil explained. "Let the young man know we're coming. Insure that he's there waiting for us. Perhaps even present the problem of the Spear to him so that he can be thinking about it in advance of our arrival." Madame began to protest, but Basil held up a tactful hand. "I know that Madame Guderian has doubts about her ability to farspeak over great distances—as well as farspeaking on the intimate mode. But it's occurred to me that we might utilize your other friend, Elizabeth, in a telepathic relay."

"Say!" Claude exclaimed.

"You did tell us, Madame, that you perceived Elizabeth's farspeech shortly after Group Green arrived in the Pliocene. Surely by now the woman's faculties must have recuperated to the extent that she could receive your own transmission on— er—tight beam, even if it were a bit wavery, so to speak."

Madame said, "I doubt that I have the competence. Elizabeth's thought flickered past me in an instant. I did not—how shall I say it?—store the data of her mental signature."

Felice jumped to her feet. "I could help you, Madame! We wouldn't have to farspeak Elizabeth on the intimate mode to get her attention. A simple shout at top volume on the human command mode would do it. All Elizabeth needs to know is that we're out here hollering. Her seekersense could surely zero in on us and then pick up Madame's weakie-squeakie on the very narrow focus."

The old woman frowned at the eager girl. "Other minds might be equally capable of tracking down the source of our telepathic loudhail."

"Not if we handle it my way! Felice exulted. "What we do—early tomorrow we synchronize timepieces and I go ten or twenty kloms back up the North Road. *Then* we simulcast at predetermined intervals! If we farspeak that way, the Tanu can't possibly get an accurate fix on the double shout. But an operant like Elizabeth shouldn't have any trouble sorting the mental patterns of the two of us and tracking Madame when she throttles back to the intimate mode."

"It could work," Amerie said.

Chief Burke growled, "None of this makes much sense to a poor old redskin shyster like me. But let's try it."

"It sounds medium crafty," Khalid said, "provided Felice and Madame can mesh brains . . . and provided this Aiken Drum can be trusted with our precious petards."

"You're crazy if you tell him the whole plan," Claude said.

"Why must you always be so cynical, Claude?" Amerie complained.

The old man sighed. "Maybe because I've lived so long. Maybe I've lived so long because."

"Claude," Madame asked, "would you trust Elizabeth's judgment in this matter?"

"Absolutely."

"Then it is simple. Tonight we rest, tomorrow we attempt the communication. If we make contact, we will request Elizabeth's own assessment of the character of Aiken Drum and proceed as she advises. D'accord?"

Her dark glance flashed around the circle. The other ten members of the expedition nodded.

"That's settled," said Chief Burke. "You leave at dawn, Felice, and we'll schedule the big broadcast for noon. You dress up in your armor and all and take Basil and Uwe and Khalid as your gray-torc escort. Any Tanu get nosy, you're just looking for your Uncle Max among the refugees. While you're putting some distance between us, Madame and the rest of us odds and sods can go down to the Roniah wharf and scout out a suitable boat. Gert and Hansi know the kind of vessel we'll need."

"Don't be late getting back to camp," Felice cautioned them. "And try to get some more blue lacquer at the Fair. The stuff that Old Man Kawai used to coat the Spear is starting to peel off."

They relaxed then, and as the midnight moon came up over the Rhône, Fitharn and Firvulag returned with forage and fresh food. Madame took the gnomish little exotic aside and told him such of their plans as seemed expedient.

"So you see," she concluded, "that in a few hours most of our people will be embarked upon the river, while Claude and I conceal ourselves near Castle Gateway and await the day when we shall deal our double blow against the Tanu slave-masters. And now you are free to leave us, my friend. Take with you the profound gratitude of our company . . . and of all free humanity. Tell King Yeochee what we hope to do. And bid him for me—farewell."

The little man squirmed within her mental clasp, crushing his pointed red hat between his hands. His alien consciousness, so hard to read even when the screens were down, was now all but walled off. The images that flickered through the near-opacity were colored with conflicting emotions.

"You are troubled," Madame said softly.

"Angélique . . ." The gnome's words and thoughts made a jumble: fear love loyalty mistrust hope doubt pain.

"Dear little friend, what is it?"

"Warn your people!" Fitharn burst out. "Tell them to trust no being too far! Even if they are successful, tell them to remember my warning!"

His face looked up at hers for one last instant. Then he disappeared into the night.

8

THE GOLD-TORC LADY AND HER STEWARD HOVERED BEFORE the Firvulag jeweler's display while the rest of their retinue, guards and serving women, prevented the fairground multitude from pressing too close.

"I wonder if this one is suitable, Claudius?" the woman asked. "Or is it perhaps so large as to be vulgar?"

The old gray-torc looked with disdain upon the amber paperweight that the jeweler's assistant proffered on a velvet cushion. "It has," the steward declared, "*bugs* in it."

"But they are part of the originality of the piece!" the jeweler protested. "Caught at the moment of their ancient mating hundreds of millions of years ago! The two insects, male and female, united in their nuptial embrace forever within this glowing gem! Is it not poignant, Exalted Lady? Does it not touch your heart?"

The lady peeped askance at her steward. "Do you find it touching, mon vieux?"

The jeweler waxed rapturous. "It comes from the darkest depths of Fennoscandia, from the Black Lake's haunted shores! We Firvulag do not dare to harvest this amber, my Lady. We obtain it!"—he paused dramatically—"from *Howlers!*"

"Tana have mercy!" the gold-torc lady whispered, eyes wide. "So you really do trade with the wild ones! Tell me, good jeweler . . . are the Howlers really as hideous to the eye as rumor has it?"

"To see one," the artisan assured her, keeping a solemn face, "is to go mad."

The lady bent a satirical eye upon her silver-haired servitor. "I have suspected as much. Ah, yes."

The jeweler's assistant ventured to remark, "Some persons

believe that this year—because of the unrest y'see—the Howlers have even dared to come south!"

The lady squealed in alarm.

Her captal, a huge man with a face like seamed cordovan, slapped his sword hilt. "Now then, Foeman! Beware how you attempt to frighten our noble mistress!"

"Oh, Galucholl is quite right, brave Captal," the jeweler made quick to say. "And let me assure you that we of the True Folk are quite as alarmed about the matter as you. Té only knows what the ugly devils want. But we shall be alert lest they come slinking among us during the games."

The woman shivered in delicious dread. "How exciting! How terrible! We will purchase the amber, jeweler. I am most taken with the doomed insect lovers. Pay him, Claudius."

Grumbling, the steward took coins from his belt wallet. Then his eye fell upon a tray of rings and he began to smile. "We'll take two of those as well, I think. Wrap them up."

"But, sir!" protested the Firvulag. "The carved-jet rings have a certain symbolic significance that you may not be aware—"

The old man's icy green eyes blazed under their white brows. "I said, we'll take them! Now get those fornicating termites under wraps and be quick about it. We're going to be late for an appointment!"

"Yes, yes, right away, Worthy Master. Get a move on, Galucholl, you young lout!" The jeweler bowed to Madame Guderian as he handed the soft pouch to the steward. "Good fortune attend you, Exalted Lady, and may you enjoy your purchases."

The old gray-torc laughed. In a manner overly presumptuous for one of his status, he took the woman by one elbow and signaled for the escort to close in around their mistress.

When the customers had disappeared into the crowd, Galucholl said, "Well, he *could* have been buying the rings for someone else."

The artisan gave a laugh that bespoke long experience. "Oh, my boy. What an innocent you are."

Gert stuck his sandy head and one arm into the tent. "Here y'go, Madame. All sliced neatly in half. Didn't even disturb the poor bugs."

"Thank you, my son. Claude and I will finish the work. Since it is almost noon, you and the others had best take your positions on the high rocks around our campsite. At the slightest sign of alarm you must notify me so that I can cease the transmission."

"Right you are, Madame." The head vanished.

"Here's the message." Claude held out the ceramic wafer. "Just like yours, but with my signature. You have the cement?"

She bent over the pieces of amber that lay on the decamole table. "Violà," she said at last. "It is ready. One for you to carry and one for me, par mesure de sécurité. I shall keep the one with the pathetic termites, even though you have signed it. It is fitting."

The two of them considered the message carriers. Shining through the reddish-gold fossilized resin were the words of the sandwiched wafers:

PLIOCENE EUROPE UNDER CONTROL OF MALIGN EXOTIC RACE. CLOSE TIME-GATE FOR THE LOVE OF GOD. IGNORE ANY SUBSEQUENT MESSAGES TO CONTRARY.

"Will they believe us, do you suppose?" she asked.

"They can check our signatures easily enough. And, as you said, two witnesses are better than one. Nobody'd ever suspect a straight old lace like me of pulling a hoax."

They sat together, saying nothing. It was very hot in the closed tent. She brushed a lock of graying hair back from her brow. A rivulet of sweat trickled in front of one ear.

"You are a fool, you know," she said finally.

"Polacks are suckers for bossy women. You should have known Gen! Sector chiefs were known to flinch like whipped curs before her black wrath. Besides, I'm too old-fashioned to compromise myself with a piece like you, hiding in a trapdoor-spider burrow for a week with my poor old nuts singing the 'Marseillaise' while the rest of my equipment tries not to stand at attention."

"Quel homme! C'est incroyable!"

"Not for Polacks." He consulted his watch. "Fifteen seconds until noon. On your mark, old woman."

Elizabeth and Dionket the Lord Healer looked down on the black-torc child in its cot. A fullblooded Tanu, it seemed to the human woman to be older than its actual age of three years—not only because of the longer limbs, but also in the overglaze of suffering on its still-beautiful face.

The child was naked except for a towel laid over its loins.

A water mattress supported the swollen body as comfortably as was possible in this tankless medical technology. The child's skin was a dark red; peripheral body parts such as digits, ears, nose, and lips were almost black with congestion. Beneath the small golden torc, the neck was blistered, clotted with some white salve applied in a futile attempt at soothing. Elizabeth slid into the ruined infant mind. Livid eyelids opened, showing fully dilated pupils.

Dionket said, "Removing the torc would only make him worse. Then there would be convulsions as well. Note the degeneration of the neural linkages between the cerebellum and the limbic areas, the anomalous circuits from the torc to the premotor cortex, the chaotic firing within the amygdala that has frustrated our own attempts at analgesia. Onset of the syndrome is typically abrupt—five days ago in the case of this boy. Death will ensue within approximately three weeks."

Elizabeth rested one hand upon the hot blond curls.

Ah baby there baby lie easy poorlambie let me see let me in to look to help ah there the relentless conduits between gold and charged flesh where misery ramps to and fro poor baby . . . ah. See. I quench it sever the controlinterface between highbrain and low admitting peace so rest now wait now and sleep until they come bright to carry thee away poor baby matured at last in the light.

The small eyes closed. The body relaxed into flaccidity.

Elizabeth you have removed his pain Tanabethanked.

Refusing as always to meet his mind, she turned away from the cot. "He will still die. I can bring no cure, only relief until the end."

But if you stayed longer if you experimented . . .

"I must go."

You could have gone but you have not. Shall I tell you why you have stayed with us even though your balloon waits for you in the room without doors?

"I have stayed to teach Brede, as I promised." Nothing— no shred of empathy passed her mental screen. But Dionket Lord Healer was old, and there are other ways of reading souls.

You have stayed with us in spite of your professed disdain in spite of your selfish self because you have been touched . . .

"Of course I've been touched! And repelled! And I *will* go away. Now—shall we continue to waste time in futile sparring, or shall we see whether I can help you with these wretched babies?"

Elizabeth Brede is so close to understanding her vision if you would only help her to interpret—

"Brede is a spider! The Host of Nontusvel warned me of that. At least they're honest barbarians, making no bones about their antagonism. But Brede weaves metapsychic webs and I say to hell with her!" The spill of bitterness was swiftly reconfined. "Shall we get on with it, or not? And speak out loud to me, please, Lord Healer."

He sighed. "I'm sorry. Brede—and all of us—have only sought to keep you with us because of our great need. We have not given proper consideration to *your* need. Forgive us, Elizabeth."

She smiled. "Of course. Now tell me what percentage of your Tanu children are afflicted with this terrible thing?"

"Seven. The syndrome that we call 'black torc' may appear among purebloods at any age up until the approximate onset of puberty, after which the adaptation to the torc is presumably in homeostasis. Most of the cases are under four years of age. With the hybrids, there is never a danger of black torc, only of the incompatibility dysfunctions that pureblood humans may experience when wearing the device. Severe though the dysfunctions may be, with careful redactive treatment they can usually be remitted. But we have been powerless to help these black-torc children . . . until now. Your execution of the erasures and cutoff was astounding! You of the Milieu are advanced far beyond us in deep redaction. Even if you will not stay—may I hope that you will at least relieve the rest of these suffering little ones before you leave us?"

O Yes? Immerse in more innocent agony breast more wailing dumb endurance so useless unchanneled unproductive evil rending of me and it poor babies *why* so ungodly why these everbedamned torcs?

It is our way Elizabeth the only way we know how could we turn away from even this simulacrum of operancy once knowing it *could you*?

Their massive egos confronted one another, naked in power for the most fleeting instant before veiling. But she had looked down on Dionket the Healer in her mightiness, and he had abased himself and entreated and offered—what was it he offered?—and he had shown her how many others there were like him.

Tears started to Elizabeth's eyes. She would have lashed

out, but she knew that this man at least was no manipulator. And so her response was gentle.

"I can't play the role you ask of me, Dionket. My reasons are complex and personal, but there are practical considerations that I will point out to you. The Host of Nontusvel still means to kill me, even though they know that Gomnol's scheme of mating me with the King has been forbidden by Brede. The Host is even more worried now that I might bear children by Aiken Drum—or team up with him somehow during the Grand Combat! You know me well enough by now to see the impossibility of either notion. But the Host think only of their dynasty. Right now, they're too distracted by Combat preparations to mount more than an occasional attack on me, but I'm still not safe sleeping anywhere but in Brede's room without doors. You and your faction could never protect me from Nodonn and a massed thrust coordinated by him. When I'm sleeping, I'm vulnerable. And they're determined. I won't live the rest of my days imprisoned in Brede's house or fending off mindbolts from that pack of mental savages."

"We are trying to change the old pitiless ways!" Dionket cried. "You could help us in our struggle against the Host!"

"My mind-set is wholly nonaggressive. As you know. Bring about your great changes first and *then* ask me to help."

"As Tana wills," he said, resigned. "When do you depart from us?"

"Soon," she said, looking down again at the sleeping child. "I'll take care of all the rest of these black-torc children for you while you and your best people observe. You may be able to learn the program."

"We will be deeply grateful for your guidance . . . And now, if you will agree, we will leave this chamber of mind-hurt for a time. Even though you screen it away, I know that you are diminished by contact with the black-torcs. We will go to the terrace, beyond reach of their pathetic aura."

The towering form in red and white walked from the ward into cool stone corridors, past screens of marble filigree and onto a great garden balcony. There was a stupendous view of Muriah from up here on the Mount of Heroes, and they could see a long stretch of the Aven Peninsula, the saltflats, and the lagoons all spread below in the clean loud scorch of the noon sun. The crying of the pain-filled young minds was blotted out in the solar emanation. The light so dazzled Elizabeth that she faltered, momentarily blinded—

—and perceived the call.

Elizabeth Orme Farspeaker respond.

Dionket said something solicitous. Taking her arm, he guided her into a shaded corner where there were wicker chairs.

Elizabeth! Elizabeth!

So faint, so garbled, so human, but who?

"Your experience with our poor little ones has affected you, my dear. It's no wonder. Sit here and I'll fetch a restorative."

Could Dionket have heard? But no. It was on the uniquely human mode and almost beyond her own perception, much less his.

"Just—something to drink," she said. "Anything cold."

"Of course. I'll return immediately."

Elizabeth!

Whoyou whereyou I Elizabeth respond.

Me/us! Felice/AngéliqueGuderian! ThankGoditworked O damn quick losing mindmeld t u n e nar r o w An gél i . . .

I have you Madame Guderian.

Grâceàdieu we were soafraid we called solong noresponse listen we are someofus coming to you sabotage torcworks require help AikenDrum if trustworthy do you think can you vouch?

Aiken?

Yesyes himalone le petit farceur! Ifonly wecantrustOlisten this how thisway it is . . .

Elizabeth listened in astonishment to the faint babbling thoughts inexpertly squirting data, smearing a crazy quilt of mind-pictures and clumsy subvocalizations, the whole so clogged with anxiety, so wavering and distant that only a Master could have made sense out of it. What an incredibly bold plan! But these human rebels had already accomplished the incredible at Finiah, hadn't they? This scheme, too, might succeed. But— Aiken Drum? What could she tell them about him, his mind now impervious even to her, doubtless of masterclass potential, perhaps even gone fully operant by now. What could she tell them about the laughing little nonborn chosen of Mayvar King-maker?

    Brede?

      Elizabeth I hear.

    Prognosticate. (DATA)

      Do it.

    Harmless?

Never that nonhuman is.

Harmless forbest myfriends humanity atlarge?

(Irony.) Longview affirm falsealoof Elizabeth.

Damn you . . .

Madame Guderian?

Yes Elizabeth.

I will relay your request to Aiken Drum without telling him more than he needs to know about your plan of action. I believe it to be in humanity's longterm best interest to include him in your scheme. But there may be shortterm danger. Be wary. I will continue to do what I can for you for as long as I can.

Othankyoumerci butit will be dangerous pourl'amour dedieu be withus Elizabeth we cannot/mustnot fail (fear guilt hope). Elizabeth?

Be at peace Angélique Guderian. And all of you my friends . . .

"Here now!" Dionket proffered a tray. "Cold orange juice should be the very thing to restore you. Vitamin C, potassium, and many other good things in this splendid Earth fruit."

Elizabeth smiled and accepted the crystal tumbler. The faraway mental voice had disappeared amid the bedlam of other thought waves.

Seized by uncontrollable laughter, Stein fetched his companion a herculean whack on the back. The small figure dressed in gold stood as firmly as a metal statue.

"Aiken . . . kid! Isn't that the damnedest absofuckinlutely *greatest* news you ever heard in your life? They're coming! Our good ole Group Green pals are coming with their pockets full of iron and a friggerty big zapper that we can blast the chickenshit Tanu into orbit with! *And they can cut off our torcs!* Sukey and me can be free! All of the humans who don't want to wear these things can be free! Would you believe it?"

Aiken Drum smiled his golliwog smile. "That's what Elizabeth says."

The two of them were on a balcony of Mayvar's apartment in the Hall of Farsensors. Their interrupted lunch lay uneaten on the table before them. The high hot sun shone upon the holiday-decked capital city, aswarm with Tanu and human visitors. Out on the shimmering White Silver Plain to the south, thousands of small black Firvulag tents spread in serried ranks, together with larger pavilions of ochre and rusty red and other earthen hues that sheltered the nobility of the Little People. Great bleachers with awnings colored scarlet and blue and purple and rosy gold were being completed on both sides of the great Field of Lists where the sporting contests were to be held prior to the blood events of the Combat proper.

Stein, bareheaded and wearing only a lightweight tunic, clutched his cup of iced mead so firmly that the silver threatened to buckle. "How about it, kid? Do you really think you can recharge that photon cannon thing they're bringing?"

"Can't say for sure until I eyeball her, Steinie. But if it's just a matter of figuring how to open a fewkin' powerpack like Madame said, it should be el cincho to a genius like Me."

"Hot damn!" The giant tossed his drink off and slammed the goblet onto the table. "I'm sure as hell gettin' in on the blanket party for the torc works! Think they might let me do the zapping? There's nobody can teach this boy any tricks in how to handle light-blasters . . . or were you figuring to join the zorch yourself?"

Aiken's grin became bemused. He took a daisylike flower from the table centerpiece and started to pick off the petals. "Who, me? Strike a blow for human freedom and the destruction of the Tanu kingdom? Me use the Spear of Lugonn? Pissy patoot, my man! I probably couldn't even lift the fewkin' thing." He dropped petals into the congealed gravy on his plate. "You know, Steinie, that Spear—the zapper, I mean—is really a sacred thing to these exotic folks. Humans using it in war has caused the biggest stink since the Tanu first came to Earth a thousand years ago. The Spear was one of two photon weapons the exotics brought here from their home galaxy for ceremonial fights between great heroes. The second one is smaller, called the Sword of Sharn. Used to belong to an old Firvulag warlord. Now it's only used as a championship trophy in their Grand Combat. Nodonn's got it."

Stein smote the table. "We'll show *that* bastard! We'll show the whole bunch of 'em! No more human slaves. No more filthy breeding schemes. Without a steady supply of torcs, this whole goddam Tanu setup is gonna fall apart!"

Aiken inspected the shredded blossom with comic dismay. "Sure seems like that's what would happen . . . Poor li'l flower. All ruined."

Stein shoved back his chair. "Let's go tell Sukey! She's been worrying her heart out, hiding away there in Redact House."

"Maybe we better hold off on that," Aiken said casually. "You know. The fewer who know a secret..."

"She'd never tell."

"Not willingly." Aiken did not look at Stein. "She's safe where Dionket and Creyn put her. But there are other redactors—unfriendly ones—floating around that place, too. If Sukey's thoughts just happened to drift a little one day, a really top digger like Culluket Prettyface might get wind of our little conspiracy. All Sukey would have to do is imagine the Spear. Conjure up an image of you shooting it, for instance."

Stein was stricken. "Sweet Jesus, Aiken! Can't we bring her over here with us?"

"I couldn't cover her the way the friendly redactors can. She'll have to stay there until the northerners get here with their iron chisel. Then I can cut off her torc, and yours, too, and you can sail away into the sunrise just like I promised. I gotta confess, kiddo—until we got this crazy flash from Elizabeth and Madame, I didn't have the least fewkin' idea how I was gonna carry out my promise to you two. But with your torcs off so you guys are out of the Tanu mind-net, so to speak, it won't be that hard."

"Can't get this thing off fast enough for me." Stein gave a futile tug at his own gray collar. "Lately, just in the last week, like, I been getting these screwy feelings. And it's this torc, kid! I know it is. I'll be doing nothin' special and all of a sudden an ordinary thing like a shadow makes me jump like a goosed moose. Or I'll feel like the worst goddamn monster in the world is right behind me, reachin' out. And I dassn't turn around and look, because that's all that keeps it from jumpin' me..."

"Don't sweat it," the trickster said. "Four, five days, you'll be bareneck and free as a bird and on your way to the Spaghetti Islands with your lady."

Stein gripped the arms of the little man in gold. "And you, too, right, Aiken?"

"Aw." The mischief-maker's eyes slid away. "*I* was having fun here in King Arthur's Court. And the Combat's nearly here. I think I might just be able to take some of these turdlings. Win myself a fair lady or a spare kingdom or something."

Stein roared with laughter. "And end up with stir-fried brains! You can have your kingdom, sweetheart. What's left of it when me and Madame's gang get finished!" He started for the balcony doors. "I'm going to Sukey. I won't say a word about the zapper. Just tell her things are looking up. Okay?"

Aiken held up the mangled stem of the daisy. Slowly, it straightened. The bruised disc plumped and restored itself. Lavender ray-florets sprang out anew, crisp and perfect.

"And we thought you were a goner, li'l flower!" Aiken chortled. "It just goes to show—don't jump to conclusions!"

Rising off the ground, he tucked the flower behind Stein's ear. Then he returned to the normal mode of human locomotion and strutted away, whistling, "Over the Sea to Skye."

They did it around the campfire at nightfall, since it had been decided that the two old people would have to leave Roniah and go into hiding that night, with the rest of the party embarking for the south at dawn on the morrow.

"It's appropriate," Amerie said when they were all together, "that the traditional Introit for this service should be King David's prayer for victory. It can serve for all of us as well as for Claude and Angélique.

> May the Lord send you help from his holy place
> and defend you from Mount Zion!
> May he grant you your heart's desire
> and make all your plans succeed!

Now repeat after me: 'I, Angélique, take thee, Claude...'"

9

Lord Greg-Donnet came scampering into the computer room of Creation House as Bryan and Ogmol were feeding in the very last of the data. His turquoise tailcoat was fresh and clean and he had a huge white rose in his buttonhole.

"I've been looking all over for you to tell you the news! And then Katlinel said you were in here, so I hurried as fast as—" He broke off as he caught sight of the dog-eared notebooks and storage-plaques that Bryan was packing away into his wicker portfolio. "The *survey*? Don't tell me you're ready to finalize it!"

"Why, yes, Greggy." Bryan smiled. "We could have spent months more on it, but King Thagdal was explicit about having some sort of results before Combat time, so we're doing the final digest today. The King will have two weeks to study it and confer with us before he presents it to the High Table, or whatever."

"How exciting!" crowed the Genetics Master. "Will you let me order the printout, Bryan? Will you?"

"Why, certainly. Just give Ogmol another minute or two."

Greg-Donnet began to jump up and down, hugging himself. "I love it when the plaques come pouring out! Can we print scads and scads?"

"Only three for now, I'm afraid," the anthropologist said. "The survey must be confidential until King Thagdal approves it for general circulation. His Majesty was very firm about that."

Greg-Donnet's lower lip thrust out pettishly. "Spoilsport! There's no fun when the computer prints only *three*."

"Greggy published five thousand copies of his new plot of the metapsychic latency coefficients," Ogmol remarked, looking up from the input mouthpiece. "Better hurry up and reserve yours, Bry. There are only about four thousand nine hundred and ninety-one left . . . That's the last of our stuff. We're ready to go."

Bryan gestured to the control console. "Be our guest, Greggy. But only three: one for the King, one for Ogmol, and one for me."

The madman seized the mouthpiece. His little old baby face regained its usual good-humored expression. "Stand back, everyone! . . . *Begin sysprint plaque opren-three-shutpren sem end*. Wheee!"

The machine, stoically ignoring the last indigestible byte, labored for six seconds and brought forth a trio of ten-by-sixteen-cent rectangles of pale-green plass, entitled:

SOCIOECONOMIC STRESS PATTERNS DEMONSTRATED IN TANU-HUMAN CULTURAL INTERACTION

—A Preliminary Survey—

BRYAN D. GRENFELL
Centre for Anthropological
Studies
London 51:30N, 00:10W
Sol-3

OGMOL urJOHANNA-
 BURNS vulTHAGDAL
Guild of Creators
Muriah 39:54N,04:15E Sol-3

"Doesn't that look *authoritative*?" Greggy squeaked, snatching one of the plaques from the hopper. "Just like back home! Let me read just the abstract, Bry. Pretty please!"

Bryan lifted the book out of the Genetics Master's hand before he could press the contents activator and stuffed it into the inside pocket of his own jacket. "I promise you'll be the first to read it after the King gives his approval. You'll just have to be patient, Greggy."

Ogmol took his own copy of the book and the one intended for his royal father. "This is sensitive material, Greggy. Not to be bandied about lightly."

"Oh, cockypop!" the adult infant cried. "I've a good mind now not to tell you my news! That's why I was looking for you two. So you wouldn't miss the fun. But if you're going to be such meanies—"

"When the King gives his consent," Bryan soothed, "I'll see to it that you get your very own copy in a fine red leather case. Stamped in gold. With your name on it."

Greggy beamed. "Oh, very well, I was only joking. I wouldn't want *you* to miss Lady Mercy-Rosmar's formal challenge to the Crafsmaster!"

"Omnipotent Tana!" Ogmol exclaimed. "So she's really going through with it? Going up against Aluteyn at the Combat in the manifestation of powers?"

"You bet!" said Greg-Donnet. "The King and Queen are here to watch the challenge, and ever so many others."

Bryan could only stand stunned into silence. But Ogmol was saying, "Does the grapevine give her a chance for the presidency, Greggy? I've been so out of it working on this survey that I can hardly separate one intrigue from another any more. I suppose Nodonn's behind the challenge. Mark my words—he and the rest of the Host won't rest until they've taken over all the Guilds! Just look how Riganone keeps crowding Mayvar over at Farsense. And Culluket would challenge Dionket as Lord Healer if his psychopotential only measured up to his power-itch."

"Mercy's brought the cauldron and all," Greg-Donnet said. "She'll give us some kind of demonstration, bet on that, Creative Brother. It should be quite a giggle! I feel sorry for poor old Aluteyn, though. It's tough to do your best for years and years in a hard job when people aren't all that fond of you—and then have some charismatic young charmer come along."

Ogmol laughed. "Bryan knows all about the lady's charm! Secure the data, Bry, and let's go."

The anthropologist seemed to snap out of his preoccupation. He spoke his private locking-encodement into the computer's input, shut the machine down, took his portfolio, and started to follow his exotic coworker.

Greg-Donnet was rummaging in a cabinet. "You go on ahead, colleagues. I want to bring some of *my* reports down to the rotunda. Everybody's there! It's a wonderful chance to corner people, ha-ha!"

After the two had gone, Greg-Donnet let his own plaque-books fall to the floor in a heedless clatter. He darted to the rear of the computer and slid open a small door in the opaque glass of the data storage module. Inside was a miniaturized manual terminal, part of the maintenance system of the ancient machine, which had been transported piecemeal to the Pliocene by a notably persuasive technician during the earliest days of the auberge. The stylus for the tiny stallboard had disappeared years ago; but Greggy, who had been a great and good friend of the long-dead computer technician, had tucked an old gnawed pencil stub inside the redundant terminal as a substitute. It was quite adequate for tapping out any number of outré and useful instructions, including overrides of lock-codes.

Greg-Donnet pecked:

```
EXEC 'ALGOVERIDE' LLLL
BEGIN RETRIEVE DT (T)
   AUTHORS:
   GRENFELL + OGMOL;
BEGIN SYSPRINT PLAQ (1);
BEGIN EXPUNGE;
END
```

There was a ruminative buzz. A single pale-green plaque fell with a muted click into the hopper. The computer made no sound at all as it obliterated from its memory the entire body of data that Bryan and Ogmol had stored within it.

Greg-Donnet patted the machine, tittering, and tucked his copy of the survey into a pocket beneath one of the tails of his clawhammer coat.

"Tidy graphs and learned jargon! Statistics and correlations and extrapolations of dire, dire portents! No surprise to me, of course. Who needs an anthropologist to point out the deluge coming? Naughty humanity! Imagine poor Thaggy thinking we'd been good for his people! Won't he be shocked to find that Nodonn was right about us? And here it is—all spelled out by clever Bryan and simple Oggy—the fate of humanity and the Tanu-human hybrids writ so plain that even the most thick-headed of the Host will understand . . . Ah, Bryan. With Oggy riding herd on you, you'd just tamely hand the thing over to the King and trust in his good sense not to do the obvious. Or do you even *see* the obvious, Bryan? . . . And they call me crazy!"

He went back to the scattered books on the floor, formed

them into a neat stack, and skipped away with it. With a little luck, he wouldn't have missed any of the fireworks.

Ogmol led Bryan through a secret passageway that eventually opened into an alcove hard by the dais of Creation House's great rotunda. The nook was shielded by curtains of an ingenious weave that provided a one-way view into the chamber.

"An old guard cubbyhole from the Times of Unrest five hundred years ago," Ogmol whispered. "All the Guild headquarters have them, and the secret passages, too. But no one bothers with them any more except Gomnol and his coercers. You know how paranoid about security they are."

Bryan was paying little attention to the explanation of his companion, nor did he waste much time on the High Faculty already seated on the dais around the empty throne of silver encrusted with beryls that was the accustomed seat of Aluteyn Craftsmaster. The anthropologist recognized perhaps half of the top-ranking creators: the aged musician Luktal, Renian Glasscrafter, Clana the illusion-spinning daughter of the Queen and her blood-sister Anéar, Seniet the Lord Historian, Lord Celadeyr of Afaliah, Ariet the Sage, and the two talented hybrids of the High Table, Katlinel the Darkeyed and Alberonn Mindeater.

The rotunda proper was jammed almost from wall to wall with hundreds of Guild members, dressed in various permutations of their heraldic blue-green with white or silver. There were also a great many outsiders of high rank who had, Ogmol explained, either wangled guest passes or simply crashed what should have been strictly an inhouse ceremony.

"See there?" Ogmol pointed. "Those two in the hooded white cloaks? The Thagdal and Nontusvel in mufti! Dressed like that, they're officially nonpresent, so no one need pay any special attention to them."

The royal incogniti had, however, been accorded front-row standing room next to the dais.

"Here's Lady Eadone," said Ogmol. "Now we'll begin."

The tall silver-clad woman, flanked by two male attendants in silver niello half-armor, came out and stood at the right side of the stage. Somewhere the chain jangled. There was dead silence. Bryan now had no difficulty understanding Eadone's speech.

"Creative Brothers and Sisters! We are in extraordinary

assembly. According to the most ancient rules of our fellowship, I stand forth as speaker until the matter of this meeting shall find resolution. Let my action be noted."

"The action of the Dean of Guilds is so noted," declared all of the members.

Eadone said, "Let Aluteyn Craftsmaster, President of the Guild of Creators, come forth and assume his rightful place."

There was a low murmur from the crowd. From the wings opposite the alcove where Bryan and Ogmol hid came a stout figure in a richly jeweled caftan. Aluteyn posed for a moment in front of his throne, his silvery-gold hair and mustache abristle with static. In a loud, harsh voice he said, "I take my seat, yielding the speakership freely to the Fivefold Benevolence of the Lady Dean." He plumped himself down, spread his legs, and hunched forward with arms angled and hands resting on his knees. He looked as though he was ready to spring at the first sign of restiveness in the ranks.

"Lord President and fellow Creators," Eadone declaimed. "There has been presented, with due process, a challenge." The throng uttered a sound like a wave breaking gently on an offshore bar. "Let the challenger come forward and be heard."

A small commotion broke out on the side of the rotunda opposite the dais. The crowd opened an aisle leading toward the throne. The creators and the curious aristocrats of Muriah craned their necks. A few even had the bad manners to levitate slightly in an attempt to get a better view as Mercy entered.

"Way!" sang a herald near the entrance. "Way for the Exalted Lady Mercy-Rosmar, Creative Sister to us all, wife to Nodonn Battlemaster Lord of Goriah, and challenger this day before the extraordinary assembly of the Creator Guild!"

Watching her, Bryan felt his heart contract within him. She had put off the rose-and-gold colors of her awesome husband and assumed those of her adopted guild. Her long gown was silver tissue cut at the edges in long dags and scallops resembling butterfly wings; like wings also were the patterns of iridescent greenish blue that made great swirls and eyespots which appeared and disappeared on the fabric as she approached Aluteyn. Her auburn hair hung free. Mercy was followed by four brawny gray-torcs in the livery of House Nodonn pushing a wheeled trolley of polished wood. Upon it reposed a large and ornate cauldron, apparently made of gold.

"It is the Kral," Ogmol whispered, "the sacred vessel of our Guild which is usually seen by the commonalty and membership only at the Grand Combat. Traditionally, the Lord Creator must fill it at that time for the edification of all Combatants."

"What's Mercy doing with it now?" Bryan demanded. But Ogmol only gestured for him to watch.

The human woman had reached the foot of the dais, where an area perhaps ten by ten was opened for her. She made a sign. Her attendants placed the cauldron on the floor in the center of the space, then stepped far back so as to leave Mercy standing alone with the great kettle beside her.

"Speak your challenge, Mercy-Rosmar," said Eadone.

The pale face lifted. Bryan imagined that he saw the sea-colored eyes go wide and wild.

"I challenge Aluteyn Craftsmaster to defend his presidency of the Guild of Creators! I bid him stand forth at the manifestation of powers during the Grand Combat, contending with me in the exercise of creative metafunction, until by the express judgment of the King, the Dean of Guilds, and our noble membership, one of us shall be declared supreme over the other and shall assume the presidency; while the one vanquished shall choose between the quitting of this Kingdom of the Many-Colored Land and voluntary life-offering to the Goddess, whose Will shall in all things prevail."

There was a roar from the crowd. Bryan turned to Ogmol. "What did she mean, for God's sake? Life-offering? Isn't that your orgy of ritual executions at the end of the games? Do you mean that the loser in this damned manifestation of powers forfeits his life?"

"It *is* the most honorable course. But a few, such as Minanonn the Heretic, who was deposed by Nodonn, and Leyr the former Lord Coercer, overcome by Gomnol, have chosen the ignominy of banishment."

Bryan cried out, "Mercy!" But Ogmol held him behind the concealing curtains and the sound of his voice was lost in the tumult.

"You should feel the Craftsmaster's thoughts!" Ogmol fingered his golden torc. "Very bad form to let your hostility show like that, even if one is a First Comer. Watch this now, Bry. The validation, we call it. Can't have just any young upstart making the challenge, you know."

Aluteyn had risen from his throne and now moved forward

until he was able to look down upon Mercy from the front of the dais.

"I accept your challenge, Creative Sister—subject to your filling our sacred cauldron here and now, demonstrating the validity of your right to challenge. And first, you shall extirpate the thing *I* place therein!"

There was an explosion and an ammoniacal stench. The woman leapt back as a slimy apparition materialized out of the golden kettle. Its body was sinuous but without scales, dripping foul mucus. There were pores along the heaving sides like small portholes. Groping filaments the size of elongated human fingers fringed its head. It resembled a monstrous eel, perhaps meters in length and nearly a meter in diameter, oozing forth from the cauldron toward Mercy while Aluteyn watched with folded arms and a sour smile. The creature had no proper mouth. Its head terminated in a species of funnel lined with carunculated ridges; inside gleamed row upon row of sharp triangular teeth. From the gullet of the monster protruded a tongue-like member as thick as a human forearm, studded with rasps.

"Good God, what is it?" cried Bryan.

"A lamprey fish, I'd say—or a simulacrum of one, more likely, unless he had this fellow stashed away and magnified him. Not a particularly ingenious effort. Perhaps Aluteyn thought your lady's sensitivities would be overcome by its horrid appearance. But she doesn't seem to be intimidated . . . ha! Watch!"

Mercy stood her ground with resolution as the thing hung over her, its horrid lips aquiver and tongue groping for prey.

"The Craftsmaster has given you a fish!" she cried in a loud voice. "I will give you its accompaniment!"

There was a second detonation, together with a great cloud of steam that swathed Mercy and the giant lamprey swaying above the cauldron. Abruptly, the stench in the air vanished. There was another aroma, one that was not only pleasant but mouth-watering—and quite familiar to Bryan the former Londoner. The vapors parted and there stood the auburn-haired sorceress with her huge kettle filled to the brim with small things that were golden-brown and smoking and giving off that delicious fragrance together with a complementary smell of fried potatoes.

Mercy began scattering the kettle contents to the crowd.

Bryan collapsed in laughter against the wall of the alcove,

as much from relief as from any other emotion. "Oh, my dear! That's showing him!"

Ogmol said, "I presume this is some human in-joke."

The throng of Guild members and nobles were catching the tidbits that Mercy threw and devouring them with hilarious cheers. Aluteyn turned his back on the scene.

Lady Eadone declared, "Let it be noted that the challenger, Lady Mercy-Rosmar, has demonstrated her right to meet Lord Aluteyn Craftsmaster in the manifestation of powers. Until that time, let the two of you dwell in the peace and fellowship of our Guild. This extraordinary assembly is now adjourned."

"Lady Mercy-Rosmar farspeaks you through me," Ogmol said to Bryan. "She has perceived our presence behind the curtains because of the—er—cri de coeur you uttered when you realized she was placing herself in peril by issuing the challenge. She wishes to reassure you. She further asks that you meet her tonight in the Creators' Forecourt, where she will arrive in her calèche at twenty-one hundred hours. She wishes to discuss important matters with you."

"Assure her that I'll be waiting."

The Tanu-human bowed in a strangely formal manner. "I must go now to present the results of our survey to my Awful Father."

"Yes, of course. Well, why don't I wander back to my rooms for a bit—and then a swim. Will you join me later?"

"I fear not, Bryan. The interview with the King may take some time."

"Well, give him my compliments." The anthropologist was jovial. "Later, I'll tell him myself what a good job you've done. I've never seen anyone pick up cultural theory so quickly. Perhaps the King will authorize us to do a broader study along these lines. I'd like to continue working with you, Ogmol."

Still displaying the air of distance that was at variance to his usual friendliness, Ogmol held out a golden-furred hand for Bryan to shake. "I've enjoyed working with you, too, Bryan." He opened the secret door and held it while the anthropologist slipped inside. "Good—good luck to you, Bryan! And thank you for the hangover pills!"

Before the startled human could reply, the sliding panel closed in his face. He was alone in the dim passage between the walls.

"Funny." Bryan took out the pale-green rectangle of his

survey and stared at it. "We did a workmanlike job, given the short time available. An interesting overview, all in all. Old Thagdal should be pleased with it."

But why, then, had Ogmol seemed apprehensive? Bryan hadn't a clue. "Perhaps I've been too close to the study during these hectic weeks," he told himself. "As a half-blood, Ogmol may be making a subjective evaluation of the survey relative to some exotic criteria of his own."

Well, a little relaxation and he might noodle it out. Nothing like a good swim in Oggy's private pool to refresh his fatigued cortex. And then a drive with Mercy in the cool of the evening.

He got to thinking about her and the fish and chips, and went off chuckling. The puzzle of Ogmol—and the plaque in his jacket pocket—were completely forgotten.

On the dark summit of the Mount of Heroes there was a small open meadow between twin crags, far above the College of Redactors and the city and the gunmetal lagoons. They sent the old carriage driver away to wait and stood side by side in the utterly silent night. It seemed that they had come to a place between two different skies—the one above all distant and frosty and old, and the one below warm and exciting with the twinkling lights of three kinds of people— the olive-oil flames lit by humans, the jewel-lamps of the Tanu, and the massed bonfires of the Firvulag making a festive display out on the southern flats.

"I think," Mercy said, "that my favorite thing in all this Many-Colored Land is the faerie look of the lights . . . and best of all when I see them from up high. Like this, from a mountain, or when flying with my Lord."

She took a small backward step so that his arms could come around her. Her hair met his lips as she swayed back against him. "But I forgot that you've never flown with us, Bry. My poor earthbound one! When I'm able to go alone and lift another, I must take you. But in the meantime, we have this here tonight."

She turned to him. The still-incredible thing began to happen again. Their minds and bodies came together in the ecstatic conjugation that seemed as far beyond ordinary sex as music was beyond noise. They lofted into ever-ascending levels of life-energy where balls of colored light pulsed and sang, clinging and crying out—she in triumph and he in wonder and a kind of defiance that dared the love to become love-death if this was the only way to prolong it infinitely. But it could not be, never was, and always there was the brink and the tumble into deep dark while the glaring colors shrank and receded and went out. And he, swallowed, sated, was enfolded within her and flown safely back over the hollow waters, hearing her hush him as he mourned the end (again), ever asking, "Why doesn't this sea reflect the stars?"

"Hush, love," she said. "Never mind."

They lay quietly on her soft cloak. When his mind steadied. he was able to look at her starlit face and very nearly recall what the fulfillment had been like (again).

"It's enchantment, Mercy," he said. "You've bewitched me. Are you killing me, too?"

"Does it matter?" she laughed, taking his head into her lap. A fold of fabric wiped his eyes and she kissed the lids.

"It can't go on, can it?" he asked. "After the Combat, he'll take you back to Goriah. Or will you stay if you become Lady Creator? Is there a chance you'll stay, Mercy?"

"Hush."

"Do you love him?" he asked after a while.

"Of course," she replied, her voice warm.

"Do you love me?" He spoke low, his mouth partially muffled in her gown.

"Would I be here with you if I didn't? Ah, my dear. Why must you always talk of loving and staying instead of the joy? Haven't you been happy? Haven't I given you all that I could, all that you could bear? Do you want the whole of it? Will nothing else satisfy you?"

"I can't leave you. Oh, Mercy."

The corners of her mouth turned up. "And you'd do anything for me, would you?"

He gazed at her smile and could not speak. She began to hum, and the words of the familiar love ballad formed in his mind by the power of hers:

> Cupid is wingèd and doth range
> Her country, so my Love doth change.
> But change the earth or change the sky,
> Yet will I love her till I die.

"And now we'll have one another again, sweet Bryan, and after that go down into the city. And you'll give me as a gift the little book you've written, the book that promises such terrible things for my Tanu people if they continue on as before with the humans and all. But you never intended your book to apply to me, did you, Bryan?"

"Oh, no. Not you."

"I'm one of them, after all, and always have been. *He* knows that and so do you."

"Yes... both of us know what you are."

"But it's really a most upsetting thing you've written, sweetheart, particularly if the wrong people such as Culluket or Imidol should read it and misunderstand. Not even Nodonn can control the entire Host. And they believe all humankind to be harmful. Even me. Even the dear loyal hybrids. But you weren't to know that, were you? How your little book could be the death of us all. You'd never foresee such an interpretation... so earnest, so civilized and sane, my love."

Bryan was puzzled, lost in his dreaming. The survey? That was only his *work*. "It has nothing at all to do with us, Mercy. Nothing to do with you. Enchantress."

"Then give me your copy of it. Give it to me and never tell that I have it."

Of course he did. And she lifted his head from her lap, laughing, and then leaned over him kissing and leading him on. When they had gone there and back (again), she summoned the carriage and driver and they drove down the mountain. Outside Redact House, as she expected, Nodonn and Culluket the King's Interrogator were waiting.

"He's asleep," she told him. "The only other copies of the survey are in the possession of Ogmol and the Thagdal—and stored in the computer, of course."

"Ogmol can wait," Nodonn said to his younger brother. "And the King has his own reasons for keeping the matter secret. But he will seek the life of this man, this unsuspecting witness for the prosecution. You must keep him safe until the culmination of the Combat, Redactive Brother. He is vital to our cause. See that he is kept happy and unaware."

The Interrogator nodded. "I understand fully, Brother Battlemaster. Our company cannot fail to be impressed when the human cancer affirms its own existence." He smiled at Mercy.

Two red-and-white-clad attendants appeared and lifted the unconscious anthropologist from the calèche. Nodonn mounted and took the place next to his wife.

"Until later, then, Brother. We two will go to Creation House and see to the computer ourselves."

Culluket inclined his head. "Until later." He turned to lead the way into the caves deep within the mountain and the men carrying Bryan followed after.

10

NAKED AND WEEPING, THE SILVER-TORC GIRL CAME RUNNING from the King's chamber.

"Oh, dear," said Nontusvel, casting a significant glance at the Master of the Royal Bed. "Not again."

"It wasn't my fault, I swear, Queen and Mother!" the girl wailed. "I did everything! Everything!" She fell on her knees. The Master of the Royal Bed gestured and a gray-torc valet came up to wrap the shivering love-gift manquée in a robe of white satin.

"Get her out of here," the Queen ordered. "I'll see to His Majesty myself tonight."

The Master bowed. He and the servant hurried away with the sniffling girl. Nontusvel extinguished all the lights except one candelabrum of pink jewels. This she lifted on high and carried to the tall door embossed with the golden bearded mask. It swung open before her.

"My King, it is I," she said. "Be of good cheer."

Only a few scattered gleams, like ruby and gold embers, lit the bedchamber of Thagdal the High King. There was an odd sound, a little like a gulping sob, and then a noise of someone blowing his nose.

"N-Nonnie?"

"Yes, dear."

The King sat on the edge of the bed, his mighty shoulders hunched, head down. "Failed again. The sword undrawn, the bow unloosed, the mightiest champion of them all laid low and humiliated. I'm done for, Nonnie. Finished. Not even that damned Lalage and all her tricks could conjure up a glimmer."

"It is all in your mind, beloved. You've been worrying too much."

212

She set the candelabrum down on the bedside table and stood before him, magnificent and comforting in a flowing peignoir of peach color trimmed in gold. Her flaming hair hung down, her arms opened wide, welcoming as her mothermind with its invitation: Rest in me.

She drew him up and they went out onto the balcony. It was very late. The moon was old, an ochreous sickle near the horizon, giving an unhealthy tinge of brass to the lagoon.

"You must not be down-hearted," the Queen said. "What has changed? Are the Foe yonder on the salt any more confident of victory than they've been in years past? Hardly. We are strong and we will crush them, as always."

"It's not that."

"Aiken Drum, then? A clownish gadfly? Mayvar is senile and it is high time dear Riganone took her place as Lady Farsensor and Kingmaker. The boy knows quite well he would have no chance against the Battlemaster. Has Aiken Drum issued any formal challenge for the manifestation of powers? Of course not! And he won't challenge by Mêlée Rules at the Combat, either. Nodonn will remain your heir—patient and loyal as always. And soon you'll recover your good spirits and your vigor as well."

The King shook his head. "It's not Aiken Drum. Two new things. I—I didn't tell you."

"Will you tell me now?"

"Brede has emerged from the room without doors. I may *not* have the operant woman, Elizabeth."

The Queen's screens shot up to conceal her elation. "The mating scheme with her is then—"

"Brede has placed Elizabeth's genes under the strongest taboo. The Shipspouse claims that the woman's destiny has been revealed to her. That it's not in accord with the scheme Gomnol and I favored. I haven't told Gomnol yet, either. I was afraid to! Can you imagine that? My genes plus Elizabeth's were going to engender a new superrace under Gomnol's guidance. And now she's taboo and I'm—I'm—"

"Gomnol's vision is undoubtedly flawed," said the Queen with some sharpness. "He *is* only a human being, for all his coercive power. And an aging one. Only a few years more, and Imidol will be deposing him."

The King's thought was perceptible even under the screen: another patient and loyal son of yours?

"Now, Thaggy," she chided, slipping an arm around his

massive waist. His belly muscles contracted and he straightened his shoulders. One or two static sparks danced in his hair and beard.

"Never mind about Elizabeth," Nontusvel said. "She is beautiful and I can understand your disappointment. But that kind of woman isn't your type, vein of my heart. A Grand Master metapsychic! How too off-putting! I don't suppose Brede said what would be done with her?"

"She wouldn't tell me. Said it would be obvious after the Grand Combat. Bloody two-faced enigma! What can you expect from a female who marries a damn intergalactic *worm*?"

The Queen giggled and pressed next to his naked torso.

"And then another blow this afternoon," he muttered.

"Not Rosmar?"

"Of course not. That creative lout of an Ogmol! Come inside and I'll show you."

They returned to the bedchamber. The king kicked aside the rug, then used his PK to manipulate the lock of a floor-safe. A small greenish plaque floated up into the Queen's waiting hands. She pressed the SLOW activator in the upper righthand corner and studied the glowing pages as they rolled across the plastic. Now and then she stopped the flow to study a chart or graph.

"Skip to the end," the King said. "The conclusion."

She pressed the upper lefthand corner and the pages spun quickly. Then a touch from the REVERSE and she had it. "Oh, dear!"

"Exactly! How's that for an unwitting scenario of doom? That besotted idiot of an anthropologist didn't realize the implication. But Oggy did—and he nearly wet his pants begging me to believe that it wouldn't happen. That he and the other hybrids and the torced humans would remain loyal."

The Queen whispered, "All you need do is extrapolate the trends a bit farther than Bryan has already done."

"And add the focusing factor he doesn't yet know about—the iron. I'll wager my right nut that hybrids are immune to it just like humans. Does that suggest anything to you?"

"Dear Tana, not that! Can nothing be done to stop it? Our beautiful Exile world! *Ours!*"

She threw herself into his arms and wept. The King held her in a mighty grip. His eyes had begun to shine in the dark. The tendrils of his sparkling beard stirred, and something else. "We'll stop any human-hybrid coalition before it's ever born.

That thing of Bryan's is only a scientific survey, not an oracle. But it's a danger to *me* in a way I hadn't anticipated. Dammit, Nonnie—I'd hoped to calm Nodonn's fears about humanity. That's why I commissioned the survey in the first place—to prove that the advent of humans was beneficial to us, not a racial menace as Nodonn maintained. I mean, *common sense* showed we'd made marvelous strides since the opening of the timegate. Technical progress as well as genetic. The anthropologist was supposed to confirm what Gomnol and I had been saying all along. And instead—"

"Dearest husband, Nodonn only wants the best for our Many-Colored Land. He doesn't mean to threaten *you*."

The King grunted. "This survey can be used to prove all of his doomsaying is justified. It's a clear contradiction of my stated policy. It may seem far-fetched to you now, but this little book could be the death warrant of every human and hybrid in the High Kingdom—and if *they* go, so does the economy of my realm! It's back to the wilderness strongholds for us Tanu, my lass."

Nontusvel raised her tear-bright eyes. "You said yourself that the survey isn't an oracle. None of these dreadful contingencies need happen at all. You won't let them."

"I won't!" he vowed. "Our Many-Colored Land will not be taken over by Lowlives! I'll see to it! And I'll accomplish my purpose without any of the damn draconian measures Nodonn advocates. There must be a way that Tanu and humanity can continue to prosper together—and I'm going to find it. *I have said it!*"

"Thaggy—?" the Queen ventured breathlessly.

"Come here, woman!" he bellowed.

When dawn came and both of them were drowsy and at peace, she murmured to him, "You see? Everything's perfectly all right. It *was* all in your mind."

"Mm-mm," the King agreed. He raised one of her hands and kissed each dimpled knuckle.

"As to your problem with the silvers . . . I think you simply need a change. These silly human strumpets with their meager little duglets are not in tune with your present mood of high seriousness. You require an entirely different type of consolation. A gentler, more reassuring sort."

The King said sleepily, "Remember that chubby black-haired one who sang the Welsh lullaby? I liked her. I kept expecting her to be sent around, but she never came."

"The very thing," Nontusvel agreed. "I'll make it my personal business to find out what's happened to her. If Dionket thinks he can keep her for himself—why, Nodonn and Culluket will simply point out a few realities to him!" She smiled at her half-dozing Lord.

"Good old girl," Thagdal said. He let her hand fall. His eyes were closed. "And I'll gather up all copies of Bryan's report and have them destroyed, and Gomnol can take care of the anthropologist as well. Too bad about Oggy, though . . . He was a good . . ."

"Sleep, my King." The Queen drew the silken sheet up to cover them both. "Sleep for now."

Eusebio Gomez-Nolan leaned back in his Victorian armchair and blew three slow smoke rings. They floated across the desk toward the person sitting opposite, turned solid, and fell to the pseudo-Oriental rug with soft thuds.

"Hope you don't mind, Lord Coercer," said Aiken Drum. "Can't stand tobacco."

Gomnol made a gracious gesture. His cigar extinguished itself and he placed it in the onyx ashtray. "My boy, events in this Cloud-Cuckoo-Land of ours have taken some engrossing turns of late. I believe it's time that you and I had a long chat."

"I thought you'd never ask."

"I've revised my earlier opinion of you considerably during the past week or two. Mayvar has been most eloquent in your behalf. And so has Bunone Warteacher, whom you impressed no end on the Delbaeth Quest. Both of these ladies feel that you will be a formidable contender in the upcoming games. They were also fervent in their praise of your—uh—nonmartial arts as well."

Aiken's grin was wicked. He lounged back in his seat with one leg draped over the chair-arm and studied the fingernails of one hand. "So what else is new?"

"I might mention," Gomnol said smoothly, "a rumored disability of our Awful King, provoked—so it's said—by intimations of mortality as much as by the collapse of my late genetic scheme."

"Brede screwed you, eh?" The little man snickered. "Now I get it. The old sinking ship syndrome. With poor old Thaggy cast as Titanic and you as Chief Rat."

The Lord Coercer's guffaw was entirely good-humored. "You are going to require a great deal of help, my boy. I'm prepared to offer it. All I ask is that you think over my proposition carefully." He took a fresh cigar from the humidor and twirled it between his fingers. "We are, I believe, approaching a pivotal point in the history of this Exile world. The Finiah attack was only the overture. And if there is a power struggle in the offing, doesn't it make sense for all of us humans to stick together?"

He took a clipper from the drawer and operated deftly on the cigar. Then he tossed the silvery little gadget to Aiken Drum, still smiling.

Aiken caught the cigar clipper and Gomnol's unspoken thought simultaneously. He peered at the thing and saw letters incised in the metal: SOLINGEN—INOX STEEL.

11

GERT CAME BACK TO THE PASSENGER COMPARTMENT LOOKING grim. "Hansi thinks we'll be into the next batch of bad rapids soon. You'd better put the skipper back together again."

Amerie was bent over a supine figure. "We're working on him now. Five minutes." Chief Burke held one arm and Felice the other. Uwe and Basil were ready to grab the legs. "Here we go," the nun said. She applied the stimulant to the unconscious boatman's temple, then got another injection ready. The little monitor taped to the man's forehead began to change color in all of its four quadrants.

Blood-rimmed hazel eyes snapped open. From the puffy lips came a croak. "Gawd . . . ah, Gawd!" And then he screamed, a sound of bitter hopelessness and physical agony. His body contracted in a superhuman heave that had the four restrainers using all their strength to keep him pinned to the deck.

"*Ahh!* Wotinell yer bleedin' sods done? Wotcher done? Yer tookit *orf*, y'filfy buggerin' baboons! Thass wotcher did. Iss gone! Gone . . ."

Tears poured down the stubbly seams of his cheeks. The boatman howled like an animal as Amerie watched the forehead monitor, white with anger at what they were having to do. The thin grizzle-haired man's once natty green tunic was now stained with vomit and blood and dust from the ordeals he had endured under his kidnappers. Around his tanned throat was a band of pale flesh where the gray torc had been.

They had been on the river two days and this was the sixth time they had brought the boatman around. Gert and Hansi could handle the boat on the smooth stretches of the Rhône; but in rough water they had to have the skipper's help—and every time they woke him, the screaming was worse. Only a few of the de-torced Finiah prisoners had displayed withdrawal symptoms as severe as this man's, and those people had been heavily sedated during the earliest, most painful part of the separation.

But the Rhône boatman could not remain asleep.

"For God's sake," Chief Burke said, "hit the poor meshugeh with the trank!"

Amerie said, "He has to absorb the first injection properly. Do you want him to crash on us? He's on the brink now. Just look at that vital-signs monitor . . . Felice! Go into his mind!"

The cries thinned into a gurgle. The nun turned her patient's head so that he could cough up thin bile. Felice's eyes dimmed and sweat started out on her brow. The boatman's frenzy began to diminish under the drug and the pressure of the girl's coercive power. The colors of the forehead monitor shifted again.

"Good," Amerie said. She slapped on the tranquilizer, then carefully administered the blend of euphoric and energizer. The skipper seemed to relax.

"Come out of him when you think the medications have taken hold," the nun told Felice.

"Jeez, what a balls-up." The athlete let go of the limp arm she had been clutching. Burke and Basil hauled the groggy boatman to his feet.

Uwe said quietly, "Will he last? How's he look inside, babe?"

"All I can do is coerce the guy," Felice said. "I'm no good at redact. This man needs a top-stem refit and I'm not capable. I think he navigates now by the seat of his pants. If he's not totally insane, he's next door to it."

"Rapids ahead!"

Vanda-Jo sang out from her lookout position on the extended mast, where she clung to a squirrel-climb apparatus installed by Basil. Khalid came limping to assist her down. The two of them dismantled the climbing gear and locked the plass roof panels of the boat back into place. The mast sank into its housing.

"Don't stand there!" Chief Burke told them. "Everybody buckle in and be damned sure all the seals are tight. Come on, Felice."

They dragged the skipper into the wheelhouse. Hansi slipped out of the captain's seat and the barely revived boatman was fastened in. Webbing from one of Basil's alpine slings served to strap Felice to a smaller pilot's chair.

"I'm all right," Felice cried. "Get back to your seats, quick! I can handle this bird. And I think I can just about hold the boat with my PK now, in the straight stretches."

The others ran aft. A great roaring filled the air, reverberating from steep canyon walls that rose sheer at least 600 meters on either side of them. Even though it was only early afternoon, dusk filled the misted slot where the Rhône boiled along in ever-accelerating flow. The vessel tilted forward. Black boulders with collars of fountaining spray went past in a blur. . .

Listen to me Harry listen to me Harry you are going to drive your boat just like you always do drive it along safe and sound between the rocks Harry through the rapids just like you always do safe and sound do you hear me Harry drive the boat you're a good skipper Harry you're the best this is nothing to a whitewater ace like you Harry bring her through safe and sound do it Harry do it . . .

The red eyes of the boatman narrowed. He spun the wheel to starboard and the craft heeled around a looming obstruction, raced toward the canyon wall, then corrected at the last moment to pass through an opening spill between two colossal standing waves that looked like yellow whalebacks. The boat zigzagged through a churning welter of rock and foam, shot around a curve and headed for a wider section of the canyon where the water seemed oddly calm—until at the last moment Felice saw that the flood poured over an abrupt shelf into misty opacity. She let panic rule her for an instant before she caught sight of the safe bypass channel that was hidden in the cloud and spume—

—but by then it was too late. Harry had escaped her grip. The boat went over the lip of the falls, turning end over end until it landed *spang* on its roof panels and seemed to buckle amidships like some great broken trampoline. The skipper named Harry was now laughing in hysteria. But there was no time to do anything to him, with the rest of them back there yelling and cursing and hanging in their harnesses upside down in the dark bubbling yellow gut.

It took every bit of her psychokinetic power to turn them back over, so tenacious was the grip of the cavitating surge in the undercut rock below the cascade. But finally she hauled them free of it. They flew along on the river's surface again, and she tried to catch Harry and put him back in control—

—but oh, God, there ahead it stood! And there was no way they could maneuver in time not to hit it! And—*spung*! The pneumatic craft caromed off a great jagged monolith with water shooting in through one broken panel while they held a fifty-degree bank around a sharp curve in the Rhône.

At last the boat wallowed into straight and level motion. The waters slowed, flattened, opened out two kilometers wide in the midst of a valley with brown steppe hills.

The boatman was still giggling. Felice tore off her straps, lurched to him, and slapped him with a fury that nearly sent him unconscious again.

"You stupid fuckard!"

The man's subvocal thought defied her through pain and maniacal triumph: You were afraid ha ha afraid monstercunt and I *gotcher*!

Aloud, he groaned and spat blood from his bitten tongue. Hansi and Gert came staggering in to take over the helm.

"Ah, shit, she breached," Hansi exclaimed, spotting the broken panel.

"We can fix it," his partner said. "There's a tool kit and spare plass underdeck. All we have to do is demount the broken piece."

Gert took the wheel while Felice and Hansi supported the limp body of Harry. "What happened, Felice?" Hansi inquired. "Guy suffer a relapse?"

"The only relapse happened to yours truly," Felice snarled. "I let the bastard get away from me. He must have been waiting his chance all this time. And when I saw that damn dropoff just ahead I panicked and let my control slip. That was all he needed. He took us over the falls on purpose."

Hansi said, "No real harm done. No use kicking yourself for being scared. These cataracts would make Genghis Khan holler for his mommy."

Chief Burke, his ruddy complexion faded to gray, reeled up and clung to the frame of the wheelhouse door. "That was a bitchcatawampus, Felice."

"We broke a panel," she said. "We'll have to moor someplace for repairs. And figure out how to keep the Ancient Mariner, here, from committing suicide and taking us along."

"So that was it." The Native American and Felice dragged Harry to the passenger compartment and dumped him without ceremony onto the deck. The exhausted girl dropped into a seat and closed her eyes. Harry drooled and cursed until Burke and Basil tied and gagged him.

The boat steered toward a heavy stand of willows on the left bank. They came into a quiet backwater where curving branches of great trees made a cave of green luminosity. There was a tiny sandy beach.

"That was a bad one," Uwe observed. "I thought the boat was going to fold over on us like an omelet."

"Felice lost control of Harry," Chief Burke said.

Her brown eyes went wide and she jumped to her feet. "I was distracted! All right—I was *scared*! Old Fearless Felice lets the bad vibes get to her at long last. So what are you going to do about it, Red Man? Try me in your kangaroo court?"

Amerie came and put a hand on Felice's shoulder. "Peo isn't blaming you. The boatman was docile enough on the other runs. You couldn't know he'd try something on this one. Your nerves are ravelled after shooting rapids all day, and it's a wonder you did as well as you did."

Felice looked mollified. "I *was* able to turn the bloody boat rightside up again, anyhow. My PK's coming on fast. But the damned coercive function gets tangled up in my emotions too easily. We really miscalculated when we took old Harry's torc off. The Tanu have the right idea with their pleasure-pain circuits. I could have had him biddable as a baa-lamb in the torc, and he wouldn't be cold-turkeying all over us, either."

"Day before yesterday you said you couldn't hack it," Khalid reminded her. "And what if he'd let loose a telepathic warning to any golds or silvers in range? Don't forget that the Great South Road is somewhere up on the west bank. There are Tanu caravans up there—and Tanu on the river, and silvers at the plantations. Quit kicking yourself."

Vanda-Jo peered at the jungly bank. "Do you think it's safe to camp here?"

"It better be," said Hansi, coming from the wheelhouse. "I don't want to go one klom farther until Gert and I give this tub a complete checkup. God knows what else we broke when we came slamming down." He began removing the roof panels preparatory to mooring.

Ducks fled as they nosed in. "I might pot us a few waterfowl for supper," Basil suggested. "We didn't," he added with a rueful chuckle, "retain much lunch."

"We can all use rest and food," Amerie said. "Then tomorrow we'll be in good shape for—whatever lies ahead. And what does, by the way?"

Khalid said, "If we've passed six big rapids, then only one stands between us and Lac Provençal. I haven't been on it, but it's said to be the longest and worst of all—the Donzère-Mondragon stretch."

"Kaleidoscopic," groaned Felice.

"After that there's only the Glissade into the Med Basin. I did ride that when I was taken to Muriah. It's steep but not difficult. Only needs a steady hand at the tiller. Gert and Hansi can handle it easily. But we'll have to depend on this boatman's skill one last time tomorrow."

They all looked down at Harry. His hair stuck up in diabolical spikes. His eyes bulged and he strained and grunted against the gag.

Amerie sighed and reached for her medical kit. "Poor Harry."

"Poor us," Felice retorted.

A half kilometer downstream from the grove of willows where the boat was moored was a jumble of large rocks, overgrown with tamarisk and acacia, that protruded out from the shoreline and made an excellent lookout. They decided to keep watch there, at least until late evening, to be sure that no other boats happened upon their hiding place.

Amerie's turn came when the sun had been down for an hour and it had become cool. She was glad of the chance to get away from the others—especially the wretched boatman, whose vital signs had stabilized under renewed sedation and a veinfeed. She made her orisons under brightening stars. A few insects shrilled and the Rhône burbled beneath the riverside rocks. Little herons squawked in the shallows while chasing their supper.

Across the broad waters the hills were dark. There must be plantations in this likely valley, Amerie thought. But no lights were visible from her vantage point. No boats came by during her watch, either. Night traffic was normally nonexistent on the river. Still, there was the small chance that the nonarrival of their skipper at his usual stops would be noted by his fellows—hence the watch. Burke and the others had not made too great a point of it, but it was obvious that the farther downriver they progressed, the greater the suspicions of the other rivermen might become when good old Harry failed to appear at some accustomed rendezvous. All of the craft on the Rhône were distinctive; Harry's, although of a common express design, had a spruce-green band around its silver hull and its name, Walloping Windowblind, painted in large letters on bow and stern. They had debated disguising the boat. But in the beginning they hoped that its owner would be cooperative, enabling them to bluff their way clear down to Muriah. Now, of course, it was too late to do anything but press on. When they passed other boats, they tooted greetings on the airhorn, hoping that the absence of a telepathic hail between skippers wouldn't be remarked during the busy Truce season...

There was a small sound among the lower rocks.

"It's only me." Felice clambered up to the high perch. "I'll take the last trick."

"Not a soul on the river that I've seen. Only birds. All in order back in camp?"

"Your patient's fine, if that's what you mean. The boat's back in good shape, and Gert and Hansi have gone off into the bushes to celebrate. VJ was in a generous mood, too, but only Uwe took her up. And I think that was mostly sweet charity on the old puffer's part."

She plopped down cross-legged beside the nun, who did not comment on the badinage. "Nice night, isn't it? The weather in this Pliocene world is pyrotechnic! I suppose they must have a rainy season in winter, but it couldn't be lovelier now. Probably why the exotics have their Grand Combat this time of year. Perfect weather for a war."

The nun did not reply.

Felice said, "There'll be a lot of fighting, once we've hit the torc works and closed the time-gate. Those Tanu slavers are going to get what's coming to them now that we've got their number with the iron. I have other ideas, too, that I haven't discussed yet with the others . . . Like, maybe forming a coalition with any of the silvers who'd be loyal to humanity instead of the Tanu. Elizabeth could sort them out for us and we could re-torc them with stolen gold and have a human elite corps ready to counter any mass Hunt the exotics might mount. Human metas versus exotic metas! We could take over the whole corpuscular kingdom!"

Amerie was still silent.

Felice came closer. "You don't approve. It's not your Christian ethic. You think we should try to gain our freedom by some kind of negotiation. Sweet reason and brotherly love! . . . Why have you been avoiding me, Amerie? Have you decided I'm a monster, too, like the others?"

The nun turned. In the starlight her face was kind. "I know just what brand of bullshit you're getting ready to serve up, Felice. Please don't. I've tried to explain to you how it is with me. I know you have your needs and you've been frustrated by missing the Finiah fight and driven half-bats by the poor boatman. But you can't use me to relieve your tensions. Not through cruelty, or through sex either. I have a right to my own commitment. I don't expect you to understand it, but you're damn well going to respect it."

Felice's laugh was uncertain. She sat very still, her tanned face contrasting with the halo of pale hair. "So much," she said, "for the brotherly-love pitch. Thanks for nothing, Sister. For a while there, I thought you cared."

The nun rounded on her and grabbed the slender bare shoulders. "You impossible child! Of course I love you. Why do you think I came?"

"Then, why? *Why*?" Felice's voice rose to a wail. For an instant, her coercive power stabbed out. The nun jerked away with a cry of pain. Felice exclaimed, "I'm sorry, Amerie! I'm sorry! I won't do it again. Don't look at me—don't *think* at me like that." The bright head sank. "Never ever. Either one of us. Why? Why is it so wrong to find a little happiness and warmth? We might be dead tomorrow and that'll be the end of it."

"Felice, I don't believe that. Whether we live or die, I don't believe that's the end. That's one of the reasons for my renunciation."

"Your religious mumbo jumbo! Who can prove there's a God out there? Or if there is, who can prove he cares—that he's not some game-playing horror? You can't prove it! You're an educated woman, a doctor. You know there's no proof!"

"Only in human psychology. In our need. In our instinct reaching out. In our very odd veneration for the love that gives without taking."

"I need your love! You won't give it to me! You lie when you say you love me!"

"I have to be true to myself, too. To love myself, Claude called it. I had to come to the Pliocene to discover that I was worth loving. And you . . . dear Felice. You've never learned to love at all. Not in human ways. Your need is different and— terrible. My kind of love can't satisfy you and what you call love would be an injustice to me. I want to help you, but I don't know how. All I can do is pray for you."

"Wonderful!" The girl's laugh was rich with scorn. "Go ahead, then! Let's hear how you pray for poor damned inhuman Felice!"

Amerie reached out, took the resisting girl in her arms. The chant was soft in the night.

"Lord, how great is your constant care. We find protection under the shadow of your wings and are filled with the good things you give us. You have let us drink from the river of your kindness, for you are the fountain of life. In your light we will find light of our own."

Felice cried out, "Oh—*shit*!"

She wept and Amerie rocked her. After a long time, the girl pushed away and wiped her face.

"Tomorrow . . . it's going to be tough. I was scared out of my mind this afternoon and I'm going to be even more scared tomorrow. If I let that damned Harry get away from me again, we're all going to be drowned or dashed to pieces. And I might not hold him. I—my confidence is going. And that's fatal when you're playing mind-games. If you're afraid that you might fail, then the whole thing comes apart and—what am I going to *do*?"

"I'll keep praying."

"Fuck your nonexistent God! If he knows everything, he ought to help us without our asking! Or are we supposed to grovel? Is that what *he* needs?"

"It's good for us to reach out to him. To *will* his help in getting things that we need."

"So your God is a psychologist! And praying is just metapsychic focusing, so that if you have enough faith you move the bloody mountain! Who needs a God at all if we end up answering our own prayers? I should pray to myself, then— right? But I don't believe in me, either!"

"Felice, I don't want to bandy semantics or theology with you. If the word 'pray' seems ridiculous to you, forget it. Just keep the psychic validity behind the concept. Tomorrow, try to reach out and demand strength from the Mind of the universe, from the life-source. Never mind whether it's aware of you or not, who it is or what it is. You have a *right* to share in its strength—not just for your sake but for the sake of all the rest of us who are depending on you."

The girl said slowly, "I think I could do that. I can believe in Mind. I can feel . . . that much is real. I'll try, Amerie."

The nun rose to her feet, lifting Felice with her. She kissed the girl on the forehead, then looked beyond, across the river to the hills black against a purpled western sky. "Felice— there's something over there."

The girl turned. On the far shore was a manifestation like a glittering string of beads moving in and out of the trees.

"The Hunt," said Felice.

They watched it in silence. It was moving southward through the bottomland that lay between the Rhône and the Great South Road.

"I can farsense them a bit," Felice said. "They're out of a place called Sayzorask down beyond the gorge at the head of a big lake. They're lóoking for us."

Amerie started to say, "You mean the overdue skipper—"

"They're looking for *us*. Fortunately, none of them can fly, and they don't have any hot-dog farsensors, so they aren't aware that I'm eavesdropping on their mental yammerings. Strictly a collection of provincials. But the big boys will be waiting for us farther south."

"How could they *know*?" Amerie said.

"Somebody told them," Felice said. "And I think I know who."

They left the moorage as soon as it was light, while the yellow water was still mostly buried in cotton wool fogbanks. The air cleared when they came into the next deep gorge, and they saw that they were not alone on the river; three other craft were lined up at the top of the chute, waiting for a little more daylight before daring the twenty-kilometer stretch of rough water.

"Bad news!" Gert sang out.

"Pass 'em!" Felice decided. "Peo, Basil, get that zombie up here. No sense trying to play tricks. Those other boats can't do a thing once we're in the rapids."

The noise of the cascading turbulence made it almost impossible for them to hear one another. When Harry, blue-lipped and feebly snarling, was strapped into place, Felice gave the other men a shove aft. "If we spring a leak, get everybody out of the harnesses and do the best you can."

They passed the anchored boats at a distance of twenty-five meters. Felice forced Harry to wave and worked the airhorn herself, *toodly-toot-toot*. And then they were into the rapids . . .

Take us through Harry do your job Harry do it and I'll get you another gray torc do you hear me another one just as good as the one we took only do your job Harry steer steer dodge and draw and race through the booming froth and the haystack bulges above the underwater rocks O go Harry good old boy stay off the knifeledge and the monstrous eddy whirling at the bend and the crazy tall waves filling the air with blobs of foam go on Harry go boy go and set her over broadside working the multiple rudders like organ pedals and twirling the wheel virtuoso Harry remember the new torc the old ecstasy just as good as before look out for the sluice and skim her on down Harry braving the violent Rhône all clogged with landslides and rock piles that should hold back the waters but never will come on I'm helping you Harry holding you and see not scared O no *kaboom!* sheesh all right Harry just a bouncer good recovery God there's a big mother big as a house in the middle of the channel right or left you know which is best Harry Harry Harry O you asshole get us out of this spin you Harry or I'll squeeze you until you Harry get us out Harry stop the spin I'll hurt you Jesus Jesus we're going to hit again Harry Harry you rotten *swine* I won't let you you can't do it I won't let you you can't *I won't let you*—

Die.

Felice screamed. The mind within her grasp went incandescent in a last surge of opposing rage. And then, ever so easily, it slipped away from her and went off along a way she dared not follow. Alone, she returned to the chaos of the riverboat caught in the treacherous white eddy, rotating just downstream from a great craggy mass that parted the Rhône into two thundering streams. The boat spun faster and faster. With every other revolution it whanged against an underwater obstruction, the impact causing the strong inflated hull to vibrate like a beaten drum.

Harry hung in his harness, seeming to wink at her. The vital-signs monitor on his forehead was solid black.

Felice worked the quick-release fasteners and let the body fall to the deck. She took the skipper's place, grasped the wheel, tramped the rudder pedals, and sent her PK below the hull to lift.

Ah, so hard so heavy so hard . . . trying to tear loose from the grip of the spinning water! But I am strong (do you all hear?) and you can make me stronger so *do* it! Up . . . up . . . help me lift it up. All you lives loves you must help you will. Up! UP! . . . And the two-in-one hears and helps and the many-in-All as well because it is not only for me and the drumbeats stop and the scratching hiss of the muddy gravely water stops and the whirling the rocking the buffeting all countermovement stops.

I lift. We float.

I am able to hold us (thank you) even pull us higher now. Faster and faster until we fly! And the frustrated water writhes underneath and the amazed canyon walls lean over to get a better view of the magic.

Ahead of us the walls fall away. Water jets out in a great round plume, creamy as rich milk. It arches down and down and down, so far into the vapor that clothes the great hidden lake. The terminal gush of the Rhône is swallowed below us without a trace.

We soar! High above the mist-country, we soar safe in sunlight. Our enemies are stifled and blind below and the happiness is so great that I burn—I burn for joy.

Amerie and the Indian Chief come at last into the wheelhouse and warm themselves at my fire. And then they put hands on me to still the shuddering and say, "Take us down, child."

And I descend. Softly.

12

"YOU ARE CERTAIN, MOTHER?" NODONN ASKED.

The Queen replied, "You will see for yourself. The Thagdal finished with her only a short time ago and sent her back to Redact House. Culluket got the truth from her when I farspoke him of what had happened. He is bringing her to the palace again for our scrutiny."

They were in the Queen's morning room. She was still en déshabillé, while the Battlemaster, summoned from the arena, wore a light practice cuirass with vambrace and pauldron for his unshielded right arm and shoulder.

"A *new* human conspiracy!" he mused aloud. "The audacity of the Lowlives almost passes belief. That Guderian woman is at the bottom of it, of course. The human-Firvulag entente, the use of the holy Spear . . . and now this!"

Nontusvel said, "It was a vengeance-thought that the girl Gwen-Minivel let slip, you see, when the Thagdal was filling her full of his grace. The gist of it was, 'You won't be able to do this to human women much longer when we destroy your torc factory and shut the time-gate. We will free all human slaves.'"

"It was fortunate that you were within range and caught her thought."

"It was heavily screened. But I am the Mother of the Host."

"Exactly who *is* she, that she should have had knowledge of this plot?"

"Alas—a most promising young healer. She was reserved from the customary bidding by Dionket himself. She should have been sent to the King's couch long ago. But for reasons that are not yet clear to me—you will want to investigate this— she was secreted in the catacombs of Redact House by the connivance of Mayvar and the Lord Healer. With your Awful Father in such low spirits over recent melancholy events, I bethought me of this girl as a potential source of comfort. She had stunned the entire company at the bidding banquet with her empathy. I—I confess that I saw in her reminders of my own self as a young maiden, lulling my dolls to sleep and dreaming of the babies I would some day bear... But enough of that. As it is my duty to assure the consolation of our King, I charged your brother Culluket to discover what had become of Minivel. A royal command superseded even Dionket's authority over the girl and she was duly produced. Culluket is much too forthright to deal with the mental preparations that Minivel required—your Awful Father being in the delicate condition he is, we could not risk her putting him down—and so I undertook the coercion and redaction of the young woman myself. I worked with her all yesterday afternoon, and she went to the Thagdal last night as eagerly as a nymph. He never knew that she despised him. And of course your Father never heard Minivel's deep avowal of revenge, since he was distracted by his own passion. I had her sing for him and vouchsafe the most maternal forms of solace in addition to the usual. She was a great success."

"And all unwitting," Nodonn now suggested, "she may become the key to our victory as well."

The door to the suite opened. The King's Interrogator, handsome and stern in a hooded cape of dark burgundy, pushed Sukey in ahead of him and motioned for the escort of garnet-armored guardsmen to remain outside. Culluket saluted Nontusvel and his brother.

"Awful Mother! Brother Battlemaster! I've questioned the woman Gwen-Minivel and laid bare all that she knows."

Sukey stood with a resolute face. Her eyes and nose were reddened from weeping and her hair hung in strings. She still wore the diaphanous love-gift robes the Queen's attendants had dressed her in the night before.

Nontusvel and Nodonn studied the intelligence that Culluket's mind displayed to them.

"Child, child," mourned the Queen. "Not only the treason—but a human lover as well! A lowly gray—Stein Oleson, man-at-arms to Aiken Drum. And you have conceived his child!"

"Stein is my husband," Sukey said.

The Interrogator, so like and so unlike his gentle mother, pushed back his hood. "The penalty for that action alone would be death, Gwen-Minivel. Death for you, for your unborn child, and for the father of the misbegotten. You have abased your silver torc and forfeited all claim to Tanu kinship. You are no longer Gwen-Minivel but merely Sue-Gwen Davies, an outlaw human. You and any persons who are accessories to this treason or to the larger infamies you have revealed to me will answer to our justice—no matter how high their station."

Sukey's swollen lips smiled. Her thought was clear: We lose our lives. But you will lose your whole world, even though you continue to live!

"Send her away," said Nodonn. "We must discuss this."

As Culluket turned Sukey over to the guards, the Queen said, "Let us go into the atrium where there is more air. I don't feel at all well."

The Second Redactor took his mother's arm, and the three of them went into a little enclosed courtyard that was a bower of autumn roses. The Queen and Culluket sat on the marble coping of the central fountain. Nodonn paced the flags, his armor's facets throwing prismatic refractions into the garden shadows.

"What have you done with the man?" Nontusvel asked.

"There was a row, of course." Culluket's tone was dry. "Stein and Aiken Drum were at the Coercer College, breakfasting with Gomnol, if you please! Naturally the young mountebank and the Lord Coercer claimed to know nothing of Stein's relation with Sukey—which was the ostensible reason given for my taking him into custody. Stein became quite violent, even in spite of his torc. Gomnol had no choice but to subdue him and turn him over to us, however. The truth of our accusation about the woman leaked from Stein's mind as from a sieve. He'll be imprisoned until the Grand Combat and set up in one of the gladiator events. The girl goes into the Great Retort, of course."

"And Aiken Drum?"

Culluket's laugh held admiration in spite of himself. "Now there's a cool one! You need no redaction to know that there must have been collusion between master and man in both treasons. But Drum insisted upon playing the innocent. He demanded that Gomnol and I inspect his mind together, right there on the spot. Without the proper softening process our examination had to be rough and ready—but the little wretch was a match for us. We couldn't discover a particle of treachery hidden anywhere in his mind. No knowledge of Stein and

Minivel, no knowledge of any plot against the torc factory or the time-gate."

The Battlemaster stopped his pacing and sat down beside his brother on the edge of the fountain. He stirred the water with one finger. Little simmers of steam rose. "You and Gomnol did the interrogation... together."

The Queen looked from Nodonn to Culluket. "You can't mean—".

But Culluket gave a slow nod. "It could very well be. Gomnol is capable of it! I suspected nothing... Rumors of the King's impotence have been circulating among all members of the High Table, and we know our precious Lord Coercer cares for nothing if not the main chance. He has undoubtedly realized that his earlier appraisal of Aiken Drum as a metapsychic nova was mistaken. Furthermore, the disallowing of his genetic scheme featuring Elizabeth and the Thagdal has made necessary a slight revision in his dynastic scenario."

"Oh, the ingrate!" cried the Queen. "Gomnol allied with Aiken Drum! This is what comes of admitting Lowlives to our High Table! We must do something about him at once! Imidol must issue the challenge to Gomnol at this year's manifestation of powers."

"He'd lose," Culluket said flatly.

"What then?" the Queen implored. "Gomnol will throw in his lot with the Lowlife rebels! Isn't it obvious?"

Culluket looked puzzled. "But Gomnol wouldn't destroy his own torc factory, his power base. It's counter to the man's entire psychology. Somehow, Aiken Drum has managed to keep this part of the plot from him."

"Then let's tell Gomnol!" cried Nontusvel. "Turn him against that horrid little golden beast!"

"Peace, dearest Mother." Nodonn's sun-bright countenance relaxed the agitated Queen with its warmth. "There are so many things afoot—so many intrigues and plots and counterplots— that they collide with one another and entwine in a tangle that seems to defy unknotting. The northern insurgents with their iron, perhaps with the Spear; the monstrous Felice, murderer of our sister Epone, who now wears stolen gold; the rebel general Guderian and her saboteur cohorts; Aiken Drum, whose loyalties lie Tana-knows-where; the King's schemes; the anthropologist and his survey; and the Lord Coercer—who would manipulate us all! A formidable snarl."

"But not," Culluket insinuated, "beyond your power to unravel, Brother Battlemaster?"

"I," said Nodonn, "have a Sword."

The Queen drew in a sharp breath. "You *can't*!"

"They are humans. They have outlawed themselves. Aiken Drum poses a peculiar problem because of his great popularity with our citizens. We'll need strong proof of his treason, but he can be dealt with. And so can Gomnol—much more easily, I believe. This entire mess can be turned to our advantage."

"Are you so confident of your own ability?" Culluket asked. "The iron alone is a mortal threat to our survival here. If you should miscalculate, the entire High Kingdom could be thrown into chaos."

Ever serene, the Battlemaster said, "We of the Host have agreed that it is necessary to return to the simpler way. To the old customs that we followed for nearly a thousand years. The superficial glamour of humanity's bastard culture has blinded too many of our people—even the Thagdal himself—and brought us to the brink of ruin. But Tana has been compassionate. It is not too late to turn back. The very conspiracies of these Lowlives show them up clearly as the danger we could only suspect before. Not even the most obtuse of our people will be able to ignore the human peril when I have done with my counteraction... And there is also *this*."

He held up a pale-green plaque. Culluket exclaimed, "The survey! Congratulations, Brother! May I inspect it?"

Ignoring the request, Nodonn said, "The human anthropologist has been unwise enough to deliver an honest evaluation. His survey points to the inevitable ascendency of humans and hybrids in the Many-Colored Land, should we Tanu continue to exploit humans genetically and permit them to occupy positions of power. The King has studied the survey but he still waffles over the implications. He and the other moral weaklings at the High Table may think that the status quo can be maintained simply by destroying all copies of the survey and the computer file of data, and doing away with Bryan Grenfell and Ogmol. But thanks to my darling Rosmar, we have not only a copy of the book—but also the anthropologist himself safely tucked away. Dearest Mother, it is my intention to force the anthropologist to reveal the truth about his own human race at the culmination of the Grand Combat. I will produce him just prior to the Heroic Encounters so that the conspirators of the peace faction have no time to prepare opposition. When the peril is made clear, the combined wrath of our entire Tanu battle-company will fall upon those who are traitors to our ancient ideals. Upon Gomnol! Upon Aiken Drum! And upon any of our other kinsmen who have become so depraved as to consider humanity essential to our survival here."

The Queen raised a hand to her lips. "But then the Thagdal—"

Nodonn was relentless. "Queen and Mother, if he persists in his folly, his time has come. I will be merciful. The choice, at the end, will be his own."

Culluket hastened to say, "You, as Mother of the Host, are wholly exempt from his fate."

Nontusvel had her mental screens up. Her eyes refused to meet those of her sons. "Sometimes . . . our ways are very hard. I thought there might be another way."

Nodonn swept on. "As for the sabotage plot in Sue-Gwen Davies' mind, there are ways to turn that affair to our advantage if we work quickly. We have no details of the proposed assault on the torc factory. Obviously, the northerners did not take Aiken Drum and his loutish crony entirely into their confidence. But we do know the date—the twenty-second, two days from now—and we can presume that the attack will take place at night when activity around the Coercer Headquarters is minimal. The second part of the Lowlife plot, the attempt to send a message through the time-gate, must certainly take place at dawn on the twenty-second."

Culluket exclaimed, "Gomnol would certainly try to stop the factory attack if he knew about it. We can beat him to the punch and take the credit ourselves!"

The Battlemaster threw back his glorious head and laughed. "Redactive Brother, what a simpleton you are! But never mind. The planning of campaigns is my duty. You'll see how well I've fulfilled it soon enough. Now then . . . you must summon all of the top fighters of the Host, who have by now arrived in Muriah. This very noon our Mother will hold a sacred re-union in order to impart a special blessing on her warrior children before the games. When we are together and secluded, I will explain the strategy that will deliver *all* of our enemies into our hands."

"The murderer of our dearest Epone," the Interrogator put in, "*she* is reserved to me."

Nodonn nodded agreement. "Extract all useful information from this Felice and then it shall be as you request. But this female monster must be able to fight in the gladiatorial games when you're through with her. It is part of my overall strategy. The others will go into the Great Retort. These Lowlives must all suffer the most public destruction, as an example to the others. I will brook only one exception. I have other plans for Guderian."

"Both she and Felice wear the gold," cautioned Culluket.

"Felice's will be removed by her own iron," said the Battlemaster. "She will wear gray as she spills her blood on the White Silver Plain. Guderian's torc will not matter, as you will shortly discover."

Nontusvel's tears had dried. She rose from the fountain's edge and said brightly, "If we're going to have a great crowd for luncheon, I must consult with the cooks at once. You will excuse me." They kissed her hands and she rushed away, trailing fragmented thoughts of hostessly menu planning.

Culluket turned a level eye to the Battlemaster. "There is still one human whose position remains to be clarified. I must insist that you be straightforward in a matter of such high seriouness."

The image of Mercy seemed to hover between the brothers.

Nodonn's glowing face was unreadable and his mind as well. "The others of the Host were too polite to question my choice of consort—or too prudent. But since you dare to be frank, I'll tell you what I have discovered about her. From my first meeting with Rosmar, I was struck by the incredible affinity, the sweet consonance of thought between us that was so different from the relationships I had known with other human women—even with women of our own race. And so after I took her to wife, I had Greg-Donnet prepare a genetic assay of my remarkable bride."

"And?"

"Mercy-Rosmar's plasm is almost identical to our own. She has more of our genes than she has of human. Tana alone knows how to account for it—but then I am no scientist."

Culluket, who was, looked profoundly shaken. His screens hid a storm of intellectualizing but could not efface the tinge of suspicion pervading it.

The insouciance of the Battlemaster melted into something black. For one terrible instant the startled Culluket was wrapped in a second skin all lined with needles, and the point of each one was the source of an electric charge that inflamed the pain receptors of his epidermis almost to the point of overload. He would have fallen, would have lost consciousness except for the grip of Nodonn's great mind.

As swiftly as it had come, the agony was wiped away, replaced by a sensation of utter well-being.

And Nodonn's thought: Cogitate as you will Redactive Brother. But never again doubt my judgment or hint that MercyRosmar is anything but loyal.

Master of every obscenity!

"Now you're behaving like a simpleton again," chided the voice of Apollo. "Just remember who it is who will be king. And never make the mistake of thinking you can teach *me* anything about the inflicting of pain."

13

TOGETHER WITH MANY OTHER SIGHTSEERS FROM MURIAH, KAT-
linel the Darkeyed went down on chalikoback in the evening
cool to wander over the White Silver Plain and satisfy her
perennial curiosity about the everyday activities of the ancient
Foe, encamped now in harmless splendor all about the northeastern end of the battleground.

She rode over the wide bridge spanning the canal. The bed
of the watercourse was paved with limestone blocks, and it ran
three meters deep with star-spangled fresh water. The flow
came from that huge spring, the Well of the Sea, whose waters
had been the rationale for the siting of the field of combat from
the earliest coming of the Tanu to Aven. Here and there the
Little People dipped buckets or filled skins. Farther downstream, some Firvulag women were washing clothes; and still
farther along, where the canal waters shallowed as they curved
east and met the Great Lagoon, were the quaint bathing tents
of the modest folk.

Katlinel let her chaliko have its head. It ambled down the
long central avenue of the tent-city where bonfires burned atop
cairns of heaped rocks. The large earth-colored pavilions of
the Firvulag nobility were here, awnings and flies fringed in
gold and silver, and embroidered designs ornamenting walls
and roof panels. Every Great One's tent was fronted by a tall
pole from which floated the richly jeweled standard of its oc-
cupant, all decorated with hair plumes and gold-plated skulls
of vanquished foemen. Every standard was topped by the effigy
of a different monstrous head, which represented the favorite
illusionary aspect of the Firvulag warrior.

The Little People were everywhere. Some wore their handsomely chased obsidian armor; but most were more casually

attired in trousers and jerkins or gem-studded robes with borders of fur (which must have been very uncomfortable in the sultry dusk). Pointed caps were the most common headgear among men and women alike. The grander ladies had veils floating from theirs, or decorated padded brims, or ornamental horns, or long lappets that hung before or behind their ears. It was customary for the lofty Tanu to refer to their shadowkinfolk as "little." But most of those that Katlinel passed were at least equal to humans in stature; and now and again she caught a glimpse of some doughty champion who far surpassed any Tanu in height and bulk. It was being said in the capital that more Firvulag than ever before had come south for this year's Grand Combat, cheered by their triumph at Finiah. The army was rumored to include certain proud fighters who had disdained to contend of late because of the contamination of the games by human participants. Medor had come out of hiding, and the hideous Nukalavee who fought under the guise of a flayed centaur with all the raw muscles and sinews and blood vessels exposed to strike horror into his opponents; and even old Pallol One-Eye the Firvulag Battlemaster had returned, breaking his twenty-year sulk.

There were supposed to be nearly 50,000 of the Little People encamped on the Plain already—nearly two-thirds of the entire Firvulag population. About half of this number were fighters, and they outnumbered the Tanu knights and their human auxiliaries by about two to one. Eventually, almost the entire chivalry of the Many-Colored Land would be arrayed against this concentration of the Foe.

Firvulag hawkers importuned Katlinel as she rode among the campfires and the jolly groups of feasters and dancers. She was offered jewelry and precious trinkets on every hand, since this was the craft that the Firvulag excelled in above all others; there were also vendors of sweets and salted nuts and hard cider and strange fortified wines. But she resisted their pleas. Only when she reached the end of the long avenue and circled around among the squat black tents of the humbler folk did she succumb at last to temptation in the shape of a goblinesque little maiden with thick blonde braids and a pert scarlet hennin, who offered flagons of carved myrtlewood filled with a marvelous perfume distilled from forest flowers.

"Thank you, Lady." The diminutive seller bobbed a curtsy as she accepted payment. "It's said among us that the Dame's

Hesperis breathes forth a scent that even the most reluctant swain finds impossible to resist."

Katlinel laughed. "I'll remember to wear it with caution."

"Well, I've heard," was the saucy retort, "that some of your Tanu gentlemen need all the help they can get."

"We'll see about that at the games," Katlinel said, and rode on, smiling.

Another chaliko fell in beside her own as she passed through an area crowded with dining and drinking tents. When a drunken ogre came carousing out and seized the reins of her mount, the rider on the other beast closed in even before she could spin a defensive illusion. One mental bolt sent the Firvulag oaf staggering into the arms of his jeering mates, who dragged him away with a breezy apology to Katlinel for the imposition.

"I am in your debt, Exalted Lord," she said, bowing her head to her rescuer.

He was a handsome figure, tall and broad-shouldered, wearing a close-fitting coif beneath a visored cap adorned with a small golden coronet. The coif hid his hair and throat and fell over his shoulders in a very short cape, all scalloped and jeweled at the edges. His hose and doublet were deep violet.

"It is my pleasure, Exalted Lady. I'm afraid that some of my countrymen take their celebrating too seriously, too far in advance."

She studied him with frank surprise as they rode on together. "You amaze me, Lord. With your neck covered, I mistook you for one of my own people."

"And which are they?" inquired the other, the faintest taunt in his fine voice.

Katlinel flushed and gripped her reins, ready to spur the chaliko away from the upstart. But the man reached out a hand and the animal stood still.

"Forgive my impertinence, Lady. It was unforgivable. But it is obvious that your beauty derives from human as well as Tanu blood. And I perceive from your silver and green gown that you are—as I—of the illusion-spinners, and one of rare power. If you will forgo your just annoyance at my crude banter and think instead of the small service lately done for you, perhaps we may yet ride on for a few moments and speak together. I have a great curiosity about your people."

"And a clever tongue as well, Firvulag Lord! . . . Very well, you may ride with me for a short time. I am Katlinel, surnamed the Darkeyed, and I sit at the High Table in the very lowest chair, being the least among the Tanu Great Ones."

"Surely not for long!" He doffed the crowned cap; the purple coif covered his skull. "I am known as the ruler of Meadow Mountain. My domain lies far to the north, on the fringes of the Firvulag realm. Never before this have I attended the Grand Combat. My people are so occupied with the daily problems of survival that they have scant heart for religious games."

"A heretical notion, to be sure. But one that I can sympathize with."

"There are those among you who are not ardent members of the battle-company?"

"Many," she admitted, "especially among the hybrids such as myself. But the force of tradition remains strong."

"Ah. Tradition. But of late the old ways seem shaken. Humanity, once so docile and useful, rises up in revolt against your High King."

"In alliance with you Firvulag!"

"The Tanu were the first to use humans. Shouldn't we as well? We Firvulag are, it's true, more hidebound than you. Why—most of my people will not even mount an animal such as this, preferring to march on their own sturdy legs."

"But you have no such scruples?"

"I've been forced to be a realist, Lady. Tell me—is it true that human scientists are honored and fostered among the Tanu? That you've used their specialized knowledge to enhance your own technoeconomy?"

"I belong to the High Faculty of the Creator Guild. Most science, excepting that of healing and psychobiology, falls within our province. We have many human scientists at work in our College, educating our young people as well as engaged in practical application of their knowledge. Agriculturalists, earth scientists, engineers of every sort, even specialists in the social sciences—all have placed their talents in the service of the Many-Colored Land."

"And geneticists?" the Lord of Meadow Mountain inquired softly.

"Most certainly."

He said, "If only we were not Foes. If only we were free to cooperate, to have a free interchange of ideas and resources. I know that we Firvulag would have much to offer you. And you . . . could do so much for us."

"But that is not the *way*," she said.

"Not yet. Not so long as the stern old battle-company rules your High Kingdom."

"I must leave now," Katlinel said.

"Will you come again and talk? There is still more than a week before the Combat begins and we officially become Foes once more."

She held out one hand and he took it and saluted her in the classic manner. His lips were cold. A flash of metapsychic insight told Katlinel that they were also illusory. But the mind that opened to her in momentary hope—that was not cold at all.

"I'll come again tomorrow night," she said. "Shall I ask for you among your friends?"

"Few here would call me that." His smile was both rueful and cautionary. "Ride here and I will find you. It would be better if none of your people knew that you condescended to have converse with Sugoll, Lord of Meadow Mountain—which humans of Elder Earth call the Feldberg."

"We of the High Table do as we please," said Katlinel. She spurred the chaliko up the trail leading from the salt plain to Aven.

14

GOMNOL PANNED THE INFRARED SPOT SLOWLY OVER THE blackness of the Catalan Gulf. "Still nothing. And the Flying Hunt will be moving their search into this area in another hour if they stick to their grid. Are you certain the saboteurs planned to land tonight?"

"Goddammit, yes," growled Aiken Drum. He squatted in an embrasure between a pair of battlements, peering through an ordinary lens-ocular. He and the Lord Coercer were on the highest turret of Guild Headquarters. "Arrive tonight, farspeak me to whatever rendezvous seemed safest, confer about the best way to crash this place, then mount the assault during the wee hours Monday morning after a day's rest and recon. Don't dump on me if your spies were too incompetent to locate 'em."

"I believe your friends are here already," Gomnol said. "They could have come in obliquely along the coast with the traffic from Tarasiah and Calamosk and Geroniah and the rest of the Spanish cities. Suppose they sailed southwest into the Catalan backwaters after shooting the Glissade, then simply doubled back along the Aven shore? If they're down on the coast now, we'll never spot them—and neither will Nodonn and the Host, airborne or not. There are half a hundred little creeks and inlets along this northern side of the peninsula, and all full of caves where they could hole up out of farsense range." He shut off the power of his big viewer. "You'll just have to wait for their hail, even if it does increase the chance that the Host might find them first. What a pity your saboteur friends didn't trust you to fly out and meet them as soon as they reached the Basin."

"Aw, shut up," said Aiken. "I'm trying my seekersense on Felice's pattern. She might not be too good at screening yet."

"And then again, she might! We'll have to be very cautious with *that* one . . . And that great booby, Stein! If our block in his mind doesn't hold—if Culluket recognizes it and gets other redactors of the Host to join in a multiphase probe—Stein is going to open up! I can't risk the Host knowing my involvement in this affair and neither can you. We're going to have to put Stein out of the way."

"Gumball, will you stop griping my ass?" Aiken's button eyes held a vicious glitter. "Stein's mental block will hold. You just try killing him or Sukey and the whole thing's off between us. You grab?"

"Only too well. But I must point out the risk we're running. If the Host obtains firm proof of our treason, we will be declared outlaw humans. No rules of Truce or other precepts of the battle-religion will protect us. I know how powerful you've become—that's why I agreed to follow your leadership in this affair. But the massed minds of the Host are capable of annihilating both of us if they act in full concert under Nodonn. I've had forty years of experience with the Tanu and you've been here three months! If you won't listen to my advice, you'll end up with your head on a pike—for all your high metafaculties!"

The trickster came down from the battlement, a conciliatory smile making his teeth shine in the dark. "Gumball—baby! I told you we'd be buddies. I know I need you. Hellfire, man, even if you weren't Lord Coercer and the craftiest intriguer in the whole kingdom—*you're the boy who knows the torcs*. Who the hell wants to be king without subjects? You gotta keep those collars rolling out, sweetie! Jeez, I almost blew my cortex when old Elizabeth gave me the marvelous news about these turkeys coming south to sabotage your place. And they want to close the time-gate! Not only cut off the supply of warm bods, but their futuristic goodies, too! No more real Scotch for you and me. Sweet houghmagandy!"

Gomnol laughed. "There's scant chance of either happening now. You and I and the Tanu may have our differences, but the valuation of the gate and the factory is hardly one of them. Not even Nodonn would dare go against the King and public opinion by treating these sabotage threats lightly."

"But he might try to muscle in on our act," Aiken warned. "Just like he did with the Delbaeth Quest. He'll try to make it look like *he's* the one who sniffs out the plots and snuffs 'em, and we can't let him grab face from us. We've gotta catch these human saboteurs redhanded doing their thing so we can show what loyal citizens we are."

"It would be more prudent to take the factory saboteurs as soon as we discover their hideout. But your idea does have PR advantages. I've arranged for neutral observers—Lord Bormol of Roniah and the Lord of Swords—to witness our brilliant defense. Both of them belong to the Coercer Guild and they'll be able to vouch for my zeal in case that scheming hothead, Imidol, attempts to say later that I was in league with the invaders."

"I wish I could be here to help." Aiken spoke with every evidence of sincerity. "But you can't fly, and one of us has to handle the time-gate operation personally. We can't just warn the castellan and hope for the best. This Madame Guderian isn't any dummy, the way she orchestrated Finiah. She'll have something sneaky planned. Probably wild diversions while she creeps up on the gate invisible. But with *me* waiting to pop her illusion—have no fear!" He added quietly, "Just be sure you do as well with Felice, Gumball."

The Lord Coercer was replacing the protective pod over the infrared scanner. "I'll have my best human golds ready for her. Iron weapons won't do the saboteurs a bit of good against *them*." In a nonchalant manner, he asked, "What do you suppose became of the Spear and the aircraft after Finiah?"

Aiken lifted his golden shoulders. "Haven't the faintest! Sure as shit the rebels would've kept on using both of 'em in other attacks if they were still operational. I thought Velteyn claimed to've shot the plane down."

"He said he penetrated the craft with his ball lightning," Gomnol corrected. "But no one saw the flyer crash and no wreckage was ever discovered. We certainly must find out what happened. If the weapon and the ship are still usable, we could be in very serious trouble, my boy."

"Aaah," Aiken scoffed. "If they still had a zapper and an aircraft, would they come down south by riverboat and try this lamebrain attack on your fortress?" Aiken was reasonable. And his mind was artistically screened. "You got nothing to worry about. We'll worm the whole thing outa Felice and her ragtag commandos and you can have your reception committee and observation team all primed and ready . . . And save a few prisoners for questioning—okay? Even if the bird and the zapper they used on Finiah are a terminal fewk-out, it would be awfully nice to know where they came from. There might be others!"

The strange bedfellows eyed one another for a long minute. Neither one could detect the presence of any suspiciously screened chicane in the other. They were both experts.

"Well—guess I'll do a little eyeball scan," Aiken said at last. "I'll get down to the shore and be ready when Felice and her gang give a shout." He flipped a hand at the Lord Coercer in farewell.

A longtailed moth, lime-green with windowpane eyespots, went fluttering from the high tower, down the northern cliffs, and over the dunes and badlands to the shore of the Catalan Lagoon.

O Aiken.

Hey! That you sweets? Longtimenothink! Thought you long gone.

How *could* you Stein/Sukey trapped Cullukettorturer?

Elizababe misread me not! Blame me not having done damnedest under friggertytough chew! Sukey leaked to Queen re Stein so Cull pounced. Options for me: [1] Let Cull take Stein; [2] fight & get us *both* taken. Yes? Yes! Threw good mindblock Stein won't betray others/me. He/Sukey secure for now Cull thinks he knows all. Before Combat I spring pair detorc ship off to save lovenest + unborn Steinling happily-everafter.

And Gomnol?

Elizacraftybeth you know.

AikenDrum + Gomnol = KingYou + GrandVizierHe. Why not?

Permit probe implementation?

You can't probe longdistance and I'm too busy now to come. What matter no trust little ConYankeeMerlin anymore?

Not allied Mordred.

Who he? And why you care anyhoo GrandDropoutMaster?

Aiken don't betray ourfriends! Beware not only for theirsake for yours O trickster-selftricked unto the end dear Aiken don't.

Relax Elizababeballooner. When I king all well but interfere not thwart not ambitions gods/superfolk lest juggernaut squish you grab?

O you Aiken do what you must but woe to you because of what you must do.

You oracles all alike anal pain. Keep aloof overflying like before whynot? You got balloon now so take off get lost! But let me alone nothing stops me now nothing not you not Brede not ArchangelNodonn not old GroupGreen gangomine not even chocolatekryptonite by friggertydamn!

. . .

Elizabeth?

. . .

You gone?

. . .

(Laughter.)

The longtailed moth followed the call to a deep cavern on an inlet of the northern coast of Aven. The saboteurs, like the Firvulag, knew that the simplest way to escape detection by Tanu searchers was to hide underground. Felice guided Aiken to them by means of a gossamer mind-thread, tuned nicely to his intimate mode, which no other being could possibly far-sense. And when the gold-clad little figure appeared with a silent snap on the other side of their shielded campfire, Felice was standing there in the looted blue-glass armor that Old Man Kawai had adapted to her small stature, the Spear gripped in one gauntleted hand—and murder in her eye.

"You tipped 'em off!" Her coercive power closed like a bear-trap.

"Me? *Me*?" He squirmed in her mind's clutches. She was stronger than he had expected. A lot stronger. He could break free—but was it wise to let them know how his powers had matured? And *now* what the hell had she done? A big muffer of a boulder plugging the cavern exit! Where had it come from, so silently, so soon? Goddammit, was she a creator, too—or had that been just a deft bit of the old PK?

"Felice, baby, you are making one helluva booboo. *Yhhh!* Lay off the marbles, kid, for chrissake! I didn't tell 'em! Give me a chance to *explain*!"

She relaxed her holds, both coercive and psychokinetic. A great cage of light-blue flame sprang up to encircle him. (Well, that was that. She could create.) For the first time he paid attention to the others standing behind Felice, disguised as guards and serving women. He only recognized the nun.

"Amerie!" cried the shining youth. "Tell her she's gotta let me explain!"

"Talk fast, Tricky-Pockets," Felice said.

He seemed to bare his innocence to the gold-torc fury. Stein and Sukey—*they* were the ones who had inadvertently blown the gaff—not him! Since the information he gave Felice was basically the truth (and since he was marvelously adept at concealing the seams that joined truth to semitruth and falsehood), the girl's redactive power, weakest of her five metafunctions, could find no fault with his recital. Still glowering, but reluctantly won over in spite of her deeper instincts, she turned off the cage of astral fire and set him free.

Aiken whipped a snowy handkerchief from one of his pockets and wiped his sweating face. "My sweet Lord, you're a brute, Felice! Really learned how to use your collar in a hurry, didn't you?"

She did not answer.

Aiken assumed his most ingratiating air. Addressing himself to the others, he said, "Everything's all set, guys. We've got an inside man—a gold-torc who's lived here for years pretending to be loyal, just waiting for a chance to strike a really valid blow for humanity. He's going to deactivate the lock on a very small service door that hasn't been used in years. They used to shovel their rubbish out of the keep and right over the edge of the cliff, see? There's a little narrow trail giving access to the door but you can walk on it all right. I checked. You'll have to come onto the trail from above, through town. But for the getaway, you can rappel right down the cliff face into the old dump and hightail it into the badlands. A little luck and there'll be such a reeraw going on that you can make it back to these caves before they even know you're gone."

With a magician's flourish, he hauled a large sheet of durofilm out of another pocket.

"Look! I brought you a complete map! City, Guild buildings, interior of the headquarters block showing your route from the service door to the torc-making rooms. See—this is where you are, and here's the old dump, and here's the Coercer HQ at the edge of the cliff and the door. You just come into town in your disguises—you look bonzo, by the way!—and lose yourselves in the greenway bushes just west of the Coercer House wall."

He spread the map on the floor and most of the saboteurs hunched down to study it. But Felice said:

"What about the Spear?"

Aiken was offhanded. "Oh. Right. Is that it you got there? Big sonuvabitch, isn't it?"

"If we could get it working," the girl said, "we could hit the Coercer headquarters from a distance. There'd be no need for a penetration at all."

"I gotcha. Oh, absolutely. I kinda forgot all about that old zapper, what with our having an inside man at the skonk works all ready to let us walk inside."

"Who is it?" asked the biggest of the desperados. He wore the blue cloak and bronze half-armor of a captal of the provincial guard.

Aiken frowned in anxiety. "I can't tell you his name. If any of you got captured, there's no way you could avoid giving him away. And we can't let that happen. This guy is not only loaded with metafunctions, but he's also in a high position. A perfect undercover agent for later on, see? Now lemme give this a good think. Like I say, I'd almost forgotten about this Spear. A real long shot—but if I *could* fix it and warn our inside man to get out of there..."

Felice silently handed the great glassy lance to Aiken. Chief Burke brought up the powerpack and its cable, which they had toted from Hidden Springs in a leathern chest. Aiken stroked the blue-laquered weapon with steady fingers, lifting the caplock to inspect the studs, hefting it into his right armpit and pretending to take aim at Felice's big rock plugging the entrance.

"Pam!" he ejaculated. A wavering little spark, the size of a firefly, emerged from the business end of the device and drifted through the air. It collided with the rock and fell into an impotent shower of red-glowing dust.

"So much for refueling the zapper with my mind-power!" He gave them a sprightly wink. "Now let's have a look at the juice box."

He jabbed and thrust at the pack's peculiar sunken fasteners with several of the tools that he carried in his golden suit. "Gonna take more than I've got here to get it open," he said. "Tell you what! I'll change it into a piece of straw and myself into a bird and take it back to my workroom. If I get it open and figure how to recharge it, I'll bring it back here before midnight tomorrow, and warn our coercer pal what's up, and you can blast the place to hell and gone from out in the lagoon. But if I give you a mind-squeak at twenty-four bells telling you it's no go, you carry on with the other plan. How's that sound?"

His eyes flicked eagerly from face to face.

"I think," said Felice, "that we should postpone any decision until you come back here with the Spear. Operational or not.

And I think you should go along with us on the torc factory assault."

"I'd like nothing better," he said earnestly. "But I'm supposed to go to this combatant's banquet at the palace. These folks are just sitting down at table around midnight. There's no way I can get out of going. I'm one of the hottest contenders in the light humanweight class!"

"I don't like this," said Felice.

"You still don't trust me." Sorrow clouded the golliwog face. He gestured to the map. "What else do I hafta *do*?"

"You've got it all planned, haven't you?" she said archly. "We just follow your little red lines on the map. Time all picked, route all picked, getaway all set up. What would you say if I told you that we'd make our own penetration at our own time? Not on Monday at all? Just to make sure there's no nasty surprises waiting behind the rubbish door?"

He flung his hands into the air. "It's your gig, babe, not mine. But without the zapper or my inside man opening up for you, you'll need one helluva can opener to break into that fortress. To say nothing of losing your sync with Madame's hit of the time-gate."

Chief Burke said, "Felice, maybe I could go back with him."

"And how'd you let us know if there was any funny business?" She was sarcastic. "Farspeak me through your broken gray torc?"

"Come along yourself, then," Aiken suggested to her.

The others burst into a storm of protest.

At last Felice said, "We'll have to carry on with your suggestion about the Spear. But God save your ass, Aiken Drum, if this is one of your hookem-snivey tricks!"

"Piffle," said the golden man. He picked up the Spear and its heavy pack as though they were toys and cocked his head in the direction of the barricading boulder. "Are you going to be a gentlewoman and open your little door for a lad with his hands full?"

Felice crossed her sapphire-armored arms and gave a tinkling laugh. "Suppose you show us how *you'd* do it, Fancy Pants."

Aiken emitted a martyred sigh. He faced the cave entrance and stuck out his tongue. The mass of mineral suddenly seemed shot through with thousands of small holes that grew and grew until the huge rock was nothing but a lacy webwork. It collapsed in another instant of its own weight, making a sound like smashing glassware.

"Shoddy workmanship around here," observed the jester.

He changed into a crescent-winged nightjar. *Kutuk-kutuk!* The bird gave a mocking call as it slipped out into the night, a straw and a lump of moss caught in its claws.

None of the people inside the cave could see the direction it took: straight north, toward the mainland of Europe.

Gumball?

Yes Aiken.

They bought the house and lot and the little white fence around it too. Exactly as we planned. They'll futz around for a while when I don't farspeak back tomorrow night. But then they'll decide some monster ate me and go ahead with their plan. What else can they do? Right? You be ready when they come in that back door. Felice is in blue armor and loaded with metafunctions. Be sure your boys have their heaviest screens up. Besides her there are six men dressed as gray guards and two dames got up as servants in those stripy robes. None of them have any mental firepower at all. They'll be easy to stop if you look out for the iron.

And Felice?

Do whatever you have to do and watch your sweet petard.

I understand. You go now to Castle Gateway?

On swift little wings. Plenty of time. You just have yourself a nice day tomorrow and be sure the welcome mat is all shook out and ready at midnight. Bye-bye!

Bon voyage to you Aiken Drum.

"I knew it! I knew it!" Felice raged.

"It's half past midnight," Uwe said. "We *must* go now. It will take at least three hours to get into the city, even if we do secure mounts at the main dockyard, and more time to make our way along the cliff. We cannot wait any longer to hear from Aiken Drum."

"It's a trap!" the girl insisted.

Amerie urged her. "Try to make mental contact one more time. Try both him and Elizabeth."

Felice's wild brown eyes fixed on some distant vista. She held her fingers to her golden torc. They all waited.

The little athlete seemed to shrink smaller than ever, despite the blaze of glass armor. "Nothing. Neither Aiken nor Eliza-beth. Nothing. We can't go. It's a trap. I know it."

Chief Burke stood over her. "That little gold mamzer might have pulled a fast one at that. But there are other ways to explain his silence. He could be in a position where he doesn't dare farspeak us. Perhaps some exotics came and hauled him away to the party before he could get a word off. Isn't that possible?"

"No! I mean—maybe." Her expression was frantic. "Oh, Peo—it all depends on his farspeaking skill! And I don't know enough about this business yet to tell whether he's capable of it or not. I suppose you could be right."

"Then we're going to have to get on with it," said the Native American.

"Can't we wait? Look over Guild HQ in daylight ourselves, the way we planned to back in the beginning? Make our own plan for penetration?...My PK and creativity and coerce are coming on *strong*, guys! I think I could fuzz the minds of the guards at that place so we could walk right in the front door. Hell—in this blue rig-out and with you as my loyal escort, I'm just another Guild member to any big guns that happen to saunter by. I can shield the bunch of you easily. And by God, I'll smear that torc factory into marmalade just as soon as I get into range. Not with thunderbolts! Soft and sneaky—with PK that just liquefies the walls! Then we can escape before anyone knows what's happened. But not out that door of Aiken's—we'll go out one of the windows on the northeastern corner of the building, as far away from that service door as we can get. It'll be easy with my PK and Basil's climbing equipment."

Chief Burke hesitated.

Uwe contributed his placid opinion. "If Felice is certain that her metafunctions are equal to the task, there's no reason why we can't follow her modified plan *tonight*. Khalid knows the city. We can take a completely different route from the one laid out by Aiken Drum. The Coercer Guild complex is huge. If they're waiting in ambush at this rear door, they may be careless elsewhere."

Felice gave a crow of joy and kissed the graybeard. "Yes! As long as we don't follow that joker's blueprint, I'm ready to go tonight."

"Do the rest of you agree?" Burke asked. There was a

murmur of acquiescence. "Then hoist your little tushies and get your disguises in order. We're off to the main landing stage to steal some horses—I mean, chalikos. If my future ancestors could only see me now."

15

"WAY! WAY FOR THE EXALTED LADY PHYLLIS-MORIGEL!" THE captal sang out.

The mob of barenecks and grays and well-dressed Firvulag that crowded the central square of Muriah parted minimally to let the mounted party pass. Even in the early hours after midnight the place was a crush of commerce and amusement and carnival display. The Little Folk were by ancient custom night people; and down here in the south, where daytime temperatures in the Mediterranean Basin soared to heights that were barely tolerable to specially adapted humans, let alone a race that had evolved in cold uplands, the Firvulag were abroad almost exclusively between sunset and sunrise. Those who wished to cater to them kept a similar schedule.

There were plenty of Tanu and gold-torc humans about as well—most of them, like the Lady Phyllis-Morigel and her train, having recently arrived in the capital and seeking lodgings. Some of the Great Ones stayed in the palace; others were accommodated with relations; the keenest fighters headed for the pavilions that had been erected on the turfed racecourse northwest of the city, where they could practice their martial specialties. But the visitors with no special accommodation arranged in advance usually did what the Lady Phyllis now did: They demanded, as was their right, the hospitality of their Guild.

She and her eight attendants rode unhindered into the great courtyard of the Coercer complex. Hostlers took charge of their mounts. An urbane silver majordomo, calm in the midst of the hullabaloo, assigned the lady and her handmaids a suite in one of the dormitory mansions; the men-at-arms were directed to a barracks.

Felice's coercive power settled without trace over the will of the majordomo. "We will pay our respects to the High Faculty of the Guild, such as may be up and about, before retiring. Coming as we do from doleful Finiah, we have need of fraternal support and sympathy. You will be glad to conduct us into headquarters personally."

"I will be glad," the man repeated mechanically, "to conduct you into headquarters personally."

He led them from the basement, through the gardens, and across the plaza that fronted the looming block of the keep. The stronghold had been hung with extra decorative lights and was a veritable blaze of blue and amber. None of the Tanu or gold-torc humans outside the building paid any heed to the new arrivals. Felice's mind was apparently overshadowed by grief. Her raven standard, borne by Chief Burke, had long streamers of silver and black fluttering from its finial, the Tanu symbol of bereavement.

They came to the guards at the main entrance. The majordomo said, "This Exalted Lady will confer with the High Faculty."

The squad leader lifted his great bare sword of blue vitredur in formal salute. "The Exalted Lady will confer with the High Faculty."

"We will follow you," Felice told him.

"You will follow me," said the guardsman.

The majordomo bowed and retreated. Felice and the others walked between ranks of blue-and-gold-armored gray-torcs who stood like empty-eyed dummies on both sides of the foyer. There were no other people in sight. The bronze of the saboteurs' military harness jingled faintly. At each step Felice took, the jeweled sollerets on her feet chimed on the marble floor. She lowered the visor of her crested sapphire helmet. The others, as if hearing her mind's command, loosened iron weapons that had been sheathed in gold-plated wooden scabbards. Folding compound bows appeared from under capes; two of the men passed spares to the "serving women," who now shed their outer robes to reveal half-armor worn underneath.

They mounted a great staircase, with still no sign of Tanu or human Guild members. Felice conjured up the image of Aiken's map, then tried to verify their position with her farsight. But the effort was still beyond her and only Khalid's spatial sense kept them from getting lost in the maze of corridors. Farsensing and seeking, like creativity, were subtle things needing experience; while coercion and PK had burgeoned within the gold-torced athlete like jungle plants, long starved for light and moisture, that suddenly achieve their rampant growth under tropical sun and rain. Felice could control this ushering guardsman with ease, just as she had blanked the minds of the thirty other grays they had passed since penetrating the headquarters building. But now—

A bronze door opened. A Tanu woman in a gown of navy blue came into the corridor and halted at the sight of the procession, giving a telepathic greeting.

Allhail CoerciveSister from Ninelva and let me assist your seeking—

"Peo!" Felice cried. "I can only hold her for a second!"

The big Native American stepped forward, his face impassive under the bronze rim of his plumed kettle-helmet. He drew an iron shortsword, pulled the woman toward him with one arm as if embracing her, and sent the point of the weapon up behind her rib cage and into her heart.

The guard who had been leading them stood quietly, a blue-and-gold robot awaiting orders.

"Did she get off a warning?" Burke asked.

"No," said Felice. "Back inside that door with her, and then out of here. We've still got a way to go."

They began to trot down the corridor, turning to right and left and passing through ornamental gates and doorways until none but Khalid retained any orientation. The lighting grew dimmer. There were occasional heedless squads of guards, whom they ignored—and finally a truly massive pair of doors more than ten meters high, embossed with the heraldic male face and flanked by six grays in full blue-glass armor.

"This has to be it," Felice murmured. To their oblivious escort, she sent a coercive command: *You will unbar the entrance to this torc factory.*

I am unable to do this. No gray can do this.

"Shit!" hissed the little woman. "Stand back and we'll hope for the best!"

The six guards at the doorway pivoted right and left and marched away like jeweled mechanical dolls, followed by the gray who had led them in. Felice stood before the huge bronze valves with helmeted head thrown back and both fists clenched at her sides. The polished yellow metal along the juncture went greenish, blue, blotched purple—and then began to glow as the power of her psychokinetic faculty sent the molecules of metal to vibrating, going from solid to molten within thirty slow seconds.

The nonmetas watched it transfixed, their iron weapons ready. Heat from the melting bronze and its pungent smell beat at them, making them draw back from the small figure that now raised glittering blue arms and bade the ruined portal swing wide.

Behind the door was darkness. Felice stepped forward, ignoring the pool of still-liquid metal that smoked on the floor.

A burst of azure fire seemed to explode in the vast black beyond the open door. And then another appeared, strontium-red, and another of violet—blazing images in human form almost twice the height of small Felice. There were flashes of green light and rosy-gold and malevolent scarlet, all hovering in the dark. Crowds of them. Fifty or sixty or more, all massed in midair with swords and shields raised but visors open so that the saboteurs could see the contemptuous triumph in the exotic eyes of Nontusvel's Host.

"I am Imidol," thundered the voice of the blue leader. "Your death."

Felice sent a three-meter ball of flame rolling at him. "Iron!" she shrieked. "Iron! I'll bring down the roof!"

Four explosions rocked the corridor. The jewel-armored Tanu came flying out of the huge inner chamber like avenging angels. The invaders loosed their arrows. There were agonized shouts, falling meteors, lightning bolts, the deep rumble of falling masonry, a smell of ozone, dust, ordure, broiling meat.

Amerie, backed against the opposite wall of the corridor and blinded by fumes and metallic reek, shot her arrows wildly at tall glowing figures. Pulses of emotional energy smashed at her unshielded mind. There was a metapsychic conflict going on as well as a physical one, but she, lucky normal, could only perceive its overtones. When her quiver was empty she clutched her short-shafted javelin in both hands, consigned her soul to Jesus, and got ready to die.

A crash resounded as a wall came down—fortunately falling in toward the torc factory and not into the corridor. The meta-powered jewel-lamps along the walls had all gone out and the only light now came from the glowing armor of the Tanu, the bursts of astral flame, and occasional puddles of molten slag. The place was thick with smoke. Amerie fell to her knees and sought air along the floor. Things lay there—shattered blocks of limestone, metal lamp-fittings, pieces of jeweled and bronze armor, and softer dark masses that glistened and oozed.

Amerie crept slowly through smoky hell. Uwe Guldenzopf's bearded face shone momentarily in a lurid blaze. His head lay close to the wall. There was no body.

Sobbing, still carrying her iron-tipped spear, she followed the wall. There were more detonations behind her and a noise like an avalanche. A female voice uttered awful whooping shrieks like a warning siren. A great glowing rose-colored form went soaring over her head toward the center of the tumult—then another that shone green and white. The mental bombardment increased. She flattened herself on the floor, beyond praying. One of her feet was completely numb. The corridor was filled with a brain-blasting throb that made her teeth and even her eyes respond in a harmonic of sympathetic pain. The fumes and fire diminished, as suddenly the whole scene retreated to a distance. She floated above her body—poor thing—and saw that one leather boot was burned black, still smoking, and the sooty bronze of her cuirass backpiece had a deep indentation above the area of her kidneys. Her right arm was raw from elbow to wrist and there was a glimmer of white bone.

"What are you waiting for, angel?" she asked testily.

But she did not die. Taking up residence in the battered thing lying on the floor once again, she let her eyes open. She saw a short human figure in shining blue armor standing over her.

"Well, I'm glad to see *you*!" she shouted, joyous in relief. "Did we win after all?"

One jeweled gauntlet raised the blue visor. A man with a large nose and humorous eyes looked down at her, smiling with small, perfect teeth. She had never seen him before.

"You did not win," said Gomnol.

Amerie felt her damaged body rise from the floor, sustained by the Lord Coercer's psychokinetic power. He walked back into the inferno with her drifting after him like some grotesque balloon-doll. The smoke was pushed away before him and little flames extinguished themselves as he passed. A radiance streamed from Gomnol's face, illuminating the ruins. There were giant motionless forms clad in dulled glass lying here and there, and smaller shapes. She saw Vanda-Jo, mouth still wide in her last silent scream; Get and Hansi, mated in death as in life, were crushed beneath a stone lintel. Khalid Khan sat against a wall looking like a parody of a pietà, a Tanu warrior spitted by an iron spear cradled in his dead arms. "Salaam aleikoum, bhai," she whispered, and Khalid was lost in the dark.

"Only superficial damage to the factory itself," Gomnol remarked in a pleased tone. "It was stupid of me not to have foreseen this contingency. It's going to be a great bore having to express gratitude to the Host for having saved my bacon, especially since you people seem to have killed a number of them. Ah, well. No real harm done."

A sunburst of rainbow light now shone in the murk ahead. Amerie heard a deafening voice intone: "Welcome, Lord Coercer! Better late then never."

Gomnol came into the area where the bronze doors had been. The last rags of smoke and vapor dissipated. Dozens of brilliantly gleaming knights were standing about in negligent attitudes, leaning upon broadswords or glass lances. Chief Burke and Basil, burned and bloody, wrapped from ankle to neck in glass chain, hunched on their knees at the feet of a ruby-armored demigod. And Felice was there, flat on the floor, helmet off, eyes shut, face and neck colorless except for the soft gleaming of the golden torc and the shine of her hair.

Gomnol sent Amerie floating toward the other prisoners and lowered her softly. To the blue titan who had addressed him, he said, "Our thanks to you, Brother Imidol, to Lord Culluket, and to all the members of your Host. A timely intervention, indeed. I see that the torc factory suffered no serious harm."

"It is quite safe."

"Splendid!" A small golden container at Gomnol's waist popped open and a cigar emerged. The Lord Coercer bit off the end, ignited the tobacco with psychoenergy, and blew a fragrant plume toward the ruined ceiling with a fine air of savoir-vivre.

"My own sources of information had made me aware of a possible sabotage attempt tonight," he said. "Unfortunately, we were misled into believing that the invaders would try to penetrate from the rear of the keep. My forces were in ambush there. Lord Bormol and the Lord of Swords had kindly volunteered to watch with us. They should be here at any moment."

Gomnol swept the massed force of the Host with a confident glance. "If you permit, I'll relieve you of the tedium of the mopping-up operation. Redactors are on their way to succor our fallen brethren. Those who are not too badly injured will surely be out of the Skin in time for the Combat."

Imidol's glaring face was as carved from rock crystal. "We have lost fifteen of our sacred number to the iron. They rest in Tana's peace, beyond the help of the Skin."

Gomnol frowned, studying the tip of his cigar. "Terrible! Monstrous!" He gestured at Felice. "But I see you have avenged yourselves on the Lowlife woman."

"She is not dead," said ruby-clad Culluket. "I have her in mental bondage. Our revenge will be taken in due time."

"Aye," said all the others. "Revenge against *all* traitors."

Gomnol stood stark still. Smoke from the cigar curled playfully in the air currents entering through the breached ceiling.

"This woman showed a formidable psychoenergy," said Imidol.

"Much greater than any of us could have anticipated," Culluket added. "She killed three of our company by her mind's power alone."

"It was only with the greatest difficulty that we all combined and subdued her," came the concerted voices of the rose-gold twins, Kuhal and Fian.

"But not," Imidol concluded, "before she had perpetrated one *final* crime—you understand that this is what we shall say."

The Host blazed brighter and brighter. A certain insinuation of the Second Coercer took unmistakable form within the massed minds.

"Stop!" Gomnol cried. The mightiness of his metapsychic power roared out to prevent them, to fend them off while shielding his soul from the combined stroke of forty-seven exotic minds focused through the hatred and jealousy of Imidol, son of Nontusvel and the Thagdal, who would surely be named Lord Coercer by acclamation once the human usurper was dead.

"You cannot . . ." came the agonized gasp of Eusebio Gomez-Nolan, "You cannot . . . combine against a brother. Tana forbids it!"

No brother you but a HUMAN and a traitor and a conniver with the monster Aiken Drum we know it we are sure so die . . . die . . .

"No proof! No . . . proof!" Gomnol's body twisted, the spine bowed backward in tetany. He fell in his armor as heavily as if he had been turned to stone.

Imidol cried out, "We of the Host have our proof! Proof

for the others may come later. For now you will seem to die a hero—last victim of the monster Felice—until it suits us to reveal the full fabric of your treachery! Die, Manipulator. Die."

A last sound came from Gomnol's mouth. The contorted limbs relaxed. The face within the bizarre sapphire globe of his helmet went gray, then white. A skull with perfect teeth grinned at the Host of Nontusvel. The cigar on the floor beside it consumed itself in fragrant patience.

Culluket the Interrogator placed gray torcs around the necks of Amerie, Chief Burke, and Basil. And then the mountain climber, who of the three badly wounded prisoners retained the most strength, was forced to take an iron blade and sever Felice's golden torc.

"No gray for her?" Imidol inquired.

"Later," the Interrogator said. "It taints the pleasure if I make things too easy for myself."

16

HELPING HIMSELF TO EARLY BUGS, THE NIGHTJAR WHIPPED around the predawn sky. Behind the foothills of the Jura the sky was already pink. Mobs of herbivores down on the plateau were stirring. There was activity in Castle Gateway, too—but, maddeningly, no trace of any invisible human skulkers anywhere.

The nightjar made a futile low pass. It was a bloody nuisance that he hadn't been able to locate Claude and Madame yet. They *had* to be hiding underground. No doubt with Madame's illusion-spinning creativity reinforcing the natural psychic shield of the dense granite and hard-baked soil. But they'd have to come out to make the sortie against the time-gate. And when they did, he'd nab 'em.

As yet, none of the castle personnel knew that Aiken had arrived. He'd flown right up the valley of the Rhône, stashed the Spear in the upper branches of a big old plane tree down on the bottoms, and winged it on up here to do the search. Who noticed whether or not a nightjar flew around in the daytime? He'd hoped to spot their hideout, turn back into himself, and lead a castle search party right to the spot (tah-*dah*!).

But the damned old love-birds had foiled him. Ah, well.

It was really kind of cute, when you thought about it. Weird, but cute (I mean—of course they couldn't. Could they? A hundred and thirty-three?) It was kind of a shame they couldn't have been content to Darby-and-Joan it off in the Hercynian Forest somewhere with the munchkins instead of messing around in the games of the big boys.

But there it was. No helping 'em now. But he'd zap quick and merciful so at least they'd be spared getting dragged down to the Grand Combat and distilled alive in that glass thing the

Tanu fancied for traitors. Gomnol had tried to convince Aiken that the ceremonial death of the old folks was strategically necessary. (He *would* think so.) But to hell with him! Gumball's sadism would have to be content with the two old heads on pikes.

Aha! Activity again. The main gate of the castle was opening. Plenty of soldiers coming out, in addition to the white-garbed portal keepers. Just about dawn, too.

He banked, hunched his wings to stall, and plummeted down to keep an eye on things.

Above him, gray on gray-pink and outlined in mallow on the sunward side, was a strange cumulus cloud. Its bottom sagged in udderlike formations. One of the bags elongated like a vaporous Tanu breast as turbulence within the cloud increased. The bag stretched lower, became a dangling sleeve, then a miniature tornado with vortex winds spinning at several hundred kilometers an hour. It twisted and groped through the air, humming loudly. But morning winds were keening over the plateau and the people on the ground did not notice the new sound. They gathered formally about an area of bare rock.

The nightjar did not observe the little tornado either—not until it vacuumed him up, spun him off with a great tangential toss, and landed him in a nearly dry waterhole some three kilometers away... The stunned trickster regained consciousness a few minutes later and sat cursing the solicitous little hipparions that came to nuzzle his muddy face.

And then his mind flinched from a far, far obliteration of a familiar psychic pattern; and he knew about Gomnol. By the time he pulled himself together and flew back to the time-gate, it was too late there as well.

"Chéri, the time has come," she said.

He stretched, yawned, smoothed his silver hair back, then reached out and caught her by the wrists.

"Fou," she whispered, when she was able.

"We both are. We make a pair—like antique bookends."

She laughed softly, but that brought on the coughing which she had been at such pains to suppress. And there was blood. He said, "How long has this gone on? Angélique—why didn't you tell me?"

"I have taken Amerie's medicines. What else was there to do? You would have been made anxious for nothing. Say no more about it! It is time to go. And soon it will not matter."

"Goddammit, we'll get away!" he insisted, voice all raspy.

She kept back as he removed the top course of granite rocks from the wall, and enough from the center of the barricade so that the two of them would be able to squeeze out. An undermined acacia tree sagged down like a curtain in front of the opening. Beyond was the deep dry watercourse where she had first found shelter in the Pliocene Exile some four years earlier.

It had been Claude's idea to hide in this place, not even a kilometer away from the time-gate area. Under cover of her illusion of invisibility, they had come six days earlier during the hours that the moon was down and burrowed into the arroyo wall, enlarging the hole that had already been formed by the roots of the scraggly tree. They had walled themselves in with boulders from the streambed. From time to time during the nights, when her metapsychic senses told them that it was safe, they would venture out. The hole had been enlarged into a chamber nearly head-high, three meters long and two deep. It had suited them.

As they crept from the place for the last time, Claude heard her half-joking little murmur of farewell; "Adieu, petite grotte d'amour."

He said, "Two old spiders in their hole, you mean. But you didn't devour me, ma vieille! Still—it's just as well our time was short."

"It sufficed," said she, mind all asmile. "But now I think we have both reached the point of plus qu'il n'en faut . . . more than enough."

She handed him the amber with the message she had signed, then covered them both with her mental cloak. They scrambled up the steep wall. The surface of the savanna was fully four meters higher than the streambed. No one from the castle could have been able to farsense their hiding place, not unless there was a powerful metapsychic deliberately searching for them and alert for her illusion. They had only a short distance to walk and moments to wait before they fulfilled the duty they had set for themselves. And then, back to the hiding place, where they would hope for the best, should the alarm be raised . . .

Last night—or rather early on this morning—they had tried to find out what had happened to the saboteurs. Madame had sent her mind's ear straining over the long kilometers that separated them from the Balearic Peninsula . . . But the distant mumble refused to finetune. She could not hear and dared not call. And so the two of them had simply prayed for their friends, made love again, and slept. She muffled her coughing in the blankets. Her mental alarm woke them at the preselected time.

As evanescent as morning wind, they approached the crowd of people near the time-portal. In the east, the sky was now greenish yellow and the day would be hot. (But their cave had been cool, and they had had plenty of water and food and the soft decamole couches, and so the brief days had passed without effort. He had told her about Gen and she had told him about Théo, and then they had explored one another as only the wise old ones can, the lucky ones who are still strong and alive to danger—for the adrenals hold the great secret of old lovers, but only for those who are brave.)

They were almost at the gate. It was nearly time.

. . . And the world around them abruptly turned black.

Both of them cried out. The sound did not propagate. They seemed to stand yet on solid ground, but all around was darkness . . . until there came a pinprick of light that swelled to a sun, to a glowing face, to the face of Apollo.

"I am Nodonn."

Well, it's finished, Claude told himself. And now she'll die with the guilt.

A voice was speaking aloud. They knew that no one heard it but themselves. "I know who you are and what you would do. I have decided there must be an end to you and your meddling."

Angélique's thought was resigned: You Tanu have won this time. You may kill us, but others will come to shut this devil's gate.

"They will not," said Nodonn, "because I have chosen you." The flaming mask was enormous, its mind-light numbing. "My people have never understood the great harm you did to us in opening this way across the aeons. They would brook no interference with it. Not even *I* dared to close the time-gate by force. But now there is another way. You will do my will and at the same time achieve those goals you have set for yourselves. The goals you have both sought ever since coming to this Exile. I presume you understand."

Claude replied: We understand, all right.

"My people will believe that you two alone are responsible for the closure. The supposed calamity will be more acceptable to them when they learn that the insurgent leader and the man who bombarded Finiah have been removed from the Many-Colored Land . . . But you know that I cannot coerce you into this final deed. The torced guardians at the gate would detect my intervention. And so you will have to act freely—and visibly."

She said: Yes. It will be the ultimate proof to those at the other end of the gate.

Claude said: And I'm glad I blasted your damned slave-city! Maybe you think closing this time-gate will make you Tanu safe from any more human uprisings. You're in for a disappointment! Things are never going to be the same here again.

The sun-bright face darkened. Nodonn's voice rolled in their minds. "Go back where you came from, accursed!"

Claude said: You fool. We came from here.

And then their human ears heard birdsong again. The true solar disk was breaking over the rim of the highland beyond the Rhône. Not a stone's throw away, a shimmering block hung in the air just above the square of stones where the portal guardians and soldiers waited.

Their illusion of invisibility still intact, the two old people began to run over the dry sod. Four human time-travelers materialized within the tau-field and were assisted to alight.

Angélique stumbled. Claude seized her hand, shoving aside soldiers and bewildered timefarers.

"Jump for it before it recycles!"

One of the armed guards gave a shout and rushed forward, waving his bronze sword. Fully visible, the old man and woman stood side by side in midair, hands linked. The temporal field reversed itself and they disappeared.

In the sky above, a nightjar shrilled its furious *kutuk-kutuk-kutuk* and flew away.

Only one of the auberge clients whose trip had been so unexpectedly aborted was not suffering hysterics. Still holding his plankton net and sack of specimen bottles, he answered Counselor Mishima's questions warily.

"They were just standing there, I tell you. We only saw them for a split second when those mirrors in the machine's walls cut off. And then they were skeletons! And then dust . . . I really must demand an explanation, Counselor. The brochure states most emphatically that there is no hazard in the journey through time—"

One of the other counselors, kneeling in front of the gazebo, broke in. "Alan, come and look at this."

Mishima said, "Please go upstairs and wait with the others, Dr. Billings. I'll be with you in just a moment."

When the man had gone the two counselors bent over the pile of ashy powder. There was a peculiar gold ornament half-buried in it, a kind of barbarian necklet. When Mishima lifted it, glittering flakes—all that remained of the internal components—sifted from small openings and mingled with the dust.

"And here . . . oh, God." The other counselor had discovered the two flat pieces of amber. The writing was clearly visible within. "We—we'd better rush these things up to the director, Alan."

Mishima sighed. "Yes. And tell that Billings chap and the others that they needn't wait after all."

The twin rings carved from jet were not discovered until later, when the gazebo's dust was reverently swept up to be stored—until the investigatory panel's work should be finished—in a durofilm sack in the auberge director's safe.

Six million years away, in the room without doors, Elizabeth and Brede wept. Foreknowledge, as Elizabeth had suspected all along, had only made it worse.

THE END OF PART TWO

PART III
THE
GRAND COMBAT

1

BY THE TIME OF THE GALACTIC MILIEU THE MOUNTAIN WAS worn away to a remnant. It rose from the Mediterranean as the island of Menorca, easternmost of the archipelago that had been called the Hesperides. Monte del Toro, not 400 meters above the sea, marked its greatest eminence on eroded Elder Earth. Most of its ancient labyrinth of caves had by then been opened to the sun by wearing elements or, in the case of deeper caverns, drowned by the encroaching sea.

But six million years in the past, the mountain had another aspect. When exotic newcomers to the Balearic Peninsula first saw its shadowed mass with the twin crags flanking a summit meadow (where Bryan and Mercy would lie), they named it the Mount of Lugonn and Sharn—after the Tanu and Firvulag champions who had fought their ritual battle at the Ship's Grave. Later, the mountain was simply called the Mount of Heroes. By a rare express command of Brede, it was made the property of the Guild of Redactors. Their college of healing and mind-exploration was built on the southeastern slope overlooking Muriah and the White Silver Plain. After the Times of Unrest and the banishment of Minanonn, the very caves within the mountain were annexed—at first to serve as secure crypts for the interment of the Great Ones, and latterly for far less sacred purposes.

Felice had vowed to herself that she would never cry aloud.

Her mind's voice might rage and the Interrogator laugh; but somehow, through all the days, she remained steadfast and never uttered a sound through the jaws wedged open. She had willed this one thing: paralysis of her vocal cords; and they of all her betraying flesh had obeyed.

271

Culluket had gone slowly, learning her, utilizing both redaction and coercive power, now strumming like an artist, now thumping with overwhelming crude malice. And if the sensory overload sent her into fugue, he coaxed her back with tweaks at the core of the brainstem to restore full-alert wakefulness when it was time for the next refinement to be demonstrated.

Mental humiliation of her, he had discovered to his surprise, was not nearly so effective as the purely physical assaults upon her feminine dignity. But she was still a child, of course. A perverted child. She had yielded up the required information rather quickly (the Spear of Lugonn in the possession of Aiken Drum, the Ship's Grave and its trove of flying machines, the schemes for producing iron weapons, the fortified villages abuilding in the north); and the data were sent to Nodonn so that action could be taken following the Grand Combat.

That had satisfied the others of the Host, leaving Culluket free to satisfy himself.

To peel open her mind slowly, like a fruit, so that he could observe and then savor all of the strange humors of the alien murderess. Her secret horrors, the massive psychic wound from the loss of her golden torc (and yet that not as devastating as one might have expected), the monstrous metapsychic faculties for coercion, psychokinesis, creativity, farsensing, now walled up and latent like ravening beasts in squeeze-traps, never to be freed again.

Taste the rage! Watch the agony deepen at the forced sharing.

Flay, open to reveal the unsatisfied needs, the infant deprivation short-circuiting the pleasure and the violence pathways deep within the cerebellum. Delicious possibilities there! Realize them. Replay from multiple vantage points the filth, until even she, wretched Lowlife, understands her own vileness. Inhumanity proven by a nonhuman male, exquisitely skilled.

He worked her, shock following shock, pain piled upon pain, her body's degradation translated into maceration of ego; her hatred and fear of other beings clarified as hatred and fear of her self.

Leave her bereft of everything she has ever valued, waiting for dissolution. (Her body had to be unharmed, of course; but he would fulfill his promise to the Battlemaster if he delivered her able to fight in the Combat as a petit-mal automaton.)

But she would not go mad.

Piqued, he rummaged in the wreckage, trying to discover

the explanation. He almost missed it. But there—a minute spark barricaded within a stubborn shell of screening that resisted all his attempts at puncture. Diminished and encapsulated, the being that was Felice continued to abide.

If only he could make her speak, cry out! That was the way, the key. He knew it! One voluntary sound and the last defense would fall.

But she would not. After days had passed and the Combat was almost upon them, he dared go no further for fear of extinguishing life, along with that stubborn remnant of shielded identity.

"Keep it, then," he said, "for what good it will do you."

And after pleasuring himself with her one final time, he clamped the gray torc of slavery around her neck, released her jaws, and had the attendants take her away to a cell in the deepest of the catacombs.

. . . Steinie?

Lovelove you're awake. "Does it still hurt, Sue?"

He knelt on the damp stone floor next to the niche with its straw-stuffed mattress and took her by the hand. There was just enough light to see her, cast by the single Tanu jewel-lamp set like a sad star in the high ceiling of the cell, surrounded by stalactites.

"There's only a leftover ache now. I'll be all right. Lord Dionket said there was no permanent damage. We'll be able to have others later on."

But not him Sukey not my first unbornson. "It *must* have been my fault. We shouldn't have . . . after we were sure you were pregnant." Stupidstupidselfishprickbabykiller!

"No!" She struggled up, sitting on the edge of the stone bed and taking his face to kiss. "Never think it was your fault. I'm certain it wasn't." (And *will* the certainty into his mind through the silver torc still worn; but hide the reality. O never let him find that out.) "You must stop thinking about it now, love. Get ready for the escape! The Combat starts tomorrow. I'm sure that Aiken has waited until the last minute so that the Tanu won't bother to come after us."

Stein growled deep in his chest. He shook his head, like a bear warding off attacking bees. Alarmed, Sukey perceived the random neural firing within his brain that signaled the onset of a spasm induced by his maladaptation to the gray torc.

"Damn Aiken Drum," Stein groaned. "He said . . . he promised... but first you, now me... *Christ*, Sukey, my skull's exploding—"

She held his head to her breast and plunged within his mind, as she had at ever-shorter intervals during their time in Muriah. Once again, she was successful in stopping the threatened conflagration. But if the torc stayed on him much longer, he would not survive.

"There, Steinie. There, love. I've got you. I've fixed it."

Water dripped from the ceiling of their prison cell—regular, musical. The wild beating of Stein's heart slowed and his rough exhalations eased. He lifted his head to meet his wife's eyes.

"You're sure that it wasn't my fault?"

"Believe me. It wasn't. Sometimes these things just happen."

Still kneeling beside her, he sank back to rest on his heels, great helpless hands turned palms up, the image of a shattered giant. But Sukey was not deceived. She could see into his mind.

If he could not blame himself, he would look elsewhere.

Aiken Drum hoisted the heavy Spear of Lugonn easily, menacing the ornate chandelier in Mayvar's audience chamber in the Hall of Farsensors. The glassy lance shone golden, now that the last of the disguising blue lacquer had been cleaned from it. The powerpack was fully charged.

"Take *that* for your yoni, witch!" he chortled, striking a wicked pose.

Mayvar's smile was indulgent. "Tomorrow, my Shining One. Tomorrow it all begins. But there will be five days of it, remember. And you can use the Spear only at the very end, after midnight on the fifth day when the Heroic Encounters take place, and even then only if Nodonn decides to use the Sword. *And* if you survive to meet the Battlemaster at all—"

"If? If?" he squealed in mock fury. "You clapped-out old seeress! Are you going to renege on your own Making? Do I have to prove myself to you again?"

He cast down the photonic weapon with a ringing clang and launched himself, suddenly naked as a fish, at the scarecrow figure lounging on the amethyst throne. There was no one else in the chamber and the seat of power was quite large enough for two.

"Enough... enough!" she wheezed, laughing until tears

trickled through the furrows of her cheeks. "At least let me live to share the triumph and give you your name!"

He let her go, still feigning vexation at her apparent lack of confidence. Perched on purple velvet cushions with his legs crossed, he stuck two fingers under his golden torc and pulled. The metal stretched like an elastic band, then sagged as limp as half-pulled taffy. He began to fling the gold about, spinning it thinner and thinner, catching loops of it on the toes of each bare foot and weaving cat's cradles with the flexible filament that had been a golden torc.

"So doubt me, Hag! And I'll give back this silly gift of yours and go my own way. Who needs you? I've got my quiverful of powers all honed and ready at last and I'm a match for any of 'em now! Bring on the Firvulag spooks! Bring on Thagdal and Nodonn!"

"If you would be king, you must play by their rules," she said flatly. "If they suspect that you are fully operant without the torc they may yet combine against you. And strong as you have become, my Shining One, the massed minds of the battle-company could kill you, given the incentive."

"The fighters are crazy about me. And the ladies think I'm cute!"

"But the Host spreads rumors. They say you co-conspired with Gomnol and Felice's saboteurs. They say that your inept handling led to the closing of the time-gate. Far more ominous, they say that you would mate with the operant woman Elizabeth and engender a race of fully operant humans here in the Many-Colored Land."

"Me and the Ice Lady? What a detumefying thought!"

His smirk was as jaunty as ever, but the golden skein melted back into a circle, which he replaced about his neck. He began to put his suit of many pockets back on. "But you may have a point at that. A good thing Elizabeth is about ready to pack it in and fly. I can't understand why she's hung around this long. Not unless she really does give a damn about us after all."

"Don't think of her." The crone patted his head. "Don't think of anything but the Combat. Your participation in the preliminaries should present no special hazard. And no one may challenge you in the manifestation of powers if I nominate you Second Farsensor. But once the High Mêlée begins you will need to muster all the bravery and cleverness and meta-psychic power at your command. It's not enough for you simply to survive the fighting. You must show yourself an inspired leader and a destroyer of the Foe. Then, as the Combat draws to its climax, contingents from all the guilds may rally to follow *your* banner rather than that of Nodonn! Thus you will be seen as a valid kingly aspirant in the Heroic Encounters at the end."

Aiken said in a wistful little voice, "You *sure* I can't use iron?"

Mayvar cackled. "Oh, you jester . . . on the day when you become King of the Many-Colored Land you may do as you please. But never dream of using the blood-metal in this Combat. It would be said that you were allied to the Lowlives in the north. Why do you think I cautioned secrecy when I gave you the weapon to use against Delbaeth?"

Aiken laced his fingers behind his head and rocked back and forth, contemplating limitless vistas.

"When I'm king we'll change all kinds of rules. With a cohort of gold-torc humans armed with iron, we'll mop up the human rebels and take care of the Firvulag, too. But we won't slaughter 'em—hell, no! Now that the time-gate's closed, I'll have to scrounge up subjects anywhere I can. And look at all of the neat things the gnomies make! Fancy jewelry and chaliko tack and booze that's just stone faraway! Nope—I'll pacify the Little Folks by threatening 'em with the ultimate weapon and we'll have one big happy kingdom under Good King—"

He stopped rocking. His black eyes widened and his mouth dropped in stunned surprise. "Oh, *damn*," he whispered. "Mayvar—can you hear it? It's mostly on the intimate human mode but enough slops over into the gray band for you to pick up if you spread it out and listen sharp. You grab? It's Stein."

"Vengeance," Mayvar said. "He blames you. Incredible!"

The golliwog youth sat stiffly on the edge of the amethyst throne, farsensing for all he was worth. "Still no firm conclusion. But mulling it over, the stupid ox . . . How I promised to keep Sukey safe. But she wasn't kept safe. Ergo, my fault! Can you beat that for idiot logic? Sure as shit, that little broad is unconsciously leaking some part of the truth to him. Women! It'd be enough if she just hinted the miscarriage wasn't spontaneous. Looks to me like there's only one thought moving Stein—blame it on somebody besides himself."

Mayvar said, "You did promise no harm would come to Sukey. The word of a gold-torc nobleman and royal aspirant—"

"What about your precious rules?" he exploded. "Play by

the rules, you said! Are you tellin' me now I should have gone against the King *and* Queen just to spare Sukey a little hough-magandy that shouldn't have done her or the kid any harm? If Stein wasn't such a thick-headed—"

Mayvar had cocked her head, still farsensing. "Hear what his mind cries out! This is no joke, Aiken Drum."

His tirade against her forgotten, Aiken focused again. The farspoken maunderings of the half-crazed Viking were mostly being broadcast through his torc on the uniquely human spectrum, and they were so chaotic that even human listeners would have been unlikely to expend the effort needed to decipher them. But if a person were patient and lifted aside the ramblings and mutters and the mixed-up business about Sukey—there was something else.

The saboteurs coming to invade the torc factory, thinking they would receive Aiken's help with the Spear. Aiken's cosy arrangement with Gomnol.

"Oh, Christ," breathed the trickster. "His mind-block's going. And with Gomnol dead, my puny redact isn't going to be able to nail the lid back down tight enough."

"You must act at once. If Stein's thoughts are brought to the attention of the Host, they will use him to prove you reprobate and unworthy of aspiring to the kingship. They will serve you as they did Gomnol."

"God... I'll have to get both Stein and Sukey out of here tonight—not wait till after I'm king, like I planned."

"It is late for that course of action." She showed him what the safest course would be, at the same time trembling at her test of him.

"I couldn't," he told her. "Not Stein and Sukey!"

"Alive, they will always be a threat to your sovereignty."

"No! There's gotta be another way!"

"You feel an obligation to them? Your honor? Your half-jesting promise? Your pride?"

"Not them! Anybody else I'll zap to charcoal, but not them." Not the crazy dumb lovers see how they suffer because of one another shrunk/enlarged by the giving but what would it be like? Poor doomed damned saps wondered at but denied by the safe avoider as I avoid/deny you dying womanbodymind.

He repeated, "Not them."

Mayvar rose from the throne and swayed there hooded, looking like the calyx of some huge, unopened violet flower. He knew but could not see her fresh tears. "Blessed be my

Making. I knew that you were not as Gomnol . . . and there is another way."

He bounded up and grabbed her by the arms. "What?"

"Remain here and make ready for tomorrow. Trust me. I will see that your friends are sent out of Muriah tonight."

2

ON THIS COMBAT EVE, EVERY TRUE MEMBER OF THE ANCIENT battle-company had thoughts only for the coming clash of Foes, the joint celebration of life and death that they believed was their reason for continuing existence in the Many-Colored Land. But there were a few who had rejected the ancient traditions, and these came together—even one who had not set foot in the capital city for five hundred years—to consider whether or not this year's Grand Combat might be the great turning point foreseen by Brede.

To their exasperation, the Shipspouse herself would not attend the meeting, would not confirm or deny the possibility. "The Combat itself will manifest the Goddess's Will," she had told Dionket, "and then you will know what you must do." But the Lord Healer had not been satisfied with that. What did a mystic know of power struggles? Her vision was so disconcertingly *long*.

And so he had summoned the leaders among the antibattle faction, even the pair long banished, to a secret chamber deep within the Mount of Heroes; and when Katlinel dared to bring in the two outsiders, the extraordinariness of the times excused it and even lent it a mad kind of suitability.

DIONKET LORD HEALER: Greetings to you all, fellow traitors and peacelovers, and especially to our Psychokinetic Brother Minanonn Heretic, and our Coercive Brother Leyr, so long absent from our cabals, and our distinguished Foeman—
SUGOLL: Ally.
DIONKET: —now so fortuitously allied, the Lord Sugoll, ruler of Meadow Mountain, and greatest of those called How-

279

lers . . . Sisters and Brothers, we are indeed poised on the brink. Say, Mayvar.

MAYVAR KINGMAKER: Aiken Drum is ready. The human youth is fully operant, possessed of all faculties save redaction in a truly remarkable degree. I believe no single Tanu or Firvulag champion will withstand him. Failing catastrophe or a mass attack by the entire battle-company—which cannot happen unless he is attainted unworthy according to our ancient code—he will become king five days hence after defeating both the Thagdal and Nodonn at the culmination of the Grand Combat.

MINANONN THE HERETIC: A human . . . barely more than a child. A trickster, if rumor does not lie! *This* is your pivotal figure?

MAYVAR: I have tested him in all the ways. He is flawed— and who among us is not?—but he will be worthy.

ALBERONN MINDEATER: Kid's got good stuff. Nerve. Heart.

BUNONE WARTEACHER: Jisum! Both kinds.

MAYVAR: He can be cruel, but he is capable of love all unrealizing. I have been true to my Making.

LEYR THE BANISHED: But—a little human mountebank?

KATLINEL THE DARKEYED: You loved a human once yourself, Father. And our races are merged, for better or for worse.

MAYVAR: Aiken Drum will engender operants. Not so many as Elizabeth might with her fuller penetrance, but enough.

GREG-DONNET GENETICS MASTER: Have no fear, kinfolk! Aiken's genetic assay is *colossal*! I mean—compare him to Nodonn, for instance. The Battlemaster is gorgeous, but we all know how few pureblood offspring he's sired. And his hybrids haven't a High Table candidate or even a first-class power in the lot.

BLEYN BATTLE-CHAMPION: Who wants to be the one to remind Nodonn of his deficiencies?

(Rueful laughter.)

LEYR: Well, you've seen this boy fight and I haven't. But it's hard to swallow the notion that *any* human could stand up to Nodonn, much less this stripling with a silly name.

MAYVAR: He will receive another name, according to our custom, after he survives the High Mêlée.

MINANONN: Look here. Granted this Aiken Drum licks Nodonn in the Encounter—and I'm not nearly so sanguine as you seem to be on that point, Kingmaker—both the post of Lord Psychokinetic and the governorship of Goriah will fall vacant when the boy assumes the throne.

DIONKET: Exactly. And now that Sebi-Gomnol is dead, the Coercer Guild must also seek a new leader.

LEYR: Almighty Tana! Is *that* why you got Minnie and me back here?

KATLINEL: Father—surely you can best Imidol in the manifestation of powers. His coercive will is much weaker than Gomnol's was.

LEYR: Ye-es, but don't underestimate the enemy, Katy-girl. Imidol won't settle for a simple manifestation the way someone like Aluteyn would. He'll want a battle-trial—minds *and* weapons—during the Mêlée.

DIONKET: This is true. And you are much older than Imidol, Coercive Brother, and there is considerable risk. But we know your mind. If you were victorious and reascended to the High Table you would play a moderating role . . . no matter who became High King.

LEYR: Dammit—Minnie's the peaceloving heretic, not me!

ALBERONN: But you'd never favor the extermination of humanity—nor of us hybrids—as does the Host of Nontusvel.

LEYR: Of course not—!

KATLINEL: And much as you love Combat between equals, Father, you have scant heart for the senseless slaughter of the Hunt, or the perversion of the Low Mêlée that has come about since the advent of torced human fighters, or the unsporting tactics used against the Foe in the High Mêlée itself.

LEYR: Bad business, those gray shock troops and the whole matter of mounting our fighters on chalikos. Small wonder the Foe sulks and makes Lowlife alliances.

DIONKET: The Host must not be allowed to dominate the High Table! We appeal to you, Leyr. And to you also, Minanonn.

MAYVAR: We stand at a crossroads, Brothers and Sisters. We may choose our turning or have it forced upon us.

LEYR: Very well. Perhaps I'm getting soft-headed in my old age . . . but I'll challenge that young brawler Imidol.

MAYVAR: And you, Minanonn?

MINANONN: You see me allied to your cause in the event of Nodonn's defeat, contending against Kuhal Earthshaker for the leadership of the psychokinetics.

MAYVAR: You have the power. You were Battlemaster once.

MINANONN: Five hundred years gone, before my enlightenment. And you know me little, Kingmaker, if you think that I would sacrifice my principles now to to become a killer once more.

DIONKET: For an end to killing!

MINANONN: Not even for that.

MAYVAR: If the Guild presidency might be decided in a peaceful manifestation of powers and not in battle-trial?

MINANONN: That will never happen under the Thagdal's regime.

MAYVAR: But if our faction forces a change of the rules under a new king?

MINANNON: Then I would willingly aspire. However, until the dawn of that unlikely new day, I must take leave of you, Sisters and Brothers. I fly back to my place of banishment in the wilderness. Farewell.

(He goes.)

BUNONE: Until we meet again, dear Brother Heretic! When our faction controls the Many-Colored Land and I forgo my war-teaching for fancy embroidery!

ALBERONN: That you may, and pink and blue to boot, Lady, if you undertake further Quests with Aiken Drum.

BUNONE: Shame on you, Creative Brother, for not considering the feelings of the Kingmaker.

MAYVAR: I have no illusions about the sexual faithfulness of my human protégé. I see him as he is.

DIONKET: Tana help us if you do not.

LEYR: Yes—how about that, Kingmaker? What happens if this trickster of yours plays his own game once we've put him on the throne?

BLEYN: We can all move into Minannon's cave in the Catalan Wilderness.

MAYVAR: He *is* worthy! I am certain of it! Under him, we will be able to inaugurate a new era. The only questionable factor was the influence of Gomnol—and he is dead. With the time-gate closed, we will push gradually for the emancipation of the grays, an end to involuntary human concubinage, abolition of the Hunt, and peace between Tanu and Firvulag at last. What was impossible under the Thagdal or Nodonn is not only feasible but certain if Aiken Drum is King of the Many-Colored Land.

SUGOLL: Let us speak of others who also share this land.

GREG-DONNET: Oh, listen! This is marvelous—and *so logical*, from a eugenic standpoint! Positively elegant! I couldn't contain my enthusiasm when Katy came to me. Of course, she and Sugoll will be only a token of what might follow as the old racial prejudices are broken down. But later— the results will be very similar to the injection of Aiken's genes insofar as ultimate improvement of the metapsychic phenotype—

LEYR: What the *hell* is this little capon blithering about?

KATLINEL: Sugoll and I, Father. The merging of all three gene pools.

LEYR: Katy?! Do you mean to tell me that you and this—this Firvulag—

KATLINEL: Howler.

SUGOLL: My body is, of course, an illusion. Like all of my subjects, I am a mutant. Katy accepts me as I am. But let there be no masking between us, either, father-in-law elect. Look.

LEYR: (!) Compassionate Tana.

GREG-DONNET: Their children will be beautiful. Their minds, at any rate! And I'm off with them to the North Country this very night to look into the teratogenic thing and see if it might not respond to a little fiddling. Anyhow—monster is as monster does.

LEYR: Katy...oh, Katy.

DIONKET (embracing her): Blessings, Creative Daughter. And upon you, Lord of the Howlers. You take with you the flower of our High Table. Be with her a bridge.

SUGOLL: Threefold, we may hope. Farewell.

(He goes, with Katlinel and Greg-Donnet.)

BUNONE: Cheer up, Leyr. At least they'll be out of this mess. You can work off your steam on Imidol. I rather like that Sugoll fellow myself. A lot of style for a Firvulag...

MARY-DEDRA: Then we only wait? Wait for Aiken Drum to conquer?

ALBERONN: Some of us take the active role in his cohort during the High Mêlée. There are numerous volunteers, admirers of his prowess, especially among the hybrids. But Aiken Drum will require captains following his banner as well. Bleyn and I have offered ourselves.

BUNONE: And I.

LEYR: Oh, hell. Why not? I'll throw in with him, now that the world's turned upside down...But there's one tradition they haven't dared to meddle with: warrior's privilege! How about it, fighters? A little practical preparation for the Grand Combat, hey?

ALBERONNE + BLEYN + BUNONE: Warrior's privilege! No

noncombatants allowed! Roll out the barrels!
(They go.)

DIONKET: The rest of us will have other work.

CREYN: And may I remind you, Lord Healer, that some of the work awaits to be accomplished yet this night.

MAYVAR: You have secured it, Mary-Dedra?

DEDRA: It is here, Lady Kingmaker, in this golden box.

MAYVAR: As a human, Dedra may touch it without peril. Open and show us, child.

DIONKET + CREYN: Ah.

DEDRA: It was where Elizabeth farsensed it, hidden beneath a granite sett in an obscure corner of the Coercer House base-court. Lord Gomnol must have put it there himself long ago against—some contingency. No one saw me remove it.

CREYN: And it is certain, Lord Healer, that this tool of the blood-metal may safely remove torcs from humans?

DIONKET: I have it from Elizabeth, who learned it from Madame Guderian herself. Both silvers and grays have been liberated by means of iron in the north. As to the safety of the operation . . . that depends upon the individual's reaction to the withdrawal. We will give the tool to Sukey and hope that her redactive powers are sufficient. When the fugitives are safely away and she is certain that she need not coerce Stein for his own good, she will cut his torc, removing him from Tanu influence and mind-hearing permanently.

MAYVAR: But we will give *her* another option, poor little one. It is the wish of our future king.

DIONKET: I see. Gold, instead of the silver she now wears. She would retain her metapsychic powers and still be free, while her mate remains a bareneck. And she must make the choice . . . This putative Crown Prince of ours is a fiend!

MAYVAR: It is late. Long past midnight. We must act.

CREYN: I will fetch them. They will trust me—even Stein.

DIONKET: Culluket is away, engaged in a premature warrior clebration with the Host. It will be safe. And Elizabeth is already waiting on the mountaintop.

DEDRA: *Elizabeth?*

MAYVAR: We have had to change the plan for the liberation of Stein and his wife. A boat could be too easily intercepted. And Elizabeth's hot-air balloon carries three.

The hellad drawing the calèche let out a whicker of surprise when it came to the dark summit and saw the huge thing moored there, swaying in a gentle west wind.

"Creyn?" Elizabeth was standing next to the gondola. Her red jumpsuit, like the scarlet balloon, was black in the light of the waxing moon.

"Make Stein walk, Elizabeth. I'll help Sukey."

"I'm all right," Sukey insisted, climbing down from the carriage. "I just thought it would be safer if Steinie were out..."

"I have him," Elizabeth said. "The balloon is ready. Thank God you're a small person, Sukey. This will be crowded, but we'll be all right if we keep Stein sedated while we're in the air."

"Elizabeth—" Creyn's voice broke.

"Upsy daisy, Stein. Now you, Sukey. No—don't touch that cable. It opens the maneuvering vent, dumps hot air that we need to rise."

The tall exotic was still standing by the carriage. The hellad drooped in the traces. "Elizabeth!"

"Yes, Creyn?" She came toward him, thinking he wished to say goodbye.

"Brede . . . charged me to explain that . . . *this* was not foreseen by her. Nor planned by the rest of us. Believe me! The cell next to Stein and Sukey . . . I could not help but perceive how little sanity was left to her, for all her uninjured body, and how the Combat would surely snuff it out whether or not she survived physically. And remembering that she had been your friend . . . I consulted Brede. She said that the choice must be your own."

He lifted a blanket. Curled up on the floor of the carriage, frail and vulnerable as a sleeping child, lay Felice.

He said, "You could force-feed the balloon piloting data to Sukey . . . a few minutes' work for a Grand Master. The hazard for them would be very small—"

Brede!!!
I hear Elizabeth.
You did this!
It is as Creyn avers. I did not not foresee it, did not plan it. It is the work of the Goddess. Of God.
No. No! Oh—*damn* you! All of you!

The balloon rose, wafting unseen as the westerly breeze took it over the lights of Muriah. As it gained altitude above the Great Lagoon it met a wind-shear. The semidirigible envelope shuddered, caught momentarily in opposing currents. Continuing ascent injected it fully into the other airstream.

It changed direction away from Corsica-Sardinia and sailed southwest, toward the Isthmus of Gibraltar.

3

THEY WAITED FOR DAWN.

Tanu and Firvulag and torced humanity gathered in splendid array on the Plain, which was pearl-colored now because of the traditional Mist of Duat that the creators of both battle-companies had conjured as a sky-canopy. A low droning sound, part growl and part minor chord, swelled on the still air. The commonalty of the Firvulag, standing on the sidelines all mingled with the Tanu and human non-combatants, were voicing their ancient overture to the Combat.

Firvulag warriors in obsidian armor all decked with gold and jewels stood in a vast mob some 20,000 strong, dwarfs and giants and middle-sized stalwarts all mixed together, some bearing the ghastly effigy standards, some clutching naked weapons. Their great battle-captains were massed nearest to the east-facing stage where the royalty of both races had assembled. On the opposite side of the marble platform waited the Tanu army. Disdainful of the informality of their shadow-brethren, they were ranged in elegant ranks according to their guilds: the violet and gold farsensors, the blue coercers, the ruby and silver combatant redactors, creators amored in beryl tints, and glowing rose-gold psychokinetics. Up in the front rank of the Farsensor Battalion, an impudent little human posed among towering jeweled champions. His armor of gold-lustre glass was adorned with amethysts and canary diamonds, and his cloak glittered uniquely black with a violet edge. He bore high his banner with its strange device.

The light in the east brightened behind thick mist. The chain of silence rang.

Eadone Sciencemaster came forward from the group of Most Exaltered Personages and raised some small instrument to her

287

eyes. Thagdal and Yeochee stood immediately behind the Dean of Guilds, the Tanu monarch attired in blue-white diamond armor, the Firvulag wearing sharply faceted black.

"The First Day begins," Eadone declared, bowing to the Kings and stepping aside.

Thagdal gestured. Nodonn Battlemaster came to salute the two sovereigns, trailed by gigantic Sharn-Mes the Young Champion—who as representative of the losers in last year's Combat had only a subsidiary role to play in this opening ceremony. Nodonn carried a glass weapon similar to the big two-handed swords used by both exotic races; but this Sword had a great flaring basket-hilt and a thin cable leading from its pommel to a box worn at the Battlemaster's waist.

Glowing like an aurora, Nodonn formally offered the Sword to Thagdal. The King declined it with equal solemnity, saying, "Be thou our deputy. Open the sky to this Grand Combat."

Nodonn turned, facing east and the veiled sun. He lifted the photon weapon. A brilliant emerald beam stabbed the low-hanging cloud deck, piercing the gray and allowing a widening shaft of solar radiance to spotlight its summoner, the two Kings and the Firvulag general standing behind him, and the rest of the Most Exalted Personages on the platform. Warriors and noncombatants together sang the Song, the soaring Tanu chorus counterpointed by the deeper, more sonorous voices of the Firvulag. The break in the clouds expanded, just as it always had for long thousands of years on the foggy planet Duat, where the ancient rivals had been accustomed to use both mental force and laser beams to insure a sunny sky for their annual ritual war.

The Song ended. The vault of the Pliocene heavens glowed blue above the White Silver Plain. Fighters and spectators gave a mighty cheer, and the First Day of the Grand Combat began.

Felice awoke to stillness. Physical. Mental. Emotional.

She was half-sitting on the bottom of some cramped container, crushed up against the sleeping form of a disheveled young gold-torc woman she had never seen before. Standing like some herculean statue almost on top of her, but looking out and away, with mind a singing blank, was a man both gigantic and familiar.

But he was not the hated Beloved not him.

Human-hairy legs rising to a grubby green tunic. A waist cinched by an amber-studded belt. Great hunched shoulders.

Hands resting on the padded top rail of the box. Motionless homely blond head.

Above, the blazing gridiron within the mouth of a vibrant scarlet gut. A blue sky.

What? Some new amusement of the tormentor? But *his* mind was no longer with her. He was gone and she remained. The strength had been given to her and she remained.

The gridiron thing was of a peculiar complex design, glowing with such heat that the air for meters around it was all ashimmer. It was mounted at the tip of a decamole frame that was attached to the decamole container that imprisoned the three of them. There were silvery cables depending from a wide ring around the red maw's opening, and these were also attached to their open-topped cell. Beside her, projecting from the wall of the box, was a fat shelf. She raised herself painfully and saw a digital instrument cluster:

ALT—2104.3; TER CL—2596.1; VAR— + .19; ENV—77[green]; AMB AT—17.5; PO FX—37:39N, 00:33E; GD SP—66.2; HDG— 231; F RES—2299.64HR; ZT—07:34:15

She and Stein and the woman were in Elizabeth's balloon. Free.

Felice pulled herself upright and stood beside the rigid man. There was absolutely no sensation of movement through the air, no wind. The heat generator above their heads was silent; but if she strained her ears she could hear minute cracklings as hot air swirled within the semidirigible envelope, and a tiny zip when a high venting panel gaped momentarily and then closed.

Free. And her mind . . .

Fingertips touched the cold gray circlet around her neck. She smiled. Unfastening the knob-catch, she removed the dead torc, held it over the rail of the gondola, let it fall into the deep basin of the Empty Sea.

Now grow, small cherished thing.

So fragile, so deceivingly meager, the kernel of her identity within the brain-vault opened. Psychoenergies gushed forth in giddy torrents. The strictures, the wounds, the debris from the torturer's work that seemed to presage madness (so Creyn the redactor had believed) were swept away. A fantastic new edifice that was the unwitting legacy of the Beloved reared in glory. It expanded, it filled, it recovered and restored and reorganized as it grew. In seconds only, the mental seedling burgeoned into a mature and executive psycho-organism. She was whole. She was operant. And he had done it! She was coercive, psychokinetic, creative, farsensing—all thanks to him. Willing destruction, he had engendered life. Crushing her to near-nothingness, he had forced her into Union (and poor Amerie had been right about that much, at least).

She abode in midair and delight. Gratitude warmed her. She loved him more than ever and thought about how to show her thankfulness. Reach out? No, not yet. But later, yes. So the Beloved and all his kin would know what she had done, just before they died.

The method...

She looked over distances. There could be no return to Muriah, the White Silver Plain, and the Combat. She could deal with many of them in direct confrontation, but never with them all. And it would have to be all.

Under the soaring balloon the Southern Lagoon narrowed toward the Long Fjord that lay south of Cartagena during the early Pliocene. Milky waters, dull-gleaming in early sunlight, had swallowed her gray torc. The alkali flats were punctuated by eroded volcanic necks from which jagged walls of old lava radiated. Where the short Spanish rivers dropped from the Betic Cordillera, the shores were stained with black and brown and vermilion alluvial fans. Receding on her right hand lay Aven. The Dragon Range of its midsection was still visible back in the haze. Somewhere on the other side of the peninsular neck would be the large city of Afaliah and the rich plantations of its dependencies.

Were human minions even now tending herds or overseeing ramas who mined ores in those mountains? Would they recognize the drifting speck of the balloon for what it was? Probably not—but her illusion-spinning power rendered the big red envelope invisible, just in case. Firvulag? There would be wild ones in the Betic highlands who had scorned to attend the Combat. But they could be no threat at such a distance, and their powers of farspeech were so weak that they would surely be incapable of spreading any alarm. Tanu? None. They were at the Grand Combat. All of them. All gathered together on the salty plain deep in the Empty Sea...

Yes, of course.

That was how. And so fitting, like a reverse birth, with the amniotic flow initiating. It would not be easy, even for her as she was now. But—yes! Stein had been a crust driller. He would know the great earth faults, the zones of instability.

She smiled up at him. The bright-blue Viking eyes stared unseeing ahead. Every five seconds they slowly blinked. The unconscious mind of him below Elizabeth's expert restraints cycled easily, at peace. Felice could now admire the Grand Master's handiwork that had shunted to harmlessness all but the sustenance circuits of the gray torc. There remained certain grave dysfunctions within Stein's brain, but they were capable of being healed.

And the little woman? His wife, of course. Gently, Felice went probing among the secret places of Sukey's sleeping mind. After a time she found the well-concealed thing that would motivate Stein to help her engineer the murder of the Tanu race.

The estuary below narrowed rapidly. The fjord, deep and blue, snaked through a region of ancient vulcanism that linked Europe with Africa. Eroded cindercones, ash beds, and areas of dark rubble made a kind of sill across this part of the Mediterranean Basin. West of the fjord-pierced barrier, below the region that would be called the Costa del Sol by inhabitants of Elder Earth, was a sizable lowland; there lay the islet-studded Great Brackish Marsh, with its areas of open water where Bryan and Mercy had once anchored their yacht. Farther to the west the waters shoaled into playas and then blazing alkali deserts. The active volcano of Alborán poked up amidst barren wilderness, smoking in a desultory fashion. Beyond was a deep evaporite basin; and then the abrupt southerly curve of the Betic Range, which joined the two continents at the narrow and precipitous Gibraltar Isthmus.

A thin forest grew along the fjord. It looked like a lonely and pleasant place to stop.

Scanning Sukey's mind once again, Felice perceived the simple maneuvers needed to land the balloon. Heat reduction and cutoff, vent action, her own override of the vagrant low-level wind currents that threatened to send the balloon into an undesirable area. There! Into a sheltered nook below one of the old volcanic cones. A spring greened level and ashy soil. The bottom of the gondola touched down, lifted, came securely to rest. Holding the envelope in position with her PK, she tugged the deflation cable. The apex gaped and residual hot air vomited from bellying scarlet fabric. A normal human would have seized a line and jumped out to deck the still-stiffened envelope so that it could be secured or completely deflated; but the masterclass psychokinesis of Felice simply lowered the thing by mind-power. The touch of a stud began evacuation of the structural members of the envelope. Within a few minutes the decamole bag of the red balloon stretched tidily at one side of the gondola, flat and expired.

"Wake up, everybody!" Felice cried brightly. "Breakfast time!"

Bryan had been imprisoned in a comfortable suite in the highest level of Redactor Guild headquarters. The sleeping chamber was windowless, extending into the flank of the mountain; but the sitting room had a balcony that overlooked the southern section of Muriah and the orchards, olive groves, and suburban villas that extended from the city outskirts to the land's-end promontory where Brede's small residence stood. Beyond that curved the White Silver Plain. He could not see the Combat, of course. The ritual battlefield lay nearly three kilometers away and below the peninsular rim. But as the sun climbed there were occasional heliographic flashes from that direction; and now and then, when the wind shifted, he thought he heard distant sounds of thunder and music.

If truth were told, Dr. Bryan Grenfell was deeply disappointed at missing the Grand Combat, even though the handsomely sinister Culluket had explained that he was going to play a very special rôle later in the celebration and so had to remain offstage, as it were, until his time had come. But almost every anthropologist delights in ritual spectacle, and Bryan, whose specialty ordinarily kept him busy studying statistics and other less colorful manifestations of culture, was at heart a sucker for a good show. He had looked forward to this stylized brawl between the exotic races ... but here he sat in glum conventry on the balcony, imbibing pale Glendessarry with the sun still on the wrong side of the yardarm, while almost every other human or exotic inhabitant of Muriah was out cheering the preliminary sporting events that were taking place down on the sparkling salt.

She came through the locked door, found him, and laughed. "Mercy!"

"Ah, your face, my darling love! That dear, astonished face!"

She ran to him, trailing cerise and gold gossamer, and reached up to kiss him. Her wired and jeweled headdress was so elab-

orate that he felt he was caught with her inside some fantastic
bird cage where dangling ornaments tinkled and chimed. With
her auburn hair concealed beneath a golden hood, she looked
unfamiliar, alien: Lady of Goriah, wife to the godlike Battlemaster, aspirant President of Creators—all these, easily. But
where was his lady passing by?

"Silly juggins," she said. There was a snap and she stood
transformed, wearing the simple long dress of the portrait he
had carried next to his heart.

"And is this better?" she inquired. "Now do you know me?"

He let his arms gather her in, and it was as always (again),
the soaring into light and the inevitable fall into darkness, from
which he returned a little later each time.

They sat together on a shaded divan on the balcony when
he had recovered, and he explained to her about the picture he
had used in searching for her, and the strange reactions of the
people he had shown it to. They laughed over that.

"I tried to imagine your life in the Pliocene when the computer first gave me your portrait, back in the auberge," he said.
"You and your dog and the sheep and the strawberry plants
and all. I visualized you in some idyllic pastorale . . . and I'm
afraid there were even times when I was Daphnis and you were
Chloë, God save the mark."

Once more she laughed, and then kissed him.

"But it wasn't at all like that," he said. "Was it?"

"You really want to know." The sea-eyes were opalescent
this day, still slightly misted from the ecstasy. When he nodded
she told him how it had been—how the Tanu examiner at
Castle Gateway had been astonished, then terrified at the result
of her mental assay, throwing the entire establishment into a
swivet. How she had been granted the unprecedented honor of
being flown to Muriah, where the members of the High Table
had themselves confirmed her enormous creative potential.

"And it was decided," she said, "that after I had been filled
with the Thagdal's grace, I would go to Lord Nodonn. He came
to fetch me, having in his mind to make me just another of his
human ladies. But when we met—"

A smile of wintry satisfaction touched Bryan's lips. "Enchantress."

"No . . . but he could see within my brain the differences.
There was love, too. But Nodonn would not have made me
his true wife because of that alone."

"Of course not," Bryan said dryly, and once again she laughed.

"He and I are not as romantic as you, dear Bryan!"

Not as human, something hiding inside him twitted.

She said, "By the time we reached his domain of Goriah we were pledged to each other. He took me as consort in a faerie wedding that seemed the fulfillment of every wonderful dream I'd ever had. Ah, Bryan! If you could have seen it! All of them dressed in rose and gold, and the flowers and the singing and the joy..."

He held her tight against his breast, looking over her head to the horizon where the mirror flashes were. He knew he was dying of her, and that it didn't matter. The elfin lover was as nothing, her metapsychic powers were nothing, not even her imminent ascension to the High Table of exotic nobility mattered. With one small portion of her heart she loved him, and she had promised that he could stay until the end.

She shattered his reflection with a droll commonplace. "Deirdre had pups! Four of them. They're all over the palace, the little devils, snow-white and full of the dickens. Fortunately, we Tanu love dogs."

He had to burst out laughing, restored to the still improbable here and now of a bright sunny morning, October 31, six million years before the time of their birth.

"Shall I show you the games?" she asked. And then in quick explanation, "Ah, no, love—I can't take you to the White Silver Plain as yet. But I can project images of what's happening for us to watch together. It'll be just like a glorified Tri-D, but with all the sensations. I needn't return to the others until tomorrow, when they have the manifestation of powers."

"And you go up against Aluteyn?"

"Yes, my dear. But I'll win over him, never fear. The poor man is old, more than three thousand, and tired. His time has come. He's as much as admitted to Nodonn that he'll welcome the life-offering."

"And will the Thagdal as well?" Bryan asked her. "Aiken and Nodonn are bound to meet in this Combat. No matter which one wins, the King himself must be challenged by the victor. I can't believe that Nodonn would continue to defer to Thagdal after a victory over Aiken Drum."

Mercy's bright gaze turned aside. "Nor would he. If my Lord wins—and he must win!—he will become king and restore the old ways. Matters have . . . progressed too far for him to consider any other course."

For only a moment, the scientist in him prevailed. "Mercy, the old ways can't be restored. The human advent, the adulteration of the exotic culture by our technology, the hybridization of the races—it can't be reversed! Nodonn must see that."

"Hush, Bryan. No more of such portentous talk!" She waved her hand and the distant tournament sprang to life in the thin air beyond the parapet. "Look! We'll watch the games together and between times you'll love me again and again from the excitement! But don't fear that your civilized sensibilities will be too affronted, for no people meet death in the First Day Events. All the wonderful violence is only for the sake of sport."

"So I'm civilized, am I?" Laughing they fell back again onto the cushions. All around spun the preliminary contests of the Combat—the Tanu knightly jousts and chariot races and chaliko races; the ramshackle Firvulag hurling competition and the Little People's gnomish version of highland games; the Contest of Animals in which Tanu and Firvulag and gold-torc humans matched purely natural skills against fierce Pliocene beasts (and could Bryan believe his dimming eyes when he saw who was to be the opponent of the giant ape?); and then the Fray of Warrior-Maids, wherein Tanu and human gold-torc women contended against one another in the lists with horrific illusions and genuine weapons, stopping only short of ritual decapitation so that the losers could be restored by the Skin in time for the real hostilities on the day after tomorrow.

Bryan and Mercy watched the spectacle all afternoon and on into the night, for no one seemed to sleep during Grand Combat time when the days lasted from dawn to dawn. And she was right about the excitement inflaming them, and when she rose to go he was so sated that he could not be roused.

"Oh, you've truly found that which you searched for," she told him, kissing his forehead. "So you won't begrudge me my share of the bargain, will you? Wait until they come for you, dear love. And after it's over, we'll meet one final time."

Her magnificent court costume restored, she went out through the locked door just as she had entered.

4

AS THE LAST OF THE CHARIOT RACES ENDED, THERE WERE DEAF-
ening cheers from the Tanu stands and flower garlands draped
around the necks of the three blue-dyed chalikos; and a trophy,
of course, and the royal accolade from the King himself. Only
the bookies reacted to the victory with understandable ennui—
not that the race was fixed, but what kind of odds could you
give against the Queen? They always let her win the last one.

"Congratulations, Nonnie," Thagdal said, kissing her as she
alighted from the gilded wicker vehicle. "You showed 'em
again, old girl."

But he didn't want to watch the Tanu youngsters in their
point-to-point, or the humans and hybrids boat-racing while
Fian Skybreaker whistled a breeze and the noble ladies shuddered delightedly at the occasional dump into the perilous chop.
They debated for a moment whether to view the Firvulag caber-
tossing or the sword dance—for there was always the chance
that a careless contestant would split a gut or get a foot chopped
off. But even these diverting possibilities had little appeal to
the King.

"I'd rather just go into the pavilion and take it easy for a
while," he confessed. "I'm in a rotten mood, Nonnie."

She led him away. Once they were secluded within the white
silk, she wove metapsychic screens and blotted out the carnival
hurly-burly. They served themselves lunch, for none of the
little ramas were allowed on the White Silver Plain lest their
sensitive minds be damaged by the emotional tempests of the
Combat; and the gray-torc servants and barenecks, by long
tradition, were free at this time to watch the games and indulge
their gambling lust.

The King did not eat much. His apprehension was so patent

that Nontusvel finally made him lie down on the royal camp bed so she could administer the sovereign remedy. And in the self-revelatory murmurings that followed, he told her all the bad news. About the defection of Katlinel and the Genetics Master, which had come to his attention just before the Opening of the Sky. About the message from Redact House, disclosing the escape of Aiken Drum's minion, Stein, together with the latter's ingrate paramour and Felice . . . and even Elizabeth.

"There's real trouble brewing, Nonnie. These are bad times and the worst is yet to come. Aiken Drum denies any knowledge of the escapes—and would you believe it? Both Culluket and Imidol confirm that the little bastard's telling the truth! But if Aiken didn't free the prisoners, who did? And where's Elizabeth? She's not working with the healers any more. Has she gone off with Felice? Or is she hiding, getting ready to connive with Aiken Drum in the Combat?"

"Oh, Thaggy—surely not! Elizabeth is nonagressive. Riganone determined that when the woman first arrived here in Muriah."

But the King, not listening, only raged on. "And that damn Katy! Look what we did for the half-human chit, raising her to the High Table and all! And she goes and confirms everything Nodonn's been saying about untrustworthy hybrids. Tana knows why she took Greggy with her, but there's been hanky-panky in the computer room."

Nontusvel said anxiously, "You don't suppose Greggy managed to get his own copy of Bryan's survey?"

Thagdal chewed his ornately braided mustache. "If he did, he'd be in a pretty position to play both ends against the middle. The human middle! And you know who's perched right there on the divider grinning at the lot of us . . ."

"Greg-Donnet is too dear and simple to fall in with any of Aiken Drum's intrigues—even if the boy were able to muster a following."

"Hah! I've had my doubts about the simplicity of Crazy Greggy for some time now. And Aiken is popular with our petty nobility, make no mistake. Did you see where he's going to fight the ape?"

The Queen looked shocked, then began to giggle. "The gigantopithecus? Oh, Thaggy! The clever little devil. I mustn't miss it!"

"Nobody wants to miss it," the King said gloomily. "That little joker has the crowd in the palm of his hand before he even gets into the blood events. They *like* the runty bastard, I tell you! And when he really starts to put on a show with his damned masterclass metafunctions in the battles, they'll respect him as well as lionize him. He'll romp through the High Mêlée giving a good account of himself and attract enough opportunists under his banner to support him in his bid for a Heroic Encounter with Nodonn."

"A few urban dilettantes and hybrids!"

Thagdal shook his head. "He's got at least three High Table champions lined up already. And contingents from Roniah and Calamosk and Geroniah and Var-Mesk have declared for him, too. Mayvar's made sure all the provincial lords know about Aiken Drum's golden balls."

"They'll never choose that clown over Nodonn!"

"Face it, Nonnie. Our son the Battlemaster has metafunctions to burn and more panache than me and my Awful Father and my Unspeakable Grandsire all rolled up in one. But eugenically speaking, he just doesn't cut the mustard. And that's all those hinterlanders think about: strong genes, more kids, population growth to keep us ahead of the Firvulag horde. No . . . we've got to be realistic. If Aiken survives the High, he'll go after Nodonn in the Encounters. And if he should win, the whole damn company'll accept the kid as Battlemaster by acclamation. Then *my* ass'll be on the line."

"Nodonn will defeat Aiken Drum," the Queen declared. "He's your designated heir. If necessary, he can invoke ancient privilege and use the Sword!"

But then Thagdal had to admit to her that Aiken had the Spear.

For a long time after that they sat together hand in hand, each contemplating the end apart from the other, and finally, with some measure of serenity, admitting that it might be more bearable if shared.

The balloon riders decided to camp on the fjord, at least until the next day. Felice assured Sukey that it would be impossible for any hostile observer to penetrate her illusionary defenses. She further invited Sukey to enter her mind and discover something of the wonders newly wrought there. All that Sukey knew of the ring-hockey player had come second-hand from Stein. (This poor little child with the big brown eyes and tattered chemise—*this* was the ball-breaking bull dyke Stein knew back at the auberge?) Any misgivings Sukey might have entertained were dispelled by the aura of goodwill and kindly power shining from Felice's mind.

Resting for a day [thought Sukey] would give them time to assess one another, get cleaned up, and make rational decisions about where to go from here. Most especially, it would provide the opportunity for that delicate operation, the removal of Stein's torc.

The double-level steel cutters were in one of the gondola lockers.

"I'll be able then to complete most of his mind-healing myself, even with his torc off." Shyness made Sukey hesitate before explaining to Felice. "There are certain mental lesions that Elizabeth couldn't mend, you see. Very old injuries made worse by the torc. But their cure is not so much a matter of redactive skill as one of . . . love."

Felice gave a light laugh. "Stein's a fortunate fellow! If you like, I'll work the cutter so you'll be free to concentrate on his mind. If there's a need, I can coerce him into quiet as well."

Sukey nodded. The two of them bent over Stein, who lay with eyes wide open on the wiry turf. At the severing, the giant cried out. But the caregiving mind was there with her soul-mortar and balm, guiding his psychoenergies into the channels prepared by Elizabeth. There would be no serious postaddictive trauma for Stein. The anomalous brain-circuitry of the torc and all trace of its insult melted away before Sukey's healing. More whole than he had ever been, Stein Oleson lived.

"He'll do for now," Sukey said. "I'll wake him."

Stein's eyes saw her. For a long time they saw nothing else.

Felice left them together and went to study the fjord landscape, the porous blocks of lava and masses of unconsolidated ash and scoria supporting meager vegetation. It was not until hours later—long after Felice had washed their clothes, and Sukey had collapsed in a brief reactionary episode, and Stein had taken his turn as comforter—that Felice began to speak in a matter-of-fact way about her plan for genocide.

They were sitting around a little fire in the shades of evening. The huntress had shown casual power by zapping a lagomorphic creature resembling a short-eared jackrabbit. They had grilled it for supper, and with the sweet biocake from the balloon rations they had had tangy wild grapes. Stein and Sukey, enjoying digestion and sweet peace, sat cradled in each other's arms not really hearing what Felice said to them.

"... and the torc factory was essentially unharmed by our attack, so the third phase of Madame Guderian's great scheme remains unfulfilled. Humanity can still be enslaved by the torcs. It doesn't matter that the time-gate's closed. Don't you see? All the Tanu have to do is rescind their ban on human-human reproduction, and in time the pool of potential slaves will be bigger than ever. And don't think that only torced humans cooperate with the exotics! You should have seen the bareneck human finks blubbering to go home after we blasted Finiah. Thoses stupid pathetickers *preferred* life under the Tanu!"

Stein said to Sukey, "We could go to Bordeaux. Where Richard and me figured the wine-loving exiles would live. There could be free people there, like Madame Guderian's bunch. Only not making war with iron weapons. Just living easy. Sorta Robin-Hooding it. I could build us a nice cabin—"

Felice interrupted. "You haven't been listening to me."

"Sure I have, Felice. You could stay with us. Both Sukey and me owe you. So do all the human beings in Exile. What you and the others did—"

"We weren't able to finish the job, Steinie. As long as that torc factory is intact, no bareneck human is safe from slavery. The Tanu will be Hunting for us as long as they're top dogs in Exile. And remember that human traitors wearing torcs aren't poisoned by iron. They're no more vulnerable to it than ordinary bareneck folks are. All the Flying Hunt has to do is spot concealed human settlements from the air, then send in parties of torced humans to do the dirty work."

"Aw, hell. There's gotta be someplace wild enough to be safe. Not all *that* many of the Tanu can fly. The big guns like Nodonn'll be up north where Guderian stirred up the hornet's nest—not in Bordeaux. That's a good spot. Richard and me were worried about ordinary human outlaws in the Pliocene. You grab? We wanted to pick a secure site for our base of operations. So we noodled with one of the geology boffins at the auberge and came up with Bordeaux. It has big tidal swamps with islands of good high land. Richrd figured the place'd be perfect."

"Do you know where Richard is now?" Felice's smile was dreamy. "I do. I can farsense him easily with my new power. He's in a broken-down exotic flyer in a parking orbit forty-nine thousand kloms out, going around and around the world with the dead body of his lady. He looks at the environmental readout every now and then and laughs. And it is pretty funny, when you think of his costume and all. Because the oxygen is nearly all used up."

Sukey, shocked to wakefulness, broke from Stein's clasp. "Oh, *no*! Felice, how can you—how can you sneer at him in such a heartless way? Richard was your friend!"

For the first time, Sukey dared to assay a strong redactive probe into the girl. The mental lancet shattered on impervious smoothness. Sukey uttered a soft cry of pain.

"Don't do that, dear. I'd rather keep my thoughts private until I choose to reveal them. I believe that's a simple courtesy among the metas of the Milieu. Richard is unimportant." *And so are you, Redactorwife, so take care!* "But Stein *is* important . . . to a certain plan of action that I have in mind. I know how to bring about the real solution to all our worries."

Stein and Sukey stared at her.

Felice said, "I want to wipe out all of these Tanu bastards once and for all—while they're gathered in one place for the Grand Combat. And as a bonus, we'll get quite a few of the Firvulag, too. I never did trust those little friggers and neither did Madame Guderian."

Stein said, "If you expect me to go along on another invasion of Muriah, don't hold your breath, sister!"

"Oh, no, Steinie. Nothing like that." Her fingers caressed the hollow of her throat. "I had a golden torc. It made me operant, with wonderful powers. And then I was caught and the Tanu took my torc away and tried to punish me. But their tortures backfired, Steinie. I'm a strange sort of person, you know. The suffering made me fully operant. Without a torc. I'm as good as the metapsychic world shakers of the Galactic Milieu. My PK and creativity are stronger than the powers of any of the Tanu Great Ones."

"No shit," he drawled. "So buck for Queen of the World at the Combat!"

Once again, the dreamy smile. "I have a better idea. That's why I need your help . . . I want to pop the cork at Gibraltar and let the Atlantic into the Med Basin. Drown the exotics like rats in a barrel. I'll do the heavy blasting, and you'll show me where to put the shots so the walls come tumbling down."

The Viking gave an involuntary shout of exultation. "And Pharaoh's army got drownded? Sweet Christ!"

"*Stein!*" wailed Sukey.

"I thought it might appeal to you," Felice said smugly.

"No!" Sukey cried.

He took her in his arms again. "Don't be silly, babe. What d'you take me for? There's human beings in Muriah! Elizabeth and Raimo. And Amerie and those two guys that got caught with her. And even the Fancy Pants Kid! He needs a swift boot, all right—but not drowning."

Felice said, "Aiken Drum is almost certain to beat Nodonn in the Grand Combat and become king. Do you think *he'll* close down the torc factory? Or free the slaves and deprive himself of all those trusty human subjects? Don't make me laugh!"

"Dammit—the others!"

"Amerie and Peo and Basil were terribly wounded. They're as good as dead. The only way they could survive would be if the Tanu put them into Skin. And why should the exotics do that? They plan to roast them alive in the life-offering in four days' time."

"Raimo . . . Bryan," Stein protested.

Felice laughed. "They're goners, too. Let's say they loved and lived. As for Elizabeth . . . she could save herself if she wanted to."

Stein's brows lowered in truculence. "You gotta give *her* fair warning. She helped Sukey shrink me. She gave us her balloon."

The little athlete waved one hand in dismissal. "All right. A farspoken warning once the thing is in train and she can't do anything to stop me."

"Stein, you can't!" Sukey cried. "Felice is—inhuman!"

"Oh, yes," the girl agreed. She stirred the fire with a long stick. The tepee structure of burning pine branches collapsed in an eruption of orange sparks. "But so are the Tanu and Firvulag inhuman! If I let in the sea, the Tanu will be virtually wiped out and the Firvulag reduced to a manageable small population. Free human beings will still have to fight against the torc wearers that remain in the mainland cities. But with the exotic masters and the torc factory gone, at least we'll have a chance. *You'll* have a chance."

Not looking at his wife, Stein said, "Sukey—she's right."

"Steinie, what about all the humans in Muriah who'll be drowned?"

He scowled. "All of 'em that I had anything to do with were Tanu-loyal to the toenails."

"But Felice is talking about the murder of nearly a hundred

thousand living persons! You can't help her, Stein! Not if . . . I
mean anything to you. Felice is insane! Culluket had her for
a week. That's enough to—" She broke off, biting her lip.

Felice was unruffled. "He tortured you, too, Sukey. And
you didn't go mad. Did she tell you about that, Stein? About
the interrogation ordered by the Queen? Don't you want to get
back at the people who tortured Sukey?"

"Stein knows all about what Culluket did," Sukey cried.
Sudden fear blazed up. But Stein didn't know about—

"And don't you want revenge on Thagdal, Steinie?"

Puzzled, he said, "On the King? But why? He was always
a pretty good old buffer. A real sport on the Delbaeth Quest."

"Felice, don't!" Sukey pleaded. "Don't!"

"Sukey didn't tell you what happened *before* her interrogation, though—did she, Stein. She didn't want you to do
something foolish and get yourself killed by the Tanu . . . or by
anybody else. Ask Sukey how the Queen found out about the
sabotage party."

"Don't listen to her, Stein! She's lying!"

"Am I lying, Sukey? I can see the whole thing, right there
in your memory bank. Too bad Stein's torc is off, or I could
relay it right to him. You've tried to wall off that memory.
But I can read it. Do you know that you've been letting it leak?
Something in your sneaky little subconscious let just the smallest bit of the memory seep out for Stein to catch! You wanted
him to catch it. And he did, too. Just a suspicion. A need
to . . . blame."

"Please," Sukey whispered. "Don't do this to him."

"Blame?" the Viking's forehead wrinkled. "How could I
blame Sukey for betraying the invasion? I never should've told
her anything about it. Even Aik warned me not to. I blame
myself—blame him, too, for putting—"

"Ass!" Felice hissed. "Not blame for *that*. For the baby."

Sukey hid her face on Stein's chest. His arms dropped away
from her body. He seemed to see something deep in the dying
campfire. Resin in a burning brand popped. Sukey's sobs were
quiet, hopeless.

"King Thagdal," Stein said at last. "In spite of what Aiken
and Mayvar and Dionket promised. He had Sukey."

"When she was already pregnant with your child. And some
women—they have to be careful in the first weeks. Before the
little embryo is latched on tight. So now you know who to
blame."

Big arms came up, enfolding the shuddering form. Stein did not look at Felice nor at his wife. He watched the flames. "We'll have to do a recon from the air. Surface, too, maybe. Can you make the balloon go any direction you want?"

"Of course."

"Tomorrow, then." He repeated: "Tomorrow. Early."

Elizabeth returned to the room without doors.

There was nowhere else to go unless she was willing to wait passively in Muriah until the Host finally deciphered her personal snuff-sequence and finished her off. Since the escape of the balloon, they had had a dozen top-line farsensors locked onto her, so there was no possibility of her slipping away from Aven by ordinary means. And the Shipspouse had declared, with every evidence of sincere regret, that she was incompetent to teleport her to safety. It was a pity, Brede had lamented, that Elizabeth herself did not possess more PK! For a very short time, Elizabeth had believed the exotic woman's protestations.

But then the sly Two-Faced One had given herself away. Her great racial vision—her foresight—if only Elizabeth would help her to make the last clarification! There was a role to be played by one of them, or both . . . and if they studied in Unity, they would surely discover the truth.

Elizabeth would have fled Brede's room—and Dionket had offered her sanctuary in his conspirators' hideout up in the Mount of Heroes. But she knew that even the natural shielding of the rock was insufficient to shut out the hostile ones. Nodonn now coordinated more than two hundred of them with growing sophistication. If any of them happened to discover that one pattern of assault, and launched it while she was asleep, she would never awaken.

Only in the room without doors was she safe from them. As for Brede . . . there was a way to be rid of her importunities as well. Away, false Unity. Away, seductive two-in-one with your cheating prolepsis that led only to another *using*. Elizabeth would accept no comfort if the price was responsibility. Not in a situation so hopelessly barbaric, so alien to her human metapsychic nature. True human beings would always be defeated in this Exile that was controlled by exotic races. And Elizabeth was too weary and heartsick to condemn herself to a wait of six million years.

The mind-voice of Brede kept calling: We need you! All

three races do! Only look and see how it might be. Look and take comfort.

I will not look. *I will not be used*. You tricked me once to attain full operancy, to become adept. And not for the sake of your people, as you said, but to gain access to *me*. To be able to reach me with your temptation, O well-named Two-Face. But I will not be your savior, exotic. Such a role cannot be coerced. You have no comfort for me. My comfort is six million years distant and this Pliocene theosphere is inhuman and untempered by incarnation. So let me alone. Let me alone . . .

Cocooned in the old fire, Elizabeth drifted away. Brede's calls became fainter and fainter, finally dwindling into silence.

5

"THE STRAIT WAS ONLY ABOUT TWENTY-FIVE KLOMS ACROSS in our time," Stein told Felice. "And that was after six million years of scouring by ocean currents. You won't be able to blast a gap anything like that wide, you know."

The two of them leaned over the rail of the gondola. The red balloon, held motionless by the girl's PK, was poised 300 meters above the crest of the Gibraltar Isthmus. The heights were rounded by erosion. Cedar trees grew in the western downslope valleys. There were dunes and rippling grassy hillocks on the Atlantic side of the land-bridge, but on the Mediterranean flank the isthmus was barren, falling off in an awesome escarpment with sharp buttresses and a tumble of great shattered blocks at the foot, below which were smoother sediments dipping to the Alborán Basin.

Felice said, "The terrain-clearance readout and altimeter put that Gib crest at only two-sixty-eight. If you're right about the isthmus being riddled with caves like a Swiss cheese, I should be able to rupture it. Looks to me like it's overdue to crumble from natural causes. And that eastern dropoff goes way below sea level."

"We could see Gibraltar from my satellite," Sukey said. She smiled into the blue, cloudless sky. "The place where Europe kisses Africa, we called it! We were very sentimental about Earth."

Felice ignored her. "Where would be the best place for my first zap, Steinie? Don't worry about the shockwave hitting the balloon. I'll spin a big bubble-shield around us. How about if I blast that little headland sticking out?"

"Hold it, dummy!" he exclaimed. "You want a real tidal

306

wave? Or just a slow-creeping thing like a friggerty filling bathtub that gives 'em plenty of time to make a getaway?"

"Did you see my satellite up in the night sky when you worked in Lisboa, Steinie?" Sukcy asked. "Up above the world so high?"

"Hydraulic pressure!" Stein said, smacking left fist into right palm. "That's what we need, kid! A good head of water. A great big surge that comes crashing through the estuary of the Southern Lagoon to the White Silver Plain and floods the battlefield fast!"

"My thoughts exactly," Felice said. "I'll torch the isthmus in a lot of different places. The gap's bound to widen and let a zillion tons of water in. For crissake, the whole Atlantic's pushing!"

Sukey said, "Most of us on ON-15 spent a lot of time looking at Earth. Especially the people who'd never been there. Fourth-generation satelliters like me. Odd that we'd want to do that, wasn't it? We had everything we could possibly want in our beautiful satellite."

"Little Miss Smartass! Even if you hit the fault lines, touched off a major subsidence, you'd never get an opening here more than five-six kloms wide to start with. Okay! The sea squirts through and you got the most hellaceous waterfall in history. But Muriah is almost a thousand kloms away from here! And you saw that big bugger of a dry basin between here and Alborán."

"You mean—it would swallow the surge?"

Sukey said, "Our lovely hollow satellite. Wherever you stood on the inside surface of the cylinder, the central axis was up. It spun to simulate gravity. Sometimes the strangeness of it drove Earthsider visitors crazy! But we were used to it. The human brain is an adaptable organism. For almost everything."

"That damn basin would kill our head of water deader 'n Saturday night in Peoria! So don't go zapping this isthmus yet, baby. First we gotta go back and seal up the fjord. Get the picture?"

"Build up *another* head of water?"

"Checko. With the fjord shut, that old volcanic line between the Costa del Sol and Africa forms a natural dam. A kind of threshold maybe two hundred and fifty kloms north to south— but not very wide, not very high. The marsh is west of it, taking the outflow from that Spanish river. The fjord is— what?—a hundred meters deep? So if we plug it, we got a long, long dam! And not made of tough rock like Gibraltar, either. Just unconsolidated ash and cinders and lava hunks."

"It would be much safer inside Hollow Earth than at Bordeaux, Steinie," Sukey said. "It's still not too late for us to find the way."

"I think I understand," Felice said, nodding. "When we get a good head of water behind this soft dam, *then* I rip the thing open."

"If you got the gigawatts, kid."

"Wait and see, big boy! You're sure the dam will hold until I'm ready to blow it?"

"Looked like it. And if you're as good as you say you are, you could always shore it up if it started to crack too soon."

"Kaleidoscopic! Let's highball it to the fjord and I'll show you how good I am!" Felice began to manipulate the heat generator. The balloon mounted rapidly into the air.

"They might not want to let Felice into Hollow Earth, Steinie." Sukey's face was anxious. "Violence isn't allowed in the peaceful realm of Agharta. Only kindness. But what'll become of her if we don't take her with us? Poor Felice...all alone with the dead ones!"

Stein took his wife's shoulders and gently pressed her down. "You rest awhile, Sue. Take a nap, maybe. Don't worry about Felice or Hollow Earth. I'll take care of everything from now on."

Sukey's mouth trembled. "I'm sorry you can't go, Felice. Steinie's changed now. He's gentle and good. He'll fit in. But not you...Let's go to Agharta *now*, Stein. I don't want to wait any longer."

"Soon," he assured her. "Try to sleep." He made her as comfortable as he could on the floor of the gondola.

Felice's creative metafunction conjured two air masses of dissimilar pressure. A wind began to blow from the Atlantic, carrying the balloon directly toward the fjord. Felice's eyes shone. "If I pedal real fast, Steinie, we can be there and back before lunch. You're *sure* this ploy will do the job?"

"When that clinker dam lets go, you'll have one vicious granny-banger of a tidal wave chargin' down that narrow Southern Lagoon. Make old Noah eat his heart out."

Sukey buried her head in her arms. One gleam of hope shone through her nightmare. Elizabeth! With this new golden torc, it might be possible to—

Silly fool! (Sukey's sanity tottered.) Don't you think I've

been expecting you to try something like that? (You can't get me—I'm running!) I've got you screened so thick you couldn't even spit without my say-so! (But you'll never catch me where I'm going.) Warn them, would you? You little hypocrite! Deep down inside your stupid virtue you want this just as much as we do! (No, no, no.) Yes, yes, yes!

Escape. . . .

Sukey tried to drag Stein along with her. But his torc was gone. She could no longer pull him like a child. She could only beg, plead with nonmeta rationality, and hope that he would change his mind and follow her as she retreated.

Deep down there, the way to Agharta still had to be open.

It was something to keep him busy, and it did not require moving about on his rudely splinted broken legs, and so Basil spent most of his waking hours scraping away at the solid rock wall of their prison cell with a vitredur spoon.

By the seventh day, he had made an indentation approximately fifteen centimeters long, four high, and one deep. Chief Burke, in one of his last fully lucid moments, had told him, "Keep working! When you break through, we'll be able to post a letter: 'Help. I am a prisoner in a dungeon in Middle Earth.'"

But that about marked the end of the brave jests and stiff-upper-lipping, for Burke became delirious and addressed Basil from then on as "Counsel for the Defense," shouting tirades that apparently reprised his wittier pronunciamentos from the bench. Amerie was less noisy in her ravings, only leaning toward the more bloodthirsty psalms when the agony from her suppurating burns was most intense. By the tenth day of their imprisonment, the nun and the big Native American were helpless and incapable of speech. It was left to Basil, with only one of his fractures compounded, and that not even gangrenous yet, to remove their single daily meal from the turntable door-wicket, exchange the full slop bucket for an empty one, and tend to his dying friends as well as he could in pitch-darkness.

When these melancholy chores were done, he would return to his patient scraping at the letter slot.

Sometimes he dozed when the pain permitted it, and dreamed. He became an undergraduate again and punted on the Isis; squabbled with other dons over esoteric fripperies; even climbed mountains (but always with the summits out of reach—alas for the Pliocene Everest!).

He might have dreamed the bizarre woman as well.

She was gowned in metallic red and black all adorned with flameshapes and beadwork, and wore the butterfly-shaped padded headdress of the middle fifteenth century. She was not a human being, not a Tanu either, and she seemed to have two faces—one comely and one grotesque. He tried to warn her tactfully about the slop bucket as she came shimmering through the stone wall, but like many an apparition, she only smiled and looked enigmatic.

"Do tell me how I can be of service to you, then," Basil said, resting on his elbows in the muck.

"It's ironic—but I really do need your help," said the woman. "Yours and that of your friends."

"Oh, hard lines," Basil said. "You see, they're more or less dying. And I think my left leg's finally going off. Getting rather noisome where the fibula ends protrude from the flesh."

The woman glowed. She had a kind of haversack, all bejeweled like the rest of her, and she took from it a considerable quantity of very thin transparent membrane, resembling plass. With no ceremony, she knelt down on the floor amidst the garbage and stinking puddles and smears of excrement and began wrapping the unconscious Amerie in this stuff; and when the nun was packaged like a choice cut in a butcher case, she enswathed Chief Burke.

"They're not quite dead, you know," Basil protested. "They'll smother."

"The Skin does not bring death, but life," the bizarre woman said. "You are needed alive. Sleep now and have no fear. Your gray torcs will be gone when you awake."

And before he could open his mouth in further demur, she had *him* entangled in the membrane, and then the dream of her faded away along with Peo and Amerie and the dungeon and all the rest of it.

Up until the time that Felice blew up the fjord, Stein had lived his whole Pliocene experience as some misbegotten culture-drama.

It had been wilder and scarier and more vivid than the immersive pageants he had been thrown out of way back in the Milieu of his young manhood; but when you came right down to it, life in Exile was just as stone friggerty unreal. The bloodletting in Castle Gateway, the fever-dream sequence culminating in the deep-redact by Elizabeth and Sukey, the auction banquet and the fight with the animal in the arena and the

slaying of the dancing predator and the Delbaeth Quest . . . unreal!
Any day now, any minute even, his participation in the show
was going to come to an end and he would turn in his Viking
costume and go out the exit and back into the real world of
the twenty-second century.

Even at this moment, with his mind convalescent and suspicious, some evaluating segment of the cortex refused to accept the balloon journey as anything but an extension of the
dream. Down below lay a pretty fjord entrance of colored lava
cliffs. A big cindercone at stage right. Fakey-looking ever-
greens like overgrown bonsai clinging to the heights. Small
wooded islets with flowering shrubs and mangrove thickets
dotted here and there on mirror-smooth water. A big flock of
pink flamingos over in the shallows, scoffing up lunch.

Unreal! He could see the posters:

SAVOR YOUR ANCIENT FAERIE HERITAGE
IN FANTASTIC PLIOCENELAND!

But all of a sudden, while he still floated in reverie, Felice
leaned from the gondola and pointed a finger.

Their balloon was enclosed in the metapsychic shielding.
But the flash, the concussion beating around them, the clouds
of dark dust and fountaining earth and rock—they were not
make-believe. He had known this kind of destruction before.
He had caused it. The blasting of the fjord and the small volcanic cone next to it shocked him more profoundly than anything else he had lived through since passing the time-gate. He
saw with vision new-born the roiling dust and steam, the ruined
marshland, the bodies of the birds. His ears, preternaturally
acute, heard Sukey's sobs and the mad giggling of Felice.

Real.

One of his hands reached out to the balloon controls and
increased the output of the heat generator. They began to rise
and shortly it was possible to survey the results of Felice's
strike. What had been the entrance to the channel was now
piled deep in rubble. Stein's earth driller's eye estimated that
the landslide from the demolished cindercone bulked at no less
than half a million cubic meters.

Felice grinned at him. "Now do you believe, Steinie?"

"Yeah." He turned from the gondola rail. His guts were tied
in the old familiar knot. He tasted bile as he knelt to comfort
poor cowering Sukey. "I believe, all right."

"We'll fly slowly over to the eastern end of the fjord, then. I'll whomp up quieter slides to block the rest of the passage— but I couldn't resist trying one little zap over here. My first shot! Did I blast rock like a pro?"

"One—little—zap?" Stein muttered.

"Well, actually I was afraid to really let loose this close to Muriah. I mean—only six hundred kloms away! They might have seismographs or something. It wouldn't do to let them know that something unnatural was going on. But a single small zap can pass for an earthquake. Right?"

"Sure, Felice. Sure."

Sukey clung to him, shivering. Ghostly drumrolls, relics of the monstrous explosion, still flailed and echoed among the ashy hills. Real. It was real. Sukey was. And Felice was.

After a time, the little blonde athlete extinguished the protective bubble and let the ambient atmosphere in again. She hung partly out of the car, laughing as she triggered rockfalls. Dust floated up on the thermals and settled all over the decamole surfaces. That was what made Stein's eye water, what set his teeth on edge.

"Oh! Sorry about the mess, guys." The bright goddess banished the sifting grit in a flourish of psychokinetic power. "All finished here! Now we'll hurry back to Gilbraltar and get down to serious business."

"You see, Steinie?" Sukey whispered to him. "*Now* do you see?" But he said nothing, only held her very tight.

Westward again flew the red balloon, impelled by Felice's wind. Over Alborán and its train of extinct subsidiary cones; beyond the deep dry basin; up the slope that rose to the Gibraltar rampart; across the crest and out over the sea, to stop suspended above the Atlantic, where white scallopings of surf fringed the great beach that stretched unbroken from the margin of the Guadalquivir Gulf in Spain south to Tangier.

"Now come up and stand beside me, Stein," Felice ordered him. "We're far enough out over the ocean to be safe from the fallout. Show me where to begin . . . Come *on*, Steinie!"

"Yeah, yeah." Sukey was gripping the front of his tunic with extraordinary strength. He unfastened her fingers.

"No," she begged. "No, Stein, no."

"Stay down," he told her, kissing the white knuckles of her hands. "Don't look."

Felice took hold of the load cables and clambered aloft. She stood barefooted on the rim of the gondola, facing the shore. "Show me! Show me right now!"

He pointed. "Where that deep straight-line ravine comes down north of the little point. Can you—can you see under the ground at all? Through the rocks, like Aiken could?"

She gave him a startled look over her shoulder. "I never thought of it! But if he could...*oh!* It's like—funny great piles of lights and shadows! Huge sandwichy chunks leaning every which way. Other darker stuff, some blobby, some too opaque to see through at all. How marvelous!"

His jaw tightened. He was as far away from her as he could get in the small gondola, the instrumentation shelf jabbing into his rump. He did not dare to look at Sukey.

Felice burbled on. "Those are rock formations that I see, aren't they? Under that straight ravine is a great big surface that slants away underground toward the south. A kind of meeting place between two gigantic slabs of rock that are—bent."

"It's one of the faults at the continental-plate boundary. You start by hitting the strata above the slanting interface of the slip. Bust the whole thing up. You'll need a string of strong shots. Start deep under the water if you can, then come ashore underneath, still blasting, and continue right into the hillside."

"I get it. Ready? There—!"

Stein closed his eyes. He was under the sea again himself, riding his drill-rig in armor, in control of emerald fury. When he blasted, great blocks of planetary crust moved or were melted. Muted thunder spent itself harmlessly against the sigma-fields that sheltered him. He torched his way through the lithosphere, the screen of the rig's geodisplay showing the Earth's structure in three dimensions—

"They're cracking, Steinie! Way down there! But not the rocks on top. What's wrong? There are only tremors on top. The isthmus is still solid!"

"Dumb broad. You think this is gonna be easy? Keep hitting it north of the slip. Farther inland!"

"All right—you don't have to get nasty!"

The ground quivered. There were a few minor landslides. A peculiar change came over the pattern of Atlantic waves reflecting from the small pointed promontory.

He said, "That's enough. Now get this damn balloon over onto the east side of the isthmus."

The gondola lurched but Felice clung easily to the web of

cables. The balloon seemed to be dragged through the sky by a genie force. It crossed the Gibraltar crest a kilometer high and came to a halt in emptiness above the dry Alborán Basin.

"Now look under the rocks again," Stein said. "As deep as you can. Tell me what you see."

"Um . . . the shadows make this big bend. A huge U-shape lying between Spain and Africa. The bottom of the U points to the Atlantic. But the cracks are all different here. There are smaller ones branching out of the U's curve. And way, way down is this hot thing—"

"Stay the hell out of that! You're starting to blast at the surface now. But below sea level, on this eastern slope. About where the yellow rock layer is. You grab? Tunnel in. Push the junk out of the way. Hit the caves. Then blow the roof out. Never mind about making the cut wide or straight. Just dig deep and head in the general direction of that other slanting fault you were working on."

She nodded, turned her back to him. There was a fearful blaze of light and unending noise. The balloon's gondola swayed gently as the girl shifted position; but the other two passengers felt none of the shock waves, tasted none of the dust. They floated unscathed while Felice smote the earth and debris boiled up. The easterly wind carried streamers out over the Atlantic. The girl sent bolt after bolt of psychoenergy into the landbridge which was, at sea level, perhaps twenty kilometers wide at the narrowest part. She hacked out a long crevice, never more than fifty meters across except where some great cavern's roof was undermined, creating a sinkhole. Clogging masses of rock exploded into dust for the winds to scatter.

She struck. She struck! Five kilometers in. And ten. Carve and rend! Make a sluiceway for the cleansing waters. Fifteen kilometers in. Blast. Blast! Slower now, through the heart of the rotten isthmus. On to where the Atlantic waits. Strike. Strike. Wearily now, but continue. Find the energy somewhere. In some other space, some other time? Who cares where the power comes from. Only focus. Hit! Hit again. Again. And now so close. And now . . . now . . . yes. Through.

Through?

Laugh. See, Felicia Tonans, ignorant child-flinger of mind-bolts! See what you've done, boobing it!

You've let the cut become shallower and shallower as you drove westward, weakening. And now the breakthrough, when it comes, is a ridiculous anticlimax. The penetration is a scant meter below natural sea level. The Atlantic enters diffidently, trickling along the rough hot floor of your incompetent chasm. It has been long millions of years since the waters flowed in this direction, toward the Empty Sea. The way is strange...

"Felice! For God's sake! You gotta do better than that— it's just piddling through! Plane out that friggin' gradient!"

She drooped, still clutching the balloon cables. The protective bubble attenuated. Around them, heat rose. With it came a smell of rock dust and molten minerals.

"Tired. So tired, Steinie."

"Get on with it! The rock underneath is busted to hell along the main fault. Keep going! Hit the sucker, I tellya! The rock'll rupture from water pressure if you just get the cut deep enough. Can't you *see* that with your damn X-ray vision?"

She didn't reply, didn't even cuss him out, only swayed a little with her eyes shut and her little bare dirty feet trying to grasp the gondola's padded rail.

He screamed at her. "*Do* it, you almighty bitch! You can't just stop. You said you could do it! God—you said you could do it!" The car rocked with the vehemence of his rage, his fear, his shame. Oh, shame.

Felice was nodding slowly. Somewhere, the strength she needed might be found.

Call for it, seek it. Search it out among these infantile, asynergic sparks of life-force that are Earth's Pliocene Mind. The two-in-one (now oddly separate) refuse you, as you knew they would. And the many-in-All so much farther out, who had also helped before on the River Rhône, now withhold and try to show you other ways. But you have chosen and it must be, and there is one other source of the energy, so bright, so early-rising, who will not turn away. Here then is a better Unity for you, here is power to brim your height and depth and breadth at least until the end. So you accept. The energy comes. You harness it with your creative metafunction; mold, compress, convert. And then you hurl it down...

With no metapsychic shield in place, the balloon caught the full force of the shockwave and was thrown far up and away. Stein gave a great shriek and so did another. Bodies inside the gondola flopped as helplessly as dolls, crushed against deca-mole surfaces, against bruising human flesh and bone.

Deafened, Stein and Sukey struggled together in the tossing basket. Neither could help the other. The tough envelope billowed, struck the hot grid of the generator but rebounded unscorched, whirled in a vortex. Spiraling upward, the balloon broke free at last from the storm-cell of ionized turbulence. What had been a distorted, kiting scarlet blob smoothed and reexpanded. It sailed in the high thin air, slowly descending to its altitude of equilibrium.

Stein dared to rise, to look out.

Below, the waterfall of the western ocean flowed.

All of the smoke and dust was streaming over the Atlantic, making it easy for him to see what they had done. The gap in the isthmus widened even as he watched. Brown and yellow rocks on either side appeared to melt like sugar in the torrent's press. To the east, the cataract outflow poured into the Empty Sea across a front nearly ten kilometers wide. A blanket of mist, grayish tan from suspended dust that muddied the droplets, hid the Alborán Basin floor.

He heard Sukey's voice. She climbed to her feet and stood beside him. "Where—?" she asked.

He said, "She *might* have been able to fly. Like Aiken could. Try with your golden torc."

She pressed the warm collar, looking down at the streaks of wrath streaming westward from the sundered isthmus. Unless the surface winds shifted, no one at Muriah would see the smoke.

"There's nothing, Stein. Nothing."

The balloon continued its descent. Seeming not to have heard her, he consulted the instruments. "Three-five-two-eight meters, heading oh-two-three. Another airflow up here. Pretty close to the direction we want to go." He manipulated the heat generator.

"Steinie, I've *got* to tell Elizabeth!"

"All right. Just her. Nobody else."

The balloon attained equilibrium. The ground-speed display told of their progress, but it seemed to the man and woman that they hung motionless in the clean blue sky.

"She doesn't answer me, Stein. I don't know what's wrong! My farspeech isn't very strong, but Elizabeth should be able to receive it on the human mode—"

He gave a sudden start, grabbed her by the upper arms. "Don't you try calling the others!"

She squirmed. "Stop it, Steinie! I didn't. Nobody else can —" She gaped at him. He was opening one of the lockers, taking something out. "Oh, no," she whispered.

"I love you. But you can't stop it. Even without Felice to

break the dam, the flood's going to happen. The whole nightmare wiped out. Elizabeth . . . if she's still there, she'll save herself. You don't have to worry about her. You don't have to worry about any of them anymore."

Cold metal touched her neck. Her vision of him, of the anguish-scarred and merciless Viking face, blurred with her tears.

"Don't be afraid," he said. "It's better this way."

With great care, he slid one blade of the steel cutters behind her golden torc. He began to close the handles. The double levers worked.

Brede! her mind cried. *Brede!*

He shorn torc fell away, hurting. But even with its loss the reply came:

Be at peace Little Daughter it will happen as foreseen.

6

THE SECOND DAY OF THE GRAND COMBAT INITIATED THE FIRST
of the battles to the death: the Low Mêlée, also known as the
Contest of Humans. In the time before the opening of the time-
gate, these preliminary fights had served to showcase the talents
of. novice Tanu warriors of special expertise; but now only
gray-torcs took part in them. Hundreds of male gladiators and
a small number of gray women contended in elimination bouts
that featured every conceivable form of martial art. One section
of the ritual battlefield was partitioned into smaller courts so
that the spectators could savor the blood sports at close range.
The bookmakers had their finest hour; but a groan went up
from human and Tanu fans (especially the Finiah refugees)
when it was announced that two of the top-ranked gray contenders had been scratched. Neither Stein nor the infamous
Felice appeared in the lists and no explanation was given for
their absence.

The fighting continued from dawn until noon, accompanied
by much festivity and culminating in a bloody free-for-all symbolic of the original character of the event. Victorious grays
who were without injury retired to prepare themselves for the
High Mêlée on the morrow, where they would join the silvers
and golds and veteran gray warriors in the ritual war pitting
Tanu against Firvulag. Battered gladiators who had acquitted
themselves well in the tournament were escorted by redactors
to the medical pavilions, where they joined the recuperating
warrior-maids in the Skin wards. The handful of badly wounded
losers who still lived and the cravens were sequestered in a
handsome glass structure resembling a box-seat section cano-
pied in silver and black cloth, which stood at the far southern

end of the battlefield on top of stout scaffolding. Its walls were transparent and unbreakable.

In theory, the remaining time of the Second Day was devoted to choosing Combat leaders by means of manifestation of powers—after which the Foes separated for a final War Feast and invocation to the Goddess prior to the start of hostilities at sunrise. In practice, the great captains had all been selected hundreds (or even thousands) of years ago and now merely stepped forward to dare any upstart to usurp their privilege. If a challenge was forthcoming, both parties might manifest their metapsychic powers on the spot and be judged by the battle-company of their race. The reigning champions also had the option of dueling contenders with both weapons and meta-functions at any time during the High Mêlée.

As overall losers in the previous year's Combat, the Firvulag presented their captains first. The regal platform was expanded into a much larger Dais of Challenge with the two Kings and noncombatant nobility enthroned well back out of range of any stray thrusts. Rivals were supposed to confine their psycho-energetic coups to one another—but accidents had been known to happen; and so a squad of shield conjurers from the PK Guild took up positions around the perimeter of the stage to protect the crowd with an invisible wall. The Tanu Marshal of Sport then introduced the Firvulag Great Ones, who simply stood forth and then retired to applause from the triracial assembly when no challenges came from the ranks.

The presentation of the Firvulag leadership was swift, almost perfunctory. Medor, Ayfa, Galbor Redcap, Skathe, Nukalavee the Skinless, Tetrol Bonecrusher, Bles Four-Fang, Betularn of the White Hand, and finally Sharn-Mes all accepted plaudits and stood down unchallenged. Lastly, in a major but fully expected break with the tradition of recent unhappy years, the Firvulag Battlemaster was proclaimed by King Yeochee. Not Sharn the Younger, who had undertaken the thankless job during the past twenty Combats—but Pallol One-Eye himself.

The irascible old First Comer, gigantic in his full suit of obsidian mail and monstrous crested helm, ascended the Dais of Challenge to tumultuous acclaim. There were many—Tanu and Firvulag as well as human—who had never seen his power manifested. Others, now that he had returned to the Combat after his long absence, jested that his faculties must surely have atrophied from disuse. No one dared challenge him; but as a

technical neophyte he was obliged to demonstrate his primary
metafaculty before the assembled field.

Pallol stood with legs wide apart and spike-studded arms
flung out. He leaned back so that he appeared to be gazing
directly at the high sun. His visor remained shut but the hushed
onlookers knew, nevertheless, that it hid not one eye—but
two. The right was a normal orb having an iris colored deep
red. The left was of a color unfathomable, usually shuttered
behind a patch but now beyond doubt naked and dreadful.

Clouds summoned by the awesome creative power of the
old ogre materialized in the sky. They were thick and dark and
low-hanging, with unnatural ruddy lightning blinking in their
depths. The black-armored monster did not move. Of its own
volition, his helmet visor slowly opened.

Twin purple discharges scorched down from the clouds into
Pallol's gauntleted palms, begetting a shattering clap of thunder. From the gaping helm a coherent scarlet beam blasted
skyward, carving a tunnel through the cloud in the manner of
a cannonball punching through a snowbank. The sun illumined
Pallol's Eye. His visor closed. The sky brightened to blue.

"Slitsal, Pallol!" cried the chivalry of the Firvulag. "Slitsal,
Pallol Battlemaster! *Slitsal!*"

King Yeochee arose from his throne and roared out, "We
confirm Pallol One-Eye as Battlemaster, to defend our racial
honor in this Grand Combat!"

Thus ended the Firvulag manifestation of power, and the
Tanu prepared to take their turn upon the Dais of Challenge.
At this point in the proceedings in years past, many of the
Little People among the spectators had tended to drift away
discourteously, being by that time of the day ferociously hungry
as well as sweltering in their armor or heavy clothing under
the Mediterranean sun. But on this occasion the Firvulag held
their places. The grapevine had promised a widespread shakeup
in the Tanu hierarchy and none of the Little People wanted to
miss the fun.

Things began tamely enough as the lowest-ranked among
the Tanu Great Ones ascended to acclaim. Bleyn the psychokinetic hybrid was unchallenged, and after him came Alberonn
Mindeater, another mixed-blood who had earned his place at
the High Table through creative mastery in battle. And then
there stood forth Lady Bunone Warteacher in her silver-green
armor and hawksbeak helm, and Tagan Lord of Swords—these
two being most directly responsible for the training of the gray-

torc warriors and cheered most loudly by the humans and hybrids in the crowd.

After the fighting specialists came the Guild Presidents. These could, by ancient custom, delegate a Combat deputy if they were not inclined to take to the battlefield in person. Any challenge, however, would have to be answered by the principal in a manifestation of power.

The Marshal of Sport announced: "The President of the Guild of Redactors, Dionket Lord Healer!"

Unarmed and empty-handed, the gaunt figure in simple scarlet-and-white robes ascended the dais.

"Is there a challenge?"

There was not. Dionket gestured and a tall warrior wearing ruby armor came and stood beside him. "I delegate Lord Culluket the King's Interrogator as Second Redactor, to defend our Guild's honor in the Grand Combat." The two retired to cheers from Tanu and humankind. The Firvulag hummed mockingly.

"The President of the Guild of Psychokinetics, Nodonn Lord of Goriah!"

The rosy-gold one came forward, not to claim leadership as Lord Psychokinetic, but to await challenge. There was none, of course, and so he delegated his brother Kuhal Earthshaker as Second, since he himself would undertake the role of Battlemaster. As the two stepped down the Tanu cheers were louder, the human distinctly subdued, and the Firvulag humming more vicious.

"The President of the Guild of Coercers, Sebi-Gomnol Lord Coercer!"

The crowd noise chopped off.

King Thagdal rose from his throne, diamond armor ablaze. "Our dear son Sebi-Gomnol having been gathered unto Tana's peace, we declare the Presidency of the Guild of Coercers vacant and call for aspirants to stand forth in this manifestation of power."

Imidol the sapphire titan mounted the dais to howls of Tanu acclamation. Then came another tall form, his blue armor and helmeted head cloaked and hooded in dull-bronzen brocade. The Marshal of Sport cleared his throat.

"Awful King and Father! Noble battle-company of the Tanu! Here before you aspirant stand Lord Imidol—"

Cheers and jeers.

"—and Leyr the Banished, predecessor to Sebi-Gomnol in the Presidency of the Guild of Coercers."

Gasps and hoots came from Tanu and Firvulag alike as the bronze fabric fell away. The deposed Lord Coercer stood decorous beside his louring young rival.

For a long moment Thagdal was silent. He had known what was in the wind, of course. And thousands of years ago on far Duat, another unseated and exiled Great One had dared to attempt a comeback, so there was precedent. He addressed the two: "Will you manifest here and now or will you duel?"

And Imidol responded, as was his right as a member of the High Table, "We will duel unto the death in the High Mêlée at such moment as the Goddess may choose."

Tanu spectators applauded stiffly while the Little Folk whooped and screeched at the evident discomfiture of the Foe. The blue-armored coercers stepped down.

"The President of the Guild of Creators, Aluteyn Craftsmaster!"

The stout old Tanu in the jeweled caftan came forward as the Marshal called for any challenge. Gulls flew overhead, uttering creaky cries in the ensuing silence. A light eastern breeze blew Aluteyn's silver-vermeil hair and long mustaches back from his stony face. He glared over the heads of the vast crowd and seemed to contemplate the pale lagoon that lapped the White Silver Plain in shallow harmlessness.

"I challenge," said Mercy.

The crowd opened for her. She came up to stand facing Aluteyn, wearing for form's sake a delicately wrought suit of parade armor, silver-lustre glass all embossed and enameled with green ornamentation and inlaid with emeralds. Mercy's head was bare except for a narrow emerald diadem, and her glorious red hair floated free.

"Awful Father! Lord Creator! Noble battle-company!" cried the Marshal. "Here before you challenging stands Lady Mercy-Rosmar of Goriah, wife to Nodonn Battlemaster."

"Will you manifest," Thagdal inquired, "or will you duel?"

"I will manifest," declared Aluteyn Craftsmaster. "Let the Kral be borne forth."

The ceremonial cauldron, which Creator Guild personnel had kept covered at one side of the dais, was placed between Mercy and Aluteyn. The Firvulag throng was now almost out of control, straining close to the platform on their side of the field and making an uproar of derisive twitters, growls, and a deep bourdon drone of humming that now reached a crescendo of maddening whole-tone intervals.

The chain of silence was shaken again and again. Finally Mercy was able to speak.

"I, Mercy-Rosmar, call upon Aluteyn Craftsmaster to devastate if he can the creation I will manifest here before you."

She and the old man confronted each other across the huge kettle, arms extended. An emanation like a wispy rainbow began to stream from Mercy's mailed fingers. In response, a flood of blackness flowed out of the Craftsmaster's hands, enveloping not only the small colored whirlwind but Mercy and the entire cauldron as well. The Tanu spectators gave a triumphant shout. Torced humans and Firvulag groaned and hissed.

The black tide swelled into an inky amoeboid blob. Beneath it, the side of the platform nearest the Firvulag commenced to fizzle and flame as though the white stone were being attacked by some ectoplasmic acid. The Little People shrank back as the PK shielders made a gesture.

Aluteyn laughed.

But something was glowing within the dark mass like a rare green star emerging from a coalsack nebula. The blackness thinned. Mercy reappeared, poised in vapor above the dissolving dais, and the cauldron was there with her. She glowed more brightly. Her rainbow vortex spun into the depths of the Kral and started something to sparkling and tinkling down there. The black tide went splashing back to menace its creator.

Aluteyn cried out. A great thing like a hammer of night came smashing down on Mercy and the Kral. But this creation of the Craftsmaster, like the other, frittered away to impotence. Mercy's rainbow tornado now rose from the cauldron and grew until it was more than four times the height of the Lord Creator. It began to show thickening clots of multicolored light. Aluteyn caught it in a huge black net and pounded it with psychoenergies, trying to force it back into the kettle or turn it upon the woman. But it eluded him. It expanded and solidified high above the heads of the throng . . .

And manna rained on Tanu and Firvulag and humans alike. The air was filled with a soft hailstorm of rainbow bubbles, countless thousands of them, which when seized and broken open released sweetmeats, cold fruits, rich little cakes, and a whole cornucopia of other delicious edibles that were greeted with jubilant enthusiasm by the famished spectators of all three races.

"Slonshal, Rosmar! Slonshal, Rosmar Lady Creator! *Slonshal!*"

She stood with lowered eyes, having fully restored the dais, with one silver hand resting on the brim of the empty cauldron. The mob was still yelling and grabbing, for never before at the Grand Combat had any creator produced fully tangible organic matter that endured instead of quickly fading away. (Mercy's astral hors d'oeuvres were far from illusory; the stomachs of the throng testified to it!) And so her talent was hailed not only for its novelty but also for its practical value.

"I delegate," she said at last in a small clear voice, "Lord Velteyn of Finiah as Second Creator, to defend our Guild's honor in the Grand Combat."

The Tanu contingent made such a bedlam hailing the bereaved former ruler—now presented with a perfect means of restoring his damaged prestige—that few heard the second part of Mercy's speech:

"And I call upon Aluteyn, late President of the Creator Guild, to choose between exile from this noble company or life-offering to our compassionate Goddess."

"I choose the offering," said proud Aluteyn. Virtually unnoticed, he walked without escort to the Great Retort and joined the other condemned ones who waited inside.

Mayvar Kingmaker stood forth unchallenged as leader of the Farsensor Guild. None were surprised when she designated Aiken Drum to lead the Guild's fighters, rather than the Host's nominee, the female warrior Riganone. Finally Thagdal the High King came forward, proclaiming Nodonn to be Tanu Battlemaster, and the manifestations ended.

With one last thundering cheer, the crowd dispersed to the two tent-cities that now stood on either side of the Well of the Sea. There they would spend the rest of the day and most of the night in feasting, drinking, and amusement, until dawn would begin the Third Day of the Grand Combat and the opening skirmish of the ritual war.

Some eight hundred kilometers to the west of the White Silver Plain, scorpions and spiders and alkali ants that lived on the slopes above the Alborán Basin were drowning by the millions. Small flying predators such as wasps and brown-flies survived longer, keeping ahead of the creeping saltwater until night coolness loaded their wing membranes with condensation and forced them down.

7

IT LACKED A FEW MINUTES UNTIL SUNRISE. THE ARMIES CON-
fronted one another, poised and ready.

The overwhelming numbers of Firvulag were on foot as
always, dancing and leaping in undisciplined mobs around the
battle-captains of their choice like great black-armored insects.
The effigy standards with festoons of gilded skulls bounced up
and down, daring the Foe to seize them—for in this manner,
as well as in the taking of heads, was the Grand Combat victory
judged. The Little People were armed with dark glittering
swords, spiked clubs, chain-flails, and halberds with odd-shaped
blades. They carried no bows and arrows or other projectile
weapons, these, as well as the war-steeds, being contrary to
their traditions of battle. Many of them had spears; but they
were accustomed to fling these at the Foe rather than thrust,
and so the weapons usually caused little damage to the heavily
armored Tanu riders and mounts.

A few Firvulag could not resist shape-shifting in anticipation
of the Mêlée. A ghastly winged serpent shot up amidst the
cohort commanded by Karbree the Worm. In another part of
the field, a stinking explosion heralded the temporary appearance of a cyclopean horror that splattered the salt with foul
ichor, prompting obscene protests from its indignant comrades-
in-arms. Out near the lagoonside flank, a formless mass of
yellowy-green protoplasm went rolling and bumping along,
hooting like an insane calliope.

The Tanu force faced this trollish rabble with dignity and
splendor. In the front ranks, armored in bronze and glass and
bearing colorful pennons, were the troops of gray-torc cavalry
and the human charioteers; all were armed with bows, spears,
and blades, and responsive to the mental commands of their

hybrid and gold-torc human officers. Behind them the five great battalions of the metapsychic guilds sat their steeds, both warriors and chalikos aglow with near-florescent brilliance. The coercers and psychokinetics were most numerous, the creators somewhat fewer in number, and the farsensors and combatant redactors constituted the smallest units, since most of their membership undertook support roles during this part of the Grand Combat.

Contingents from the various Tanu cities gathered around local champions bearing banners that must not fall into the hands of the Foe. Certain knights of high repute had their own adherents, Tanu and human; and besides the golds and silvers there were among them numerous glass-armored grays who had proven themselves in the Low Mêlée. Later, when the battle heated up, the regional groups and even the guild segregation would be abandoned as fighters gathered to follow the banner and mental commands of the heroes who acquitted themselves most valiantly—and also showed the most powerful defensive shielding ability. The royalty and field generals of Tanu and Firvulag stood well apart at this early stage, ready to observe and evaluate strategy and commend noteworthy feats.

The sky above the Great Lagoon was golden. As the upper limb of the sun appeared, there was a vivid green flash that persisted for a full twenty seconds before dissolving into white dazzle.

"Omen! Omen!" Screeching like banshees, the Firvulag horde leaped forward. Their mailed feet raised a din that caused the salt to tremble.

The Tanu waited in arrogant rainbow array, banners high and chalikos held firmly in check.

The sunlight strengthened. Nodonn Battlemaster rose into the air mounted on his armored charger, blazing to rival the solar disk. His mind and storm-loud voice sounded the ancient Tanu war cry:

"Na bardito!"

Glass trumpets held by the fighting women blared. Seven thousand gem-studded shields rang like bells as they were struck with the flat of vitredur swords. The uncouth bellowing of the Firvulag was overwhelmed as the tall exotics and their human allies repeated the cry.

"No bardito! Na bardito taynel o pogekône! *Forward, fighters of the Many-Colored Land!*"

The armies swept together, beginning the three-day encounter of massed minds and weapons. The clash of their meeting could be heard far away on the Mount of Heroes by those who had ears to hear.

"This year it will be different!" Sharn-Mes had vowed to Pallol.

The Firvulag Battlemaster, clothed in his illusionary guise of a monstrous black otter having six legs, flaming fangs and claws, and a coruscant opal the size of a dinnerplate lidding his Eye, professed scepticism. But then, he had not been there at Finiah!

The young general and the old, surrounded by aides and cronies, watched from behind a formidable screen as the early skirmishes took place. But after the first hour, even Pallol had to admit that the Little People were handling themselves with singular éclat. There was a marvelous and fresh sense of valor among them. Finiah had lifted their spirits—and even more, it had opened them to new ideas.

Sharn, wearing the shape of a three-meter albino scorpion, all waxy translucent, with glowing organs in his body cavities, pointed out an impending engagement with his farsense.

"They're coming close to us, Battlemaster. But no more tactical retreats now! Just you watch our lads when the Lowlife cavalry charges!"

A troop of gray-torcs came galloping hell for leather, ready to cut and trample a tight phalanx of some sixty Firvulag, who appeared to be making their customary stubborn and futile stand. But on this occasion, just before the mounts' pounding claws slashed down on the mound of overlapping black shields, the foot-soldiery scattered and went dodging among the tall animals, slashing at unarmored bellies with pole-knives, or swinging axes at the vulnerable leg tendons of the chalikos.

"I'll be damned!" interjected Pallol.

The gray-torc charge disintegrated. Hamstrung and mortally wounded steeds threw their riders and then staggered, screaming and tripping over their own gushing bowels, until they died. There were still the unhorsed humans to contend with; but in hand-to-hand combat the superior numbers of the Little People gave them the advantage, even though the grays were often physically stronger and compelled to fight to the death by their banner-carrying officers. Visions of battling goblins and other ghoulies and ghosties came and went in the midst of the struggle. The aether throbbed with hideous mental projections. The gold-torc human officer in coercer blue managed to zap out and hack to death half a dozen of the Firvulag before disappearing beneath a pile of stalwarts, but it was plain to see where the advantage lay now.

"That belly-sticking maneuver's not bad," Pallol had to admit.

"The humans used it at Finiah," Sharn said. "It was an innovation of some Lowlife metalcrafter who acted as an ad hoc leader. He said later that the tactic was traditional among members of his ancestral ethnic group. The hamstringing was suggested by a Lowlife holy woman, of all people. She had seen it used by the terrible Morigel in her murder of Epone."

"Morigel? *The Raven*—? Oh, you mean that human monster, Felice." Pallol shook his fierce carnivore head. "Té be thanked *that* one's out of the picture! Rumor has it she escaped the clutches of Handsome Cull and flew away in a big ball of scalding-hot blood. Damn superstitious claptrap! But wherever she's gone, I hope she stays there."

The Firvulag had finished butchering the last of the cavalry troop, and now raised thirty severed heads, still in crested bronze helmets, at the ends of their lances. One head wearing a blue-glass burgonet with draggled golden plumes was impaled on the pike of its own standard. The visor of the helmet was open and the dead eyes seemed to look down on the bloodied azure banner with mild astonishment.

The phalanx of Little People came rushing up to the knot of leaders. "Manifest, Battlemaster!" howled the dwarfs, dancing around Pallol and Sharn. "Manifest—like in the good old days!"

"You fellows...I'm prouder'n hell of you!" croaked the demon otter, swallowing a lump in his throat. "You bet I'll manifest for you!"

He lifted the opal lid from his Eye and zapped the waving heads to white bone. The skulls flew up and spun like a swarm of meteors just over the cheering warriors' speartops, then swooped down to land in a pyramidal pile on the sidelines, surmounted by the disgraced blazon. Every one of the skulls now was plated with gleaming gold, ready to be picked up by the trophy makers.

"Slitsal, Pallol!" yelped the phalanx. Brandishing their freshly cleaned weapons, they went dashing off to seek a new engagement with the Foe.

* * *

In a tangled heap lay two Firvulag bodies and one human being only pretending to be dead, the latter praying that he would be able to hold out until sundown, when it might still be possible for him to desert.

With great caution, Raimo Hakkinen groped again in the region of his high-rising rump. Once more there was only the dull *ching* of a glass-plated gauntlet striking the skirt of articulated tassets that armored his derrière. Damn! Forget again. He had no hip pocket. He had no flask of good old Hudson's Bay Demerara. No water, even. Nothing to drink at all unless you fancied blood. From the ventilating slot in the visor of his pink-glass sallet came a faint sob. It went unheard in the battle tumult all around him . . .

They'd had to coerce him into it, of course.

Those giggling Tanu she-fiends had dragged him away from the War Banquet and stripped his poor emaciated husk of a body right in the middle of the armorer's showroom while they selected a suitable PK harness for him. A gray squire had snickered while dressing him in the undergarments: first a cotton singlet and briefs, then the beautifully engineered suit of padding, tough woven-gauze fabric enclosing pea-sized plass bubbles, fully protective, airy, and weighing only a few grams. The six exotic women themselves had strapped on all the sliding plates of gold-chased pink glass, telling him how brave he was going to be and how gloriously he would prove himself on the White Silver Plain. Armored to the neck, he had to kneel before them while they mockingly dubbed him "Lord Raimo" with a big sword of rosy vitredur. Then he was forced to pleasure all of them in the only way left to him, and after that humiliation was over they clapped on the magnificent crested helmet that rather resembled a visored sou'wester, sheathed his sword in a scabbard hanging at his side, and hustled him outside to the skittish armored charger all ready to bear him off to battle. The chaliko had its coat dyed a violent fuchsia with acid-yellow mane and fetlock featherings, a parody of the Psychokinetic Guild's heraldic rose and gold. When the women teleported him into the saddle he barely had time to grab the reins before the great brute reared, nearly flinging him ass over teakettle backward.

Somehow he stayed aboard and was rewarded with six separate zonks on his silver torc's joy-buzzer.

They all trotted over to the Plain together from the Tanu encampment, joining the vast parade of bejeweled fighters and well-wishers streaming along the torch-lit and bannered avenue in the gray false dawn. The six ladies waxed symphonic on his happy-circuits to work him up to a fine pitch of euphoria; and when they reached the staging area of the battlefield they switched abruptly to the hypothalamic trigger, charging him with adrenalin and insane hostility toward the Firvulag Foe that lurked less than a kilometer away in the murk. He joined the Muriah-town ranks of his fellow silver PKers, hyped to the eyeballs with battle ardor.

Then the army waited in place for another whole hour. And with the passing of time and the withdrawal of the women to the distant sidelines his frenzy weakened and what remained of sanity began to assert itself. He discovered that the Tanu witches had forgotten to turn control of their man-toy over to Kuhal or Fian or some other officer of the PK battalion. He was unfettered! No one was coercing him any more!

When the charge sounded at last and he was off and running, waving his sword with the amok multitude and yelling with both voices, he was cold sober and scared out of his mama-reamin' mind.

At first, his chaliko saved him. It was a well-trained destrier, for all its evil temper, and it knew how to lash out with its claws whenever members of the Firvulag infantry came running at them. Raimo charged in a middle Tanu echelon, between the elite grays and the splendid ranks of provincial champions. By the time he was in the thick of the fighting there was enough dust and shape-shifting and preliminary slaughter going on to keep his erstwhile comrades occupied with matters other than *him*.

It was time to think about escape.

He wheeled about, slashing at the air and hiding behind his shield when illusionary monsters loomed up in the uncertain sunrise glare. Waves of Firvulag-generated terror swirled around him and blended with his own home-grown funk. He rode through a nightmarish hullabaloo where the combatants of both armies flashed into and out of view like images on a fritzed holo-projector. Only one aspect of the war was relentlessly real—the headless bodies, mostly human and Firvulag, and the dying animals staining the salt with sticky crimson and hot excrement.

Once he raised the visor of his helmet and vomited with discretion so as not to spook his mount. For the most part, the tall beast stepped carefully among the corpses while he tried to guide it in the direction of the ascending sun, which looked like a cut-out white disk heavily curtained in dusty haze. In that direction lay the eastern arm of the lagoon. If he reached the shore, it might be possible to swipe one of the Firvulag boats; and if his broken-down PK had a few watts left, he just might make it to Kersic.

Luck. Just a little luck. Didn't he deserve some after these months of living hell? Just keep up the good work, Horsie, and kick! Kick the crap outa those little turdlings when they come at us!

The chaliko fought well. And the Firvulag, he discovered, only threw their lances and never made use of arrows or darts, so he was fairly secure behind his shield in the high saddle until—

Something like a gigantic purple spider came scuttling out of the misty dazzle and got behind him. One of its appendages thrust up under the armored tailpiece of the chaliko's crupper. The animal let out an earsplitting scream and fell heavily forward, impaled by some kind of long-shafted pole-arm. Raimo was pitched from the saddle and hit the ground with a sound like a demolished xylophone. He saw the spider waver and dissolve, and then, cavorting around and around him and chortling in a falsetto squeal was a Firvulag in gore-smeared half-armor—the spitting image of Grumpy the Dwarf in Disney's 2-D cinema classic.

"Now I gotcha! Now I gotcha!" the manikin shrilled, waving a black glassy blade with a terrible notched edge.

"Help!" Raimo cried. He tried vainly to rise. His chaliko thrashed in death agonies, its great claws almost on top of him. *Helphelphelphelp* . . .

Sweet houghmagandy, Chopper! That you?

Aik! Aik, for the love o'Christ!

A beam resembling that from a sodium-vapor searchlight stabbed from the clouds of dust. It flicked harmlessly over the collapsed pink knight, but when it detected Grumpy it steadied and intensified. The Firvulag warrior's limbs flew out in spasm and his obsidian sword arced away. Orange-yellow light licked up and down the exotic body, melting the cuirass and leaving a path of smoking wound. The Firvulag uttered piercing shrieks. A voice out of thin air said, "That's a good fix," and the astral beam swiveled to shine into the transfixed dwarf's open mouth. There was a small, exceedingly nasty explosion.

"Open your eyes, Chopper. Your shining knight has come to the rescue."

Still prone, Raimo tilted up his visor. A huge black chaliko all armored in gold looked down at him, its benign eyes peering from the openings of a gilded chamfron. It had a monocerine faceted spike of amethyst mounted on its forehead. Sitting the magnificent beast was a diminutive human glowing as from a self-contained power source. He carried no weapon, no shield. But he held high a purple banner whose golden-hand blazon gave the finger to the Exile world. A black-and-violet cape rippled unstained about Aiken Drum's gold-lustre armor. He grinned as he PK-hoisted Raimo to his feet.

"There you go, Chopper. Good as new and ready to raise hell! See you later!"

"Wait—" the former woodsman pleaded. But the Shining One was gone. The battle noise intensified and so did the clouds of smoke and dust. It sounded as though some desperate engagement were coming right at him.

He stumbled about until he recovered his sword and buckler. Avoiding the thrashing chaliko and the fearful mess that had been Grumpy, he started off in the direction opposite from the worst of the psychocreative detonations, away from the clang of glass and bronze weapons, the bellowing of thousands of human and inhuman voices that filled his ears and mind. Within a few minutes he was completely disoriented. There was no clue to show him the way to the shore, no sure route to escape.

"What am I gonna do?" he whimpered.

Survive until sunset, something reminded him, and there would be a recess of three hours while the field was cleared of the wounded and the dead. If he could manage to hide until then—

He tripped over the two decapitated Firvulag and stopped his aimless flight. There was no natural cover on the Plain—so why not? Still shrouded in thick dust clouds, he flung himself down and burrowed among their dark-dripping limbs. Then he withdrew his consciousness into that inadequate little closet of refuge Aiken had taught him to use when the women drove him to the brink of madness. Unless someone beamed a thought right at him, he was safe. Almost all sensation, almost all pain ceased. Raimo Hakkinen waited.

The sun climbed high, heating the White Silver Plain and generating rising air currents that lifted the pall of dust. The warriors of both sides renewed hostilities. Great deeds of her-

oism were accomplished by Tanu and Firvulag alike, but the
gray-torc levies were being decimated by the new tactics of
the Little People, which placed the Tanu in a potentially dangerous position.

Raimo lay unmoving, even though some skirmishes took
place only a few meters away from him. He suffered cramps
and heat and thirst. Flies descended to feast on the blood and
lay their eggs in dead flesh, and some of them crept into his
helmet. Rousing from his stupor for a moment, he used the
shreds of his psychokinetic power to squash them against the
insides of the sallet. From time to time he groped deliriously
for booze. The fuchsia and yellow feathers of his helmut crest
shaded him slightly, but he still broiled in his shell of pink
glass until late afternoon when the sun declined at long last
and silhouetted the spine of Aven against blood-red light before
it disappeared.

A single horn sounded a silvery note that reverberated in
his mind.

The noises of battle faded. A wind of luxuriant coolness
came rushing over the salt. The armies withdrew.

Soon, Raimo told himself. Soon—when it was a bit darker.

He was wide-awake now but still lying motionless. Unfortunately, he had concealed himself in a spot precariously close
to the huge Tanu encampment. Redactors and farsensors on
missions of mercy were spreading out onto the quiet Plain,
guiding bearers to the wounded Tanu and human knights. And
there were others as well, leaders mounted on fresh chalikos
assessing the results of the first daylight action. If any of *them*
detected him—!

He tried to suppress all thought projection, shrinking back
into his little skull-closet. I am a dead thing let me be I am
dead pass me by ignore me go away go away . . .

"Oh, you are, are you?"

The voice was in his mind and ear. He refused to open his
eyes.

Laughter. "Come on now, Psychokinetic Brother. You don't
look as badly wounded as all that!"

The Firvulag bodies, those precious sheltering bodies, shifted.
He began to slip down onto the salt; but someone held his head,
compelling him to look out through the opened visor of his
sallet.

Two Tanu women—one in purple, one in redactor's red
and silver. Behind them, a pair of stolid male barenecks with

a litter. The stiffened Firvulag corpses lay like discarded headless mannequins beside him.

"He is not wounded at all, Sister," said the farsensor. Her deep-eyed face was grim and shadowed beneath the hood of her cloak.

"It's true," the redactor confirmed. "His mind also is untouched by the Foe. He is a malingerer. A craven!"

In a panic, Raimo scrambled to his feet. The cramped muscles of his legs refused to hold him up. He fell—and then the full force of Tanu coercion flowed from both women to his torc and held him in thrall. He stood perfectly still, a statue encased in jeweled pink plates crusted with other people's blood.

"You know the penalty for cowardice, Lowlife," said the farsensor.

He had to reply, "Yes, Exalted Lady."

"Go to the place then. Go where you belong!"

He turned from them and began to trudge across the battlefield, to where the Great Retort of glass stood waiting on its high scaffold.

Seven hundred kilometers to the west, the body of a young plesiosaur lay stranded on the rocks of the Alborán Volcano.

It had been hunting tunny-fish in the Atlantic, oblivious to any danger. And the tunnies themselves were chasing flying squid, and the squid in their turn had pursued a shoal of silver sardines that had been browsing upon the microscopic organisms of pelagic plankton. The unexpected current had seized them all, large creatures and small, and sucked them into the Gibraltar rift.

For a hellish quarter of an hour they had been buffeted and churned and then they were flung over the incredible waterfall. The young plesiosaur's graceful neck snapped as it impacted into the foaming pother of the new Mediterranean Sea. It died instantly. The tunnies, torn and battered against submerged rocks, succumbed not long afterward, as did the squid. Because of their small size, most of the sardines managed to traverse the falls shocked but physically unharmed. When their brains regained a measure of equanimity they attempted to go about life as usual, but the turbulent water filling the Alborán Basin was so full of silt that their tiny gills were clogged and every one of them suffocated. Of all the creatures that had been pulled through the newborn Straits of Gibraltar, only the hardy plankton survived.

The body of the plesiosaur had floated eastward until it came ashore on a slope of the Alborán Volcano that had once stood 600 meters above the floor of the adjacent dry basin. Gulls and carrion crows feasted on the carcass before the rising flood reclaimed it and set it adrift again in the misty dark.

8

IN THE RECESS BEFORE DAWN, NODONN FLEW OVER THE BAT-
tlefield with Imidol and Kuhal and Culluket, studying the dis-
mal results of the first round of the High Mêlée. The nearly
full moon was setting and the stars shone dim. In keeping with
their mood, the four brothers had dulled their own metapsychic
illumination and rode the sky like wraiths.

Firvulag medics, firefly lanterns bobbing, were busy among
the masses of dark bodies. Over in their camp was a great circle
of bonfires signaling a warrior's collation in progress. The Little
People were singing a loud polyphonic chant, punctuated by
throbbing drums.

"I don't recall hearing that one," Imidol remarked.

"One of their fight songs," Kuhal said sourly. "The kind
they sang when they used to win every other Combat back in
the days when you were still clinging to Mother's skirts and
learning to coerce black beetles. The song's a victory lay,
actually. Let's hope it's premature."

"That they should dare to voice it at all—!" Culluket's face
blazed momentarily crimson.

"We're not even behind in the banner tally," Imidol protested. "It was a shame about Velteyn, but Celadeyr of Afaliah
can take over his Creator Battalion."

"What's left of it," Kuhal snarled.

The Battlemaster had offered no observation. Now he led
them lower, to a large area where the scarlet-and-violet glow
of Tanu agents of succor had concentrated. He said, "Velteyn
was an impetuous fool to underestimate Pallol. He of all our
battle-captains should have known the new mood of the Foe.
And do not minimize the disaster, Youngest Brother! The ranks

337

of the creators have been reduced by fully one-quarter of their number—and Celadeyr is not one of the Host."

Culluket was a shade too neutral. "Well, it was your idea to have Mercy designate Vel as Second Creator. I warned you about his impaired judgmental outlook."

"And now," the truculent Kuhal appended, "our late brother of Finiah overlooks the Firvulag revels! Doubtless from empty, gold-socketed eyes."

"We have two more rounds," Imidol said, radiating confidence. "This fiasco with the gray-torc cavalry was a fluke. We'll bounce back."

"The Skin pavilions are overflowing," Culluket warned.

"I've been considering that," said Nodonn. "The most seriously wounded Tanu and human golds will have to be transferred to the healing rooms up in Redact House so that the field medics can devote their skills to patching up the battleworthy. We will undertake a second innovation as well. Culluket—you will farspeak the Lord Healer and instruct him to begin admitting the best of the fighting grays to the Skin. The wounded incompetents of our own race must resign themselves to sitting out the rest of the Combat in Muriah. We'll have no time for aging has-beens and bunglers in *this* war."

"Tana's teeth, Brother!" Kuhal exclaimed. "Thaggy will supernova if you go against tradition like that!"

Nodonn was adamant. "Our customs can stand a little bending. We have more to worry about than the injured pride of traditionalists—or even the Kingly honor. I admit now that I made a serious mistake putting Velteyn in a position of command. I was moved by sentiment, and you saw how popular his designation was at the time."

"Celadeyr is a good leader, even if he isn't of the Host," Kuhal said. "But we've lost a sure High Table candidate in Velteyn, and we'll have to look sharp from now on...And I'm talking to *you*, Youngest Brother!"

Imidol blustered, "I'll take care of Leyr when the time's ripe! You just watch your own psychokinetic ass, Brother!"

The eastern sky was deep violet. Venus hung over the gunmetal smoothness of the lagoon.

"This day," Nodonn told the three, "we must all take great care. The battalions will be fragmenting as the pressure of battle builds and the Firvulag Great Ones emerge to do personal combat. With so many grays and creators gone, we are even further outnumbered—but we still have the advantage in total mindpower. When you take to the field yourselves, be more prudent than our luckless brother, Velteyn. He erred in trying to gather outguild fighters to his personal banner too early by means of spectacular but foolhardy tactics. He gambled and lost. But let me remind you that there is another gambler fighting amongst our ranks . . . and he is playing a masterclass game for the highest possible stakes."

The four brothers talked over technicalities for some time after that, letting their steeds drift in the dawning. Down below, the Plain was being cleared rapidly. Firvulag dead were loaded into special coracles on the lagoon strand, to be immolated on the water during the return journey of the Little People to the mainland of Europe. The headless Tanu and human bodies were shrouded and stacked beneath the glass box of the Great Retort, where they would fuel the distillation of the imprisoned in the ultimate Combat offering of life and death.

For a hundred years, the eggs of the brine shrimp and the spores of minute algae had waited for rain.

Safe beneath the cracked saline crust of the playa, they had husbanded their tiny portions of life-force, resisting heat and drought and chemical action until yet another extraordinary once-in-a-century rainstorm should drench the Pliocene Betic Cordillera, swell the Proto-Andarax River, and fill the Great Brackish Marsh to overflowing.

Then for a few short weeks the thousands of square kilometers of dry lakebeds that lay between the normal western boundaries of the marsh and the gentle Alborán Rise would burst into teeming life. The brine shrimp and the algae and a few other hardy aquatic forms would thrive until the waters drained and evaporated away, leaving fresh eggs and spores entombed in the sediment to await the next Hundred-Year Storm.

No rain fell. The Pliocene sky of early November was clear and the bed of the Andarax carried only a thin trickle from the Spanish heights into the basin of the Mediterranean.

Nevertheless, the playa filled. The water spread and deepened in a manner unprecedented.

Brine shrimp hatched by the billions, ate algae, and hastened to lay the softer-shelled eggs that they produced in a well-watered environment. The water was muddier than usual and it harbored alien competitors, oceanic plankton that vied with the shrimp for the drifting greenery and even tried to prey upon the little crustaceans themselves. But the creatures of the playa had no true awareness of that, nor of the fact that they would never have to endure the long drought-sleep again.

"Trust me!" said Aiken Drum, amid the fire, smoke, mind-bellowing, and carnage.

"If this doesn't work," Bunone Warteacher told him, "there's a good chance that Nukalavee will nail you."

Aiken jabbed his saucy banner skyward. "Fear not! Just keep your fewkin' illusions intact and see that none of the gang here tries any heroic chivalrous bullshit to louse up the ambush. You hear me talkin', Tagan baby?"

The Lord of Swords said dryly, "We are so menaced by the Foe that I will bow to any expedient giving promise of reprieve. Even to you, Aiken Drum."

"Attaboy, Coercive Brother! Look sharp, then. I'm off!"

The golden figure on the magnificent charger vanished in a puff of purple smoke.

Lord Daral of Bardelask said, "Have confidence, Lord of Swords. Aiken has led us with brave ingenuity all this day. We have more than twoscore of the Firvulag battle standards through following his banner—as well as the head of their hero, Bles Four-Fang!"

"Lying in ambush isn't our *way*," grumbled Tagan.

"It's a way to win," Bunone shot back. "You old soldiers give me a pain in the—heads up!"

Out of the dusty imbroglio surrounding the six depleted Tanu companies emerged a new sound—an infuriated roar from more than a thousand throats, carrying over it a whistling squeal that reminded the human fighters of a king of Brobdingnagian electronic feedback. In an instant, all of the five hundred or so mounted knights disappeared, transformed into piles of miscellaneous corpses lying on both sides of a fairly clear corridor perhaps thirty meters in width and nearly ten times as long.

"The illusion is firm," Celadeyr told them. "And now—en garde!"

Into the cleared area came galloping a hipparion, one of the donkey-sized three-toed horses of the Pliocene Epoch. It was bridled and plumed and caparisoned with purple and gold garniture. Standing upon its back, waving a small-sized version of his digitus impudicus banner and laughing like a maniac, was Aiken Drum. He was wearing his golden suit of many pockets.

Charging hot on his trail was a legion of monsters, Firvulag stalwarts clad in their most fearsome illusions, led by a towering apparition resembling a centaur from which the skin had been flayed. Its raw muscles and sinews and red and blue blood vessels glistened and throbbed; the eyeballs started from its skull in frenzied rage; a lipless mouth with broken tusks gaped as it voiced its appalling scream. Nukalavee the Skinless, one of the premier Firvulag champions, pursued the small figure on horseback, flinging lightning balls that hit some invisible metapsychic barrier around the fleeing jester and exploded into harmlessness.

"Nyaa-nyaa!" cried Aiken Drum.

The hipparion galloped flat out. The youth bent to peer backwards through his legs and stick his tongue out at Nukalavee, clinging to the reins with one hand and flourishing his midget banner with the other. Then he dropped the flap of his golden suit.

Nukalavee's feedback howl soared to a hundred and ten decibels. The trampling Firvulag mob came to be entirely encompassed by the twin lines of corpses.

Bunone and Alberonn and Bleyn gave a simultaneous mental command:

Now.

"Wake up, Bryan. Can you hear me? Wake up now."

The dream of darkness began to fade, that cavern swallowing him with sweet and awful finality. He opened his eyes and there were Fred and Mario, the silver-torc redactors who had been his warders. And there was Creyn, now setting aside a small golden censer from which lingering acrid fumes swirled.

"I'm quite all right," Bryan said. (But soon to return to be engulfed.)

The deepset exotic eyes with their flat-blue pupils were very close to him. "Tana be thanked, Bryan. We had feared for you."

Good old Creyn was concerned. But why? She had promised to come for him.

"You have been asleep for three days, Bryan."

"It doesn't matter, really."

"No," the Tanu healer replied in gentle agreement. "I suppose it doesn't. But you must rise and prepare yourself now. Mario and Frederic will help you dress appropriately. It's time for you to leave Redact House. In an hour, after the sun sets, we will have the second Recess Before Night. There is to be a gathering of the entire Tanu battle-company in extraordinary conclave. You are summoned to the White Silver Plain."

Bryan managed a slight smile. "Another command performance before Their Awful Majesties? I should think they'd have . . . more diverting entertainment these days than the likes of me."

"You are summoned by Nodonn," Creyn said. He extended one bony hand all covered with rings and lightly touched the fingers of the still recumbent anthropologist. "You have no torc and so I cannot reach you in the fullness of fellowship, nor heal you even if it were allowed, or possible. You are unaware of what you have done, and in Tana's mercy you may never know. So go, Bryan. Receive your last gift. Goodbye."

Bryan's wondering gaze followed the exotic man to the door of the suite. And then Creyn was gone and Fred and Mario were helping him into the sumptuous bathroom.

"They weren't listening to me!" Bewildered, Thagdal sank back into his throne.

The banqueting pavilion was a turmoil of conflicting thoughts and shouts. Nobody was sitting formally at table any more; they were jumping up on top of them to deliver impromptu harangues; or gathered around this champion or that, consuming heroic quantities of liquor as they debated and quarreled about the remarkable events of the day, the Tanu comeback in the face of lengthening odds and what—or who—had been responsible for it.

"I thought it was a lovely speech, dear," Nontusvel assured him. "Setting differences aside and all working together. What could be more logical?"

The King only gave a hollow laugh and drank from his gilded-skull goblet. Morosely, he stared into the inset carbuncle eyes.

"Remember this good old boy? Maglarn Wrinkle-Meat. Ugliest mother's son of the whole Firvulag tribe, and a fighting fool. I finally zapped him through the gizzard after we'd walloped each other for three mortal hours in the Heroic Encounters. Now *that* was Combat! None of this hole-in-a-corner sneaking around and dirty tricks. But now—! The Foe fights dirty, and so do we. And unless some miracle supervenes, the dirtiest trickster of the lot will end up King of the Many-Colored Land."

"Here's Nodonn," Nontusvel said softly. "He has . . . brought someone with him."

The King looked up and uttered a mild blasphemy. "I might have known who had that anthropologist stashed away! My boys combed the whole city and half of Aven and couldn't find hide nor hair of him."

Nontusvel regarded her husband with sorrow. "But they found poor Ogmol, didn't they?"

The royal beard sparked ominously. "You're an innocent, Nonnie. I was trying to save us all."

The arrival of the Battlemaster inspired cheers from the thousands of feasters, and a single impudent *nyaa*. Nodonn made his duty to his parents with accustomed serenity and then took Bryan around to a prominent position in front of the High Table. The human scientist appeared dazed; an odd smile touched his lips and from time to time one of his hands strayed to his open collar, from which came a telltale golden gleam.

"Noble battle-company!" intoned the storm-loud voice. The chain of silence was not needed. "We have suffered defeats in this Grand Combat . . . and victories!"

Plaudits and groans and not a few drunken curses.

"The first round of the High Mêlée saw us faced with disaster when our gray-torc cavalry and charioteers faltered in the face of novel tactics from the Foe. The misfortune was compounded when the commanders of the gray levies, half-bloods and gold-torcs, as we know, failed to rally their troops according to the tenets of our ancient battle-religion."

Catcalls and shouting of indignant denials, mingled with taunting epithets and a scattering of "Shame!"

The Battlemaster held up one mailed fist. "Let those deny it who will! The ranks of humankind were shattered. And as a consequence we suffered grave setbacks. The blame, however, lies not with humanity, fellow warriors of the Tanu, but with ourselves!"

The hubbub, which had been swelling in intensity, suddenly fell away to silence.

"We have come to depend overmuch upon humanity in our Grand Combat. We have become lax and decadent as we adopted first their domesticated animals as battle-mounts, and then their very selves. Yes . . . we adopted humanity. They fight our battles, they grow our food, they operate our mines and factories, they administer our commerce, they infiltrate our sacred guilds, they mingle their very blood and genes with our own! But that is not all. We are faced with the ultimate humiliation—and once again, we have brought it upon ourselves. For a human now aspires to our High Kingship!"

In all the vast tent there was no sound. And then came the mighty bellow of Celadeyr, Lord of Afaliah: "And is this to our shame, Battlemaster? When Aiken Drum goes himself to meet the Foe, unarmed and unafraid, while certain Exalted Personages rest secure behind impregnable screens, dithering about antiquated tactics that no longer dismay the Firvulag— much less defeat them?"

A thunderclap of mental and vocal shouting greeted this sally. Celadeyr added, "The Foe has consorted with humans. This is how Finiah fell. This is how their pikemen learned to devastate our cavalry. Shall we then return to the ancient ways you champion and all lose our heads—rejoicing that at least our honor is intact? Or shall we follow this golden youth, the chosen of Mayvar, and know victory?"

This time the outcry made the very walls and ceiling of the pavilion billow and the cups and plates dance on the tables. The face of Apollo was apparently unmoved; but Nodonn was now glowing so furiously that those closest to the High Table fell back, shielding their eyes from the rose-gold glare.

"I only wish to show you," the Battlemaster said, and now his voice was very soft in the reborn silence, "what the price of such a victory must be. You will see and hear what future lies ahead of us from the lips and mind of this human scientist, who enjoyed the highest reputation in his own Galactic Milieu. His survey of our relationship with humanity and the attendant stresses was commissioned by the Thagdal himself in the hope of confuting my own long-stated opposition to human assimilation. This scientist carried out his analysis freely, without prejudice. Many of you were interviewed by him or by his associate, our late Creative Brother Ogmol."

Now Nodonn held high the book-plaque that had been Bryan's love-gift to Mercy.

"Here is a copy of the survey he recently completed. He will explain it to you himself. He wore no golden torc while he worked—and he wears one tonight only so that you may examine his mind yourselves and see the truth of his statements. Because I compel him through the torc, he will carry out the survey's extrapolations in full, including the impact of humanity's use of the iron. Listen to what this man, Bryan Grenfell, says. It will not take long. And then return to the White

Silver Plain for our night affray and *think* as you contend against the Firvulag! When dawn brings the final day of our Grand Combat, you may then choose which banner to follow until the end—that of your Battlemaster, or that of our true Foe."

The marshgrass flats and the lotus beds of the Great Brackish Marsh were gone now, and mangrove jungles were the ibises and egrets and pelicans once nested were completely submerged. Only the highest islets still poked above the rising waters; here crazed animals fought one another in the dwindling space until they were drowned or pushed off to swim for their lives. The luckier of the refugees found sanctuary on the great dam of volcanic rubble; but it was necessary for them to keep climbing higher and higher up the clinkery slope as the water continued to rise. Once the summit had been attained, many of the animals were too weary and traumatized to go farther (and down the eastern flank of the dam it was all desert, anyway); and so they crouched there beneath the moon that lacked one day to fullness—the tusked water deer and the otters and the pygmy hippos and the aquatic hyraxes and the long-bodied felids and the rats and the turtles and the snakes and amphibians and a myriad other displaced creatures—not one showing aggression toward another, instincts of predators and prey alike dulled by the devastation of their world.

The water rose higher. The weight of it thrust against the natural dam; water seeped into every crevice and percolated through the coarser strata of ash. Some found its way among the debris clogging the Long Fjord. When this reached the head of the narrow Southern Lagoon estuary, a thousand little jets of water squirted from the rubble-face.

The water in the erstwhile Great Brackish Marsh was now more than eighty meters deep where once the flamingos had waded. For the first time in more than two million years it was possible for a fish to swim from the cliffs of southern Spain to the Morocco shore.

9

He was summoned again from the warm dark.

Why oh why couldn't they simply leave him in peace? Leave him to savor the last of her alone? He had done the sun-god's bidding, explaining to the barbarians why the shutting of the time-gate was good, why the Tanu should wean themselves from their overdependence upon human technology.

Ingenious, the way that the Battlemaster had twisted the statistics to his own ends; but of course he had to spare Mercy and the loyal hybrids. Pogroms were so wasteful and Apollo ever a prudent husband-man.

But Bryan had justified it all, speaking through his golden torc. Poor Oggy had been so right about it being a boon to communication. (And so it was, provided you had angelic backing when it came to sloughing over the dicey bits without getting caught.) When the little lecture was finished, the mood of the crowd was turning away from Aiken Drum. Bryan wasn't surprised. Barbarians were a hot-headed and fickle lot, and this tribe was almost as mercurial as the Irish.

Nodonn had taken him then to the place where Mercy waited. And she had shown him what he had been missing by not accepting the golden torc before. Even knowing that it was the end, that he would not survive the cave this time, he had gone freely to her, into the bright flight and the long fall.

Free but never free of you with your wild wild eyes, Mercy. And will I love you till I die.

"Come out of it, son. Help a little. I'm not the best redactor in the realm, but there's a few tricks left in the old man's bag. Come on, Bryan. You remember me."

I die I did but die I see her passing by I die . . .

346

"He's not gonna stop free-wheeling until you zorch him in the stem, Craftsmaster."

"You shut up, you damned male trollop. I pulled *your* marbles together, didn't I?... Come on Bryan. Open your eyes, son."

A great round irascible face, hair and trailing mustaches of silvery gold, all backlighted by a yellow morning sky with strange streaky red clouds. He closed his eyes, willing the memory of her and her warm dark to return.

But it would not, not yet. In an unsteady voice, Bryan said, "Hullo, Lord Aluteyn."

"That's good!" An arm slipped around him, lifting. A glass of water, not very cold, was held to his mouth.

"I'd rather be left alone," Bryan whispered. Oh, let me go down, down! But where was that sea unreflecting of stars?

"No you don't son. Not yet."

He peered out of the mind-cave resentfully. A crowd of people, looking very seedy, crouched all around him. Gold and silver and gray torcs and now all of them able to *feel* at his mind in the most disconcerting way. "Do stop that, all of you," he told them peevishly. "It's not decent when—when I'm—"

"You're not quite ready to shuffle off, son. I've patched you up a little, as well as I could. Just tell us what happened at that conclave last night. What's Aiken Drum up to? There's something very odd going on. Since I'm deposed, I've had a block put on my metafaculties to restrict my range to the immediate vicinity. But I don't need my powers to feel the ground tremors and the changes in the local earth currents, and see those anomalous clouds. Has your young friend Aiken Drum been doing any fancy mucking-about with Aven's geology?"

Now Bryan's eyes were fully open. He began to laugh, then trailed off in feeble coughing. The glass of water met his lips. "I should think... Aiken Drum had quite enough on his plate already... without conjuring up earthquakes." He sank back against the Craftsmaster's arm. A singular pang shot through him. *What if he wasn't going to die?*

A contemptuous voice. Raimo? Yes, it was Raimo Hakkinen, that poor devil.

"He's no help! Maybe we can get some fresh dope when the next batch of losers is tossed in here at sunset. Though what difference it makes to *us*—"

"I thought I was beyond caring," the Craftsmaster said. "But I do care! I'm one of the First Comers, and I care! If there is a genuine danger, then I must give warning. My honor demands it!"

The Raimo Hakkinen voice was muttering something scornful. Other voices, other thoughts, came sloshing in disorderly waves against Bryan's brain. A few persistent interlopers picked through the ruins like bored ghouls.

"A really big earthquake might crack this thing so we could escape!" the Raimo voice said. Exclamations. Protests. And the probing. How many of them were there mauling him?

"Mercy," he groaned aloud.

Something like an arm of silver-and-green light swept all of the prying minds away from him and showed him how to put up the screen. He did. But when he turned to descend again he could not find the cave. His mind and voice howled, anguished, *"Mercy!"*

Run search cry hunt the dark with the golden torc's horrible light driving it back whenever he spotted it afar off. She would not wait. She was gone. And he might not die.

"Mercy," he whispered again, and woke to the compassionate gaze of the old Craftsmaster. After a long time, he asked, "Where is this place? What is it?"

"It's called," Aluteyn said, "the Great Retort."

Brede Shipspouse led the three humans along the deserted corridor deep within the secret wing of Redact House. They were free of their gray torcs, dressed in fresh clothing, and at a loss to know who she was or what she wanted of them.

"My identity is unimportant," said the masked exotic, stopping in front of a closed door. "The only one who matters lies within, lost now in a reverie of self but soon perhaps to awaken."

Brede's brown eyes fixed on Basil. "You are a man of action and ingenuity. In a few brief hours your talents will be called on. When the time comes, you will know what to do. All of the things you will need—including maps and many sophisticated devices confiscated from time-travelers—will be found stored in lockers inside this room."

The headdress of the Shipspouse tilted far back as she addressed Chief Burke, and her eyes crinkled with humor at the big Native American's expression of suspicion. "You will organize and lead the survivors. It will be difficult, for there will be the Skin patients to care for, and even the able-bodied will be reluctant to follow a bareneck human. But you will lead them, nonetheless."

Brede's hand now rested on the latch of the door. She said to Amerie, "Your task will be the most difficult of all, for you will have to help her during the terrible time of adjustment. But you were her friend—and you are the only one of the original group left for Elizabeth to turn to. You will understand her, even though you are not a metapsychic. She does not need a fellow initiate now. She needs a friend... and a confessor."

The door opened. Within was a large dimly lit room, three of its walls carved from the living rock. The wall at the far end had a long horizontal slot, glassed over, that revealed a late afternoon panorama of Muriah and the salt flats to the south. There were storage lockers lining the side walls and in the center of the room, a low cot with a figure in red denim lying on it.

"Remain here until tomorrow morning. Do not leave this place before dawn, no matter what should happen. You will not see me again, because I must go down to be with my people in the hour that I have foreseen. When Elizabeth wakes, tell her this: *Now you are free to make a true choice*. Guard her well, for she will soon be the most important person in the world."

Brede faded from their sight, enigmatic to the last. The three of them exchanged glances and shrugs, and then Amerie went to examine Elizabeth while the men opened the lockers.

With the Fifth Day now winding down to the final hours of the High Mêlée, both armies were inflamed and hopeful of victory, even though the Firvulag knew very well that the odds were lengthening against them.

King Yeochee spent most of the afternoon in the darkened Tent of the Seers, where talented crones used farsensing powers to project choice bits of action for the noncombatant Little People to view. The duel between old Leyr and Imidol of the Host had been particularly gripping... and poignant, too, for Yeochee remembered well what a firebreather the old Lord Coercer had been before his banishment by Gomnol. Even though Leyr was one of the Foe, that had been a hard way for him to go—sliced up slowly like a salami and then forced, by the superior metafaculty of the young coercer, to open his gorget and cut his own throat. Ah, well. Youth would have its day.

He left the seers and rambled on to the field hospital where the wounded were being treated preparatory to disembarking for home. Boats had already begun to leave Aven, and many more would sail before the Combat had its official finale at dawn. The post-Combat Truce, like that prior to the games, was only one month in length—and overland travel with the wounded was a slow business, especially since they could not utilize river boats on their homeward journey.

Yeochee wandered up and down the rows of battered and bloody gnomes. A word of cheer from the Old Man always seemed to bolster the warriors' spirits, and they needed all the help they could get. There was no magical healing Skin in the field hospital of the Little People. All they had were their rough and ready surgical skills, fortitude, and the superior resistance of a tough race that had matured in a natural environment fraught with hazard. Nearly half of the original Firvulag complement was now hors de combat. But the Foe, King Yeochee reminded the smirking casualties, had lost almost the entire 2000 of their gray elite corps and most of the 1500 silvers— as well as a respectable number of the rash and punier-powered among the Tanu and human golds.

"We still have a chance!" the King asserted. "We're not licked yet. This might just be the year that the Sword of Sharn comes home!"

The broken warriors croaked and gargled and whistled. Yeochee hopped on top of an empty bandage crate, knocking his crown askew again.

"So we haven't got as many high-point banners as they do! So we've only got four skulls in the 'Most Exalted' class! Damme if two of 'em don't belong to the Host—and one of those a High Tabler! Velteyn and Riganone are worth ten extra points right there, and that offsets our loss of poor old Four-Fang and Nukalavee. We've still got the Heroic Encounters to come, and one good upset there could wipe out all the Foe's advantage in the Petty Nobility tally. If they do beat us, it'll be by a squeaker. But they won't beat us! We're going to fight, and we're going to win!"

The tent rang with ragged cheers. One game soul even managed to turn on his sparkling centipede apparition for a moment.

Wiping away a furtive tear, Yeochee stood proudly and let his regal aspect come slowly upon him. His dusty fur-trimmed robe turned to obsidian parade armor, blazing with a thousand gems. His tall crown (sitting foursquare) sprouted its ram's horns and beak of enameled gold, and brushed the roof of the great hospital tent as he attained his full stature, dark and terrible, eyes glowing like green beacons.

"This is the end of my term in office, warriors. And I confess that I never dared hope to see the old days of glory restored before my retirement. But those days are at hand! Even if we fall a little short this time . . . *just wait till NEXT year!*"

"Let's hear it for Yeochee!" somebody yelled. And the maimed and mangled hauled themselves up and hailed the Soverign Lord of the Heights and Depths, the Monarch of the Infernal Infinite, the Undoubted Ruler of the Known World.

Illusionary aspects flashed and flared and the tent seemed crowded with a thousand monsters. But then as quickly as they had appeared they were extinguished, and the little man in the dusty robe with the tilted crown was saying, "Té lift your fighting hearts, lasses and lads," and all the brave demons turned again to bloodstained and weary gnomes.

Yeochee slipped outside into the evening calm of the Last Recess. He would still have to get something to eat and say his prayers and then get into harness to join Pallol and the generals overseeing the last of the Mêlée. In the four hours before midnight, the free-for-all battle would have its wild climax. Some of the Firvulag shitfires were sure to be bucking for the empty champion slots—and Yeochee wanted to be there on the spot with the commendation if any of them came through. No proxy accolading for him!

The sky looked rather strange. Wispy cloud-tails coming out of the west still showed purplish against indigo. It was too early for the rains, though. The King shook his head. The big full moon was sullen orange in leftover dust and smoke blown out over the lagoon. Bearers with the newly wounded and the decapitated dead were wending their way from the battlefield, across the Well-of-the-Sea Canal, and past the great pile of skulls encircled by exultant bonfires. The heap of gilded trophies had never been larger. And how fine those captured banners would look hanging among the old soot-stained blazons draping the stalactites at High Vrazel! Perhaps they wouldn't win back the lost Sword of Sharn. But they would at least have acquitted themselves with honor.

"And that's the important thing!" Yeochee whispered fiercely.

Out on the salt, the glowworm processions carried in their burdens.

10

AT MIDNIGHT ON THE WHITE SILVER PLAIN, WHEN THE SILVER moon rode high behind thin clouds that rippled like watered silk, the two armies lowered their weapons and finally disengaged. Bareneck hostlers led all the war-chalikos away. Swift psychokinetics cleared a great circle of bodies and debris. All around its perimeter the rank and file of Tanu and Firvulag gathered indiscriminantly in the fellowship of utter physical exhaustion.

The Kings came forth with their entourage of noncombatants, Thagdal bearing the trophy Sword. And after them swarmed the commonalty from the camps who wished to view the Heroic Encounters with their own eyes. At the last, in an action so unprecedented that it defied comment, Brede came.

No one needed to have the tallies posted; each mind knew what the Mêlée score was—the Tanu holding to their precarious noble bodycount lead, which would be overtaken if there were any significant upsets during the Encounters. The great champions of the sibling peoples would now fight individually; they were nearly equal in metapsychic as well as physical prowess. None of the Firvulag heroes were of the gnomish build; they were all massive and some of them were giants. The Tanu (with one exception) were also outstanding physical specimens, their somewhat lighter musculature outweighed by the wider range of their mental powers. So well matched were the Great Ones of the two battle-companies that the winners of the Encounters were almost always adjudged on points. It had been many years since any hero had been slain in the Combat's final scoring event.

Referees from both races took their positions. Heralds sounded a fanfare of glass and silver and the Firvulag drums

began to beat. Out of the black-armored multitude came Pallol
One-Eye, bearing his terrible effigy battle standard, which he
implanted in the salt. The nine Great Ones of the Little People
emerged from the throngs of their adherents to declare fealty
to their Battlemaster: Sharn-Mes, the veteran Medor, Galbor
Redcap, the female heroes Ayfa and Skathe, Tetrol Bonecrusher, Betularn White-Hand, and—newly accoladed in place
of the defunct Bles and Nukalavee—Fafnor Ice-Jaws and Karbree the Worm.

While the cheers for the Firvulag champions still resounded,
Nodonn came forward to plant his sun-faced blazon. Those
who gathered beneath it were Imidol, Culluket the Interrogator,
Kuhal Earthshaker, and Celadeyr of Afaliah, field-promoted
to the High Table and now Second Creator, who had chosen
to follow Nodonn after all. But then, with the crowd's murmur
building to a new crescendo, Aiken Drum strolled out and
planted *his* banner, and to him adhered Tagan Lord of Swords,
Bunone Warteacher, Alberonn Mindeater, and Bleyn.

The assembly erupted. This partisan division among the
Tanu heroes signified that Nodonn's position as Battlemaster
and heir apparent was challenged by the little gold-clad human.
Tanu and Firvulag viewed such a split in leadership differently;
among the Little People, there would have been a popular
election to settle matters, just as in their choosing of kings; but
the Tanu resolved their intramural conflict on the field of honor.
The Heroic Encounters between Tanu and Firvulag might not
be broken for partisan jousts, and so the total performance of
each aspirant's attachés would decide whether Nodonn or Aiken
Drum ultimately met Pallol. The ensuing Encounter of Battle-
masters would bring to a close the scoring; and following would
be the awarding of the victory trophy by Thagdal—who would
either yield up the Sword to King Yeochee or keep it himself.

This officially marked the end of Grand Combat hostilities.
But not the end of the fighting—for the two rivals for the field
leadership of the Tanu would then have their duel, the winner
earning the option of declaring fealty to the reigning monarch
or challenging him on the spot.

The prospect of provoking the downfall of Tanu royalty
gave a nice added incentive to the already victory-hungry Firvulag heroes and they began stamping their mailed feet on the
salt in a gesture of defiance that was immediately taken up by
all of the Little People among the spectators. The ground shook.
The Tanu knights blazed in furious retaliatory display. The

aether and air vibrated with insults and it seemed that a riot might break out.

Then from the crowded area where Thagdal and Yeochee stood, there stepped a woman dressed all in black and red with her face hidden. The chain of silence was held unmoving between her outstretched hands. The mob fell back and the mind-storm calmed.

The Marshal cried out: "Let the Encounters begin!"

Now there was frantic whispering and a cudgeling of wits among the spectators, trying to compute the odds for this decisive event. Poor Karbree was bumped from the field because of the Aiken Drum-Nodonn combination, leaving eight subsidiary heroes on either side. As each Firvulag contestant stepped forward in order of reverse seniority, Thagdal—as present custodian of the victor's Sword—was entitled to name a Tanu opponent. It was a time of suspenseful calculation. Would the King succumb to the temptation to shave points in favor of Nodonn's boys? Would he risk the loss of the Sword in order to beat out the little human? Past matches between Nodonn and Pallol had been very close, pointwise. Was it possible that the small golden manikin had stronger metafaculties than the glorious Apollo? (Physically, there was no comparison.) And yet—the upstart must have something going for him or he wouldn't be in a position to challenge at all! Not since the Times of Unrest had there been such a wild windup to the Grand Combat; and a heretic aspiring to the Tanu throne was nothing compared to the prospect of a *human* King of the Many-Colored Land...

Thagdal raised rainbow-glinting arms.

"For Fafnor Ice-Jaws—Culluket the Interrogator!" (It figured; the novice Firvulag versus a High Tabler notorious for his mind-tricks and dubious courage.) "For Betularn White-Hand—Celadeyr of Afaliah!" (Two codgers, but the edge clearly belonged to mean old Celo.) "For Tetrol Bonecrusher—Alberonn Mindeater!" (Nod to the Firvulag. Was Thaggy getting sly in this match?) "For Galbor Redcap—Tagan Lord of Swords!" (Nope, guess not. Tagan had beaten this boy before.) "For Skathe—Bunone Warteacher!" (A tossup. Nothing harder to handicap than battling broads.) "For Ayfa—Bleyn!" (Now there was a real mismatch! Sharn's wife would take that hybrid apart like fried chicken. This one could finish Aiken Drum.) "For Medor—Kuhal Earthshaker!" (Now the big guns. Pretty close, but this Tanu threw a helluva PK punch.) "And for Sharn-

Mes—Imidol Lord Coercer!" (Anybody's fight, Imidol being so young. But coercers were a nasty lot and this boy was overdue.)

"You will come forth," Thagdal said, "contend throughout the allotted time, and then withdraw promptly before the next contestants. And may the Goddess of Battles look upon you, judge your valor, and make her choice!"

"Listen to me, Coercive Brother!" the Craftsmaster pleaded. "The ground tremors! The electromagnetic changes in the crust! Can't you feel them yourself?"

The cherry-faced human gold in the blue armor shrugged. "With the fans making such a brouhaha over at the Encounters, I should bloody well hope the Earth would shake! It's two losses and two wins for Aiken Drum's folks now, and the lads of Nodonn have a win, a loss, and a tie between Kuhal and Medor. So you see we're down to the wire in this last tilt with Imidol versus Sharn-Mes—not only in the Battlemaster sweepstakes but very likey in the whole friggerty Combat to boot! And I'll thank you to stop impeding me in me duties so I can get back to the action!"

Gray soldiers herded into the great glass enclosure the last of a draggled column of men and women, cleared from the dungeons and lockups of Muriah and brought to the White Silver Plain to make their last offering. There were not fallen nobility or craven fighters, but the saddest dregs of the realm— the traitors, the criminals beyond rehabilitation, the rebellious barenecks too feeble to provide sport in the Hunt, women worn out by childbearing, and above all the mind-burned, who shuffled along through the impetus of their gray or silver or gold necklets to stand in neat lines along the show-window front of the Great Retort and stare out at the moonlit battleground with empty eyes.

"Read me!" shouted Aluteyn to the commander of the guard. "Check my mind! There's something funny going on, I tell you! Just give me permission to farsense the King—or Lady Eadone Sciencemaster."

"None of your guff now," warned the human coercer. "Just ease off, old fellah-me-lad. Cash in your chips like a man." He sent a mental order to the soldiers, turned his back, and hurried outside to where his mount waited.

"I told you it wouldn't do any good," Raimo said gloomily. "But nice try, Al."

Aluteyn's teeth ground together as he looked out of the thick, clear front of the Retort. "Damn them! Damn them! This Mediterranean Basin is unstable! Over to the east, between Kersic and that long archipelago that you future people call Italy, there's a zone of crustal instability I've had my eye on for a couple of hundred years. What if it has a major disturbance? There could be a seiche in the lagoon!"

"What's a saysh?" asked mystified Raimo.

"A tidal wave. A little one," said one of the craven gold knights, chuckling. "Wouldn't that be a kick in the nuts for all the brave gladiators on yon battlefield? Och, we know how the Tanu love to get their little trotters wet!"

"The lagoon's too shallow to slosh up much," somebody opined.

"It might make things too wet to light the fire under the Retort!" another shouted.

"Not bloody likely. You ever *see* one o' these here conflagrayshuns, cockie? Ask old Al Tub-o-Guts Craftyfuckinmaster here! He usta be the one to touch off the corpse pile every year. Goddam psychoenergy from the whole goddam Guild o' Creators'll broil us in the goddam box even if it pours goddam pups and pussycats!"

"I must give warning!" Aluteyn cried. "It's my duty! If I could only communicate—"

"Send 'em a stargram C.O.D.," a harsh voice suggested.

A woman said, "We could act out your message in charades when they come to light the bodies!" Her giggle was hysterical and infectious. Laughter spread.

"Testify like those muffers Shadrach, Meshach, and Abednego! Too bad we got no Nomex angel in here like them old-time Israeli cats had!"

The rabble of the doomed cackled and taunted and wept.

Meanwhile, Aluteyn Craftsmaster, former Lord Creator, used what was left of his metapsychic power to etch a warning message on the inside of the Retort's smooth front pane. It probably wouldn't do any good, but he had to try something.

"You *lost!*"

"It was a lousy Firvulag trick he pulled on me, Battlemaster," protested Imidol hotly. "I really had Sharn-Mes worried, him and his damn scorpion suit, and if I'd just had three more seconds—"

"You lost, and your bungling and inexperience may have cost us the Grand Combat!"

The sapphire titan removed his helmet and dumped a bucket of cold water over his still-smoldering hair. "You know you can beat Aiken Drum in the one-on-one."

"Fool!" The Battlemaster raged to incandescence. "Have you forgotten the Firvulag? They now lead us in the point-scoring!"

In the minds of the eight Tanu champions and Nodonn hung the telltale scorecard:

CULLUKET	(LOST)	*vs.*	FAFNOR
CELADEYR	(WON)	*vs.*	BETULARN
ALBERONN	(WON)	*vs.*	TETROL
TAGAN	(WON)	*vs.*	GALBOR
BUNONE	(LOST)	*vs.*	SKATHE
BLEYN	(LOST)	*vs.*	AYFA
KUHAL	(TIED)	*vs.*	MEDOR
IMIDOL	(LOST)	*vs.*	SHARN-MES

The Battlemaster gestured to the four allies of Aiken Drum who stood around the defeated coercer hero. "And thanks to our turncoat brothers and sister here, we must send a puny trickster into the Encounter against Pallol One-Eye!"

There was a puff of purple smoke. "I thought I heard my name taken in vain," chirped Aiken Drum. "Don't tell me, Brother Sun-Face, that you have doubts about me being able to put a lid on the Big Eyeball?"

Nodonn said, "He is five times more mighty than his blood-cousin, Delbaeth, who led us such a merry chase on the Quest. And he does not strike and run away, as the Shape of Fire did. He stands! Do you think that your mind will be able to shield you indefinitely from that Eye? Are you confident that your psychocreative power is a match for his? Or will you expend yourself in defense, human youth, using all of your strength to fend off his energies while he demolishes you with a single blow of his armored fist?"

"How would you like *me* to kill *him*?"

The eight champions and the Battlemaster broke into bitter laughter.

Aiken frowned. "No. Seriously. I could kill him. Just like I did Delbaeth. I'd have to do it in a human way, and you and the rest of the High Table have to all agree that I can do it my way without getting zapped by the lot of you for breaking some holy fewkin' rule."

Nodonn's face within the fantastic rosy-gold helmet was bright with contempt. "You may not use the Spear on Pallol, Lowlife. Only against me."

Aiken flipped one finger toward the Battlemaster. "That's not what I meant. And don't be impatient, Sun-Face. Your turn's coming!" He glared at the champions in turn. "Well? Am I going to pull your baked patoots out of the fire and win this damn shindy for you—or not? My trick's no more dirty than the ones the Firvulag and their human pals pulled on you guys at Finiah." And Aiken's mind showed them what he proposed to do. "Yes or no, dammit? Give the rest of the Table a holler or I'm gonna just take off like a skyrocket and leave you here with your thumbs in place."

"Go and be damned!" Imidol yelled. "The Battlemaster will meet Pallol if you default. And he'll win!"

"Are you sure?" inquired the jester softly. "Will he win by enough points to clinch the ball game? Nodonn can't decapitate Pallol. But I can. And you know what that'll do to our score. We win, walkin' away!"

"I will confer with the High Table," said Nodonn.

Fifteen seconds later he said, "You will fight Pallol One-Eye in your human way, without prejudice."

The moon was descending now, having done its work. It still shed light on the Mediterranean Basin, but its tidal effects, so long inconsequential on the shallow water, were just beginning to make themselves felt in the area west of Aven where the dark waters lapped a crumbling lava crest.

11

AIKEN DRUM ADVANCED ON PALLOL ONE-EYE.

The giant did not bother to shape-shift. He waited, an ebon monolith planted in the middle of the white-salt circle, and chuckled. The sound reminded some of the hushed spectators of a metal dustbin caroming down a long flight of stairs.

Fools! What fools the Tanu were, sending this puny creature against *him*! They had forgotten, that was it. His long absence from the field had dimmed their memories, just as their fatal contact with Lowlife humankind had softened their wits. This insect, this gaudy midge in his golden glass and jaunty purple-feathered crest, was not even worth toying with. He would die in a single thunderclap thrust, incinerated by the incomparable blast of psychoenergy from Pallol's Eye!...

Aiken Drum had come to a standstill. He had no lance, no amethyst sword, no weapon at all that Pallol could discern save a small golden ball and a dangling leather strap wide in the middle and thinning toward the ends.

Holding up one admonishing forefinger in the universal gesture that begged a moment's wait, Aiken transferred the strap to his teeth and concentrated on trying to manipulate the ball in some way between his mailed fingers. Still laughing, Pallol removed his awesome helmet, tucked it under his right arm, and with the other hand raised the patch over his Eye.

ZAP went the scarlet beam. It struck an invisible meta-psychic barrier, a three-meter dome covering Aiken, and disintegrated into a web of lightnings.

Aiken scowled, continuing his struggle with the ball. Was he trying to unscrew its halves? Press some button or lever countersunk in it?

ZAPP!! This time, one portion of the psychokinetic screen glowed an ominous blue. The ogre bellowed in glee. "Now we'll see how well you hide, you insolent little pismire!"

A salvo of coherent radiation beams sprayed at Aiken's mental shield. Globs of energy like great static discharges hit the screen from all angles, making it glow blue, green, sickly yellow. The crowd of spectators emerged from their fascinated trance and began to shout. Tanu clanged their shields and tooted horns. Firvulag whooped and smote their tomtoms until the drumheads split. The great white-salt circle of the fighting-ground was walled by a mass of shining colored bodies and leaping nightmare shapes.

At long last the two halves of Aiken Drum's golden ball fell apart. He grinned up at Pallol in a friendly fashion, paying no attention to the ferocious bombardment of the metapsychic screen. The barrier was fading from vermilion to dull lake red, the signal of imminent collapse.

"There we go, Goliath baby! All set now!"

Aiken placed a small silvery object in the wide section of the leathern strap and swung the sling around and around his head. Something flew through a hole in the screen, flickered among the light beams, and struck Pallol smack in his normal right eye.

The Firvulag Battlemaster roared. Both gauntleted hands clutched at his face. The awful left Eye closed and from the right one spurted blood that was black in the pallid moonlight. The ogre's howl diminished in strength, and slowly, as a monumental structure folds and crumples when the charges of demolition engineers undermine its supporting members, the monstrous armored form bent, sagged, and crashed to the salt.

Mayvar Kingmaker came out of the crowd with Aiken's own purple-glass sword and presented it to him. He cut off the head of Pallol with a single swipe and held it up. The once-potent Eye was shuttered. In the other socket something silvery glittered in a mass of bloody tissue. Delicately, Aiken plucked the fatal missile out. He zapped it with his creative faculty so that the late Lord Gomnol's cigar cutter was as shiny and clean as ever and the long vision of the farsensors in the crowd could read what was stamped on the metal:

SOLINGEN—INOX STEEL

"Here's to the new era," said Aiken Drum. "Long live Me."

Six hundred kilometers to the southwest of Muriah, the long natural dam that stretched between Spain and Africa was finally starting to give way—not in one spot but in a hundred, all along its waterlogged and crumbling length. Stressed unbearably by the weight of the ever-deepening water, great slices of the ash and scoria barrier went sliding forward down the eastern slope. As the impounded sea gushed over, the breaks grew and merged with one another until it seemed that the entire unstable dike would be shoved into the estuary of the Southern Lagoon by the pent-up pressure.

Saltwater crashed among dark lava buttes in the desolate country east of the vanished Long Fjord. It flooded across moonlit flats, found new drainage channels among gypsum dunes and spindly towers of striped evaporite. The ground trembled and the air was filled with a stupendous roar as nearly 200 kilometers of dike-length subsided within fifteen minutes.

The volume of rushing water was too vast for the narrow estuary of the Southern Lagoon to accommodate and the flood rose higher and higher in the phenomenon called hydraulic damming. Ahead of the catastrophic surge flew a hurricane blast of air. The pale waters of the long lagoon seemed to recede in horror before the onrushing dark wall, then surrender, rise to meet it, and merge at its nearly vertical face. The wave was 230 meters high.

Freed of their last restraint, the waters of the Western Ocean raced toward the White Silver Plain.

The throng of Tanu and humankind sang the Song while all of the knights held high their glowing jeweled swords. Beneath the waving white banner with its golden face stood Thagdal and Nontusvel, and behind them, seeming to generate her own shadow in spite of the multihued dazzle, was Brede. The Tanu Great Ones were also there; but of the Foe, only King Yeochee and the noncombatant Firvulag nobility stood waiting for the latest and most disappointing in a long-unbroken string of similar humiliations. The Firvulag champions, and many Little People among the spectators as well, had withdrawn—too overcome by sorrow even to stay for the rare spectacle that was soon to follow.

Aiken Drum plucked Pallol's standard from the ground. With a psychocreative flourish he removed the demon-otter effigy that had been mounted amid the dyed scalp locks and dangling chains of skulls. Displaying the head of the fallen Battlemaster to the crowd one final time, Aiken made a magician's pass. Pallol's head was transformed into a golden death mask; in the socket of the left eye was a star ruby the size of a grapefruit. When the head was impaled upon its own battle standard, Aiken Drum raised it high and approached King Thagdal.

Before he could speak, a gaunt figure in purple robes came from the ranks of Great Ones and stood beside him.

The Marshal of Sport, already flustered by the outrageousness of the whole affair, seemed to choke on his stately announcement.

"Awful King—and Father! The referees and—and judges of the Tanu and Firvulag races have—conferred and made their last accounting. And—uh—the victory belongs to the noble and valorous Tanu battle-company of the Many-Colored Land!" After a pause for cheering, he resumed. "Here before you, craving your royal accolade as Premier Champion of this Grand Combat, stands Lord Aiken Drum—"

"No," said Mayvar quietly.

There was a breathless hush.

"No longer Aiken Drum," she said, "for now I bestow upon him at last his Tanu name—that taken by every human admitted to our battle-company and fellowship. I have kept Aiken Drum's true name hidden in my heart for so long because I wished to let him show you himself that he is worthy of it. I, Mayvar Kingmaker, have never had doubts of him. And on this field of battle he has proved that he is truly one beloved of the Goddess . . . Therefore, with confidence and love I call him! He is the Shining One! He is the Young Lugonn."

The crowd, stunned first by incredulity, began an uproarious clamor of voices and minds, horns and beaten shields. There were those who rejoiced and those who shouted enraged exception; but the tumult was so vast that no one could say where the hearts of the majority lay—with the young Battlemaster or with the old.

Thagdal stepped forward, his face stiff as that emblazoned on his royal banner. He accepted the Firvulag standard from the hands of the little golden man and passed it immediately to Bunone Warteacher. Eadone, Dean of Guilds, now came to the fore bearing something upon a long velvet pillow. The crowd noise ceased. This was the moment they had been waiting for. Would Aiken Drum—Lugonn—pick up the holy Sword of Sharn and pass it in fealty to the Thagdal, as Nodonn always had done? Or would he—

The shining small figure lifted the huge thing, leaving the

tethered powerpack on the pillow that Eadone still held. Taking
the hilt in both hands, he pointed the Sword blade-down and
drove it into the salt at the feet of the King, then turned his
back on Thagdal.

There was a slow letting-out of breath. The throng seemed
stupefied, as did all of the royalty, both Tanu and Firvulag,
gathered beneath the emblems of the two Kings.

Into this void stepped the dark personage who had guided
both races for a thousand years. Her garments of scarlet and
black repeated the colors of the sky, for it was nearly dawn.
Her face, clearly visible, was wet with tears.

"Let it be, then," her mind and voice spoke together, "as I
have foreseen. Let the two heroes contend with Sword and
Spear on the White Silver Plain in the last Combat."

Mayvar led out the four Tanu champions who had declared
for the Shining One in the Heroic Encounters. They carried
with them the Spear. Bleyn fastened the jeweled baldric holding
the powerpack around the little human's shoulder and hip.
Nodonn materialized out of thin air and stood next to the Sword.
He pulled it from the ground and held it high while Kuhal,
Imidol, Culluket, and Celadeyr girded him in the harness.

The throng drew far back. Impelled by some psychokinetic
force, the heroic pair separated, gliding a few centimeters above
the salt, which now had assumed a dull-red luminescence in
the overcast dawn. Visible haloes of defensive mental energy
englobed the tall rosy-gold apparition and the diminutive form
of the trickster. Both stood ready.

"Begin," said the Shipspouse.

There were twin bursts of emerald fire and simultaneous
concussions that forced all of the torced spectators to shield
their senses for an instant. When the audience recovered, the
thunder still reverberated over the Plain. Both contestants stood
firm, psychic barriers and glowing armor intact.

Again came the green explosions and the monstrous clap of
sound—but this time the echoes did not dwindle. The deep
rumbling became louder and the ground shook under the heroes'
feet. A wind rose out of nowhere, adding its howl to the deeper
note. The red-and-black sky suddenly was obliterated all along
the western horizon.

Thagdal the King saw the wave and cried the first mental
warning. Summoning every erg of his metapsychic power, he
erected a wall. "To me! To me, all of you!"

They joined him—Firvulag and Tanu and torced human—

in a massed mind-thrust never before attempted in Exile. Nodonn lent his psychokinetic strength, and Lugonn, and all of the Little People strove with their creativity to shore up the King's mental bastion that held back the onrushing sea, to prevent it from breaking over them all. But the dark water mounted higher, higher, and the weight of it pressing their defending minds was unimaginable millions of tons...

The wave broke.

"I am still King," Thagdal told Nontusvel. The sea crashed upon them. Drowning, he was content, and he sent the last of his dwindling force in a touch of comfort to the Queen, for he had not let go of her hand.

The primary wave-front rushed on into the sunrise, losing height rapidly as it spread into the expanse of the Great Lagoon. A secondary surge washed the shoulder of the Aven Peninsula, flooding inland for several kilometers before draining away down the cliffs. The waters caught those still remaining in the city by surprise, and most of them perished, including all but a handful of the ramapithecine slaves.

Amerie would have rushed out of the room high on the Mount of Heroes, except that Chief Burke seized her and held her tight, and she fought him and screamed until she was exhausted and could weep no longer. And then Basil came and crouched there with them under the terrible window. Both Amerie and the rugged old lawyer understood when the former don whispered his ancient prayer.

"Elevaverunt flumina fluctus suos, a vocibus aquarum multarum. Mirabilis elationes maris. Mirabilis in altis Dominus."

Together, they waited for Elizabeth.

12

THE MIND-CRIES AS THEY PASSED!

They reached Elizabeth even within the cocoon of fire. The first scattered leavetakings at the start of the Mêlée came like tentative drops introducing a storm; and then whole gusts of them went flying by in increasing numbers—crying out, afraid and disappointed and raging and eager. There were lulls. And then the death gales rising again, rushing past her refuge. All those disembodied minds hurrying beyond space and time to the many-in-All that she had shut out, and a very few spinning their own fiery cocoons to drift apart from the stream, denying, going their own lost way.

But she was not free to follow the river of Mind. She was anchored yet to Earth. When the final disjunctive cataclysm happened, she felt the shock even within the hiding place, and had to let her mind's eye observe. Too amazed to grieve, she watched and heard the torrent passing.

Many of them were persons she knew. And at the end of the great storm-surge of mortality there came one that was all too familiar. Brede's mind swept by her with a final appealing touch. And then Elizabeth saw an alien thing, vast and bright and loving, come to meet its mate, an escort into irresistible light . . .

Elizabeth awoke.

The face leaning over her belonged to Sister Amerie, and it had the drawn, haunted expression that comes after there are no tears left.

"I know," said Elizabeth.

The nun extended her hand, touched Elizabeth's tightly clenched fingers. "There was—an exotic woman. She knew this would happen. She healed us. Brought us here to you.

And there was a message: 'Tell Elizabeth that now she is free to make a true choice.' I hope you understand."

Elizabeth sat up. After a moment she was able to rise from the cot and walk to the window in the natural bunker where Basil and Chief Burke stood, now unable to take their eyes from the scene below the mountain.

Morning had broken fully and the heavily clouded sky gave a gray and pitiful light. The White Silver Plain and both tent-cities and the entire expanse of carved and sparkling sediments that had once rimmed Muriah from its cliffs to the lagoon shores had vanished. In its place was a sea. It was the color of dull jade and its white-capped waves ran eastward toward the far horizon. Driven by the strong wind, breakers crashed over the small curving point of land at the peninsula's end where Brede's house had been. Muriah was now beyond reach of the waves; however, smashed houses and trees and pools of draining water showed where the earlier surge had devastated most of the capital city.

Now you are free to make a true choice.

Outside the door of their room was noise. Her mind perceived the anguished jumble of thoughts. It was hard—well-nigh impossible, given the unbearable emotional load of them—to distinguish Tanu from human, or these from the Firvulag who were apparently gathered among them. There were no masters and slaves, no friends or Foes; there were only survivors.

"I think we should go out now," Cheif Burke said.

Elizabeth nodded. The four of them turned away from the window and walked to the door. Burke lifted the latch.

Now you are free to make a true choice.

There stood Dionket and Creyn and others wearing the garb of redactors. Behind them milled numbers of the survivors. Elizabeth gently fended their minds, met the eyes of the two healers.

"Give me just a few minutes." She gestured to the red balloon jumpsuit she still wore. "I'd like to find some other clothes."

Torn from its base, the huge glass box that was the Great Retort wallowed in the flood, the bodies inside of it tumbling and piling with each violent oscillation. Eventually the Retort settled on a fairly even keel. Half of its bulk was below the waterline and the conscious ones among the prisoners felt they were adrift in some bizarre parody of a glass-bottomed boat.

The black and silver awning that had roofed it was all tattered and it snapped as the gale took hold of the ornamental super-structure. The benches and tables, the commodes and food dishes and water jars were all flung together with the bodies of the condemned.

Raimo Hakkinen spat out saltwater, salt blood, and a tooth. He lay up against the front wall, close to the door. Water was leaking in through crevices around the jamb.

"Come on," he croaked, stripping off his undershirt and ripping strips from it with his teeth.

Only one person from the pile of casualties nearest him responded, a woman dressed in a suit of armor-padding. They bit and tore apart her short gambeson; the collapsed plass bubbles made excellent caulking.

"That ought to hold her," Raimo said, offering a gap-toothed smile.

"She floats!" The woman stared in a dazed fashion at the brownish water, swirling with unimaginable debris, that surrounded them outside the four transparent walls. "Just like some crazy aquarium—except—those things on the outside aren't fish—" She turned away and was violently sick. Raimo backed off on hands and knees.

"Maybe I can find a water jar that didn't break."

He went creeping among the bodies and the mess. Quite a few people were alive, but there were plenty of deaders, too. He located a container of water snuggled amid three corpses. And wasn't that one over there—

He turned the body over. "Bryan? You all right?" The lips smiled. "Bryan?"

"He cannot hear you," said the voice of Aluteyn Crafts-master. "Your friend has passed into Tana's peace."

Raimo shrank back, holding the water bottle. "Uh—too bad. We came down to Muriah on the same boat together. And if the rumors I heard about him and Lady Rosmar were true, maybe the two of us—well, sorta suffered the same way."

Aluteyn gently unfastened Bryan's golden torc. "Not quite the same way, Raimo. But neither of you has to suffer any more." He put the torc around Raimo's neck, removing the silver one he had been wearing. "I think Bryan would have wanted you to have this. Your brain is mending, thanks to my little patch job, and we may find more skilled redactors among our fellow survivors. Or—later."

"You think we'll make it? You think this damn glass box'll float long enough to take us to shore?"

"Those who programmed restraints on my metafunctions are doing so no more. I can generate a moderate PK wind, even keep out the sea by reinforcing the walls of the Retort, now that I have recovered my full consciousness." He gestured to the sprawled bodies. "If you will help me to sort out the ones who still live—"

"Let me go get the dame who was helping me to caulk the door." Raimo grinned and tottered off. The floor of the Retort lurched in the fierce currents, setting the bodies to rolling.

The Craftsmaster gave one last look at the smiling face of the dead anthropologist. Then, groaning with pain and resignation, he began to work again.

She was a strong swimmer and a woman of courage. Using her fatigued creativity, she could still fashion twin bubbles from a portion of her court dress and position them behind her arms so they would help to buoy her up. And when the sun came out at last to shine on the swirling muddy waters and she began to faint from weariness and shock, Mercy called out:

"My Lord! Where are you, Nodonn?"

No answering thought came. It was hard, almost impossible, to muster the control needed for long-range farspeaking. She was so deadly tired! But finally she gathered the strength and called again. "Nodonn! Nodonn!"

O come daemon lover, angel of light, come. How can you be dead and I not?

She floated in the midst of the flood. Faint thoughts, faraway and garbled, made a vertiginous twitter in her brain. None of them were his thoughts.

"Nodonn," she kept whispering. And once, "Bryan."

Her head flung back, hair trailing like tendrils of dark seaweed, Mercy drifted in the sea. Finally the sun went down and it was cold. Her legs and lower body numbed. She suffered from thirst, but she was so weakened from shock that she could separate the sweet water molecules from the salt with only the greatest effort. Creativity, of all the metafunctions, is most vulnerable to trauma and sorrow.

"Then I will die along with his world," she decided, "for it's all gone now, all the brightness and the wonder and the song."

A small yellow light.

It bobbed, flickered, grew. She decided to wait, since the radiant entity gave evidence of having farseen her, even though it stayed coyly beyond her own mental sight. After an hour or so the glowing thing drew close by. She saw it was the Kral—that great golden cauldron sacred to the Creator Guild—and she cried out.

"Creative Brother! Do you know if Nodonn lives?"

"Is that gratitude?" asked Aiken Drum.

He leaned over the rim of the kettle, extended an arm all covered in golden pockets, and painfully lifted her up. She was deposited in a heap on the curved metal beside him and he grinned down at her.

"Sorry to be so crude on the teleport, Merce lovie, but I'm feeling a little wonky myself yet. Lie still and I'll see if I can conjure you dry."

"You," she said. "*You* live."

"The baddest penny of them all. When I saw that we didn't stand a chance with our King Canute act, I figured every man for himself and spun myself a little air capsule. Popped up and only had enough strength left to float. This tub was a mighty welcome sight, I can tell you. I'd just about had it when it came sailing by, chirky as you please."

Slowly he dried her, cleansed her of salt and filth, clumsily restored her torn clothing. By the time he finished she was nearly asleep.

"The gown," she murmured, "is supposed to be rose-colored—not gold and black."

"I like gold and black better."

She tried to rouse herself. Her whisper retained a trace of the old coquetry. "Now then... what's in that naughty mind of yours, Lord Lugonn Aiken Drum?"

"Go to sleep, little Lady of Goriah, little creative Mercy-Rosmar. There's plenty of time to talk about that tomorrow."

Winter rains swept over the Bordeaux marshes. The great river was silty, and the fish were shy, but there were still plenty of wildfowl and the small anterless deer with the tusks, and in higher parts of the large island where the oaks and chestnuts grew, succulent mushrooms. Sukey craved them now and had nagged Stein until he agreed to go for a basketful. And then she was sorry when it began to rain so hard, and saw to it that there was a fine hot stew waiting for him and a good fire in the cabin hearth.

He returned when it was nearly dark. Besides the mushrooms, there was a haunch from a half-grown wild porker. He said, "The rest is cached up a tree. I can fetch it tomorrow. Cook this pig meat well, remember."

"I will, Stein. I wouldn't take a chance. You know that." She caught up one of the wet, callused hands and kissed it. "Thank you for the mushrooms."

"I'm all soaked," he admonished her. "Wait." He stripped off the squelchy buckskin jacket and pants and the rawhide moccasins and warmed himself at the fire while she leaned against him, watching the flames and smiling secretly. In the summer it would be born, and there would be plenty of time to search for other humans then, in the days of lasting calm weather when the great balloon would sail very slowly and land with scarcely a jolt. Next August or September, they would leave. And in the meantime, this wasn't so bad. They were all alone, completely safe, with plenty of food and a snug cabin and each other.

"Eat now," she told him. "I'll take care of your things and see to this meat."

Just before they were ready to go to bed the rain stopped. Stein lifted the door flap and stepped outside, and when she heard him returning she came to stand beside him in the peaceful, dripping dark. The stars were out.

"I love it here," she said. "I love you. Oh, Stein."

He encircled her with one great arm, saying nothing, only looking up into the sky. Why should they leave this place? They had often talked of it, but why was it necessary to seek out other humans? Who knew what they would be like? Besides, there were wild Firvulag in the mainland wilderness. He knew, for he had seen their will-o'-the-wisp dancing lights once when he had gone exploring in the dinghy.

The two of them had been very lucky in avoiding contact with exotics on their way to this haven. It would be madness to run the risk all over again, doubly mad to take a newborn infant on a journey in the balloon. A balloon was too unpredictable. It flew its own way, not yours. If an unexpected strong wind took them, they might be carried hundreds of kilometers before being able to descend safely. They could be carried southeast, all across France, over the Mediterranean...

Never. He would never return there to look on what he had done. He would never do it.

"Oh, look!" Sukey cried. "A shooting star! Or—is it? It's moving too slowly. Too late, it's gone behind a cloud! And I forgot to make a wish."

He took her hand and led her back inside their little home. "Don't worry. I made the wish for you," he said.

The lights on the orbiting flyer's display were all dead now, and the exotic alarms no longer sounded a warning. Without power, without oxygen, the craft faithfully maintained its parking orbit, going around and around the world at an altitude of something less than 50,000 kilometers.

During most of its orbit, the dull-black surface of the flyer made it virtually invisible against the backdrop of space. But now and then sunlight would strike the flight deck's front port, brightening Richard's face and causing a brief beam to reflect back to Earth.

Around and around the little broken bird went, endlessly circling.

In the Hall of the Mountain King at High Vrazel, the decimated council of the Firvulag met to discuss new business: the election of a new Sovereign Lord of the Heights and Depths, Monarch of the Infernal Infinite, Father of All Firvulag, and Undoubted Ruler of All the Known World.

"We're going to be in trouble this time," Sharn-Mes warned them.

"How so?" queried Ayfa.

He told her and the others the bad news. "The Howlers are demanding the franchise."

The great black raven spiraled downward to the place where its fellows were feeding. All along the North African shore, the scavenger birds were prospering as never before. The bounty had persisted for nearly four months now and still showed no sign of scarcity.

Pruuk! grated the newcomer. It ruffled its feathers malignantly when another bird was slow to move aside on the carcass of a porpoise. *Pruuuuuuuk!* it repeated, lifting its shoulders and opening its wings. It was a huge bird, half again as large as the others, and its eye sparkled with a mad gleam.

Uneasily, the rest of the flock moved back from the meal, leaving the great stranger to dine in solitude.

* * *

"They're coming! They're coming!" Calistro the goat-boy shouted as he dashed up the length of Hidden Springs Canyon, his charges forgotten. "Sister Amerie and the Chief and a *lot* of others!"

People swarmed from the cottages and huts, calling out to one another in excitement. A long train of riders was wending its way into the village outskirts.

Old Man Kawai heard the commotion and stuck his head from the door of Madame Guderian's rose-covered house beneath the pines. He sucked air through his teeth.

"She comes!"

A small cat came running from the box under the table, nearly tripping him when he spun about to snatch up a paring knife. "I must cut flowers and hurry to greet her!" He pointed a stern finger at the cat. "And you—see that your kittens are groomed so that you do not disgrace both of us!"

The gauze-screened door slammed. Muttering to himself, the old man chopped off an armful of the heavy June rose clusters, then rushed down the path scattering pink and scarlet petals behind him.

THE END OF PART THREE

EPILOGUE

REMEMBERING THE INCIDENT OF HIS CHILDHOOD, THE YOUNG male ramapithecine came again to the Lake of Giant Birds.

There was a trail that some larger creatures had made more than a year ago, now kept open by other animals, for it had been a dry summer and the crater lake a boon to the thirsty. The ramapithecus was not in search of water, however.

Slowly he crept out into the open area along the crater rim. There was the bird! When he crouched under it, he wondered why it seemed smaller. And the hole in its belly was gone, along with the climbing-up thing. But this was *his* bird. He knew. The memory burned within him. His mother screaming her anger . . . snatching, flinging away a precious joy that gleamed the color of the sun.

He searched. Into a bush. That bush, that gorse bush. He extended a brown-haired arm into the spiny thicket. Careful. Scratch at the dusty soil. Dig, probe.

His hand touched something smooth and hard. He drew it out with great care. It was as he remembered. The knobs snapped open, the halves turned, and this time it fitted around his neck snugly enough so that it could not be slipped off over his head. It would not be taken away from him again.

He got up and started down the path to the forest where his mate, more timid, was waiting for him. The sunshine was brighter, the smell of the maquis more pungent, the trilling of birds and insects more distinct. All of the things around him were transformed. It excited and pleasured and scared him a little, all at the same time.

I'm coming! Yes, I am!

He leaped in his joy and the lesser creatures on the trail hastened to get out of his way.

THE END OF THE GOLDEN TORC

Volume III of the Saga of Pliocene Exile, titled THE NONBORN KING, *tells of a realignment of power structures during a turbulent period in the Many-Colored Land, wherein human and exotic antagonists receive their first intimations of a new-old menace from the western morning.*

APPENDIXES

Apologia Pro Geologia Sua

Map of Northwestern Europe
During the Pliocene Epoch

Map of Western Mediterranean
Region During the Pliocene Epoch

Map of Eastern Aven (Balaeric Peninsula)
During the Pliocene Epoch

APOLOGIA PRO
GEOLOGIA SUA

THE ANCIENT LANDSCAPE DEPICTED IN THIS SAGA REPRESENTS Europe during the so-called Mio-Pliocene Regression, when the Mediterranean was at its lowest ebb prior to the opening of the Straits of Gibraltar. The timing of the latter event has not been firmly established, but it may have taken place about 5.5 million years before the present, and I have rounded off this figure to 6 million years. During the Miocene Epoch, the Mediterranean Basin received Atlantic waters via two channels that opened and closed a number of times—the Betic Channel in southern Spain and the Rif Channel, which extended across northern Morocco, Algeria, and Tunisia. The rupture at Gibraltar took place after the Rif and Betic channels had closed. With the opening of the Gibraltar Gate, the filling of the Mediterranean might have been a fairly rapid thing; perhaps only a hundred years after the cataclysm, influx from the Atlantic would have filled the basin of the Empty Sea completely, drowning the ancient Valley of the Rhône almost as far north as Lyon, and undoubtedly initiating tectonic adjustments that not only altered the Mediterranean floor into its present topography of abysses and shallows but also caused profound modification of the geology of the Italian peninsula, Sicily, and other unstable regions.*

The map of the Empty Sea that I have drawn is entirely speculative, especially in its treatment of the Southern Lagoon Estuary, the Great Brackish Marsh, and regions now known as the Alborán Sea and the Algerian Basin. There are, however, volcanic remnants that make my rubble dam at least remotely plausible; *vis.* at Cabo de Gata; at Cap de Trois Fourches, Morocco; and of course at Isla de Alborán itself.

I have postulated that Pontian flora and fauna were contemporaneous with the Mediterranean flood. The climate, geography, vegetation, and animal life of Pontian times are essentially as set forth in the novel—but geologists and paleobiologists will be quick to detect a few fudgings that I hope can be forgiven in the spirit of good fun. Ramapithecus, that enigmatic and fascinating hominid of many aliases, is placed as late as the Pontian by virtue of a jaw described in 1972 by G. H. R. von Koenigswald, to which he gave the name *Graecopithecus freybergi.*

The structure called the Ries (or Rieskessel) is the subject of some controversy—one school of thought accepting it as an astrobleme, while another holds it to be the result of a cryptovolcanic explosion that brought to the surface "meteoritelike" materials. Arguments for the latter viewpoint are summarized in G. H. J. McCall, *Meteorites and Their Origins* (New York: Wiley, 1973). The more dramatic impact hypothesis is elegantly supported in E. Preuss, "Das Ries und die Meteoriten-Theorie" (Stuttgart:*Fortschritte der Mineralogie,*

---

*The only other events remotely comparable to the flooding of the Mediterranean were the "Great Missoula Floods," which took place during the Pleistocene Ice Age in western North America. Melt waters from the Cordilleran Glacier of the Rocky Mountains flowed toward the west until they met a lobe of the Okanogan Glacier, which blocked Clark Fork Valley near the present Lake Pend Oreille in northern Idaho. This formed Glacial Lake Missoula, one of the largest freshwater bodies ever to collect in the western part of the continent. More than a thousand feet deep in some places, it inundated the valleys of western Montana until the natural dam of ice and rubble broke. Some 500 cubic miles of water drained from the lake through the Grand Coulee within a period of about two weeks, scouring the Washington landscape known as the Channeled Scablands and draining into the Pacific through the Columbia Gorge. Hydraulic damming in the gorge piled the flood waters some 400 feet above sea level in the region adjacent to Portland, Oregon. The flooding was apparently repeated a number of times. In comparing the Missoula Floods to the filling of the Mediterranean, one should recall that the Mediterranean Basin now holds about one million cubic miles of water; but in early Pliocene times, the basin is presumed to have been much shallower.

1964, 41:271–312). McCall seems not to have considered the Preuss material in his later survey. In my novel, trajectory, velocity, and mass data are from Preuss. Both K/Ar and fission-track testing of the Moldavite tektites (usually considered of identical age with the Ries) yield—alas!—an approximate age of 14.7 ± 0.7 million years.

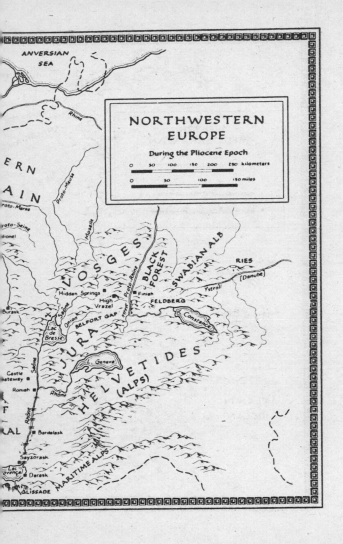

ANVERSIAN
SEA

NORTHWESTERN
EUROPE

During the Pliocene Epoch

0   50   100   150   200   250 kilometers

0   50   100   150 miles

Rhine

Proto-Meuse

ERN
AIN

Proto-Marne

Proto-Seine

Moselle

dionel

V O S G E S

BLACK FOREST

SWABIAN ALB

RIES

[Danube]

Burask

Hidden Springs

High
Vrazel

Proto-Rhine

Finish

FELDBERG

Ystroll

Saône

Onion

BELFORT GAP

Constance

Lac
de
Bresse

J U R A

Sedna

Castle
Gateway

L. Geneva

Romah

Rhône

H E L V E T I D E S

(A L P S)

Doubs

Rhône

Bardalask

Sayzorask

M A R I T I M E   A L P S

Lac
Provence

Darask

GLISSADE

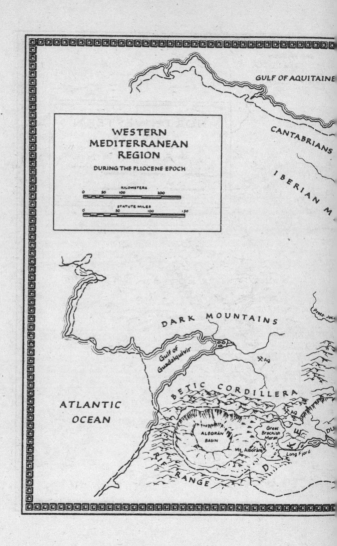

WESTERN
MEDITERRANEAN
REGION

DURING THE PLIOCENE EPOCH

KILOMETERS
0   50   100   200

STATUTE MILES
0   50   100   150

GULF OF AQUITAINE

CANTABRIANS

IBERIAN M

DARK MOUNTAINS

Gulf of
Guadalquivir

× Ag

BETIC CORDILLERA

ATLANTIC
OCEAN

ALBORÁN
BASIN

Great
Brackish
Marsh

Mt. Alborán

Long Fjord

RANGE

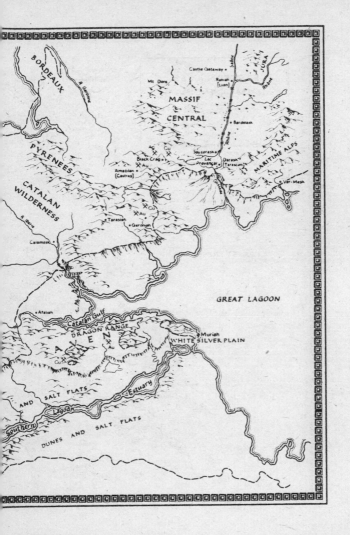

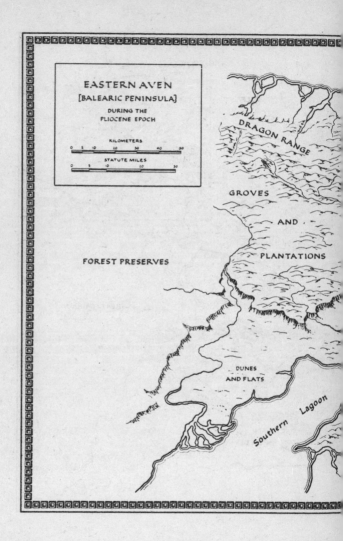

EASTERN AVEN
[BALEARIC PENINSULA]

DURING THE
PLIOCENE EPOCH

KILOMETERS

0   5   10   20   30   40   50

STATUTE MILES

0   5   10   20   30

DRAGON RANGE

GROVES

AND

PLANTATIONS

FOREST PRESERVES

DUNES
AND FLATS

Southern Lagoon

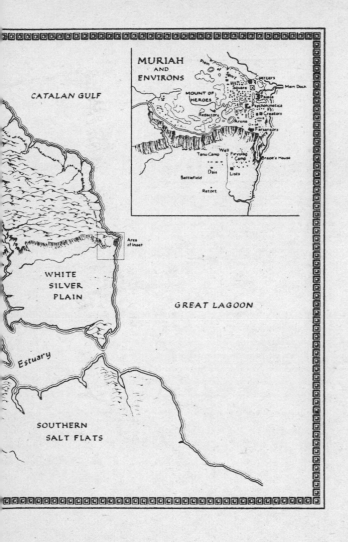

CATALAN GULF

MURIAH
AND
ENVIRONS

Plain
of
Mist
Square
Coercers
Main Dock
MOUNT OF
HEROES
Palace
Psychokinetics
(R:)
Redactors
Creators
Arena
Farsensors
Well
Tanu Camp
Finvulag
Camp
Gracie's House
Dais
Lists
Battlefield
Area
of inset
Retort

WHITE
SILVER
PLAIN

GREAT LAGOON

Estuary

SOUTHERN
SALT FLATS

ABOUT THE AUTHOR

JULIAN MAY's short science fiction novel, *Dune Roller*, was published by John W. Campbell in 1951 and has now become a minor classic of the genre. It was produced on American television and on the BBC, became a movie, and has frequently been anthologized. Julian May lives in the state of Washington.